BIRCH LANE PRESS PRESENTS

American Fiction

The Best Unpublished Short Stories by Emerging Writers

Introduction by GUEST JUDGE
Anne Tyler

Edited by Michael C. White
and Alan Davis

A BIRCH LANE PRESS BOOK
Published by Carol Publishing Group

BIRCH
F
7/90

A Birch Lane Press Book
Published by Carol Publishing Group

Editorial Offices
600 Madison Avenue
New York, NY 10022

Sales & Distribution Offices
120 Enterprise Avenue
Secaucus, NJ 07094

In Canada: Musson Book Company
A division of General Publishing Co. Limited
Don Mills, Ontario

Manufactured in the United States of America

Library of Congress Cataloging-in-Publication Data

Birch Lane Press presents American fiction: the best unpublished
    short stories by emerging writers / introduction by guest judge Anne
    Tyler; edited by Michael C. White and Alan Davis.
        p.   cm.
    ISBN (invalid) 0-55972-029-8: $12.95
        1. Short stories, American.   2. American fiction—20th century.
I. White, Michael C.   II. Davis, Alan.   III. Title: American
fiction.
PS648.S5B56   1990
813'.0108054—dc20
                                                            90-1386
                                                              CIP

This book is dedicated to
RAYMOND CARVER

Contents

Editors' Note

This marks the third edition of *American Fiction*. While several changes have been made, including our publisher and a minor change in our title, *AF*'s intent remains the same as it was when we started three years ago: to present the best of unpublished short stories, by both new and emerging writers, through our national contest. Our growth—from fifteen stories in 1987 to nineteen in 1988 to twenty-four this year—is testimony of that commitment.

This year we are again fortunate to have as Guest Judge one of the country's foremost writers, Anne Tyler. Ms. Tyler selected the three prize-winning stories and wrote the introduction. In words which echo those of the late Raymond Carver, *AF*'s 1988 Guest Judge, Ms. Tyler has written of this year's collection, "This leads me to wonder whether the present-tense, cut-and-run approach is losing popularity. Certainly none of the twenty-four is what I'd call minimalist. Maybe the American short story is returning to its traditions." We hope that it has, indeed, returned. In that spirit of continuity, we'd like to dedicate this book to the person who, more than any other current short story writer, both established its unique contemporary form and linked that form to its traditional heritage—namely, Raymond Carver.

We'd like to congratulate this year's prize-winners: the $1000 First Prize goes to Florri McMillan for "The Color of Scars"; the $500 Second Prize to Catherine Browder for "Tigers"; and the $250 Third Prize to David Mason for "Pullandbedamned Point." In addition, we'd like to congratulate the other twenty-one finalists.

We'd also like to thank several individuals as well as institutions: to begin with, Anne Tyler for her graciously accepting the role as this year's Guest Judge and for fulfilling that position admirably; Springfield College and Moorhead State University, and in particular, the English departments of each school, for both the financial and moral support they lent to this project; Irene Graves and Sonja Watkins for helping to sort through the hundreds of manuscripts; the C.F. White Family Foundation for their generous past support of this project; and finally, once again, the hundreds of writers who allowed us to read their work.

MICHAEL C. WHITE, Editor
Springfield College

ALAN DAVIS, Assistant Editor
Moorhead State University

BIRCH LANE PRESS PRESENTS

American Fiction

Introduction

BY ANNE TYLER

Luckily for all of us, I've thrown away the notes I made
while I was reading these stories. They weren't really notes so
much as identification tags—a bare-bones summary of each
plot. *Woman describes own brain surgery*, for the winner. *Cambodian refugees living in U.S.*, for second place. And for third,
Daughter visits dying stepfather + difficult mother.

Luckily, I say, because of course the bare bones are not the
point. *Woman describes own brain surgery* could be more of your
next-door neighbor's chit-chat about her latest hospital stay,
but Florri McMillan's "The Color of Scars" is the opposite of
chit-chat. It's sheer poetry—and beautiful, stark, terrifying
poetry at that.

What makes the difference is selectivity, pure and simple.
The narrator—the story's "I"—leads us through her ordeal in
a series of wide, daring leaps. She pounces tiptoe upon the
details that will most vividly demonstrate her eerie symp-
toms, her surgeon's decision to perform the operation, and at
long last her recovery. "Can't you fix it so you get color?" she
asks at the outset, but it's not television she's referring to; it's
the real world. When a resident removes her sutures after
surgery, her brain "spits white flecks of pain at him." In an
elegant sort of shorthand, her doctor masquerades as a cocky
prize fighter, and her losses interweave with the memory of
her brother Alan's loss of his fingers in a childhood accident.

> [The doctor] traces the scar exactly, in its horseshoe shape,
> with his finger, brushing the black cobwebs off the edges of

1

my vision...He fits the ball of his thumb into the hole and presses against the skin.

"It doesn't matter what you lost," he says. "It's healed now."

I can feel it, feel the edges of my skull soften.

("Take off your mitten, Alan," Grandad told him, "I want to see your fingers."

And he rubbed his thumb over the stubs, holding Alan's hand, hefting it.

"You've got a good working hand here," he said.)

Not inch by inch, but light-year by light-year, the narrator races through events, touching down now here, now there in the most graceful manner possible and ruthlessly discarding any excess baggage. What could have been a whine, therefore, becomes a glorious shout.

And *Cambodian refugees living in U.S.?* Well. Good for a feature article in the "Home" section of your local paper, maybe. But take a closer look at these particular refugees—the gossipy, ambitious, touchingly resolute little community in Catherine Browder's "Tigers."

It is the dialogue that brings these people to life. Especially, it is the mother's dialogue, which is so clumsy and stunted that we could easily fall into the trap of finding her *cute*, almost childlike—this wrinkly-faced woman with full-grown daughters.

"Teacha? I am Vonn. I so sorry that you Aunt die...When you come back?"

I listened through the pause, to Ma's tiny voice.

"She leave you everything?...Oh, I so sorry...Maybe her husband die and leave you everything."

Then we begin to realize what the dialogue is hiding—or at least, what it's gliding over. Beneath the broken phrases, the comic errors, and the parrotlike talk of microwave ovens and Frosted Flakes lie memories so appalling that Ma can dismiss the grisly scenes in the movie *The Killing Fields* as "Not hard enough. Too soft." When a chance encounter revives the past, her response is couched in pitiably inadequate English, and her daughter tells us:

I felt such sadness, like a deep, dark hole. All her one-inch words, her short and jerky sentences. I wanted to cry out, *Hush, Ma. Let me speak.*

What this story is about, ultimately, is language—both its power and its limitations. That language has the capacity to define us is frustratingly clear to anyone who's ever traveled in a foreign country and found himself deprived of the subjunctive mood. That there are some experiences that are literally unspeakable may not be so evident to the average sheltered American. But it is to Ma.

Daughter visits dying stepfather + difficult mother. Do we need this? Yes, we do, it turns out. David Mason's "Pulland-bedamned Point" draws its strength from the writer's control of his material. The central issue here is the stepfather's position in the daughter's life—a question of geometry, so to speak, whose answer the reader learns only over the course of the visit. Even the daughter isn't fully aware of her feelings until the last couple of pages.

It's significant, therefore, that the story is so fraught with signs of emotional evasiveness. Greer, the daughter, observes her own daughter flinching away from a boyfriend's kiss. ("I shouldn't have seen that," Greer reflects.) Greer and her husband enjoy their tennis matches because "It was something they did well together that didn't require talking." And Greer's mother, who seems constitutionally incapable of viewing people as they really are, first compares each of her visitors to Grace Kelly, John Kennedy, or Charlton Heston and then forces upon them a "homemade" meal that ends with a pie served up in an aluminum pie-plate.

Another bald-faced lie. It's store-bought. The dumplings were store-bought. This whole family was bought in a supermarket by the side of the road.

All the averted glances, the edginess and the sense of something *not quite right* make the emotional directness of the final scene unexpectedly moving. The story appears to unwind from a skein, in the most restrained and delicate manner. It would be a satisfyingly tidy situation if, having assigned top ranking to these three entries, I were suddenly to notice that they shared a single, striking quality. "Why!" I could say. "All three have a such-and-such type of plot!" Or, "All three have a so-and-so point of view!" But that's not the case. I'll have to take my satisfaction from another source entirely: They are just about as different from each other as possible. They prove that there is no one right way to approach a story, no neat formula for success. In the company of the twenty-one other entries, they demonstrate the variety and individualism of this country's up-and-coming writers.

It's worth noting that only one of the finalists (Cris Mazza in "Is It Sexual Harassment Yet?") attempts a noticeably innovative form. (All, on the other hand, attempt innovative content, which is exactly as it should be.) A surprisingly large majority employ the past tense, and almost as many choose to tell complete, fully rounded, beginning-and-ending *stories* (in some cases life stories, whole histories) as opposed to brief episodes. This leads me to wonder whether the present-tense, cut-and-run approach is losing popularity. Certainly none of the twenty-four is what I'd call minimalist. Maybe the American short story is returning to its traditions. Then again, maybe not. (I didn't see the other 500-odd entries, after all.)

The phrase "honorable mention" takes on a literal meaning here: There are additional stories I'd like to call attention to. Joann Kobin's "His Mother, His Daughter" is admirable both for its intelligence (the uncanny but thoroughly convincing perceptiveness of the daughter) and its subtlety. When the author refrained from stating outright the reason for the son's mysterious dislike of his mother's white bow, I thought of that wonderful Charlie Chaplin scene where Charlie, skating backward toward an abyss but unknowingly avoiding it, avoided as well the slapstick, the obvious point hammered numbingly home.

Elizabeth Evan's "Ransom" presents a character who will be hanging around the edges of my mind for some time, I suspect. Marie's spunk and her basic goodness are just part of it; I loved her theological debates, which seemed perfectly believeable, and I loved the author's audacity in trusting us to believe them. She shows the proper faith in her readers.

"Trees" is a showcase for Jane Ruiter's fine craftsmanship. Look at the rose hips, for instance—how unobtrusively they're put to work. At the start we're told that the two central characters might once have stopped to pick them for tea. Now, though, they don't give them a glance. Then at the story's end the wife—having undergone an emotional sea-change—pauses before the bushes and tastes a handful. She doesn't pick them for tea, not yet. But she does taste them. It's a moment a Fifties-style ladies' magazine might have sealed with an embrace. No question about it: Rose hips are better.

Or maps. In "Sworn Statements: The Map," it's the point of view that's striking. First there is the unusual angle—not the Jew in Nazi Germany but the Aryan, seizing his advantage without a thought. Second, there's the intimate sense of the protagonist's slant on things. Like the best of liars (there's no higher praise for a writer), Marcie Hershman convinces us by means of particularity—the casual, seemingly random name-dropping, you might call it, of topographical references.

Judging these twenty-four finalists was no easy task, but reading them was a pleasure. For that I'm grateful not only to the writers, but also to the editors, Michael White and Alan Davis, who forged bravely ahead of me with the hard part—550-some entries. Heaven knows what *their* notes looked like.

My own notes, I promise, have been carted away days ago by the Baltimore City Sanitation Department. What's left behind are not bare bones but luminous ghosts: a defiant woman in a hospital bed, a wrinkled Cambodian refugee struggling with her English, a gentle stepfather dying of cancer, and a host of others. The short story slims down or puts on weight, delves into the depths or skims across the surface, depending on the times. But in any case, it continues to enrich our lives.

The Color of Scars

BY FLORRI McMILLAN

"Close your eyes, Constance, and keep them closed," the technician commands, and her white chest spills over my face, emptying the world. I obey, but my ears cling to the tiny nylon crackles of her uniform.

White blots explode—angry spurting flashes against a humming in my brain. Flakes of snow dance flat on a black square; a television set is broken or left on all night, abandoned by the sleeper.

Pattern is in the snow. I can feel the scratch of a needle on crisp skin, tracing patterns, then gone. Behind my eyes there is no color; black and white are the same.

"Open your eyes, Constance, and keep them open." I watch a clean steel stylus pull across white paper ribbon, elegant as a fingernail; satisfying the itch between the creases of my toes, inside my brain.

There are two men wearing gray jackets, far away. I call but do not hear the call; their faces bulge toward me like expanding balloons.

"This is a thirty-four year old white female..." one says into a square box he holds. The other watches me.

"How many fingers?" he wants to know, lifting them. His flat, round face is blowing up into his cat ears.

"Do you know what day this is?" he asks, and so I tell him.

He purses his fat lips into a pink "o", the pouty tip of the balloon, as if he has expected this disappointment.

"What color is this?" the first says, holding out his little box, but I do not know what color is.

They turn to Rand, my husband, and shake his hand. They gesture to each other and say, "neurologist," but the word slips away from me into fortune tellers. The balloon man presses his thumb into the box. A noise pierces my forehead with such freezing sharpness that I close my eyes and feel the bright points of stars, the sound - ZZZT - of white hyphens scudding across black sky.

Dr. Francesca is a prize fighter. His street clothes riffle in the slip stream of his entrance like the silken hem of a boxer's robe when he makes his way to the ring. His followers trail behind and, when he halts, arrange themselves silently along the walls like caryatids, adorning and supporting this cathedral.

He is billed as Francesca, the expert contender, having performed this delicate procedure more often than anyone else in the country—twenty-six times. A couple of decisions have gone in his favor, and the judges have called several matches a draw. He has no knockouts to his credit, but this is the big time and that's the fight game. He says he is a humble man. The interns, who refer to a Francesca residency as if it were a prison sentence: "seven to ten with time off for good behavior," watch him with reverent eyes.

His green blazer is expensive, as definitely Italian as he is. Dark, crisp ringlets cover his head, just tinged with gray at the temple. He is very tan.

He looms in the doorway like a figure from classical tragedy, elevated by buskins or hidden platforms, but he is not tall. When he enters the room, flipping through pages, his teeth flash white, but he does not smile. He snaps the plastic notebook shut.

"She's having a real good day," says Ulla, the nurse, and hands him a clipboard.

He is a WINNER: his eyes, darkly alive, travel across our faces, demanding this answer. He talks to Rand, then jokes a little with the residents. He moves to the bed and nonchalantly squeezes my hand. The people in the room begin to smile a little, relieved to be in the champion's retinue. He studies my face, still holding the hand, and his eyes are turning black. From their cold depths he searches, listening and probing, for a chink in death, one thin shaft of light.

Watching his eyes, I see that he has gone away, like Roman heroes into battle, without farewell. A colorless heat has risen in my brain, spraying little electric bursts that burn out as quickly as they come. Charred fumes trickle from my lips; foul words I do not recognize, sounds I have never heard. I can smell the residue of rage. All the people in the room are backing away from my bed with horrified eyes, seeking protection in the soft vanilla walls.

"She can't help the shouting," Ulla explains to Rand. "She hardly knows she does it. All short circuits up here, you see." She points to her temple.

Rand is asking if these earthquakes of anger will harm me. His voice trembles.

"Ja," Ulla says sadly, the sympathy in her Scandanavian inflections covering like cloth. "She is afraid too, maybe."

The faces of the neurologists hang above me on a square, lighted screen.

"Can't you fix it so you get color?" my voice says.

"Television?" one asks. "Do you mean tel-e-vis-ion set?"

His lips are a pair of pudgy, horizontal rods, pushing words out slowly. I cannot quite reach them.

I have seen these rods before, losing color, floating too far away. They belong to my brother.

"Pick 'em up, Connie!"

Alan stood by the snowblower, bellowing into the storm. His fingers, pink on the snowbank, grew paler, swelling until they were white. I could not move.

"Pick 'em up. Pick 'em up!" He howled at me, his voice rough with anger. I heard the painless screams and stared at his fingers, lying separate on the snow. They were white as slugs from under the rocks, driven up and drowned by rain. The whiteness froze me to the snow. I listened to Alan's animal cries, sharp as crystal in the cold air, begging me, and watched the fingers far away, half Alan's, not Alan's, gone.

After a long time I knelt to pick them up, as if I were in church, and held them in the warm cavern of my hands—two fat, swollen rods, slimy and cold. Then I went to find Mother. She wanted to wrap Alan's fingers in a piece of gauze, but I wouldn't let them go. I held them all the way to the hospital. When we got there, I threw up, but I did not cry.

The other neurologist is sighing now, ruffling the moist inner edges of his lips. He sounds annoyed.

"Constance," he explains patiently, "I can't get you color. You know there's not a television in this room."

Mother is allowed to see me for five minutes of each hour. One morning I try to find out what happened. She flutters around the end of the bed, telling me there was a seizure (a fit, she says), and then unconscious.

"What's the matter?" I ask, and she keeps right on talking about how I cannot talk quite, can't understand always, and the artery is broken, yes, deep in there.

"Why aren't I dead," I say.

She nods, a little ducking of the head, and explains there is a blob of blood, like jello, around the break, covering it over a little, and she answers me that she doesn't know what will happen if the jello melts; yes she supposes it *will* melt, but not before the operation, she hopes.

Her voice is sparrow cheerful, but she picks at the corners of my tucked in blanket, her fingers darting like delicate claws over the wool.

"What went wrong?" I stretch my voice outward into silence.

"We just don't know," Mother says quietly, concentrating on the neat beige tucks at the end of the bed. She lifts her face, fixed firmly in the folds of love, denying panic.

A nurse is trying to insert an i.v. needle into the top of my hand. Her hands are clammy with nervous perspiration. The touch of her fingers enrages me. I hear my voice shouting, a rough edge to the words.

"Where did she learn language like that?" a resident murmurs. "She swears like a Marine."

He moves forward to rub the back of my hand with his thumb until I feel a painful, releasing jab.

"See?" he asks the white-faced nurse.

They push machines around and arrange my limbs with straps. Rand said they were going to shoot dye into my brain and take an X-ray. Then we'd know.

"Know what?" I asked him.

"Don't be afraid," he answered, but he was afraid.

Everyone in this room is afraid. Of Dr. Francesca, of death and failure. He stands close to my head, looking at me. Deliberately I meet his eyes. There is not a shred of fear there, and I see quite clearly that he can't wait.

(In this corner, weighing 170 pounds...the leading contender...)

"You can stand anything for four seconds," he says.

I slam rigid into the pain, shooting upward so hard my teeth fuse into my skull; and it crumples, a steel hull destroyed entirely. Its fragments float by, washed away in turquoise. The color is everywhere, so intense that it obliterates me: the I, the eyes, all things, no thing, nothing exists except the color turquoise.

I am lying calm in light. There is no weight or color to the air. Water has no ripples. My brain holds no pattern.

He breaks through the swinging door, leading with his shoulder, cutting a path through his own retinue. He holds the wet, black square of the X-ray high, in triumph. His eyes are shining.

"Now I know where it is," he says.

"Put your index finger on your nose and put the other finger in your ear," he says. He is leaning against the wall next to my bed. "Extend the lines until they meet. That's where it is."

He is wearing surgical greens. There are sweat stains under the short sleeves. I stare at the hairs curling along the top of his arm.

"It's a bad place," he says lightly.

I know it is in a bad place. I have seen the sick despair in Rand's eyes. The neurologists have explained that I say "Thursday Thursday Thursday Thursday Thursday Thursday Thursday," instead of the days of the week. At ten in the morning I can talk to Mother. By dark I can only make the hard sounds.

"Kick," I can say. Kick, like bones cracking. Most other words are gone, not there any more. Color is gone. Where are the words? What color is Thursday?

"This is what I'm gonna do," Dr. Francesca says.

He walks tough, like the leader of the Italian Cobras on the

Northwest side, pitching slightly forward. When he clips the
X-rays over the long white-lighted rectangle on the wall, fear
flickers around the edges of his residents' eyes, anticipation
playing across their faces because he could turn on you, this
street smart sonofabitch, he could waste you. This is his turf;
don't make mistakes.

He turns his back on the light that leaks through the slick,
black squares of film. He talks quietly to them, bouncing on
his feet. He talks fast, suddenly throwing out a shout of
laughter which releases their own. He is wearing a dark, short
sleeved shirt striped with thin lines, and he runs his palm up
and down one tan forearm while he speaks. His eyes travel
quickly across their faces, seeking the assurance that his
followers realize the war's on and they're going to *go* now and
win this alley fight before anybody else knows what's up
because they're in their territory here, a perfect place to meet
the enemy, see.

His eyes widen to include them and then, as the pace of his
speech slows, his pupils contract to sharp points in the
expressionless depths of dark brown iris. Unconsciously, he
takes a grease pencil from a drawer in the table and begins to
play with it. Holding it lightly in his fingertips, he tests the
balance, and it trembles slightly, alive in his palm.

"We'll go in here," he says, and the pencil makes a broad
slash on the slippery film, the shiv entering silently, then
ripping upward through the gut.

"And clip here," a greasy line to hold the leaking light, "and
then... *here*," slash, "and hope we can get the thing out
without removing too much of the brain."

A resident's voice lifts at the end of a murmured question.
The pencil pauses in midair.

"Well, we'll find that out, won't we?" Francesca says, the
sarcasm sharp in his tone. He pauses, still for a moment. He
studies the linoleum under his shoes, listening to another
speaker, then suddenly flings his arm toward the bed in an
impatient gesture.

"I don't care about 99.9 percent of the time, George; the
aphasia's *there*," he barks, exasperated. "She can't talk."

An intern's timid voice interrupts, and Francesca looks at
him in amazement.

"Hell yes, I want to cut," he half laughs. "I'm a cut man, remember?"

He slaps the pencil softly against his open palm as he studies the X-rays, seeking the enemy's weakness.

"I'm confident about this," he murmurs to himself, and then looks up at his residents. "I'm confident," he announces and crosses the room to my bed.

He is watching me closely. My head aches with the effort to find a word. I know that I can say kick, kick.

"Talk." I say it twice, and Francesca understands. He looks at me without moving for a long time. I wait for an answer.

"You want to go with this operation?" he asks me finally.

"Talk?" I repeat stubbornly.

He looks over at the lighted X-ray and traces the pencil lines along the side of my head with his index finger. The movement of his lips is as slight as the pressure of his fingertip.

His eyes are sad when he begins, touching the points where the burl of the electric drill will enter, but by the time he has completed the pattern, they glitter with the hard reflection of challenge.

"Alive is everything," he says.

"Go," I tell him, finding the hard G of a word I can say. Rising, he nods.

"This Thursday, then."

I lie on a narrow stretcher in a cold, cold room with white tile walls. There are other people. No one moves.

A woman whines, "I'm freezing. They're freezing me."

Two men are pushing a stretcher along a hall. The wheels bump steadily underneath me.

I feel the steady hum of electric clippers, brushing gently against my skull.

The last thing I hear is Dr. Francesca's voice:

"That's great, George! I'm ready to go here, and you want to change the whole fucking plan. Terrific!"

In the dark I hide from Death. I lie very quietly, as wild birds and beggars do, to avoid detection, to be not sufficiently interesting to her.

My eyes are always open, spreading wide to find light. It is always black, empty. I am always alone. I stare for days until white begins to flow into my eye sockets, stuffing the holes until it chokes me. I open my mouth to push it back and scream, again and again, staining whiteness with the sound of my fear.

Alan wailed like a banshee when he was baptized, and the priest, smiling, said Satan was *leaving* him with the screams. I looked for the Devil behind the chapel organ and in the choir stalls; God, too, because the priest said He was with us today.

When he discovered me, the priest lifted me up in his arms and explained that God's spirit came down from above us, and the devil had been up there too, with God, until he fell down below. I wondered if God missed him, like a lost brother or some part of himself that he dropped by mistake.

Someone is shouting. The rough edges of the voice rip small holes in the black around me. The barked commands tear the darkness into lacy, floating shreds. Beyond them is the Devil's face, surrounded by a ring of light. Dark eyes are glittering. Lips stretch wide against white, flashing teeth. I hear Him laughing, piercing the black with rising, unearthly sound, and then I recognize Dr. Francesca, the WINNER who has cut his deal—alive is everything—and he shouts, "Squeeze my fingers! Squeeze my fingers!" and I reach up to them (pick 'em up, pick 'em up), and grab his hand.

"Goddamn it, it's perfect," he says quietly, and the black opens over the high floating notes of my laughter.

When we made a deal, Alan always came out on top. I never minded. Once I traded him all the marbles I had in my Indian leather bag for his purey shooter. Mother was mad.

"Now," she explained patiently, "you don't have any marbles left at all, so how can you play?"

I held up the clear glass shooter to the light and looked closely at the perfect red, white and blue American flag inside. It was beautiful.

"I don't care," I told Mother.

"When you trade, you give one for one," she advised me. "That's the way to make a deal."

I look up at the ceiling, trying to see the color of the light;

Now I wonder if I can cut a deal with God or the Devil, whoever. Cut my losses. Alive is everything.

When we went to the woods at Christmas, Grandad came out in the cold to Alan and said, "Take off your mitten, Alan. I want to see your hand."

And he took it in his two old ones, stroking the smooth stubs gently with the pad of his thumb.

"You've got a good working hand here," he said.

It made Alan happy, but his fingers were still gone.

The color of pain is the winter sky, no end and no beginning. The muscles deep in the pit of my stomach are clenched all the time, so tight I cannot make any sound. If I move, the pain will never end. Under my closed eyes I draw a circle around the gray. It glows a little at the outer edge. I tell myself that when I reach the ring, the pain will be over. There is no one in the circle but me, pushing outward through the colorless light of pain. I do this a thousand times, and I picture each circle as a scar on my face, like the battle scars on soldiers' foreheads.

In the dark a nurse leans close, her breath warm, and whispers,

"Why are you crying, Constance? Do you miss your children?"

I am angry because she has broken my circle open and left me alone. I do not know children, and I am not crying. I am not afraid.

One of the residents, Dr. Brooks, has come to take out the black fishline stitches that climb up and over the top of my scalp. The stitches have been in for almost a month, and every time Dr. Brooks pulls a string out, my brain spits white flecks of pain at him. After each snip, just before the yank, I bellow angrily to blot out the hurt. It works beautifully. Dr. Brooks is not amused. By the time he has finished, he is frowning down at me, a very bad patient. I am having a wonderful time.

As he turns to go, a look of mild interest crosses his face.

"You never cry, do you?" he says.

When he's gone, I lift the top of the tray that swings across my bed. There is a steel mirror underneath. I have not looked at myself since the operation. I expect to see the marks of prolonged pain: ravaged eyes and deep lines around the mouth.

I can't take my eyes off my head. There is a wide flat shelf on the right side, as if someone cut a slab off the round top. And a hole. There is a deep hole the size of a Kennedy half dollar in my head. A thin layer of shiny skin is sucked down into it. Where the stitches used to be are pairs of dark dots, and thick layers of dead skin rise around them, cracked and flaking, ready to drop off. In the front chin-stubble hair is beginning to grow back in patches. It is white. I close my eyes, but I do not cry.

I meet my gaze in the mirror and recognize my physical self. The face is unchanged. My skin is smooth and firm, the contours the same. There are no visible marks of suffering. Still, there is a striking difference. I stare at myself and think about what it is. It takes almost an hour to understand. When Rand comes after work, I tell him.

"My face," I say, "is all yellow, definitely *yellow*," and he looks very pleased.

When it is clear to everyone that I am not going to die, they hire Sheila, an R.N. who works at the Rehabilitation Institute across the street, to take over the 11-3 shift. Sheila, who has special training in physical medicine, nurses people who are too sick for therapy, sort of warming them up for rehabilitation. She won't give me coffee until I walk over to the chair. She asks me questions as long as I can talk. Then, when I am tired, she reads the newspaper out loud.

There is a huge picture on the wall. I think it is of big and little flowers. Some are yellow. There are neat rows of tiny black drawings spread in rows across it. Some are closed tight and others are quite pretty, opening like flowers themselves. Sheila says that these are names. Names of my friends on a *sign* that they have *signed*. I know "friends," and "sign," but I do not understand "name." I look at the sign every day for hours. It is white.

The two doctors arrive every day in their uniforms. Their faces seem thinner. They call me "Constance" and always ask about the days of the week. Sheila usually asks me who the people are in the newspaper pictures, but I never recognize any of them. This used to irritate me, but now, sometimes, it makes me feel like weeping. The doctors always bring their square box and mumble into it. One day I say, "Don't you ever leave that dumb orange box at home?" and they look very pleased.

Sheila says I am getting much better, that almost everything I say before lunch makes sense. I remember about "name," and we name things together. She is very pleased. She calls the tiny marks on the sign and the newspaper "letters." I don't understand letters. Can I make some? she asks, giving me a paper and a pen. Suddenly my fingers are frozen. I can't move them.

In the afternoons blackness starts at the edges of my eyeballs and moves inward like spilled, spreading ink. I try to push it back, but it keeps covering my eyes until I can't see the light, or the yellow flowers on the sign.

I have lost something in the dark. If I could find it and pick it up off the ground, I would be well. I could understand what "letters" were and make the tiny drawings and even talk sense after lunch. If I knew what I was searching for. I look around all the time, but it is too hard to find anything in this seeping blackness.

When Sheila picks up her pad of paper and the pen it is close to the end of her shift. One afternoon I understand something.

"You're writing," I say, and she looks very pleased.

It is suddenly clear that the newspaper is "reading."

I look at my fingers and say, "I can't write."

And I can't read—names or newspapers. I don't know pictures or faces. I won't be able to learn to write, read, which is which.

"I can't talk."

I say it very quietly.

Yesterday, Mother brought my china christening cup, a baby's keepsake filled with flowers.

"I thought it would cheer you up," she said.

It is on the tray table by my styrofoam coffee cup. A little girl holding flowers is painted on the side. Her dress is yellow.

They have told me what it says on the cup: "Thursday's child has far to go." But I do not know that. I cannot read it. I will never know what color Thursday is.

Dr. Francesca's voice is harsh with anger.

"Sheila says you won't talk," he accuses me.

His eyes, deep in the sockets, are ignited like live, black coals.

"You can talk." He won't look away.

I stare back, helpless, thinking that once I could make hard noises with the back of my mouth; Kck.

"Cat," I say.

"Yes you can."

"Cat." I shake my head.

"Try harder."

"Cat!" I shout. "CAT CAT CAT." It is so hard to say it. I am panting.

"Can't," he says, and I answer, "Can't," exhausted, hearing my voice through water.

The water is tickling my cheeks. It is covering softly, not quite warm, washing the dirt from my eye sockets. I can see the blackness receding, flaking away and dripping with the water, out of sight. It rises in my head and then empties itself, until the darkness is washed away.

"Why are you crying?" Dr. Francesca asks me.

My pupils begin to tighten. I see his face sharpen in the rising light.

"I'm afraid," I say, hearing my voice, clear as the water. "I am afraid."

He sits down beside me on the bed and rolls the edge of the sheet between his thumb and finger.

"Take your hand off your head," he says.

"I can't."

"Sheila says you've held it there since she came this morning. Why can't you?"

"Things will spill out of the hole. I lost something."

"Some pieces of your brain."

"I can't read or write. I can't talk."

"You're a living miracle," he says, peeling my fingers off my scalp one at a time.

He traces the scar exactly, in its horseshoe shape, with his finger, brushing the black cobwebs off the edges of my vision.

"You did that before," I tell him. "With a red pencil, your finger."

"You remember that?" he asks and holds my shoulders, very pleased.

He fits the ball of his thumb into the hole and presses against the skin.

"It doesn't matter what you lost," he says. "It's healed now."

I can feel it, feel the edges of my skull soften.

("Take off your mitten, Alan," Grandad told him, "I want to see your fingers."

And he rubbed his thumb over the stubs, holding Alan's hand hefting it.

"You've got a good working hand here," he said.")

Fourteen is not the same as the other floors.

Everyone has the same horseshoe-shaped wound on one side of the head, a tribal scar which can never be rubbed out.

When I move carefully along the corridor I can see, in 1487, a tiny, shriveled woman with fingers curved into bird claws, so old that her flesh, veined like onion skin, clings tight to the outlines of her skull. A thin ribbon is tied around her scar and a few white tufts on the unshaven side of her head.

Next door there is a handsome boy about eighteen with a stubble growth of beard beginning. The white of his scar glows through his dark brown crew cut. Sheila told me he had a football injury. My eyes met his, but there is no flicker of response. Sheila says he is fine except that he can't walk.

The retarded boy in 1462, next to me, cries all the time. Sometimes his noises are like moaning, other times he sounds like angry, jabbering crows outside a window. Often, in the night, he heaves dry sobs, without tears, until he falls asleep. He has had an operation to relieve his pain. Today he is calling out to someone unnamed in a language no one understands.

I stop in sunlight to examine my fingers. I riffle them like a child playing a hand game, and it seems to me wonderful that I can do this. I lift them slowly, one at a time in sequence and I see the old lady raising her white, fluttering fingers over a piano keyboard; the retarded boy behind a podium, speaking clearly and forcefully; the quarterback cutting down the sideline, dancing out his dream. Moving the fingers of my good working hand, I weep.

I grow used to the pain. It shows up at lunchtime, like a horse-faced acquaintance who pretends to drop in unexpectedly and stays all afternoon. It will last, Dr. Francesca says, another eight or ten months, but the prospect doesn't terrify me now.

I notice that Rand has lost weight. His suits hang on his body and he walks with a slight slump at the shoulders. Mother's voice cracks often from fatigue, and she speaks haltingly, as if she's holding onto something for dear life. Rand says that taking care of four children is getting to her.

I am rubbing baby oil into my scalp, trying to get off the dead skin, when he says it. The word "children" snags on a sharp edge of my consciousness, and I see them clearly, our four children: one boy, three girl babies.

"Baby oil," I say, smiling, and hold out the bottle to Rand. The letters on it are blue and they say "Baby Oil" and they are the smell of it, the greasy touch on my fingers, and the table where I change their diapers while they look at me, those three baby girls, each with her own face.

Rand nods, "yes," and looks pleased.

"Billy is eleven," I say.

"Right."

I am rubbing the oil into my head. "Remember when he fell on that broken bottle? He was three."

"Sure," Rand answers. "I do."

Billy had a pink scar on his knee like a little smile, carved there by the sharp glass. We didn't stitch it up, how could you stitch it? and it grew with him. It spread outward with his skin and muscle, expanding, changing color until it rested above his flesh like a white, coiled worm.

"Rand," I call and I am trembling, "hold me."

Today I am going home. The morning paper is lying on my tray table with a big picture of Richard Nixon on the front page.

"What does it mean: Water Gate?" I ask, and everyone in the room looks very pleased, when who should walk in but THE

WINNER with a pink shirt under his gray doctor's smock and a silk foulard at this throat. Our laughter is like cheering because this time he might get the K.O., we can feel it coming. He stands, feet apart, with his hands on his hips, looking at me. "You squeamish?" he asks, his eyes sparkling. I shake my head.

"Get up," he commands. "I'm gonna walk you to your own case presentation."

It is black. A square of white glows in the center of the darkness. The small room is too warm, filled with the rustlings and murmurs of strangers I cannot see. A machine stands humming in the corner. I close my eyes to avoid the empty screen, and I am lying on my back, falling slowly past the white flickers of fear that pierce the darkness.

"Here he comes," a voice whispers and I feel them moving aside, the slight draft that follows his entrance.

"This is a thirty-four year old white female," he says.

I open my eyes and keep them open.

The film is in color. The brilliant purples and roses of blood flowing through arteries and veins vibrate against the gleaming steel of surgical clamps. My brain is magnified and trembling, opening like the flowers in Walt Disney's time-lapse movies.

"...clamped the artery there," Dr. Francesca is explaining, holding a lighted pointer, "...and there."

The shades of pink and violet shift and change, growing more intense and beautiful. His voice accelerates, stops, the steel knife on the screen pauses and suddenly the screen fills up again with white. Disembodied fingers, sheathed in transparent rubber, place an oval object on a paper towel, the size and deadly dull purple of a plum. The gloved hand opens to spill several items onto the towel. I squint a little to see what they are, but there is nothing but the plum to see. The fingers descend again and carefully place the black plastic cap of a cheap drugstore pen. I can see them now, white on white, short fat slugs, slightly curled and dead, drying in the sun.

"What are they?" My voice is too loud, an intrusion.

"Pieces of your brain."

"Don't I need them?"

"Apparently not," he says. All the doctors laugh.

"What's the pen cap for?" I ask.

"Scale."

Up north at Grandad's, he fed deer in the winter, when the snow was so deep even the tree bark was buried. One year when the herd came to his woods there was an albino with them. Alan took pictures with his birthday camera, he must've taken thirty. And when they came back from the drugstore, he cried because you couldn't see any albino deer at all.

He took his pictures to school, and said to his friends when they laughed at him and called him a fibber, "Connie was there! She'll tell you it's true!"

I told them the albino deer wasn't on the film but it was in the woods because we both saw it.

At home I said to Alan, very pleased, "You used me. You owe me one."

The lights are on and the doctors are filing out. I stare at the empty white screen wondering whether the white paper towel and white pieces of brain (which I do not need), are still lying on it. What I need is something I can use for scale.

Before supper I walk with Billy. He is old enough to support me or run for help if something happens. We are both very careful.

I should have been careful not to look up into the trees, the green lacy network of leaves that covers us. They are so shiny and lively in the breeze, letting the late light drop through like golden coins.

"Why are you crying?" someone says.

It is Billy's voice. I raise my hand, startled, to brush the wetness off but he stops it.

"You never cry," he says.

"I thought I never would."

"The day of your operation I went over to Peter's for dinner," he says, walking over the grass, looking at his sneakers. "And during dessert Dad called, and I didn't want to go to the phone. I almost couldn't."

(*"Pick 'em up, Connie! Pick 'em up!"*)

"I thought that Dad would say you were dead and I would start crying."

("*I'm afraid. I am afraid.*")
"I didn't want to cry in front of Peter."
("*You never cry, do you?*")
("*You can stand anything for four seconds.*")
("*Close your eyes, Constance, and keep them closed.*")

His face is tilted up toward mine. With my finger I trace the U-shaped track of one of his tears, erasing it.

"I hate to cry alone," I say.

We stand still, looking at each other, and the dark centers of our eyes, bright with tears, open wide to let the life in.

Tigers

BY CATHERINE BROWDER

For the longest time no one knew much about Auntie Bohray's new friend. On Wednesday, my older sister picked up some news at the City Market and phoned Ma immediately: Bohray's man was well off. He drove a new American car, wore a gold necklace and watch and ring. He paid the utilities and her two children's school fees, not to mention all miscellaneous expenses. The man only had two children of his own to feed. Well, maybe three, since a new one was on the way.

Ma was thrilled. "See, Dara!" she told me. "I knew something was going on." The only grudging note was that the man wasn't one of us, but Vietnamese.

By the time Ma got around to telling my stepfather, the subject had been discussed from every angle, with a half dozen friends. What she told Tom seemed a bit thinned out.

"Bohray not just widow anymore," Ma said, over supper. "No good live in Projects. Need friend. Now Bohray have friend. And bran' new microwave."

"Is that how you spent your day?" Tom said. "Gossiping about Bohray?"

("He's just jealous," Ma said later. "Men here, men there. Same-same.")

There wasn't any plot to keep Tom out. It was just the way of things, and Ma's Tarzan English. Out loud, I always called him Daddy, because Angela did. I was the only one of Ma's first family who still lived at home. In my school diary I called him Tom and Tommy-boy and Mr. Potato Head.

24

"I go Saturday," Ma said. "See microwave."

"Sure," Tom said. "But I don't like you being in the Projects."

"Bohray she live there!"

"I know and it's a shame. Somebody'll steal that microwave right out from under her nose."

Angela got out of her chair and pulled on Daddy Tom's sleeve. Angela wasn't more than five at the time. Tom just looked at her and melted. I called her the Mouse. Whenever she wanted something from him, she squeaked. She had round eyes, a puff of curly brown hair, pale skin like Tom's. Whatever Angela wanted, she got. Ma said that was natural, since Angela was his own true daughter and I was just a step. Funny word, I thought. Something you put your foot on, but he never did. Ma made sure I got my share.

"My two girls," he said sometimes, which made me feel I ought to like him better.

In my school calendar I drew a bright blue star and wrote: "By this date, Tom will buy Ma her new oven." And if he didn't? Sulks and cries in Ma's make-shift English. Hot Khmer words that could knot us girls against him. Burnt bacon. Burnt rice. It wasn't as if Ma got everything she wished for. Tom kept the purse strings tight—counting out her grocery money every Thursday night. "Dara," she told me, "you have to learn when to fuss."

That Friday, I crowded onto the bus with my friend Chantelle. Only three weeks left. Both of us were finishing up sixth grade, although I was old enough for eighth. "Small for sixth grade," someone at Church said once, which made me mad. Mother was small too, and so was Angela The Mouse, even if Daddy Tom was her father.

I felt the summer months pull toward me like a wide and empty boat. I hoped I might fill them up by helping Tom with the animals in his clinic. Chantelle dragged me down the aisle until we reached a double seat halfway back. She plopped down and said, "Whew-ee!"

"Come summer, I'm goin' to the pool every single day," she said.

"Maybe I'll go to the pool too, if my stepdad takes me."

The bus lurched and stopped. The driver stood up, his dark

glasses wrapped around his stern, black face. Most of the kids were still standing in the aisle, waving at their friends through the window.

"You kids, siddown!" he said. "You, back there. Put your butt on the seat. Tha's right. Right down *on the seat*, or we be sittin' here a long time!"

Boys in the back row started giggling. They rapped out a song, hands slapping against their legs and the backs of chairs.

> Put your butt on the seat!
> Put your butt on the seat!
> If you want to get to heaven
> You put your butt on the seat!

"I'm gonna buy me a hot pink swim suit," Chantelle said. "And those pink plastic sandals."

"Why pink?" I asked.

"Pink's my number one color. Suits me."

It was Angela's color, too.

"Blue suits me," I said. I'd been thinking about how much I'd like my bedroom walls and ceiling to be the color of a Kansas City sky. "I'm gonna have my stepdad paint my room bright blue," I said.

"He must be a nice man."

I turned my head away. Outside, groups of children chased and jumped and lined up for other buses.

"How come you don't talk about him more?" Chantelle asked. "Being as he's so nice?"

I shrugged. "Not always nice," I said. The bus pulled away, and I watched the city moving in: the brick and frame houses, fenced and unfenced, one right after the other, and none of them too tall.

"You don't talk about your real dad either," Chantelle said.

"I don't remember much."

The bus passed a block of shops that I liked to look at— Florine's beauty parlor that sold Redkein, a pawn shop, a drug store with heavy grill over all the windows and door, and on the corner Speedy Checks Cashed. I used to think that Speedy was a name. We passed Troost lake, so small, and someone always fishing, quiet and patient as a tree.

"Girl, you listenin' to me?" Chantelle poked me in the arm. "What're you gonna do this summer?"

I hadn't thought about it, only about the color of my room.

"I'm gonna watch Oprah and 'All My Children,'" Chantelle said.

"Me too." I didn't like TV, but Angela did. So did my married sisters.

I looked out at the city. From inside the bus, it was like watching a movie, on a life-size screen, everything within reach picked up by an invisible eye—cars and fences and concrete.

I couldn't remember the things my mother missed: wet farm ground with animals nearby, cabbage and fish and rice cooking in the house, the yellow-green sky the wind brought before rain and the fresh scent left behind. Dripping roofs and leaves. What I could still remember were the sights and sounds at Khao I Dang. And smells, like an army marching up your nose. I met a boy there, older than myself. He'd spent a year living in a hole in the ground. He said he could only tell when it was safe to come up by how much sweat and blood and gunpowder was hanging in the air.

The bus pulled over to the curb, red lights flashing. Chantelle gave me a quick hug and bounced into the aisle. "You call me, y'hear?"

I watched her go. She was laughing and teasing a boy who lived somewhere on her street. She was so excited, she forgot to turn and wave.

Tom drove us over to Bohray's that weekend. He waited until Ma and Angela and I were safe inside—Bohray waving from the door—before he drove away.

Bohray didn't care much for the Projects either, but it was cheap. She used to say there weren't many decent places where a Cambodian widow could live, without moving to California. Anyway, now she had her friend.

"Think of all the widows he had to choose from," Bohray joked.

"But none so pretty," said Ma.

I would have said the same thing if I'd been allowed. Auntie Bohray was the most beautiful woman I knew, even if Ma said Bohray had put on weight in the seven years she'd lived here.

"Bohray has a nice face still, but now she's got an American bottom."

Bohray led us into the kitchen. Ma cried out, pleased and jealous, both at once. She opened the microwave door, closed it, opened it again and felt the strange pebbled lining, the buttons.

Bohray took some cheese and bread and made a sandwich, put it in the oven, ran her fingers quickly over the numbers. In no time the cheese melted, seeping out the sides. The timer dinged and she gave the sandwich to Ma.

"But the bread's still white."

"You have to buy a special oven with a browner."

"When Tom buys me one, I'll make him get a browner. Next time you ask your friend for a new car."

A few weeks back, someone had smashed out Bohray's windshield, for the third time. I don't know why Ma thought a newer car would get better treatment.

Bohray laughed. "His wife's going to have a baby. I don't want to look greedy."

"He come here often?" Ma asked.

"Yes. His wife told him no more babies."

"You be careful too."

"I am. I got you-know-what from the clinic."

"Don't you want him too?"

"It's all right this way."

"But you're only a number two wife."

"It doesn't matter," Bohray said. "He's not so young, you know. I can tease him about younger men."

Ma laughed.

I was glad Angela was playing with Bohray's son in the front room. I liked it when I had them to myself. Bohray put on some rice. The sweet smell of it filled the kitchen and frosted up the windows. I drew a cat's face in the steam. Bohray thought she was being smart, but I knew what was *what*. Chantelle told me.

"Not so good," Ma said. "You need a husband. Like me and Tom."

I watched Bohray move slowly around the kitchen, graceful as a dancer at the Royal Palace. Bohray could have her pick.

"You come with me to school," Ma said.

Bohray shook her head. "I've been."

Ma waited until the evening meal to tell Tom. She served up everything he liked: pot roast, potatoes, rice, carrots cooked to pulps that made me gag.

"So-so oven," Ma said. "Cheap model. Can't brown food."

If she got one—and maybe Santa would bring her one before Christmas—she wanted the kind that took away the whiteness of bread, the pinkness of meat.

"Be nice, huh?" Her voice trilled up like a bird. "Angela she like too."

Ma wouldn't stop smiling. I had to cover my mouth to keep from laughing. Ma glared.

"What matter with you?"

"Auntie has new Nike shoes," Angela piped up. "Pink and white."

"With velcro straps," I shouted. I wasn't one to be left out.

Tom dug his fork into his roast, faced it like it was the only safe ground above the line of fire that came at him every night. There'd be hell to pay if Angela got new shoes and I didn't. He looked at Angela. I knew what he saw. He used to say the sound of her name took the chill off a room.

Tom said he didn't care one whit what they said about him at the VFW. Those old boys can come and show off their grandbabies all they want, he said, and he'd just pull Angela out of his watch pocket. *How old is Tom Mapes anyway?* they'd say when we'd passed on to another group at the Fourth of July picnic. Old men, all of them, pulling in their chins, hiding their waists under red and blue Hawaiian shirts. *A daughter, you say?*

And this Auntie business. He never understood it, complaining that Bohray was no more an aunt than the woman who came in every day to help him clean and feed the animals in the clinic. *"Auntie!"* he huffed. "You people wanna turn everyone into family!"

It's true, we didn't know Bohray until we'd all met at the Westside Christian Church. Tom's church. New arrivals, all of us. Adopted and cared for, given blankets and canned corn and ham. Sort of like the animals in Tom's kennel. Tom helped out himself, lowering the back seat of the station wagon, piling it high with cartons and old grocery bags, making the "mercy runs," he called them, from one rundown apartment building to another, in parts of the city where he wouldn't have sent either of his grown sons.

"More people wedged into three rooms than you could shake a stick at," he said. Folks with small children who had to walk up three narrow flights, kept warm by a single heater-stove in the central room.

"A dangerous thing!" he said.

Tom was carrying a stack of blankets up just such a flight when he first met Ma. She was Vonn Touch then, and if she'd married him at home she'd never had to change her name. Tom likes to tell the story on me, how I hid behind Ma, with eyes so serious they made his heart sink and swell, both at once. Of course Ma didn't know any proper English then. Just a lot of single words that hung together as she spat them out, sounding like someone punching holes in paper. He always seemed proud of that fact, that what little she knew could cover so much space. I think that's what brought him back to her, again and again. The widow man, Ma called him.

Ma was still going to school then, with Angela. Not that it did much good. Tom dropped them off at nine and picked them up again at noon. Ma dolled up Angela in pink dresses and hair ribbons and little lacy socks that would have made any man forget he had a son of thirty-eight.

"Good class. Good teacha," Ma said, and Tom laughed every time.

Ma brought her teacher bags of rice, Cambodian spring rolls, fish soup, cheese and butter and crackers that had been donated to the church, with the "sell by this date" stamp already expired.

School was the most sociable thing in Ma's life, outside the family. There were lots of other Cambodians for her to gossip with, Vietnamese with their noses stuck up in the air, Mexicans who laughed and hugged and talked all the time, and that nice Syrian lady who always wore a scarf. Ma talked with her every day on the phone, scolding and telling her how she should handle her sons and husband, how she had to act "more tough."

"You make boys help!" Ma said. "You do!"

When Tom found out, he almost lost his temper. "Vonn, honey, you can't tell other folks how to live?" I told Chantelle, imitating the drawly way he speaks. I thought it was funny, coming from Mr. All-American Do-It-My-Way Tom.

Once, when her teacher was absent, Ma came home sad and droopy. "Poor teacher," she said without telling me a thing. Ma phoned her just before supper. Angela was watching TV. I was in the kitchen, helping.

"Teacha? I am Vonn. I so sorry you Aunt die... When you come back?"

I listened through the pause, to Ma's tiny voice.

"She leave you everything?... Oh... I so sorry... Maybe her husband die and leave you everything."

Early Monday, after we'd gone to Bohray's, I heard bowls clanging in the kitchen. No one but Angela could sleep through that noise. The blender whirred. A metal spoon tinged against glass. Water ran in the sink, full blast. Tom's feet thumped down on the floor in the next room. I went in my pajamas and found Ma looking for the Pyrex cake pans.

"Bohray says no aluminum. Only glass."

Tom scuffed along the wood floor to the bathroom. I asked Ma what she was doing.

"Making a cake. I'm going to bake it in Bohray's microwave. You want to come?"

"I have school," I said.

"I'll write a note."

I shook my head and slumped into a chair. With only three weeks left, I wasn't about to miss a day. Ma brought boxes of cereal, milk, sugar to the table, brushed the hair out of my eyes.

"You come with me and Angela today. Daddy will drive us over."

"You're missing school, too."

"Yes." She giggled. "I'm a bad girl."

The clock on the stove read 6:45. Ma picked up the bright yellow wall phone and punched the numbers.

"Teacha? I am Vonn. I wake up? I no come to school today. Angela sick."

Tom left the bathroom. I ran in and shut the door. I thought Ma was being silly, calling up her teacher in the middle of the night. Telling a fib, just so she could go and play with Auntie Bohray.

I loved school. All the students in bright clothes and socks, the green chalk boards wide as walls. It made me sad to think about it ending. Chantelle wasn't sad at all.

"Dara? You there?" Ma called from the hall. "Dara! Enough time! Come out."

I left the magazine on the floor. I'd been careful. I'd replaced the cap on the toothpaste just the way Tom liked, and put the lid down on the toilet. So many fussy little ways of doing things. *You do what he says*, Mom told us. *You do!*

On Saturdays, Tom let me help him in the veterinary clinic. He liked my help—it was free—especially when Flora phoned in sick.

"She'll drop out of sight one day," he said. "Like a stone in water."

I helped him clean the cages, feed and hold the cats so they wouldn't feel so homesick. It was the animals I liked, but I let Tom think it was him.

He'd even had a young woman helping out, a vet student, full of ideas about how to lure the public and let them pay on a sliding scale.

"All I ever learned, Dara, was the essentials," he said. "Anatomy, diagnosis, surgery, treatment. Nowadays, they all want to run a business!"

Delores would put blue and pink bows on the animals after they'd had their flea baths and shots. She'd hand them over to the owners like birthday gifts. The older people loved it. After Delores left, I tied the bows.

What a peculiar world, Ma said to me, where pets, other than pigs, had the run of human feeling. Cats and poodles, standing in for babies. I knew what it was that got Ma all worked up.

I thought about asking Tom about his own family feeling. I'd write out the questions carefully in my school diary. *Do you ever think about your first wife? How often do you phone your sons or do they phone you? Did you used to see them more often? Why doesn't your daughter call you more? How come she doesn't visit? How come she lives in Milwaukee anyway?* There were other questions, too, some that I was too afraid to write.

Tom's sons had children, all of them younger than me. I used to ask Ma how come they didn't come on over to eat, like my married sisters. American boys don't do that, she said. *Grow up, move away. Strange world!*

We did go over to their houses, once in a while. Ma chatted and smiled and the wives chatted and smiled, but it seemed like someone or other was always sulking off into the kitchen. Angela got on with Tom's grandkids for about ten minutes. Then something would happen and she'd come sit in Tom's lap, in a sulk. I'd sit at the kitchen table and color or read my book.

Just like Ma's wedding. My two older sisters were there with their families, along with Bohray and every other Cambodian Ma knew in Kansas City, wearing their best silk *sarongs*. There were records and songs, and a shortened-up Cambodian wedding ceremony, after the Christian one, which took place downstairs in the Church gym. (Ma complained that we weren't allowed to have rice wine.) Tom's sons, their wives and children seemed to stand apart. His daughter didn't even come. Ma sniffed and said maybe they didn't like our Khmer looks and voices, but I don't think she was right. I saw the lonesome way they looked at their dad.

Flora phoned in one last time, to quit, like Tom predicted. Ever since Mrs. Murphy's dog had sunk its tiny teeth into Flora's index finger, she'd been touchy.

Tom told Ma she'd have to help, after Ma told him she wasn't going to allow me to, anymore. He softened the asking when he said, "It's a family business, you know. I was hoping you could learn the ropes."

"Learn ropes?" Ma said with a sneer. "You pay Dara? You pay me?"

"Not a matter of paying," he said, getting cranky. "It's a matter of helping out. The money all goes to the same place."

"What if I want buy Angela new shoes. Pretty dress."

"Don't I give you everything you want?"

"Not enough allowance. I want toaster oven! Bohray have new toaster oven."

Tom struck the kitchen table with his fist and stomped out. Ma spent the afternoon in a huff. I'd told her I'd be glad to help.

"Not your job," she said. "Tom's job."

She kept Tom guessing all day and night, right up to the

following morning. I heard her banging in the kitchen around six, boiling rice, lining up the cereal for us girls, traveling in and out of language without ever shifting gears. Tom sat down to his bacon and eggs, and Ma went to the phone.

"Teacha? I am Vonn. I wake you up?"

Ma pulled the long coiled cord and wound it around her hand.

"I no come to school right now. I help Tom. Feed dogs."

The Saturday after my last day of school, I asked Ma if I could paint the bedroom Angela and I shared. Ask Tom, she said. I waited until I sensed a happy mood.

"Why, punkin', that's just fine by me."

I told him I wanted to pick out my own color. I knew the exact shade: Lucerne Blue. I'd seen it on a color tile at Sears. I shouldn't have asked at supper. I should have waited until I was alone with Tom. Supper was the time Angela pricked up her ears.

"I want pink!" she said and swung her shoulders back and forth.

"Pink's for sissies," I said. "Pink stinks. Nobody in their right mind wants pink, An-ge-laaa."

I felt bad, speaking out against my best friend's color. Angela always made me lose my head.

She wailed and pouted, saying all the silly things you expect of someone five. She huffed around the kitchen, little hands on little hips, went up to Ma, then began to work on Tom. *Pink, pink, pink.*

I rolled up my drawing paper and chased her out of the kitchen, through the living room and into our bedroom. I swatted. I poked. Angela screamed for Daddy Tom. You'd think she was being murdered.

"Girls! Girls! Cut it out," he called. He didn't move an inch.

Ma took the fly swatter and went after us both, Khmer words hitting us like salt. We both got our legs switched. She made us sit on our separate beds and hold our tongues.

Dara always gets her way, Angela whispered.

Angela's spoiled rotten, I hissed back.

"Half-half," Ma said. "Half pink. Half blue."

"And the ceiling?" I cried. "I want the ceiling blue too. You can't have a pink ceiling. You have to have a ceiling like the sky."

"Okay."

Angela began to cry. I opened my mouth, and Ma cut me off.

"Enough, Dara," Ma said. "You too old."

Bohray called that summer, before I started Middle School. She'd seen a movie and said Ma should go. *And Dara too.*

I don't think Tom would have suggested it if Ma hadn't brought it up. We dropped Angela off at my sister Phyrun's.

Ma watched with total concentration, and I watched Ma, when I didn't want to watch the screen.

When the theatre grew bright, Ma picked up her sweater and handbag and headed for the exit.

"Okay movie," she said at Tom over her shoulder. "But not hard enough."

"Not hard enough!?" he said, once we were in the car. "How much harder can a person stand? All those empty fields of bones. Like the title!"

"Too soft," Ma said. "More killing. Much more."

He watched her as if she were some stranger who'd climbed in his car by mistake. A small woman with a sweet and wrinkled face. Nice smile, when she used it. "Brave and fiesty as a pit bull," he bragged to his sons, although at home he didn't care much for either. Now he stared. The light changed and the car behind ours honked. He was quiet the rest of the way home.

Tom sat in the living room reading the evening paper while Ma bathed Angela. I heard Angela squeal, Ma talking, her Khmer voice rising and falling, warm and open as a bed.

Tom called me from the kitchen where I was drawing. He asked me to sit down with him a while. I sat in the rocker across from the sofa. He cleared his throat and looked down into his lap.

"Your mother can only say a few things about what happened before you came here," he said. "You know...her English."

I began to rock.

"I know about the camp and how the Khmer Rouge would

sometimes come at night. I know you lost your older brothers and your fathers and others. But I don't know how or why."

"You want me to say, don't you."

You'd think I'd hit him with a stone, but then he smiled.

"I've got me a house full of second-guessers," he said. "My first wife Edna didn't say much. Not half as much as your mother. Edna couldn't guess a thing."

He leaned back in the sofa. I sat quietly rocking, staring at the floor.

"I might understand things better if you said a word or two."

A word or two. I heard words rolling back and forth as though what happened were a car wreck, a one-time thing.

"I wasn't any older than Angela," I said. "I don't remember much, except the camp. Not so nice, camp."

He knew about the camps. The Church had told them all about it. I wondered what he meant by *all*.

The floor gave a little chirp whenever the rocker traveled over the loose board. My rocking grew fast, faster, faster, as though I wanted to make that old chair fly.

In my mind, the days melt into one day that never ends.

I hear voices, the rattle of feet and guns: A group of men pulling someone in short work pants and floppy shirt; the sun against us, blotting out the face. What we see is blurry, a farmer in a field, hands tied behind his back. Two men, one on each shoulder, lead him toward some distant trees. I see a different farmer coming toward us. We are in the garden, just beyond the house. Ma says to go inside. *Soldiers. Quick.*

Through the cracks in the shuttered door I see a tall scarecrow of a man with a drooping eyelid raise a sickle. "This is what we do to traitors of the people," he says. His arm moves, bringing the blade down across my Uncle Sothea's neck. Soethea's head lulls to one side, falls and rolls a foot into Ma's garden. Ma faints, and two other women drop to the ground to help.

A home at the edge of our village bursts into flames. I remember the fire and smoke and screams, more young people arriving, dressed in black pajamas or bulky camouflage pants. Some of them carry guns heavier than themselves. A boy looks at Ma and tells her that we'd one day come with them.

Where? she asks. And why?

Learn new ways, he says. Forget the past.

When they leave, she spits in the garden dirt. Toy soldiers! she says. With young, dead eyes. Forget the past? Forget Sothea or the father of her children?

My pictures fade, sinking down in shadows. Ma keeps sending us indoors. More people come, more child soldiers. They ask Nhouk to be the village head. An odd job for Nhouk, Ma says. Too mild-mannered. They ask Nhouk, Who is sympathetic. *Sympathetic? Who to? We are all alike.* And still they come, eating and drinking and shooting Nhouk's brood sow.

Your soldiers, their soldiers? They're all the same to us. For this, Nhouk is struck, hard, in the back.

The pictures begin to spin, a movie speeding up, hot and sticky colors exploding in my mind.

They take Nhouk's boy and tie him high up in a tree. *There is still no one*, he tells them, through his tears and the keening of his wife. I am there, holding my mother's skirt. After four days, they take him down. A limp rag. Nhouk touches his lips with water and bathes his face until a girl younger than my sisters grabs the boy away.

At sundown he goes back in the tree, she says. And at dusk we hear screams from a neighboring house.

I look up. Tom was staring at me, his eyes and lips two narrow lines. The only sound was the chirp of the rocker against the floor. Chantelle used to push me in a swing as high as it would go. We're too old to swing much anyone.

"Uncle Sothea died," I said. "Killed. And Ma saw Pol Pot soldiers take my father away. So she dug the money out from under the water jug in the garden and took Phyrun and San and me... We left for Thailand. In the night."

Tom folded the paper slowly, back into its folds. He took off his reading glasses and rubbed his eyes.

It wasn't my place to tell.

Ma got Angela and me up early the next day. "Zoo today," she said. "Teacher called me Friday."

I threw back the covers and bounced up. Ma tickled Angela's feet. Angela play-whimpered and Ma yanked the covers back.

"You no get up, you no go to zoo," she said in English.

Angela stretched and rolled to the top cover. Such a lazy bones!

The bowls were ready at our places, the cereal lined up like train cars across the table.

"You want Kix?" Ma asked. Angela sulked, shook her head.

"Frosted Flakes? Cheerios?" Angela pouted.

"Okay. I give you sticks instead."

Angela grabbed the nearest box and poured cereal into her bowl until it spilled over.

A large saucepan steamed on the stove. I smelled rice.

"Teacher says we'll have a picnic too. Everybody brings something. Angela, look up. We'll see the giraffe today. You like the giraffe."

Angela made a face.

"Okay. You stay home."

"I like the monkeys better," said Angela in her squeaky voice.

"I like the tigers," I said, and grinned.

"Tigers! Terrible animals!" said Ma. "Tigers come into villages at night. Steal babies!"

"Not here."

"Why d'you like tigers?"

"Because they eat babies like Angela."

"Talk nice!"

"Maybe we'll feed Angela to the tiger today," I teased.

Angela smacked the table with her spoon, squealed, pretended to cry.

"Maybe *you* won't go to the zoo," said Ma.

"Maybe tigers took Father," I said.

Ma stopped, turned, and stood absolutely still.

"Why d'you say that?"

I shrugged and played with my cereal box.

"Yes," Ma said quietly. "Tigers. On two legs."

I looked up at her but she was staring off into space.

"Daddy Tom asked me last night."

"I already told," Ma snapped. "They don't show that in the movie. They show guns and shouting and pushing and bones. They don't show how babies die slow. They don't show how Sothea lost his head."

"It's only a movie, Ma."

"Some movie. Too soft."

I took a box of Kix and poured it carefully into my bowl. Chantelle liked Kix.

"You want sugar?" Ma asked, her voice quiet and low. I shook my head.

Most of the students and their families had arrived by the time Tom dropped us off. Ma waved at Bohray who was parking her car in the lot beside the school.

"So many new people," Ma said. "Where do they all come from?"

A yellow school bus, just like mine, stood parked across the street. I saw the driver leaning against the front grill. A black man with dark glasses. For a moment I thought he was our driver and I started to wave, until I looked close. He was shorter, heavier. I felt let down.

"Here," Ma said. "Take the bag."

Bohray's children were with her. Her daughter Rohn had brought a friend, a girl with pink cheeks and long hair the color of sand.

"I could have brought Chantelle," I whispered to Ma, angry.

"No friends. Only family. That's what Teacher said."

I pointed at the American girl holding Rohn's hand. Ma shrugged. "Bohray's business. Not yours."

I pushed away and went inside the school building. I sat down on the steps and watched the adults going up and down, everybody moving so fast through that thick August heat. I heard laughing on the top floor, the school floor. I recognized Ma's teacher, a tall woman, carrying down a cooler. "Hello, Dara. Where's your mother?" she asked.

"In front," I said. "With Bohray."

I followed her outside. Ma squealed and hugged her teacher, everyone talking at once.

Auntie said something but I couldn't hear. There was a sudden burst of voices just behind. Khmer words turned to shouts, curses, screams. I turned, backed away from the entrance and stood behind Ma.

Two Cambodian people came out the front door, backwards. A short round woman in an orange and black *sarong* pushed a man with spikey hair and crushed khaki pants. People on the sidewalk froze in mid-step, lowering baskets and bags to the pavement. Heads appeared from the office window on the third floor—one head, two, three.

The man pushed back. Ma whispered, "I know that man."

The shouting woman grabbed hold of the man's shirt and began to pull, the man swatting at her hands. When he tried to shake loose, the woman took a firmer hold, both hands pulling until the shirttail came free.

Ma ran up the sidewalk and pushed the man down. Both women were on him now, like cats on a bird. Feet kicked up, elbows stabbed the air, limbs moving so fast that no one dared to help. From behind the school bus, a third Cambodian woman screamed and ran across the street to the group struggling on the sidewalk. She tugged on the man's shoulder, trying to pull him to his feet, her own feet kicking out at Ma. I felt my body moving forward, then Bohray holding me back.

The heads in the upstairs window disappeared. Seconds later, four teachers burst out the door and fell on Ma and the other people in the street.

"Stop it! Stop it now!" someone yelled.

Ma shook loose and backed away. I saw Ma's teacher place a hand on her shoulder, ready to hang on tight. The man's shirt flapped open, one button gone, the buttonhole torn. His mouth hung open. His face looked so old.

Ma let loose a string of curses that singed our ears. Not one Cambodian moved. We stood there in a cluster, motionless and afraid. This is a dream, I told myself. A camp dream. A nightmare that would vanish in the sunlight. But the memory pushed up harder, the harder I pushed it down.

I could see the man's face now, the look of anger and fear and surprise. His wife stood flushed and small-eyed as a nursing sow, ready to trample anything that came too close.

One of the teachers, a man, began to speak, the words never stopping, his hands talking, talking. *Back up*, said the hands. *Calm down, calm down.* Bohray held tightly to Angela's hand. I came and put my arms around Ma.

"Khmer Rouge," Ma told the teachers and pointed, her finger a gun. "He give away my neighbor. Maybe give away my brother. My husband."

The man shouted back in Khmer. "I gave no one away. They came. They took. Don't you remember my son? Don't you remember the tree?"

Ma's finger remained steady in the air until it trembled. Slowly she lowered her arm.

"I call Tom," she said to her teacher. "I go home now."

I felt such sadness, like a deep, dark hole. All her one-inch words, her short and jerky sentences. I wanted to cry out, *Hush, Ma. Let me speak.*

Ma turned back slowly to the man and his wife, and spoke in a voice that shook. "May the Buddha protect you, Nhouk."

Ma sat on the curb, holding Angela. I waved at Auntie Bohray as the bus finally left. Angela whimpered.

"I want to go too."

"Not today. Daddy will take us Sunday."

"Auntie's going," I said.

"But we aren't," Ma said.

"Everything works out for Auntie," I said. "And she's not even married."

"What do you mean?" said Ma.

"Nothing."

"You say something but mean nothing? Strange child. You want to ride in the same bus with those people?"

"I don't care about those people."

"You forget your father?"

"No. I remember. A little."

"Good. You keep that *little*."

The light in my eyes turned pink and dim. I felt in them a stinging cold, as though all the winds of the world had come to blow them out. I turned my face away.

"I don't like to remember," I said. "When I try, my head hurts."

Ma took my hand and squeezed it.

"You like it here?" she asked softly, and I nodded.

"I didn't mean what I said about Auntie."

"I know. We're all just number two wives. No good being alone."

The station wagon turned the corner and stopped in front of us. Ma opened the front door, pulling Angela onto her lap. I got in back.

"What happened?" Tom asked. He sounded annoyed, like we'd somehow put him out.

"Angela sick," Ma said. Angela squealed.

"Fever," said Ma and clapped a hand over Angela's mouth. I

fell across the back seat and stuffed my fingers in my mouth until the noise that wanted to come out—the laugh or cry—was gone.

"You all right back there?" Tom asked.

"She upset," said Ma. "Can't play with other kids. I say maybe you take us Sunday."

Ma smiled up at him and laughed. "I so sorry for girls. Sunday okay?"

"I don't know," he said. "If I can get away."

"Dara and me. We feed dogs Friday, Saturday, Sunday morning. Then we go."

I sat up quickly and pressed myself between the two front seats. "Can we take Chantelle? Please?"

As the car turned onto the Avenue, I lay back down and watched the sky. A bright, clear-blue sky. Without a single cloud. I imagined the sky covering me like a blanket, covering Chantelle wherever she might be. A blue this strong makes you forget about all the other skies that come and go, the brown and black and heavy red ones that can press you to the ground.

Pullandbedamned Point

BY DAVID MASON

Nickel Thompson lay dying in the back bedroom of his house on Pullandbedamned Point Road. Greer knew it, woke up knowing it and, though she was ninety miles away, felt his presence as if he were here in Bellevue, as if his dying were a way of calling to her. But she didn't want to go to him. It was her husband, Carl, who said they had to do it. "Don't you think you should see him? It might be the last time." And now, as soon as their children were assembled, they would go. "Is it your mother? Is that why you don't want to go?" Of course it was, but Greer couldn't say so to Carl when he was being so understanding. And it was the old man dying on her like this, the way he was dying, knowing everything had been botched from the beginning.

Here for the time being it was quiet. A quiet Saturday morning, and from her kitchen everything she saw—the driveway, the rhododendrons—was just what it should be. Everyone wanted to live in Bellevue. You crossed the floating bridge from Seattle and entered a world of clean prosperity, high hedges and low crime. It meant you had arrived, and it certainly wasn't Pullandbedamned Point, not the faded little house her mother scrubbed with such ferocity.

And here I am, scrubbing, Greer thought. She had done the breakfast dishes, the washer was running, and she stood by the corner table with a wet sponge in her hands, gazing vaguely out at the rhododendrons.

She knew that there was something wrong with this life, but that the alternative, another life, would be worse. She could have married Shane Fenton and stayed in Nooksack, moving maybe a few miles away from Nickel's house, though why she called it Nickel's house with her mother there scrubbing and disinfecting was beyond her. Shane Fenton now had a shoe store in Nooksack Mall. If she had married him, she might be working Saturdays for her husband, eking out a mortgage in a tract on the north side. Pullandbedamned Point was on the north side. She might never have moved to the south side, or to Bellevue, or anywhere people didn't worry so much about money. She used to think that if she didn't have to worry so much about money everything else would fall into place. Instead it fell to pieces. Nickel was dying, holed up in that house with a woman everybody said was crazy. Even his magic tricks and stories couldn't save him now.

Pullandbedamned Point got its name from a shipwreck long before Nooksack was a town, when it was only a harbor with no breakwater and a lumber mill on the creek. There was a muddy bluff, and below it when the tide ran out, a beach slimy with sea wrack. One winter, a ship sprung a leak and turned over in a storm. The crew lowered a dory and rowed close to shore, but the tide was against them and they couldn't beach the boat. Men on the shore got a line to them somehow, and they pulled. "Pull and be damned," one of the men shouted. But the rope snapped and the dory overturned. All hands were lost.

Nickel told her the story, which he had heard in a barber shop, soon after they first moved in. Greer was sixteen, and this was their first house since running away from her real father in California. "We're going to make it here," Nickel said. "Pullandbedamned, that's us. We'll pull ourselves up and make a life of it. We'll pull through, eh Doll?" And he ruffled her hair. He was the only one she could stand to have ruffle her hair. When boys at school did it, she pushed them away.

The house stood on top of the bluff with its back to the weather. It had no view of the Sound, but looked south toward the pulp mill, the timber booms and Japanese ships, or out on Pullandbedamned Point Road, the driveway and mostly tree-less lot. Nickel had meant to grow trees in the yard, but for some reason, gravel in the soil perhaps, they didn't take. The stunted fir by the driveway never grew taller, the house was greener than the tree. "Puke green," the kids called it. But Nickel had been happy when he got a deal on the paint at Joiner's Hardware Store. Now the house looked like sea wrack flung up from the beach, askew on its bluff, and she hated going back.

The sponge in her hand was damp. Greer had been anxious to clean everything, to forget nothing, while Carl made his rounds at the hospital, and now she stopped herself mid-gesture, immobilized by her own absurdity. It's just like her. I'm acting just like Mama.

Poor Nickel. The room he was dying in had been Greer's room for her last years of high school. At one time it had known her secrets like nothing else, known where she hid her diary, now lost, known who she dreamed of and why she slept with her teeth clenched and the blankets tight in her fists. She had arranged everything in the room so that it was hers: a yearbook from the school in Portland, a box of notes from her friends or half-friends spread out living distant lives down the coast. She could play the radio softly (otherwise her mother, whom the girls called Nana, would want to come in and listen with her and talk about Elvis or Buddy Holly, talk about them until their music was spoiled by being talked about) and lie there with the wool blanket wrapped around her feet, staring at the shadows on the blue ceiling.

Greer went away to college, and Nana kept the room for her, but whenever she came home there was something more that was altered, some piece of furniture rearranged, something of the old life boxed for storage, until at last the room ceased to be Greer's. The walls were painted yellow, the old bureau refinished, its empty drawers lined with new paper. Greer had visited just a few months ago at Christmas. Nickel was strong enough to sit at the dinner table then. And after dinner, when her mother refused any help with the dishes and Carl and the girls were in the living room listening to Nickel, Greer had wandered back alone into the room. She stood in the middle of it, sat tentatively on the bed, ran her finger over the yellow bedspread, but it was like an object in the museum of another life, one of those places where you go to see how people lived way back when, only this was a museum of the days when Buddy Holly was alive and a date was a holy battle to stay at first base.

Unable to breathe, Greer had tried to rush out, but found that her mother stood blocking the door with a plate and dish towel in her hands. "Don't move anything, Hon. I've been cleaning in here for a week. This room's going to be Nickel's now."

Standing in her own kitchen with the damp sponge in her hands, Greer felt the chill of that moment, when she had realized Nickel would never get better and her old room was where he would end his life.

"We're just like twins," her mother had said. She set the plate and dish towel on the bureau, took Greer's hand and stood where they could see themselves side by side in the mirror. "People say we're just like sisters. Isn't that a laugh? I tell them don't be silly. Greer's a hundred times prettier than I ever was. I tell them you're named after Greer Garson, but you know who you really look like?"

Grace Kelly.

"You look like Grace Kelly."

But not the young Grace Kelly, Greer thought.

"People always tell me I look like Marilyn Monroe and I tell them you should see my daughter. She looks like Grace Kelly."

Though she was lean from nursing Nickel, Greer's mother looked younger than she was. With a free hand she lifted one of her breasts, and Greer looked away from this. She saw herself, the backwards image of herself in the mirror, dimly lit and standing in a dress her daughters had said was pretty.

Carl returned from his rounds at ten o'clock. "Is there any coffee?"

"I'll put some on."

"Are you okay?"

She nodded, and Carl stood by the counter with his mouth set in helpless sympathy as she started a fresh pot.

"It's going to rain."

Of course it's going to rain, she thought. It always rains.

Without looking she could sense the way he positioned his hands, one splayed on the counter, the other resting on his hip. They were thick, assured hands which he kept scrupulously clean. She had never quite been able to imagine those hands in surgery, though other doctors said he was very good at it. Tennis kept him trim, kept them both trim. It was something they did well together that didn't require talking.

"The kids are here," he said.

Stephanie's boyfriend, Ted, had pulled into the driveway in his Volkswagen beetle. He had picked up Stephanie at her apartment, or that was what they always said they did, and stopped by the dorm to get Christine. Stephanie and Ted would graduate this spring, while Christine was struggling through her first year without her big sister's grades or sense of direction. The three of them stood in the driveway for a few minutes before coming in.

Like her father, Stephanie was a trim brunette, vigorous and thoughtful, and like her father's, her hair would probably gray prematurely. Christine was a blond like her mother, a little porcelain doll who cried easily and kept her room at home exactly as she had left it. Ted and Stephanie studied marine biology together, met on a university expedition to the San Juan Islands. While they were studying tidal pools, someone had discovered a seal pup whose mother had apparently been killed. Ted had come up with a scheme to rescue the baby seal, feeding it bits of fish until they could transport it to Seattle and raise it in captivity. For a while he had kept the seal in his apartment, mostly in the bathtub, but finally he had been forced to deliver it to the zoo.

Ted was a short, muscular boy with a stutter and a patchy, comical beard. Like Carl he had strong-looking hands, and he punctuated sentences by periodically poking his black-framed glasses back up the bridge of his nose. He had a way of falling silent, as if embarrassed, whenever Carl mentioned medical school to Stephanie. Greer, too, hoped her daughter would choose something more practical than rescuing seals. But the two young biologists kept to themselves about such decisions.

They came in now with an aura of salt air about them, flushed from laughter at some joke Ted had told, and helped themselves to coffee. Christine poured a Diet Coke from the fridge and went straight to her room to find a sweater she wanted.

Greer picked up the sponge she had left on the kitchen table and wiped coffee rings from the counter. Carl went out to warm up the station wagon. Stephanie sat with the morning paper, turning to the comics, and Ted stood leaning over her. Suddenly, just as Greer turned to them trying to think of something harmless to say, she saw Ted plant a firm kiss on top of Stephanie's head. It was such an absurd place for a kiss, but what disturbed Greer most about it was that Stephanie flinched at the touch.

"Sorry," Ted muttered, and Stephanie stared almost ferociously at the paper, her neck muscles taut above her sweater.

I shouldn't have seen that, Greer thought. She had to say something, so she said, "More coffee, anyone?"

It would take them an hour and a half to drive to Nooksack. The kids sat in the back, Greer and Carl in front. When she drove alone, Greer liked to listen to the radio, but Carl preferred to drive without it, so she concentrated on the houses by the interstate, wondering how it felt to live there, or the woods south of Everett that seemed to be hiding some suburban or military secret, incest or the testing of nerve gas on dairy cattle. She liked it best when they crossed the Stillaguamish River and entered the Skagit Valley, a place of low farms and dikes, humped islands on one horizon and misty mountains on the other.

She remembered driving north on old 99, before the interstate was completed, in the car with Nickel and her mother, who chattered all the way like some lunatic bird except when she and Nickel sang. Greer could not remember what song they sang, but it was like that episode of *Lucy* where Ricky, Fred, Ethel and Lucy drove to California singing the whole way. They were like some corny vaudeville foursome, a studio projection of landscape behind them—not at all like a long car trip in real life. In the Chevy sedan that Nickel bought used in Portland, there were only two adults and a long-legged sixteen-year-old girl who sat in the back alone with her mother's magazines. Nickel would lean back every now and then and shout the name of some new place: "Tugboat Slough!"

She didn't see any tugboats then, but the slough must be that brackish inlet winding past a lumberyard by the road. And later, in flat land dotted with mossy barns: "We're in the Skagit Valley now. Jim Rice says this is the best duck hunting

he's ever had." Duck hunting was another thing Nickel never
got around to.

Farmland stretched to the Sound, from which they could
smell salt and something rotten. Earthen dikes had been
thrown up against the tides, and at one point Greer remembered a wall of creosoted pilings. The Sound's presence was so
quiet that day that it had frightened her, particularly when,
after glimpsing a snow-capped volcano beyond the eastern
hills, they had followed the road along a cliff high above the
water. As time went by she learned this was a place of floods
and landslides, where people died in the woods and where
yardwork was an endless battle against encroaching growth.

Little of this could be seen today from the interstate; the
close weather and rain turned everyone inward for long
silences.

Carl cleared his throat. "Can you kids hear me back there?"
They all said they could.

"I think you should know what you're going to see today.
The cancer has metastasized and advanced pretty rapidly. It's
all through his system. In his bones."

Greer thought she should add something, as if it would
steady her nerves to say anything at all. "Nana says he looks
awful."

"He's lost about ninety pounds," said Carl. "The pain's got
to be pretty bad, though I think they have him on
Meperedine, which is usually a good drug. Anyway, I thought
you should know it's going to be a rough visit."

The weather hovered over the interstate in gloomy strips.
Greer looked back at her daughters and saw that Christine had
begun to cry, letting Ted comfort her like a brother.

She remembered her real father in California. For a long
time she hadn't known what work he did, though she knew he
wore glasses when he worked and sometimes looked for hours
in the big book that lay on a stand of its own in the study. He
would run a finger down the page of his book and mumble to
himself. Now she understood that he was a high school
English teacher in San Diego, and that he had never been
confident of his spelling. Greer never opened a dictionary
without thinking of her father, the way his hands paused

gently over the page. She liked to think she acquired her secret love of reading from him.

"Do you want to meet him? I'll buy some plane tickets and we'll fly down."

Carl, always helpful, had made the offer a few years after they were married. She hesitated, terrified that her father would not be anything like she remembered him.

He was, yet the meeting had not gone well. They ate a dry chicken dinner at his house, prepared by his new wife, Jean, and he showed them his sprawling garden, of which Greer had no memory because she had known her father in another neighborhood. She wanted to ask him if he still spent hours with the big book, but was afraid such childish questioning would irritate him. She saw that his life had in fact improved since the morning his first wife ran away with a man from the shipyards. He seemed interested in what Carl had to say about Seattle and surgery, but when he tried to hug Greer as they said good-bye, the gesture was only woodenly sincere.

Outside in the rented car she had sobbed for what seemed like hours while her husband drove and spoke soothingly, and for the first time in months she did not resent him for trying.

Maybe it was for the best that they had left. Greer's mother was often out at night. There were arguments that poisoned the house. Maybe her father thought that Greer, too, had wanted to leave.

One day, her mother helped her dress as though for school—she was in the third grade then—and said, "Honey, I'm going to introduce you to someone special. We'll fill a suitcase just for you and go on a long vacation, okay? You're going to love him. He's so fun and he's the best dancer."

The chatter, the hurried packing—slowly Greer sensed that her real father had gone to work. Or had he abandoned them? Was he dead? Maybe he had died in a car wreck on the way to school. She seemed to have been confused on that point.

The man who met them in a shiny yellow car with white stripes on the tires was bigger than her real father, with larger hands and pointy elbows and slicked-back hair thinning at the front. He wore a bright shirt and laughed more than her real father did, and Greer had never, in all the years since, seen him with a book, except a picture book on plumbing or wiring, or a copy of *National Geographic*. At their first meeting he had stooped beside his shiny car and held out a hand like a shovel. "Why, she's pretty as a picture, Fran. She's a little doll."

"Didn't I tell you? Honey, I want you to meet Nickel. We're going to go places together and have lots of fun."

That was when it struck her. They were really taking her away, and her father would never know that Greer wanted to stay with him. She wanted them to be a family.

She remembered bawling and kicking, and how Nickel's strong hands had swept her up and flung her into the back seat of the car. "Time to hit the road. Don't you worry, Doll. We're going to have nothing but fun."

"Nothing but fun!" her mother had shouted almost hysterically. In the front seat of the noisy car, her mother adhered to this strange man who was not Greer's father. The car hummed. Greer turned her face to the seat and hummed with it.

There was a motel somewhere in a desert. Nickel sat on the edge of the bed and told her, "Know why they call me Nickel? My real name is Nigel. My people are from England, see? Well, one day I was working in Colorado Springs, El Paso County, on a survey. We were out in the scrub east of town working for the county out there. I was about seventeen, a big kid. It was my first job since leaving Pittsburgh to come out west. Out there in the heat I found a nickel on an ant hill. Right out in the middle of nowhere, this Indian-head nickel was shining in the sunlight, and I caught the glint of it and walked over to have a look. Ever found a nickel on an ant hill before? I tell you, that was something. That day the fellas on the crew said my name shouldn't be Nigel any more since Nigel's a sissy name. It should be Nickel. And I've been Nickel Thompson ever since." He laughed easily; for a moment Greer stopped being afraid. "You got to have a good eye to catch a nickel on an ant hill." He laughed again. "What do you suppose those ants were going to spend it on?"

"Hon," said Greer's mother.

"I was just telling her a story. Kids like stories."

"I know, but we got to be alone now."

"You go with your mother, Doll. I'll tell you some more stories later."

Greer's hand in her mother's. Tightly. She was led to the

bathroom and told in a whisper to stay there. "If you open that door I'll knock you, understand? Don't say a word and don't you listen to me and Nickel. This is something grown-ups have to do. Stop that. Don't you even think about crying or I'll whack you one, I swear it. That's a good girl. Sit quietly for Mama, okay? And Nickel and me will make you the happiest little girl in the world."

She sat there as quietly as she could, though there were sounds from the room beyond the door that frightened her. She climbed into the bathtub, touching her forehead against its cool surface. She slept. When she woke the air felt late. She felt she would die, crushed by the air, if she spent another minute alone in that room with its cracked tiles. She opened the door and no one punished her for it. The big bed was rumpled. An open bottle stood on the nightstand, letting its smell of sickness into the air. Nickel and her mother were gone.

Had she known they were coming back? It was difficult to say, all these years later, because of a numbness she could not look beyond. She had slept on the cot they left open for her. Sometime late that night they woke her, leaning over her with petting hands on her hair, laughing. "Wait till you see Nickel dance. He's the best dancer in the whole world!"

Nooksack hibernated in its nest of hills where cloud and woodsmoke clung to the trees. Carl took the first exit north of the pulp mill, drove toward Pullandbedamned Point through a neighborhood of Victorian houses (Greer had called them haunted houses once) and along the high bluff above the harbor where the houses were newer, except Nickel's house, which managed to look tawdry in spite of all his work on it.

From the boatworks in San Diego Nickel had gone to work in the lumberyards of northern California and Oregon. He had tried to run his own building supply company in Nooksack, but a partner who was once a friend had cheated him, and his business quickly failed. Nickel never talked much about it, except to say, "Just goes to show you don't know who your friends are. You never can tell till the going gets tough."

"He should have saved more," Carl often said. "I can't believe the guy didn't have more insurance. One of these days

some disaster's going to hit and he won't have a nickel to fight
it with."

They pulled into the driveway, parked and unloaded, and
immediately Greer's mother rushed among them, hugging her
granddaughters. She wore nothing over her light sweater in
spite of the drizzle, and wept openly, stroking Christine's hair.
"Nickel's so sick and I been nursing him all by myself. Not
that I mind. I'd nurse him till I dropped dead from overwork.
Guess that's a silly thing to say, but you know me. I'm just an
old lady, Hon, even though I'm your Nana and you love me,
don't you? And sometimes I say silly things because I'm rundown all the time. Doctor Ressmeyer says I don't get enough
vitamins and to watch my weight. You see how skinny I am?
You can feel my ribs."

"We should go in," Carl suggested.

Greer caught his glance and made one of her "here we go"
faces.

Ted stood close to Stephanie's grandmother, who was telling
him that his beard made him look just like Charlton Heston in
that Bible picture, which was preposterous. Stephanie, who
had turned so her face was safely out of her grandmother's line
of vision, rolled her eyes.

They were not even to the front door when the old woman
latched onto Carl, telling him he was a dead ringer for John F.
Kennedy. "You're just as handsome as he was, I swear. The
women couldn't keep their hands off him. Only I know you
don't have his roving eye. You're married to my Greer, so why
would you want to rove?"

Christine was crying again, hugging her grandmother who
said she looked exactly like Grace Kelly. They entered the
house to the tune of this inane chatter. Greer went in first,
hoping to keep her mother at a distance. She left Carl and Ted
to handle things with their skillful small talk as coats were
hung in the hall closet.

The house seemed dim and, despite her mother's mono-
logue, silent, as if bracing itself, waiting for it all to end. Greer
held her arms close, stood waiting for someone to make a
decision.

"We'll go see him," her mother said. "Then we'll sit down to
eat."

"Eat?"

"I've fixed a big dinner. I've baked a pie. Apple's your favorite pie, Carl, I know."

"It's too early even for lunch," Carl said.

"But you have to have some pie. And roast beef and dumplings."

Greer could hardly stand it. As if this was just another family visit, a Christmas dinner or Thanksgiving. As if anyone could feel like eating on a day like this. She tried to catch Christine's eye, to smile and find an ally in the awkwardness, but no one seemed able to face anyone else, or smile, or say anything, except of course her mother. It was all nonsense about the pie and dumplings. They'd be store-bought. Greer's mother didn't know a dumpling from a Danish.

"Well," said Carl decisively, and gestured that they should go in.

Greer's mother led them to the back hallway. "He's been so sick, Honey, and I hardly know what to do. I work myself to the bone, but he can't eat any more. Nothing stays in him. But I know he wants to see you."

The hall was dark, as if infected by the weather outside. Greer felt it like a place of hollowed earth around her, a gallery of whispers. It was so small now, not the long hallway she remembered that kept her a safe distance from her mother. Too quickly they would pass through it, nothing could prolong the walk toward that room. She stopped, feeling Carl's hand on her shoulder, and realized she was trembling.

Her mother opened the door, but it seemed they were entering another darkness like the hallway, a strange room in somebody else's house that wasn't really located in Nooksack or anywhere else. A place without weather or sound. The shades were drawn because the light hurt Nickel's eyes. Carl held Greer's arm now, and he was leading her against her will. "Just a few minutes," she heard him say.

Nickel was hardly there. So strange. The bedcovers pulled back because even the touch of blankets was painful to him. His eyes had sunken far back into his head. There were no longer gums enough to support his false teeth, and his lips flapped inward. A low sound came from him, seemingly from his encaved eyes, as Greer bent over him with her husband.

He was the embodiment of pain, but when she searched his eyes she could see Nickel somewhere inside them, his kindness and failure, as if even now he were struggling to make it all easier for her. His lips moved, and she perceived his acute embarrassment at being seen unshaven and without his teeth.

"You don't have to talk," said Carl.

But Greer had seen the word the old man wanted to say; it was "Doll." His face trembled with effort, his hands moved as if he would like to show her something, show her a trick with a deck of cards. His hands fell back on the sheets. His head shook slightly from side to side.

"I don't think you should touch him," Carl said. "It'll hurt too much."

Greer realized that her own hand had gone out, and she retracted it slowly.

"The girls are both here," she said, stepping back to let him see them.

Nickel moaned something.

"He wants to sit up," said Greer's mother.

"Let me help," said Ted, coming forward, and before Carl could stop him he had gripped the old man by the shoulder. Nickel moaned again, looking helplessly at Carl.

"Don't touch him, Ted. He can't stand it. Take ahold of the pillow."

They tried shifting the pillow enough to pack another one beneath it, but this too caused Nickel acute discomfort.

The children spoke their few words to Nickel. His eyes simultaneously drank them in and begged them to leave.

Afterwards, Greer leaned close to his ear and whispered, "I'll see you again. I'll be sure to say good-bye before we go."

They had been on the road for two years before Nickel settled on the lumber business. He worked odd jobs all over California. Greer was always the new kid in school, and just as she made friends she found she had to leave them.

Sometimes her mother and Nickel left her alone in a motel and drove off for a few days at a time. Nickel would always give her twenty dollars for food and tell her to keep the door locked and not to open it for strangers. When they came back they would say Nickel had found a new job, it was time to pack the car.

While they were gone, Greer read the two-volume en-
cyclopaedia he had given her on their first Christmas together,
or paperbacks she bought in a drugstore. Somewhere—she
thought it was in Santa Rosa—papers came in the mail that
sparked serious talks, then the drinking of champagne and
another two days of Greer alone in a room, and when the
grown-ups returned, they announced that they were married.

She had only to endure them while she was in school, she
thought. Sometimes it was terrible, her mother screaming that
Nickel looked that way (whatever that way was) because he
wanted her little girl. "I know you want her. You just came
with me because you liked her. She has prettier breasts than
me. I'm an old hag and I know it." Throwing things. Kicking
mad. Then making up with a closed door between them and
Greer, and Nat "King" Cole on the radio.

One night Nickel drove off mad, chucking a bottle from his
car as he pulled away. It broke on the gravel macadam. Greer's
mother went screaming after him, running up the road like
some kind of nut, and for a few hours Greer thought he was
really gone forever. He would never come back. She began to
imagine what it would be like to live with her mother, with
only her mother and no Nickel to tell stories and make things
better. She had seen him drive away from the balcony of the
motel, and when her mother started back to the room Greer
went in, closing the door and sitting on the bed, praying her
mother wouldn't come. But her mother did come. She knelt
beside Greer as if nothing had happened, saying, "You think
I'm pretty, don't you, Hon? Let's see what we can find here to
dress up. We'll trade clothes like sisters. He likes that sweater
you're wearing. I know he does."

Just a few more years, Greer thought. But it seemed those
years would never end.

As it turned out, Nickel was gone only two nights. By the
time he returned, Greer's mother was half-mad with anticipation and Greer lay awake at night thinking of escape. When he
came in he, too, tried to pretend that nothing had happened.
He brought a new doll for Greer and a bottle for drinks with
her mother, and pretty soon Greer was told to take a long walk
by herself, buy herself dessert in the coffee shop and stay clear
of the road.

In Portland, Greer began to make friends, though there

were girls who never liked her. She thought it was because she was ugly. But at Nooksack High they elected her cheerleader and Prom Queen, and her mother made her date any boy who asked her. In those days a date was a date, except that night with Shane Fenton in his car by the lake. Shane was nice, and she wanted to love him, and even thought what it might be like if she had his child and could move out of the house on Pullandbedamned Point. On another night, though, Shane wanted her to do it again and she felt her mother's presence in the car and couldn't. It was too awful, the thought of being like her, talking like her, running away with the first boy who said he liked her.

In college she met Carl, who was going to be a doctor like his father. One vacation, he drove her to Mercer Island to meet his parents, and Greer was so tongue-tied at dinner in that large house above the water that she was sure they disapproved of her. They seemed to pity the small voice with which she answered their questions. She should have known they would finally approve, that whatever their son wanted was all right with them. They weren't like her mother; maybe they had never known anyone like her mother. She wanted to be like them, to behave in such a way that they would have nothing to regret when she married their son.

Little was eaten during lunch. Stephanie made it plain that she was furious with Ted for having touched Nickel's shoulder. Greer overheard her saying, "Didn't you hear my father? The cancer's in his bones. He's in excruciating pain."

"I couldn't help myself," Ted said. "He looked so sad I just wanted to touch him."

All of their jauntiness and youth seemed to have gone stale; Ted looked ragged, unwanted, and completely uncomfortable. I should do something, Greer thought. I should know what to do.

Her mother served pie in an aluminum dish. "I baked it myself. I just put it in this dish because I couldn't find my pie pan."

Another bald-faced lie. It's store-bought. The dumplings were store-bought. This whole family was bought in a supermarket by the side of the road.

Greer looked at each of her daughters, at Stephanie who all

but complained of a headache, and Christine who sat with head bowed as if begging someone, anyone, to take her away from this. It's my fault, Greer thought. They were happy just a few hours ago, and now they're miserable. But who could be happy after seeing Nickel like that? No, it isn't Nickel. It's all of us. We don't have what other families have. They know how to act, and none of us knows. Carl tries, of course. He's like Nickel in that way. But nothing he does can help because we don't know what to do, and that's my fault.

She heard her mother's voice again, appalled by the fullness of her own hatred at the sound of it. Someone has to stop this. If Nickel were healthy he would be kind at least. Kind without touching. He pulled cards from his sleeve when they sat on the motel bed, just flicked them out in his fingertips, laughing at how easy it was. Or he told stories like the one about Pullandbedamned Point. "We'll come through, all right," he used to say. "Just you wait and see, Doll. I'm onto a good thing now, I can tell."

She sat still, her fork skating over her untouched pie. The whole notion of eating anything now revolted her, and suddenly she had to stand up.

"Greer?" She could tell Carl was deeply worried.

Her mother saw what she was doing. "I'll come with you, Hon."

"No," Greer said. Her voice was soft and inconclusive, so she added firmly, "I'll go alone."

She touched Christine's hair. "I'm all right. Really. I just want to see him alone."

"You can't go alone, Hon. I got to be there when you go because I'm the one who knows what to do."

Greer looked at Stephanie and Carl, then sharply at her mother, who stayed put, fidgeting with her napkin. She stepped away from the table, pushing her chair aside for fear she would stumble against it, and walked to the hallway.

It was long again, darker than before. She touched the walls for balance as she passed through it to the door of Nickel's room. Her room. Nobody's room.

When she went in she realized at once that the gesture was futile; she didn't know why she was here. This man wasn't her father. He was hardly Nickel Thompson any more. Just Nickel's bones with some breath left in them, and little of that.

In all the years she had known him, she had never said she loved him, and now, leaning over him, she saw he was asleep.

There was a chair beside the bed—had she noticed it before? She pulled it close and sat down in it. Nickel's chest rose and fell almost imperceptibly. He looked like a man who had taken regular beatings all his life yet hidden them from others. Greer put her hand on the sheet next to one of his. Her hands were darker, the veins standing out, and her ring next to his scaly fingers looked like the ring of an empress, something he could never have dreamed of buying for the woman he had married.

"Poor old fool," Greer said. "Can you hear me? Doesn't matter. How could you love her the way you did? All those years. And me, too. You loved me even more. Did you put up with her just for me? I know you meant well. You didn't always do the right thing, but you wanted to. Just pull and be damned, like you could pull us through by magic."

She stopped. His face registered no change.

"You don't have to pull us through any more. You're through with that now."

Nickel twitched slightly in his sleep.

"I'll just stay with you a while," Greer said. "Okay? I'll stay with you like you stayed with me."

They were safe here for the moment. Her mother wouldn't come. She wouldn't dare. And for as long as Greer wanted, she and Nickel would be alone.

Sworn Statements: The Map

BY MARCIE HERSHMAN

Mapmaking will always be profitable. You must remember how big the world is. For all its glories, the globe is quickly flattened, and flattened the dimensions shift. Sure, a man can make a good living by lifting one name from a land mass and carefully inscribing another, by flooding a new dye inside the freshened boundaries.

Even before the war, my work was in some demand. I'd been employed in Munich by the Schermer brothers, but on December 23, 1939, I was stopped by a sign on the building's front door. *All business suspended until further notice.* The bookkeeper in our huddled group was the most distraught. She insisted all the ledgers were in order, that Stefan and Isaac had withdrawn no more funds than was usual, but when— earlier—she'd rushed to their houses, everything was quiet, locked up tight. She hadn't wanted to peek in the windows, but it seemed the two brothers and their families were gone. Perhaps, she kept repeating as one by one we turned from the building, they'd had an emergency—and just before the holidays.

It was the push I needed. For five years I'd been relegated to working on mostly statistical maps, allowed to do topographical jobs only when a project was running behind deadline. But now I was on my own and could choose the mix I wanted.

My first thought was to open a shop in Munich, then I reconsidered. Its neighborhoods already were studded with newspaper kiosks, leafletted lampposts, and everywhere one looked there were pieces of paper appropriated for directing the populace. When a word, *Czechoslovakia* for example, began to flicker from the headlines, the boastful or ignorant didn't have to go far to find a map shop. They'd sift through the man's wares, then: *Didn't he have the new version yet? That country* (and here they'd point) *is ours.* The citizens of Munich knew where they stood and more importantly where others were to stand in relation to that. For fine art, they cared only somewhat; it was prompt correction they sought. A newspaper map, a cartoon of black and white, could do well enough. No, the more I thought about it, the more it seemed I needed to find some place simpler than Munich where I could make my mark.

After a process of elimination, I came up with three possibilities: Landau, Bensheim and Kreiswald. In the end I settled on Kreiswald, a medium-sized city between Munich and Passau, for the sentimental reason that I'd camped near it on a scouting expedition when I was eleven or twelve, some twenty years before. I remembered the surrounding woods as coniferous, dark green, valleyed, the hills flowing up from a minor tributary of the Danube. Typical Bavarian topography. Of the town, I recalled not one brick. Still, it had to be some kind of a hub because the express trains stopped there; its name was superimposed above the long, delicately vertebral line that meant *railway* on the map.

At high speeds, you can't always see that it's snowing, but you can see the accumulation—a white cast over the ground. Only gradually, as you near some destination, do flakes fill the air. I disembarked onto a platform crowded with soldiers and women. It was one of those shifting crowds a stranger can't get through because the people in it are trying to stay together until the last moment. I had to make my way around the edges and out to the street where there was, at the intersection, a news kiosk. It was early evening, and nearly dark. I picked up a copy of the local paper: *Finland Surrenders to Axis*, said the headline. Behind me, the whistle blew.

"But I just placed that notice," said the landlady almost angrily, peering through the pelting flakes. "I didn't expect someone to show up this soon. In fact, I was hoping to wait until after the next weekend."

"Are you saying you have nothing to rent?"

With a sigh, she stepped out onto the threshold, letting the front door close behind her—but not all the way. "No." She pushed a wave of thick brown hair off her forehead and gazed past me to the brick rowhouses that lined the street.

She was an unusual-looking woman, more a composite of individual features than a wholly integrated vision. She had a heart-shaped face accentuated by a widow's peak in the exact center of her forehead, those cascades of brown hair, and a narrow, pointed chin. Her eyes were almost Oriental, but blue. Her mouth, like her eyes, looked foreign—too long or maybe just too fleshy. She was slope-shouldered in the way women can get after forty or so, and though not especially short, she only came up to my chin.

Shivering, she wrapped her arms under her breasts and said, "Those rooms weren't supposed to be vacant."

My eyes dropped to the advertisement in the newspaper: *33 Ludvigstrasse. Three rooms, furnished, for immediate occupancy. Inquire: Hofflinger.*

"Frau Hofflinger, I need to get someplace as quickly as possible. If you wouldn't mind, given the bad weather..." and here I handed her the *Clarion*, "would you tell me which of the listings is the nearest? Would it be this one, the third one from the top? Is it in this neighborhood?"

She took the paper but didn't so much as glance at it. "What is your name?"

"Felix Braslauer."

She looked down at my bags: two suitcases, a small canvas duffle, an art portfolio and a paint box—all covered by a wet film of snow. The zipper on the leather portfolio was so icy that its teeth looked maliciously clenched. Inside were the Schermer brothers' base maps that I'd been allowed to keep at home in case I was given one of those jobs that had to be completed after hours. I was sure they could be used now, with my own modifications, without fear of incurring a legal suit. Not plagiarism but a starting point. With new colors, clearer symbols, a simpler lettering than I'd had to use in the past, they'd be the base for a new topographical series: Braslauer's World. And of course, there would also be the local needs, the statistical maps for civil and commercial interests, and a series on the city's environs, its streets and general property.

"Are you married?" she said.

"No."

"Then how many are you?" She indicated my luggage. "Are you looking for only one or will there be others coming after?"

There was a gust of wind. Even with my collar up, the cold still slipped down my neck. "No others." I stamped my numb feet. "I'm here alone. These are some of my supplies. I'm a mapmaker."

She smiled, the corners of her mouth barely curling. "Then certainly you should be able to find your own way around town! And to ask me for directions to those others, when we're all competing for the same tenants, well..." With a dismissive laugh, she handed me the newspaper. "You might as well take this back."

Stung, I began to gather up my bags and heard: "Wait. Give me a moment to find the keys. The rooms are directly across the street. I don't share walls with my tenants."

Loaded down, I followed her across Ludvigstrasse, trying to keep my feet in the prints she made in the piles of slush. Frau Hofflinger had thrown a sweater across her shoulders and the red sleeves flailed between us, reaching over and over for something they had no power to grasp.

"Number 42," she called, pointed with a bare elbow. "The rooms are on the ground floor. The top unit is filled."

With relief, I set the bags down on the tile floor in the building's unlit common entry. Frau Hofflinger had gone ahead, and though she stood at the door to the apartment, she made no move to open it. She had both arms around herself.

I said, "Are we waiting for someone to let us in?"

Shaking out the keys as if they were wet, she selected one silvery finger from the handful, and replied scornfully, "Who? Do you think there's someone inside?"

She pushed the key into the lock. "Tell me, do you own any property, Herr Braslauer?"

"No."

"Well, you will one day." She gave the door a sharp tug forward. "Most people want property, but why I don't know.

If my husband hadn't inherited this building, I wouldn't be doing this."

The landlady stood a second at the open door, then hurried inside, her hand over her nose and mouth.

I took one breath and did the same thing. The hallway was dim but it looked clean. There was a small table against the long wall and as the hallway widened into a half-parlor a larger table, and a small green loveseat.

"Would you please go back, Herr Braslauer, and open the window in the front room? This is the first I've been in here. I received notice only a few days ago."

I pushed aside the lace curtain. A card fell out from behind it: *My Sweetest, happy birthday, you're 19! I love you, Torgood.* I placed it back on the sill, in a square of fresh cold air.

"Here's the culprit," she called. "In the kitchen."

I went back. She was holding a geranium, limp and bloom-heavy, lying over the side of its pot. "The soil's rancid. Look! I think he poured a can of milk on it instead of water. I'm sure he meant to save the plant for my next tenant, but you know what can happen when you're rushing."

I looked about the yellow kitchen. The fire was out in the grate. The stove was cold but looked workable. A small icebox in the corner, a table and two chairs, even pots and pans hanging by their handles from a metal rack.

Continued Frau Hofflinger, "I'll have to come back to sort through things. The flat comes furnished, but some of his personal items are still here. Just look at the pantry."

"He lived here alone?"

"He had a wife. Torgood and Gerda Stella. There were two of them." Holding the geranium, she went to the door to the left of the stove and deposited the plant in the alley outside. "See how quickly it's done," she said, coming back in. Her hair was netted in fresh flakes. "That's the benefit of living on the ground floor, you can easily get rid of what you don't want." She left the door open a bit and the wind forcing through the crack whined like an agitated kettle.

"I lived on the ground floor in Munich," I said.

She smiled widely; it made her attractive, tilting her features into some kind of harmony. "Do you like this, then? You can have it if you do. It's really a sweet little place but anything empty will have a bad smell. I hate having it empty like this?"

"Is it quiet?"

"Oh, you won't be bothered, Herr Braslauer, I promise you! Nothing happens around here, at the most you get a howling cat, but these days, not even that. As for the Rauschers, upstairs, I've never had a complaint about them." The land-lady picked an embroidered dish towel from the floor and wiped her hands on it. "To be honest, the postman will be your only nuisance. He summons you to the door when he could just as easily slip any mail through the slot. I know all about the postman. Ever since August. Ever since Herr Hofflinger was sent to Poland by his company to help set up a new factory." She threw the towel onto the table.

"Now, the bedroom is at the back. I would have had everything cleaned, but if you want to move in tonight, you'll have to take it as is and I'll come by when you're gone. Do you think you'll be away from home in the morning or the afternoon? I'd prefer to come after the mail comes."

Once she let herself out, I went to the pantry and selected two of the tins of chopped ham from the shelf. I opened them right then and there, and ate them standing up. Too tired to do much of anything else, I wandered once through the apart-ment to shut the front window and then back to the kitchen to secure that door. I washed up with cold water directly in the kitchen sink, wiping my face with the dish towel already smudged by the landlady's fingers.

I wouldn't unpack, I decided. Instead, I went into the bedroom, pulled back the comforter, and with the flat of my hand, brushed the stray hairs off the bedsheet. I got in, facing the window where the snow, sharpened and ghostly against the glass, formed the infinitesimal islands that appear only in storms.

Above me, the floorboards began creaking. Then two shoes thumped down and a piece of furniture was pushed back or pulled forward and a child, quiet as an insect, began to whine.

One of the mapmaker's skills is walking with a measured stride to count off distance and surface. When I stepped from the apartment the next morning at dawn, the sky was almost lurid with the clarity that follows any kind of torment: the wind was still, the snow piled pure and white above the layer of slush, air crisp enough to snap. I pulled my collar up closer to my neck and set off, stopping at each corner to mark down street names, number of paces, direction, coordinates. In such a way, I could come to know my new city. Until you look at a map—with some of the details in the area selected and retained, others just as decisively swept out of the picture— you can't quite see the place itself; you can't see how it compares to any other place. My street, Ludwigstrasse, was from end to end 322 meters long; the juncture with Os- terstrasse which ran to the north, came at 142 meters. Oster led to Gringeld, Gringeld flowed east to Tottenstrasse and dead-ended at Franz-Josephplatz. At the plaza a cafe was open and there I went in to warm up and have breakfast. The waiter congenially gave me directions to the police station so I could register my new address. (East for 700 meters then "follow Kempener, even though Bergenstrasse is a more direct route. Cut across the commercial area; the stationhouse is in the west corner.")

But at the juncture of Kempener and Bergenstrasse, I saw a sign for a printer's shop. I needed a printer. Why should I wait to find one until after I had some statistical jobs lined up? That was the usual way, of course, but with my base maps, I could start in with the topographical work, print up the first copies in the series of Braslauer's World, and draw my initial customers that way. What a turnaround, using the dream to bring in the drudge work! More than a start, a kingdom was lying before me.

I turned left, down Bergenstrasse. And within half a dozen or so strides, I saw planks nailed across the windows and doors of Friedman Clothiers, Weiss' Ladieswear, Our Own Restaurant. Every third store was boarded. A yellow leaflet flapped from each closed storefront. *Government Action: 8, February, 1940*. All along its length, though, the sidewalk had been freshly shoveled and sand scattered so that no pedestrian would slip. Kreiswald's Jew street was still open for business. A tailor's shop—open, a pawnbroker's.

Premier Printers. A silly tinkling of bells announced my entrance through the front door. The air smelled lush and hot, though by the overcoat the secretary wore I knew it was barely heated. It was the smell of ink coming off the machines in the back room infusing everything.

"I'd like to speak with someone about a printing job. Is this firm capable of handling maps?"

"I'll get Herr Volkmann." She stood up from her desk.

"Thank you, Sarah."

She stiffened and then she nodded. Smiling slightly, she went on to the back room. On the first of January, all German Jews had been given new first names. Males took the name, Israel, females Sarah. This was only the second occasion I'd had for using the address. The bookkeeper in Munich, Frau Zweigler, was the other, when I'd asked her for the pay due me, since I was moving on.

A man no older nor taller than I entered the front room. he was in his shirtsleeves, red-cheeked and flushed, with blond, regular features. "May I help you, Herr...?"

"Braslauer."

"Herr Braslauer." His light-colored eyes flickered over my face. "I need only one moment to fix you in mind so I won't forget. Well, I'm Herr Volkmann, as you must have guessed. I hear you have some maps you'd like me to see?" And he held out his right hand, stained blue at the fingers.

With a laugh, I drew the scrap of paper only part-way out of my coat pocket. "This, I hope, will never be printed. It's just a newcomer's first survey of his surroundings. I haven't been here since I was a boy, but I'll be opening a shop very soon. My cartography is complicated, highly sophisticated, and I need to find a good printer who can handle it—at a good price."

"Ah yes, a good price." He turned slightly. "Would you get me a pen, please, Frau Gorowitz? No, wait, the one I like is still in my jacket, I'll get it." He walked over to the coat rack and from behind the lapel of a blue suitcoat, withdrew a slim ebony pen.

"I'm sure you understand how important such things are," he commented, smiling. "This one has a fine steel tip, and the shaft is well-balanced. Now, if you're talking about a four color map, and a run of let's say, fifty or more, the numbers would start at something like this. Of course, we'd need to see the work first to come to a final agreement." He wrote a series of figures on a piece of paper.

I studied it and though the prices were low, too low in fact, I held my tongue. With a little shrug, I put the slip down on the counter.

"I see." He paused. "We both know that there are other printers around, Herr Braslauer. Even as a newcomer you must have guessed that. But the reality is they're not situated here, as I am, on Bergenstrasse. And they won't be as eager to get your business—new, unestablished, with no guarantee you will have enough cash coming in to even repay..." He wet his lips. "Though anyone can see you will prove an honorable man."

"Thank you."

He tore up the piece of paper. "Let's start over. I'm sure we can come to an agreement." When he finished, he carefully put the top back on his pen.

This time the figures were even lower. "I appreciate this," I said, picking up the new slip. "I think we'll run off a smaller batch at first, rather than a larger one. Given the way things are going, I don't want to do a lot of work for nothing. I'll return as soon as I'm sure I have something that will stay current for awhile."

He looked up, eyes fierce. "The whole world isn't going to change," he said. "That would be impossible."

"Well, you could be right, but who can know?" I opened the door to the sound of tinkling bells. "I'm glad I met you, Israel. And I'll be back, with some luck, even before you think."

But whatever luck I had with Volkmann fled the moment I stepped inside the police station. I'd presented my papers and Aryan purity certificate to the clerk and had begun to swear to their authenticity when the Commandant strolled over. With his thumb, he turned the citizens' registry I'd just signed toward him. How casual he was, leaning over.

"Well, how do you like this, Prudmann?" he said, and he whistled through his teeth.

The clerk said, "Com. Terskan?" He gave a wan little smile, but a child's grin in an older man's face is unnerving.

Mid-salute, I moved away from the flag, lowered my arm.

Com. Terskan said, "Go on, finish swearing."

I did so, quickly, and turned back to him.

He pointed at the line I'd just completed in the citizens' register. "Braslauer, Felix N., from Munich?"

I nodded.

"Now of 42 Ludvigstrasse, Λ?"

"Yes."

"Recently vacant? Very recently?"

I said, "That's what I was told by the landlady. She hadn't even cleaned it up yet. Of course, I only secured it for two weeks, as a trial. I didn't bring that much to Kreiswald with me, to set myself up, I mean." I hesitated. "Is there something wrong? I don't know yet which areas of town are decent and which aren't."

"But didn't you write down here that you're a mapmaker, Herr Braslauer?" said Com. Terskan.

"Yes. From Munich."

"Well, then—*Munich*!" He shrugged in a mock-helpless manner. "Kreiswald won't mystify you very much longer then. You'll soon figure it out. It usually takes a man no more than a walk to tell the good, clean neighborhoods from those that need a good cleaning. Your neighborhood," said Com. Terskan, glancing again at the register, "is fine, but you might expect a visit in the next day or two. You might have something—oh, not that it's yours—but there could be something in your possession that its owner wants back. I'll let you know tomorrow. Would that be all right?" He smiled, his white teeth straight, square.

"Of course."

"Prudmann, see that Herr Braslauer isn't delayed any longer. Herr Braslauer," he said, with a nod.

Prudmann pulled the register over the counter, made a check by what must have been my name. Then, humming a little nursery song, he got out a duplicate book, but with a red cover, and opened it to a blank page. He began to record my information.

"Is there something..." I ventured.

"No," mumbled the clerk. "Don't bother yourself." He bent his head and continued writing. "You're done here."

I walked out, with a shaking hand closed the door behind me. The wind had picked up and with it the snow. For a second, I stood confused by the swirls of traffic just on the other side of the curb, then I headed for Kempener. Kempener to Franz-Josephplatz, to—I wouldn't take Bergenstrasse even though it was the more direct route.

I knew what Terskan had been saying. I'd acted too quickly. Too readily, I'd assumed that Isaac and Stefan Schermer were gone. But that wasn't the case. Perhaps it had been just as the bookkeeper had said, some emergency. And with it resolved, their arms and legs swinging, those large heads held high, they'd returned to their building, they took down that sign and inside again saw who—and what—was missing.

A set of base maps: missing. Felix Braslauer: missing.

I hurried, head down against the wind, not counting my strides. I'd been reported for stealing property. In front, the pavement kept disappearing, trackless and white.

The door to my apartment was standing part-way open. I could hear someone rummaging around, pausing, then rummaging around again, quickly, as if searching for something against time. I kicked off my snow-clotted boots in the common entry and left them there; my socks were damp. "Frau Hofflinger?" I rapped my knuckles against the wood.

"Come in," she called. "I'm in the parlor."

I had to stop myself from running forward. She was the only person I knew in Kreiswald.

"The mail was early." She turned around in front of the bureau; her hands were clasped before her stomach. Again, she wore the red sweater but this time she wore it fully, tightly, over a brown dress—the sleeves rounded, the buttons closed except for the highest one, at the neck. "It didn't matter." She gave that odd, slanted smile. "Herr Hofflinger is not a writer."

Steadying my voice, I said, "It's not a good time."

She wasn't sure what I was referring to, I could see. She turned her face to the side, with her chin lifted just a bit, as if that would help her to make clearer sense out of what I'd really meant. She looked as if she would concentrate very hard on what I'd next say.

I stuck my hands in the pockets of my coat. "You have to leave. I have to work and can't have you here."

"Oh! I thought we agreed that if you were out..." She hesitated. "But you're back now. Yes, of course, I'll leave you to your work." Coloring slightly, she took a breath. Her chin lifted and with the clear tone of a much younger woman she said: "I'll come by once more. But I can't just go back and forth at your whim. I have other obligations. This is at your choice."

She picked up a wastebasket filled with paper—envelopes and letters and such. "Old correspondence, I suppose." The landlady laughed in such a way that I knew she had read some of them. "I've got some weightier things packed up in the kitchen. I'll take that bag out, too."

She walked back, her shoes clicking so loudly, each heel-strike so distinctly separate one from the other, it seemed the apartment I'd rented was empty, that there was nothing in it—no furniture, no curtains or rugs to absorb the shock of anyone walking through it.

I went after her.

"Are you following me?" She turned around from the kitchen table in much the same way she had before the parlor bureau, with her hands clasped over her stomach. Calmly she said, "I'm not taking it all. I left you half the food in the pantry and a quarter of the coal in the back bin. Imagine leaving coal when there's a shortage! He could have sold it, if only back to the delivery man." She rubbed her eyes. "I'll have to return for it, but you can see how much there is. Of course I can't just carry it off in my arms."

"Bring a wheelbarrow."

She laughed. "I haven't had time to go through the rest of the apartment. When do you want me to return?"

"Tomorrow afternoon." The words struck like ice on my tongue. "Come then. You can have a free hand. Take whatever you want of theirs. It's not mine, I wouldn't touch it."

A few moments later, alone in the strange apartment, I slid the base maps from my portfolio and onto the kitchen table. The full series of the earth's surface fanned out before me. Among them: *Northern Europe /3*, *Highlights: Finland, Sweden, Norway and Denmark*. I separated it from the others. Then sitting with my back to the stove, I placed a sheet of tracing paper—that reptile's eyelid—atop it and began the work that would not only save me but also, when I was safe, give me something to use.

First: Norway, wedged high against the top frame, I brought it down just a notch. My pencil skimmed away from the Schermers' shadow-country lying two paper-strata beneath it. I pressed harder and the new border thickened. Finland (already gone) had to be drawn with a lighter hand, and where the base map maintained boundary, the new one claimed instead merger, where the shadow said: chasm, the new corrected: no, hardly a crack. I went next to Denmark. Then to Sweden, a dangling arm; it had to reach—but downward to Rostock, also ours, *already* ours. I looked again at Rostock, its position against the coordinates.

When the map was traced, but not as some slave would trace it, I stood up and went over to the stove. In my hands was the Schermers' original. It seemed to seek the coals on its own. For one breath it lay lightly atop them, then it just lifted, and petalled like an impossibly bright rose, it burned. The brief conflagration added no heat to the room that I could notice.

The work went slowly. By 5:00 in the morning, I had traced the outlines and the most common features of only a half-dozen of the European maps. So many others remained. And I was trying only for base maps, only something to build from! I had the three full maps I'd completed back in Munich, but so what? I'd have to burn what I couldn't copy; that would leave me with hardly anything. It was no use.

I wandered into the front room. Piled under the frosted window was my luggage. Everything I owned was still packed up. Seeing it like that sparked something in me. I'd leave it all here, start over somewhere else, in some different way. Perhaps just a clerk?

I went and got my overcoat. Soundlessly, with only the small duffle in hand, I let myself out of the apartment. Ludvigstrasse was frozen into position. I shivered. For a moment I stood on the stoop, stamping my boots and looking up at a lamp glowing in Frau Hofflinger's upstairs corner window. Then I was halfway down the street, walking toward the train station.

Yet as I approached the building from behind the news kiosk, the one in the middle of the intersection, I saw the two lines of soldiers flanking the front entrance. They stood with rifles at the ready; at different intervals, a small explosion of breath puffed up before each of their faces.

I glanced at the array of magazines and papers on the counter. The vendor didn't notice me; he was pinning the front page of the paper to the back wall.

"Hurry up!" someone ordered. Almost immediately, a group of about fifty or sixty civilians surged around the corner of Franckenstrasse. They were a strange group, bundled up against the cold, their faces swollen and flushed as one's face is when just lifted from a pillow after a good night's rest.

"Hurry!" It was an officer who said it, now I saw him, at the back of the group. At the sound of his voice, the soldiers raised their rifles and the people at the front of the crowd hesitated. The captain repeated his command, but this time in Slovak. As he said it, he crouched down and with both gloves scooping, flung the sopping handfuls of slush at them. "Go," he shouted, throwing again. "Get out of here. Go back where you came from!" The balls splattered against their hats and necks, and set off a flurry of small, startled cries. Awkwardly, they pressed forward, filing between the guards, the adults holding the children's hands, the oldest ones holding each other or a bag no bigger than mine. As the captain went through, smacking his gloves together, the soldiers formed a wedge before the entrance, blocking it off to anyone else. Standing to one side were two policemen; I hadn't noticed them.

As casually as I could, I put the duffle down atop a bank of snow and selected a *Clarion*. The headline was about Russia's breaking off relations with Norway.

The vendor was busy tidying his wares.

"I want this," I said, summoning him.

"Didn't see you." He shook his head. "Sorry."

I dropped the coins in his gloved hand. Casually again, I picked up the duffle and turned back, in the direction I'd just come from.

I was nearing the steps to my building when I heard someone chasing after me. "Herr Braslauer," called the landlady. "Stop."

I turned. As if in triumph, she waved an envelope over her

head. She looked as if she'd just come from bed. Clad in a thin white housecoat, with her hair loose and wild over her shoulders, she stretched one leg out and then—tightrope walker—the other along the icy pavement.

"So," I shouted back, despite myself, "you have gotten your letter."

After a taxi went by, she crossed the street and came up to me. "Not at all," she said with a little grimace, one hand against her bare throat. "You have."

I took the envelope. The flap was sealed with the gray wax imprint of the Kreiswald Police. "Frau Hofflinger." With a click of my heels, I pocketed it and turned away.

She followed, talking. "A policeman delivered it. An older man who looked very uncomfortable. I suppose he didn't want to leave it under your door. They usually don't, with official business." She paused. "They had my name from the citizen's registry. As your landlady, they must think I have some responsibility."

I didn't answer. I opened the door to the building.

"It's so early to be out, Herr Braslauer." She looked at the duffle bag as I fiddled with the keys.

"I worked through the night. It's best not to bother trying to sleep again. You can't make it up." The door swung open and I went in without taking off my boots.

But she slipped in, too, saying, "Then I'll make you some hot coffee. I know the kitchen and you look exhausted." The sharp sweetness of almond extract floated from her in a kind of homey perfume.

"Frau Hofflinger—"

"No, attend to your business, I won't bother you." She waved a pale arm over her shoulder. Her shoes left small wet tracks on the floor.

I waited until she was well back in the apartment then I took out the envelope. Just as I slid my thumbnail under the sealing wax, I remembered the Schermers' maps. They were everywhere.

My mouth went dry. I had hung myself.

"Frau Hofflinger!"

She looked up, those blue eyes wide and at the same time

narrowed. She was holding Central Europe/4 before her as if
it were a hymnal. "All the details," she said. "How do you
know these things?"

"Put it down."

She let it slide from her hands and onto the others. "I didn't
bend it."

"Bending doesn't matter. Just the oil in your fingers can
leave marks on it. That's my work, my livelihood." I went over
and began to gather my maps, corner by corner.

"It's nice that it's warm in here," she said, trying for
conversation. "Maybe it feels even warmer when the coal
comes free." Her voice trailed off. Upstairs, someone began to
walk around in the kitchen.

I looked at her. "The kettle is over on the stove, Frau
Hofflinger." Surreptitiously I slipped the few Schermer maps
remaining in at the bottom of the pile.

"Oh yes," she said, relieved, "I see it."

Back in the parlor, I separated out the two groups of maps,
and getting down on my knees, slid the originals beneath the
bureau, on the floor. My own I placed in the leather portfolio
where the others had been.

Then I unfolded the letter, the crisp paper. *Herr Braslauer:
Anything left behind in your new home should be thrown out. Heil
Hitler. R. Terskan, Commandant.*

I sat down on the floor, stunned. Was I safe? I read the letter
again and broke into laughter. "Pig!" With a whoop, I pried off
my boots and threw them across the room into the stack of
luggage. The pile wavered, toppled. I raised my hands up over
my head, victorious.

"What was that," she called.

"The gods on high," I shouted. "Bowling."

I went to the kitchen. I pulled out the chair in which I'd
worked all night and sat down, tilting it back on its rear legs.
"Tell me," I said, "is it usual for your police to meddle in the
people's business this way?" And I handed her the note.

She read it, her lips pursed. "No," she muttered.

"Well, I didn't think so."

Letting out a breath, she said, "Gerda Stella moved from
this apartment to be with Rolf Terskan. She left so fast, she

didn't take anything with her. No one talks about it, but it's true. I suppose he was trying to be considerate to her about her old attachments. That's what this must be."

The chair came down. "It wasn't the war? But the way you were speaking of his, that Torgood's, distress..."

"Not war. Adultery." Frau Hofflinger cut me off with a slashing motion of her left hand. "The marriage fell apart. They were sweet together, I can tell you that, and young. But on the other hand, Com. Terskan—he was Torgood's Commandant, you know. Well, that part is over with. He was transferred to Passau. Passau's far, but not as far as Poland. Do you take sugar?" She set the bowl on the table. "He left some."

I looked up. "Why do you say that he left it? She did, too."

"You're right, I suppose." Frau Hofflinger used the embroidered towel to pick up the hot kettle. "When all is said and done, what *has* been done doesn't matter. The sugar's here— that's all." She bent her wrist and from out of the kettle came a thin, hot stream of coffee. Though ersatz, it was richly dark.

I picked up my cup and took a huge gulp. It tasted wonderful, nearly scorching my throat. "So, Gerda took nothing from here?" I said.

She tilted her head. "Didn't you look in the closets?"

"I was focused on my work. You know what a bachelor is like. But if there is something you want that you saw..."

"I saw..." her voice trembled, and she stopped.

"Without empty space, I can't unpack." I drained my cup.

Frau Hofflinger bit her lower lip and put down the kettle. Without another word she went to the bedroom. I heard her open the closet.

"She doesn't need a scrap like this any longer," she called. "You should see how fancy she is these days."

"Let me see." I picked up her cup and took a sip.

She came back into the kitchen. Over the white bathrobe she had draped a fox wrap. The legs hung down, the tiny, flattened paws just grazing her breasts and against her bare collarbone rested the head with its buttoned eyes and thin snout. The jaws were only slightly opened. Frau Hofflinger herself was flushed. Perhaps nervously, she kept stroking the fox along its full length, where the spine would have been. "I want to keep it."

I glanced away, resettling the cup in its saucer. "Then do."

"How simple!"

I raised my head and she laughed, pale throat glistening.

"But you look lovely," I said, startled. "In this light, with your hair, and your face—already shaped so like a heart—"

Her smile faded. "You think that?" she said, and tucked the black tip of the fox's tail into its mouth as I stood up.

She was on her side, away from me when I rolled from the sheets. I got dressed as quickly and quietly as I could; I didn't want to wake her. There was so much more I could still make of this day. It was a wonderful day! I gathered up the few things I needed and as I shut the door first to my apartment, then the heavier one to Frau Hofflinger's—dear Gertrude's—building, I felt bouyant, a different man entirely from just half a day before. Briskly I walked down Ludvigstrasse, turned right and right again.

In no time at all, my hand was on the door of Premier Printers. I entered and Sarah looked up.

"I'll get Herr Volkman," she said, rising immediately.

"Do that, please. Thank you."

He came in from the back room. His face was bright and shiny with perspiration. "I'm glad to see you this soon," he said, coming up to the counter.

"I've been able to get a lot done. Two maps for certain; one other, possibly. But I'll wait on that last just a bit."

"Well, good." He paused. "May I see?"

I laid the portfolio down on the counter.

He turned the case toward him and began to unzip it. As he did, I said, "I noticed some of the property on this street is going to be auctioned. That gives me something to think about."

He looked up sharply. "Oh?"

"Sure. Maybe I will be your neighbor." I reached over to flip open the cover. Then the maps were spilling out.

Trees

BY JANE RUITER

On the last Sunday in October, a cloudless day, Fran and Richard Hollis have just finished quarreling. They are standing beneath a canopy of evergreen in the county land preserve while Fran's dog dances impatiently around their legs. Fran finally unleashes the dog—a small Black Lab mix, lively for its age—and watches as it ranges ahead.

Richard states the safe, the obvious: "Shadow sure likes to run." Then he waits for Fran to say something.

She nods in agreement, but keeps her eyes on the dog; and it occurs to her that she's known the dog longer than she's known Richard. She's known Richard eight years, been married to him for five, and they've been walking the land preserve together every weekend now for the past four months. Walking had been the counselor's idea; seeing the counselor had been Fran's.

They take the millpond path today, a narrow, unkept ribbon between rows of red pines. Fran glances at Richard, feeling distant, although they're only inches apart. He never seems to feel cold, she thinks. Unlike her. Tall, blue-eyed and bearded, Richard is dressed in Levis and a plaid flannel shirt with the sleeves rolled up, his forearm bare and tanned and corded with carpenter's muscles. Fran wears jeans and a hooded sweatshirt, as well as a quilted vest, and shivers each time the wind blows through the pines. She dreads the coming winter with its damp, cold days and early darkness, and wonders sometimes how she'll survive it, especially the holidays, when

Richard's children, all grown—and all alive, of course—will come to visit.

Richard shoves a fallen log to one side of the trail with his foot, and the smell of rotting wood rises and diffuses in the cool autumn air.

"You're awfully quiet," he says.

"Didn't sleep well." Fran could have added "again," but she assumes it's understood.

"Neither did I."

They step around wild rosebushes bowed by the weight of countless scarlet rosehips. Another autumn, they might have stopped and picked rosehips for tea or jam, but today neither of them pauses. The counselor has told them that their marriage is at risk, which they already knew, and that eighty percent of couples like them divorce, usually two to three years after the death. If that's the case, Fran guesses they've got nineteen months to go. She keeps thinking today of quarrels Richard used to have with Kenny. Underwear on the floor, hair in the sink, fingerprints on the woodwork. Fran had thought Richard was being petty; Richard had said Kenny was careless; and Kenny, at times, had seen a way to drive a wedge between his mother and stepfather. For the past five months—since Kenny's death—Fran hasn't mentioned those quarrels, but they keep repeating in her head like some stubborn tape loop.

The dog circles back to make certain they're following, then reassured, it dashes away, nose to the ground for rabbit scent, its coat red-black in bars of filtered sunlight. Fran loves the way it looks, streaking along, so single-minded and close to the earth. She listens, for a moment, to the muffled beat of its paws on the pine needles.

The forest has changed to hardwoods now, mostly oaks and birches. Fran and Richard scuff brown leaves with their boots.

"I think we should buy a dog bed."

"What's wrong with the carpet?" Richard asks it innocently enough, but the question puts Fran on the defensive.

"There's a draft already, Richard . . . and it's going to get worse this winter."

The dog used to sleep with Kenny. He'd smuggle it under his covers on cold nights and Fran would find the dog hairs clinging to the flannel sheets. The dog sleeps in the hallway now, just outside Fran and Richard's bedroom door. Sometimes, in the mornings, they trip over it on their way to the bathroom.

"Why not just a throw rug?"

"She's an old dog, Richard. Her joints get stiff when it's cold."

Fran's voice is shaking, and so are her hands. She takes a deep breath, holds it, then lets it out slowly. The first three months after Kenny died, she'd felt a numbness that she'd thought worse than anything else in the world. Now she feels a relentless anger, and she thinks it must be the worst thing, because of the way it walls her off from people she loves, especially Richard.

The dog returns, then races away again. Fran retains the brief image of it standing, panting, in the center of the trail. Maybe it's running too hard, she thinks, feeling in her pocket for the leash. Maybe not. Until the past May, she'd let the dog run free all the time, and it had followed Kenny as he jogged his five-mile loop around the neighborhood. He did this every day after high school track practice—said he had to run more, work harder, because his legs were so short. Warm spring days, when Kenny came back from running, he would drop his sweaty T-shirt on the porch and Shadow would flop down beneath the backyard willow, the first tree of the season to offer shade. Kenny would hurry inside and empty all the trays of ice cubes into a large bowl of cold water, then carry the bowl outside and set it down so the dog could drink without getting up. Most of the time, Kenny forgot to refill the ice cube trays. Later, Richard would complain there was no ice for tea.

The young man who hit Kenny was only eighteen years old, traveling the backroads in his first car on the way to his first full-time job. The curve, the shadows, Kenny's dark clothes— they simply hadn't seen each other; and Kenny, running with his Walkman on, hadn't heard. For weeks after the accident, the dog had circled the neighborhood, aimlessly following Kenny's jogging route, every time Fran or Richard had let it out. Fran had finally bought a leash and chain.

"Good weather," Richard says. He and Fran are standing on

a weathered wooden deck that overlooks the millpond. The dog lags behind. "Every Sunday," Richard adds, "it's been nice."

"Yes," Fran says skeptically. "So far." She raises herself on tiptoe, trying to see through fallen branches that mar her view.

"This way," Richard says. "Down by the water. You can see better down here."

"There's no path."

"Yes, there is," Richard insists. "Just a little washed out."

He leads the way down a gully deepened by the past week's heavy rain. Shadow pushes suddenly, eagerly, in front of Fran, who slips on leaves and mud, but rights herself before she really falls. The dog runs to the pond's edge and lowers its head to drink, but Fran, thinking of pawprints and dirt on the ride home, calls it to her and snaps the leash on its collar. Shadow whines and pulls, trying to drink the muddy water at the shoreline, but Fran tightens the leash, pulling the dog away.

Maples and willows border the millpond; its glassy surface mirrors reds, oranges and yellow-greens. The week before, they'd seen two fisherman in rowboats and a small sailboat with one blue sail. Today a lone pair of mallards skim the water and take flight, leaving the pond deserted. A single-engine Cessna, white with a red stripe, drones its way across the cloudless autumn sky.

"A nice day for flying," Richard says. "No clouds."

"But there's wind."

"Not so much."

"Seems to be moving awfully slowly."

"Student pilot, maybe. Or just enjoying the view."

Fran shades her eyes, trying to make out the call letters on the undersides of the plane's wings.

The day before he died, Kenny had run the 880 in an All-Conference meet at his high school, and on the first curve of the second lap, Fran had seen him lengthen his stride and begin to pull in front. He'd looked so beautiful running that day it had made Fran's heart pound, and she'd started shouting "Ken-ny! Ken-ny!" along with the rest of the crowd. Kenny had kicked hard down the backstretch, then swept around the final curve, and Fran had the strangest feeling, watching him, that all his fifteen years had been lived for the single moment when he sprinted across the finish line and broke the ribbon. She forgot the odd feeling, though, when she stepped onto the track to meet him. He was absolutely winded, but ecstatic; and he hugged her and spun her around in a little circle until he realized his teammates were watching. He walked away then, and sauntered into the infield to put his sweats back on. The next afternoon, waiting outside the emergency room, Fran had relived that race again and again.

As Fran and Richard climb back up the gully, the dog's pulling on the leash makes Fran's ascent easier—she tires so quickly these days. Back on the path, she unsnaps the leash and watches as Shadow lopes away. The dog returns shortly, however, panting laboriously and covered with burrs. It sways for a moment, sides heaving, then collapses on the loamy ground.

The forest air seems stifling, filled with leaf mold and decay. Panicky and short of breath, Fran lowers herself beside the dog on knees that feel like water. *Let her be all right*, she thinks. She couldn't bear for one more thing to be different.

Fran remembers now how Shadow tried to drink from the millpond, and how, preoccupied with pawprints, she had tightened the leash and jerked the dog away. Her own pettiness appalls her. We could have spread newspapers on the back seat, she thinks. We could have wiped the mud off when we got home.

The dog scrambles to its feet, shakes itself, then trots ahead, as if nothing at all had happened. Fran is unspeakably relieved.

"False alarm," Richard says, and adds, "Thank God." He gives Fran a hand up, and she feels the callouses, coarse as bark, on his palm.

She had sent a friend to intercept him, that afternoon in May, before he could arrive at the hospital; but the friend had missed him, and while Fran was in the chaplain's office making phone calls, Richard had walked, completely unprepared and alone, into the emergency room waiting area. Someone had asked about funeral arrangements for his step-son, and he'd toppled like a felled tree.

Richard had carried Kenny's wristwatch and running clothes in a blue plastic bag that evening as they crossed the hospital parking lot. Fran had remarked on the spectacular sunset, shocked at seeing such beauty when her only child had just died. After they reached home, Fran had heard Richard start the washing machine. When she walked into the laundry room, Kenny's watch was on the counter and the plastic bag was lying empty on the floor. Richard was crying as he closed the top of the washer. "I didn't want you to see," Richard said.

In a clearing overlooking the millpond, Richard reclines on a quilt of brown leaves while Fran sits, tailor-fashion, beside him. The dog is lying a short distance away.

Richard breaks a long silence. "I think pines are my favorite trees."

"Why? Why pines?"

"I don't know...I feel peaceful when I'm around pines. And I like working with the wood."

Fran watches sunlight strike the silver strands in Richard's beard. She remembers snapshots from his old life—pictures of him shaved clean, dressed in suits, and never smiling—and realizes she's never known him without the beard.

"My favorite are willows," she says.

"Why's that?"

Fran clasps her hands around her knees. "I guess because they keep their leaves longest in autumn...and they bud first in spring."

The sun slides behind a thicket of pines to the west, deepening the sky colors—gold to pink to mauve. The dog scratches, then looks at Fran and whines, anxious, perhaps, to resume hunting, or to return home.

"It's probably pretty late, Richard. Do you want to start back?"

"If you're ready."

Fran rises and brushes bits of leaves from the back of her jeans. "I'm ready," she says. "Are you?"

Richard pretends to haul himself up on the hand she offers him, and they walk on together, leaving hardwoods and re-entering pines.

"You know," Richard says cautiously, pointing to a trail off to his left, "if we wanted to, we could ski right from the parking lot to the millpond this winter."

Fran studies the sloping path, nodding. "That way," she says, "we could avoid the trails with the steep hills. Especially the one with the curve at the bottom."

"The one where I fell, you mean."

"I fell there, too," Fran says.

"I'd forgotten."

"Yes, this looks better." Fran imagines the hiss of her skis on snow, the cold air burning her nose, and the warmth surging through her body. She wills to survive the coming winter and knows she will never speak of quarrels. "Yes," she says again. "It looks like a good trail."

They climb a small knoll as the dog ranges ahead, casting about for scents of game. Fran pauses to pick a handful of scarlet rosehips from a sprawling bush, tastes the tart seeds, then picks a few more and passes them to Richard.

"Rosehips, Richard . . . look at all of them."

They walk on and fall in step, layers of dry red needles cushioning the tread of their boots. The forest, at dusk, seems hushed, almost hallowed, and Fran can smell a hint of sassafras somewhere in the pine.

Ransom

BY ELIZABETH EVANS

"There he comes," Mickey whispered to me.

"Wait, wait,wait," I said. At that distance, the car was small and dark, but it grew lighter, a dusty blue. Dad. Slipping off the road and into the wide ditch along the highway, then rolling back up again, so slow that from where we stood the motion looked almost peaceful, like an ocean wave.

"You kids!" I tucked little Krystal higher up on my shoulder and prayed she'd go on sleeping. Except for Mickey, all the bigger children had started throwing gravel from the shoulder as soon as we left the diner. Their cheeks were red with the cold, but they still laughed, they tumbled into the ditch on purpose. They didn't know what was what.

Another big truck went by, far enough from the diner now that it picked up speed. It sucked at our clothes and made things even colder. When the trucker got close to dangerous Dad's car, he leaned on the horn.

"Wow," Mickey said. He squinted down the road. "Dad's driving doesn't look so hot."

"When's it ever?" I asked. The rate Dad came on, we'd still be standing on the side of the highway when spring arrived; by the time he got there, maybe the climate would have changed entirely, Nebraska would be an underwater sea once more and the kids and I would all have flippers.

"What sort of mood do you figure he's in now?" Mickey asked.

"Ha," I said. I knew Mickey wanted to blame me for us being out here, but it was Mickey Dad was burned at *yesterday*, so mad he punched a hole in the bathroom. Dad hadn't even yet fixed the hole he kicked between the living room and the hall last summer. *That* particular hole. The little ones liked to look at each other through that hole. Sammy's idea of a good time: pull a diaper box out in the hall and watch TV through the hole. Personally, the hole made me sick: always plaster dust on the floor from the little kids picking, and the wall smudged with finger marks.

I had cried at the new hole, but when Dad said, "Stop your blubbering," I'd nodded. I wanted to be strong, strong, I wanted to move with the dependability of the tortoise and provide the children with a lifelong model of Christian tolerance—which, if I didn't have, I didn't have a thing. Except maybe the children. Maybe Krystal, now shifting in my arms on that cold and dirty road which her father traveled slow as a camel, slower.

I blew into the yellow down of Krystal's hair, made a star. I felt certain that if Krystal looked like anybody on earth, I was it. No one alive would have guessed such a perfect child came from Dad and my stepmother, Anndean. But that was the way with children: when my real Mom brought home my brothers and sisters from the hospital, they smelled sweet as bread, they might cry out for relief of earthly suffering, but they never did a truly bad or cruel thing to anybody.

"Whoa!" Mickey threw his hands up before him like somebody opening a sheet onto a bed. I looked. Dad was climbing the median, headed straight for a big pole. The children screamed. They didn't even know what had happened. They screamed because I did. They were hooked to me that way, like Christmas tree lights where if one goes out they all do.

Still, Dad missed the pole. He turned off the car. He stuck his head out the window, like he'd just found the right address, any moment someone would call out, "Come on in for a beer, Gary!"

Mickey started walking faster. "Wait," I said. "We wait 'til *he* comes for us. He can do that at least."

"But I'm *cold*, Marie."

"Of course you're cold," I told him. "It's cold out here. If you weren't cold, something would be wrong with you, so I guess you're all right."

Mickey smiled. I could always make him smile. I smiled back, to help him along, but I didn't feel like smiling. I wished we were in the diner still. Krystal would wake soon, and then what? I'd used the last diapers and bottles over two hours ago; the three littlest kids were sure to be wet by now, and pretty soon they'd notice, start to holler.

I breathed on Krystal's face to warm it. She remained as yet unspoiled by contact with us, but I imagined her in our company, simmering like a poor little pot roast until she, too, cooked clear through.

Dad started to back off the median. I asked Mickey, "If Dad died right now, do you think he'd go to Heaven?"

"Don't start," he said, "that's how we got here in the first place, Marie."

I sniffed. The sound frightened me. I looked around for Anndean. Then I did it again: sniff!

"Did you hear that, Mickey?" I said. "Did you hear me sniff?"

"Don't change the subject," Mickey said. "It *is* your fault, Marie."

"I've been infected with Anndean's gruesome habit!" I cried. "She's infected me, Mickey!"

Mickey didn't smile. Because of this morning. Anndean had wanted her coffee, but it still perked, I couldn't bring her a cup yet, so I had just sat down with her and the children at the breakfast table.

Anndean turned away from the TV to give me a dose of her fishy stare. That's what got me started. And the sniff. As always, she sniffed: *sniff*, like she understood things through her nose, or else I stunk. Anndean wasn't much older than me, and I was smarter, but marriage to Dad gave her the advantage, say, the sort a sledgehammer has over something like a microscope or a fancy computer: whatever I could do, she could put an end to it, quick.

"You!" she said, and wagged her cigarette beneath my nose. "Stop looking, you!"

"Did I look?" I said. "I didn't mean to, Anndean, but I suppose observation is my nature." This was not a lie. "You're a good observer," more than one teacher at the schools had told me. Indeed, I often found myself fascinated by the bottom line of Anndean's face, a journey which had no interest in scenery but traveled from ear to ear by the shortest distance, so that, head-on, Anndean looked like the mailbox we had the time we lived in the country.

Judge not lest ye be judged, but I did suspect that the *inside* of Anndean's head was like the mailbox, too; maybe once a day something ended up in there, but it mostly stood empty. A sweeter, more practical woman would have let us use the space between her ears for storing some of the stuff that spilled out of cupboards, and closets and boxes wherever we lived. Canned goods, I thought once, just to make myself laugh, canned goods would be my choice.

"Anndean," I said this morning. I turned down the TV despite the honking of the children. "Do you know, Anndean, I used to think and think, 'Why are we saved by the coming of Jesus?' A visit's a visit. Rules are rules, okay, but how does following them give us eternal life? How could Jesus die for *our* sins? And in so doing ransom us all from eternal death?"

Anndean flicked at my ear with her fingernails to keep me from getting close. Anndean—she was nothing like my real mother. My real mother looked precisely like a combination of the stars Raquel Welch and Stefanie Powers, except she had blue eyes. She *never* hurt us kids, and it upset her so when Dad did, she had to go in her room and just lock the door. Anndean, on the other hand, could always be counted on to possess, within easy reach, a pointed shoe, a serving fork, some item which would let her join the fray.

She didn't want to listen this morning, but I went on: "Then I figured it out! Even though God made men, He couldn't understand what it meant to be a man until He took the form of a man. And when He did! And saw how bad life was! How it stunk, and people did *lousy* things to one another, sometimes not even out of the rottenness of their hearts, but because He gave them bad equipment—why, He put His face in His hands. He just said, 'I don't blame anybody for anything!' Which was all He *could* say, since it was His fault, but the rest of us don't always behave that graciously."

I did not look directly at Anndean, but I watched for signs of absorption. Like I said, she was not bright. She thought TV programs where people sat in chairs and discussed things like Negroes and wars—I could *see* Anndean thought that those shows appeared by mistake, that she caught glimpses of them the way she might spy strangers in hospital rooms while on her way to visit a friend. ("Turn!" she'd say if I stopped to hear a little, "Turn, turn, turn!")

If my theory about Jesus relieved her this morning, she did not let on. Maybe she accepted God's forgiveness as her due, though she *had* served time for breaking and entering, *and* forgery, *and* when my baby was born one month after her Krystal—Tommy Lawrence Handsell I named him, though nobody cared, the people who adopted him gave him a name I will never know as long as I live—when my baby was born Anndean worked hard and long to convince Dad I had to give him away.

"Anndean," I said, "forgiveness and forebearance." She turned the TV back up, lit another cigarette, stubbed out the last in her jam. "Even," I told her, "for Jesus, Who made the fig tree *wither* when He was hungry and it bore no fruit!"

Anndean looked around the room at all those children waiting to be fed. She'd given her Krystal a bottle all right, she did care for Krystal. Right then, she reached over and stuck her finger under Krystal's sleeper and gave her a little tickle. Then she looked at me. Ran her fingers down her neck and into the V of her bathrobe. Rose from her chair. Opened her mouth.

"Get out!" she screamed.

She chased me into the living room with the coffee pot, throwing coffee towards me like I was moving fire, and screaming, and hitting Erin over the head with her plate.

"Out!" she screamed. "Out!"

While she screamed Dad out of bed, I helped the little kids find something to put on, and grabbed-up diapers and things. I couldn't locate a shirt so I just stuffed my nightgown in my jeans. Krystal lay on my bunk, bawling; but once I picked her up, she'd be fine. I'd been more mother to her than Anndean any day of the week. I'd meant to nurse Tommy so he'd have all the protection possible against whatever was out there, and when they took him away, I secretly gave the milk to Krystal, twice a day for a whole month, once for her night feeding and again before the rest got up.

"Out! Out! Out!" screamed Anndean.

When we started off, she came after. She threw toys and chunks of snow at the car. "Bring back my baby!" she yelled.

Dad looked in the rearview mirror, then over at me and
Krystal. His hair was mashed with sleep. He looked like he
had a fry pan stuck on his head. "Better give her a chance to
cool off," he said.

I knew if I agreed he'd stop the car and take Krystal back so
I kept my mouth shut. And prayed. For nothing more than
forebearance and forgiveness. But worried my prayers concealed wishes, had little pockets sly as those folds in your
brain scientists say contain everything you ever heard or said
or smelled, even though you don't know it.

With Krystal in my lap, maybe I secretly prayed for all the
things which would give me the peace I seemed to need before
I got forebearance. Like an automobile safety seat for Krystal.
And knowing my Tommy was safe and sound. And revenge
on Dad and Anndean.

The way Anndean acted about my theory, you'd have
thought I came up with it for my own pleasure. But think: if
everybody *did* go to heaven, heaven would just be life on earth
all over again, wouldn't it? Also, suppose you're nuts and kill
somebody. Suppose you're not, and do. Does that mean you
are?

The children had shivered and shook in the car this
morning. I'd tried to comfort them. I'd put my foot over the
rusted-out place in the floor to keep splatters of slush from
shooting up at us. If the rusted-out place had been there two
years ago, January 17, maybe Mom could not have killed
herself. I've tortured and tortured myself, trying to rust out
the metal earlier or make one of the windows impossible to roll
tight. I didn't ever want to get in a car again. I thought we
ought to become Amish. The Amish don't have cars. They
live in solid houses where if a thing wears out, they fix it, or
make another. They only have things they can fix! They grow
their food. They eat hot meals with crowds of people who
pray and believe the same things, so at least you had a chance
of turning out right for your earthly life, and didn't just figure
you'd say "sorry" before you died.

When Dad dropped us at the diner that morning—a truck-
stop place out further than I could remember going before—
he said, "Fill up. I'll be by later. Out on the highway. You
watch for me."

He knew I didn't have any money, so why ask? He drove off, and there stood the kids, six of them besides me and the baby, waiting to eat.

"May as well get whatever you want," I told them; and to the waitress; "Our dad's coming later."

I could not entirely stop the kids from spilling syrup and tearing open sugars and blowing straws. I scolded, I prayed; but our waitress still had to stand a couple feet from the table to get our dessert orders. "But which one's *best*?" Sammy cried. "Which is very *best*?"

"Sorry," I told the waitress. She deserved it. She had forebearance, like my real mom. A skinny man at the counter asked her if he could have "a beaver on rye," and she didn't frown or smile or anything. I admired her until about eleven-thirty, at which time she began to cast looks my way, like, "Where's your dad?" and "So who's paying?"

I stared out the window at all those trucks. I thought, I will be stuck in this booth the rest of my life. I've already been here forever.

"Say, darling, you watching for your boyfriend?"

A trucker across the way. Sweet-voiced. The chip of face I allowed in my sight not bad. In self-defense, I began to pray, "Lead us not into temptation..." but found I could not hold on, both prayer and temptation spun on the same globe, their edges blurred like the borders between countries.

"Psst! You in the nightgown!"

"That man wants you, Marie!" the children cried. "Marie! Marie, look!"

"Marie!" said the trucker. "Look!"

I looked. A dinner plate held up, and on its chopped steak, the words 'I love you' unwound in bright red katsup.

"Hey!" protested the trucker as a man in a blue windbreaker came between me and my view of the trucker's plate.

"Chuck Rappenhoe's the name."

I met my Mom's dad once, at Mom's funeral, and I'd say the man in the windbreaker—Chuck Rappenhoe—was about his age, forty something, a little gray, glasses. He had a gap-toothed smile, like a jack-o-lantern; but he frowned at my trucker. Who just laughed and started eating the chopped steak.

"Don't pay any mind to that joker," Mr. Rappenhoe said. I regretted the loss of the trucker, but perhaps Mr. Rapenhoe was my reluctant prayer made flesh. Maybe he'd pick up our tab.

"That's a beautiful baby," said Mr. Rappenhoe. "Is that your baby, young lady?"

The children had seen me go around big as a house, but they giggled at the question. I glared them down. They knew from Social Service calls not to correct me when I looked that way. "Yeah, she's mine," I said.

Mr. Rappenhoe put one of his big fingers in Krystal's hand. She bit it, hard. "Yikes," he said.

"Sorry," I said.

He shook his head, no problem. He acted as if he didn't even notice that, under our coats, both Theresa and me wore nightgowns, or that Erin's eye was turning black, and there was jam in his hair.

"I came here to study radio electronics," he said. "Me and my wife farm, but, on the side, I've always been good at fixing things."

He could have been a mass murderer-child rapist in disguise, but I did not believe evil necessarily better at deception than goodness. Krystal liked him, all the children liked him. While Sammy combed, this way and that, what little hair Mr. Rappenhoe had on his head, Mr. Rappenhoe smiled and explained that just that morning he had finished his final exam, so he'd come over here to celebrate with a piece of pie.

I didn't hear all of it for over by the cash register, my trucker was giving me a sign: "Tonight." Pointed his finger at me like we were a regular thing. "You be here." It gave me shivers. Was he handsome? Ugly? I watched him cross the lot and swing himself into a big blue truck. I couldn't tell if I liked one thing about him except his handwriting.

Mr. Rappenhoe frowned while he worked to untangle a snarl in Theresa's hair, but he sounded happy: "Tommorrow, bright and early, *adieu* to the The Three Bells Motel! I load the car and head on home to Arkansas!" He stuck his comb in his back pocket and smiled. He creased his napkin with his thumbnail, made a shy boy's face. "I missed the wife so a couple times I drove home in the middle of the night just to eat breakfast with her!"

He showed us her photograph. "She seems nice all right," I said. I knew they couldn't be Amish since he'd mentioned a car and electronics, still—farmers, and one of them knew how to fix things!

"How many kids you got?" Mickey asked.

Mr. Rappenhoe shook his head. "We tried, but just weren't blessed. Turns out now we're too old to adopt." He patted Krystal's cheek. She worked the hinges of his glasses back and forth like she meant to snap the bows right off. "Look at that," Mr. Rappenhoe said, very quiet, "she's a smart one, isn't she?"

Who could answer? Here sat the best dad I ever met, without even one child to be dad to! It just showed, again, the rightness of my theory, and so I said!

Mr. Rappenhoe listened, but then *he* said, as if he put away my theory entirely, "Christ came to ask us to be better. Maybe we're home free in the end, Marie, but he still asked us to be better."

The waitress stopped by the table, rag squashed in her hand, face all red. "These kids have sat here over four hours and I take it you aren't the dad?" she said to Mr. Rappenhoe.

I blushed. All the children old enough to know beans blushed. "He'll be here," I said. After she left, I told Mr. Rappenhoe, "I try to do everything Jesus told The Rich Young Ruler, but I don't honor my father. If he had been better to my mother"—I didn't want to tell Mr. Rappenhoe what Mom did, so I backed up a little—"If he were nice to her, she'd be happier."

Mr. Rappenhoe nodded. He looked serious, but not mad, like the counselor they had me talk to when I got pregnant.

A few minutes after he left, the waitress came over. "Old pumpkin head paid for you," she said. *Sniff.* And turned on her fat white heel.

"Have a good breakfast?" Dad asked as we finally weaved off down the road. He smiled, but I knew he was headed for tears, about Mom, and every bad deal he ever met, and how we didn't appreciate him.

"We've been there four hours, Dad. Sam and Erin are already asking where's supper. Krystal's crying and we're out of everything."

We sloshed into a gas station, barely missed a sign: $1.13

REG. Dad tried to honk at it, lacked the energy. I got us back on the road just as the station manager ran out.

"Anndean didn't mean nothing this morning," Dad said. "Why, you kids are all we got!"

I thought about that. Was that true? "Still," I said, "Tommy was all I got. Had." I wiped the wet off the windshield; put us together in a car and it dripped like a covered pot. I said, "Thou shalt not steal."

"Oh, hell," said Dad. He rested his chin on the steering wheel. He squinted at the winter afternoon as if it were a terrible storm, he was sea captain. "First one to spot a church gets a quarter," he said.

The secretary lady at the St. John's Episcopal said, "I see." She blushed, embarrassed for us; but she knew what to do, right away she got graham crackers from the Sunday school, by five-thirty the kids and I ate lasagna and something called green beans amandine at the home of a church family. Dry pants and bottles for the little ones and a whole case of Krystal's favorite formula on the kitchen counter.

"Quiet down!" I told the kids. That house knocked them out: toys in the basement, more in the bedrooms, a place just for fingerpainting and clay and puzzles, a clothes chute to holler down, the boy's bed topped by a frame so it looked like an outdoors tent. They kept jumping out of their chairs and going to see this or that. Nuts—even Mickey, who should've remembered other stays like this—as if we might live in that nice house with candles on the table forever.

I knew better. Dad might not come tomorrow, but he'd be back the next day for sure. You couldn't understand why, but he would. "Trouble with the oldest," he'd tell Social Service. "You know she's trouble."

While I dished myself seconds of the lasagna, I tried on the idea of me running off with all the kids, in the back of my trucker's trailer. Then I tried just Krystal, me, and the trucker. I kept it simple, but it didn't work. I didn't see how I could be good for anybody.

When the husband got up to get us more milk, I asked the church lady, Mrs. Zenor, who was pretty and nice like some dull school teachers I'd had, "What's a person have to do to be a nun?"

"We're not Catholics!" cried her son and daughter. Them I didn't like. Them I gave a look, but they kept on eating, chewed up little mouthfuls like they had all the time in the world.

"I'm not Catholic either," I told Mrs. Zenor, "I just wondered."

Mr. Zenor nodded. She tilted her head to one side: "Let's see if I can get all your names right!" she said.

Now Chuck Rappenhoe couldn't *believe* himself so lucky as to set Theresa or Krystal on his knee, while Mrs. Zenor couldn't believe anybody would ask her to return the children she fancied. She and Mr. Zenor looked across their shiny table at each with a crazy kind of happiness. Later on, while the bigger kids ran around the house and I watched TV with the little ones, I heard her on the phone:

"She's a darling, Kim! And I can just imagine your Glenn with a little brother—"

She was a good woman, but misguided. She thought taking one or two of the children would be like picking out a pair of hamsters, easy, she'd tuck them into a spare corner, gratitude would shape them into something better than what she already had.

By about nine-thirty, she began to see the error of her ways. She came downstairs in her bathrobe. Without makeup she looked older, tired. I felt old and tired myself. I propped Krystal with her bottle and the three of us watched the end of a show called *The Exterminator*.

Now and then Mrs. Zenor looked up at the ceiling. "Do you usually just let them run down?" she asked me. *Thud* went children jumping off beds. "I kissed them goodnight at about nine, but in five minutes, they all were up again."

Probably, they started arguing about who she kissed first and why and if she liked one of them more than the other. What if she thought she had to kiss me, too? Except for the children, and the person who was Tommy's dad, nobody had kissed me since Mom died.

I told her, "You may blame me that they're not better mannered, but we've been subject to bad influence."

Mrs. Zenor smiled. "I doubt you're all that bad, honey. What are you—fourteen?"

I switched the channel with the remote device. I stopped at

a couple dancing in the rain and drinking 7-Up. They made me want to cry. Was it fair for envy to be a sin? If people had everything, they could put envy out of their minds, but if you had nothing, on top of everything else, you had to worry about wishing you had something!

I imagined Mr. Rappenhoe would have a quick reply to that, and it would sound nice, but not fit me at all.

"That's a cute ad, isn't it?" said Mrs. Zenor.

I looked at her, sitting on her couch, smiling. "Didn't you think God was wrong when He asked Abraham to sacrifice Issac?" I asked.

She smoothed her hands over the lap of her puffy robe. Finally, with a little laugh, she said, "Well, He wasn't a father yet, Marie."

At first I like her answer, but then I remembered: "He was God!"

"Yes."

"And He was supposed to be *our* father, wasn't He?"

Mr. Zenor had been doing something in the basement. He came up the stairs just then, like on cue. "Girl talk?" he said.

Mrs. Zenor patted my knee. "Let's discuss this in the morning, sweetie, let's get some rest now," she said.

By ten-fifteen, except for the TV, the whole house was quiet. You would not have believed the quiet, like Krystal and I swam under the sea and all the others rode in a boat above. The weather lady said tomorrow would be the same as today, cold and clear. She acted as if she liked the prospect.

For cover, I left the TV on when I went in the kitchen. I put as many cans of formula as I could into a paper bag, along with half the Pampers, a jar of peanut butter and a box of Triscuits.

I lay Krystal on the counter to change her. "You know you're going somewhere, don't you?" I said. She bounced her heels against me and laughed.

Have you ever noticed how a baby cries and cries but doesn't understand *you* crying? Then somewhere along the line, maybe about the time they start causing pain, they get sad when you're sad, as if it takes them a while to build up enough of their own pain to understand somebody else's.

I unbuttoned Krystal's little suit. She wiggled away from me, laughing. She had bruises from times when I didn't get between her and Dad and Anndean fast enough, and a burn scar on her thigh that nobody ever explained to my satisfaction, but she was, like Tommy, like all babies, perfect, perfection.

Maybe Anndean and Dad never felt sad about another person's pain in their life. Maybe they never felt bad enough themselves. Maybe they'd suffered too much and that was why they were the way they were, and God could look at the big picture and say, "A life's a short time, they'll rest with me in eternity." I didn't care. I didn't make them. I didn't have to ask their forgiveness for what I was about to do.

After I got Krystal suited-up again, and into her jacket, I checked the address for Mr. Rappenhoe's motel. It turned out it sat on the same stretch as the diner. Since I'd already stole the peanut butter and crackers, for which I guessed I'd be forgiven, I took the change on the windowsill, too. Three quarters and one dime. Enough for a cup of coffee afterwards.

I pushed open the back door. Afterwards, at the thought, my arms felt empty and creepy, like when you stand in a doorway and press your hands against the frame, and then when you step away, up they float without your even willing.

I didn't let myself think about the other children at all.

The night was cold and clear, with fuzzy strands of stars high above. I got myself out from under them, erased myself from the world, which instantly seemed cleaner, brighter.

The Amish houses I'd seen in the books at school had been big and white with clean yards. I imagined Chuck Rappenhoe's place would be like that. I imagined myself stepping from such a house. Yes. Tomorrow night, late. My husband, Chuck, is just pulling in the drive.

"Chuck," I call, "welcome home!" Like my husband, I'm scarcely aware I radiate goodness, I'm just good, always work to be good, assume that's how it goes.

Chuck gets out of the car, grinning his old jack-o-lantern grin. "Come here," he says. Excited, but almost whispering, like he doesn't want to wake somebody. "Come here!" So I laugh and come to the car where he's pointing in the window at something I can't yet see, and saying, "Come here and see my little passenger!"

Then a big black car turned down the Zenors' street. I became Marie again. Marie stuck out her thumb.

The car stopped. The driver reached across and opened the door. "You need a ride?" he asked.

I nodded. I smiled. Mild as a lamb, sure as a tiger. "We do, indeed, and if you don't mind, sir, we'll just sit up front with you, in case you need directions."

Little Sinners

BY THOMAS E. KENNEDY

My ninth summer, in 1952, I ran with a kid named Billy Reichert, a classmate from The Christian Brothers Boys School. We were thieves. We used foul language. We smoked Lucky Strike cigarettes purchased with stolen quarters. We pored over the dirty pictures on a pack of Tijuana playing cards Billy had secreted in his basement. It was a lovely summer.

I loved stealing. You had to be quick and brave. I loved that feeling in my stomach just before I made my move. I glanced at whatever it was—a Milky Way bar, a cap pistol, a comic book—walked past, scanned the shop in front of me, turned, scanned behind, and if the coast was clear, *zip*! I moved, shoved it in my pocket, under my shirt, down my pants. Then I hung around a while as a precaution, but also as part of the fun: that incredible sense of power it gave me to stay there, moving slowly amongst the enemy, the loot on my person— the danger, the triumph, the sheer belly-tingling risk! I asked the shop clerk, the guy with the pencil moustache and underslung jaw at Gerstie's, say, the price of some impossibly expensive item, HO gauge electric trains or a glittering package of handpainted tin soldiers in red coats, looked wistful, wandered out with my head down. I understood from overhearing my father, who was a legal counselor for the State of New York, that the law said you could not be arrested for shoplifting until you were actually out the door, so I was prepared to put the booty back on the shelf again at the least suspicious glance. But none ever came. I was too quick. Me and Billy could lift just about anything—coins out of the cigar box on the brick and plank newspaper stand in front of the Roosevelt Avenue cigar shop, comic books out of Gerstenharber's, cupcakes and Mission sodas from the A&P or Frisch's Market, toys from the glass shelves of Kresge's or Woolworth's, and assorted junk, mostly mysterious small automotive gadgets, out of Sears & Roebuck's which, for some reason, we called Searsie's. If there wasn't anything in particular we desired, we would lift any old thing, just for the joy of it.

Billy was a nice-looking good-natured boy, blond and tan and blue-eyed with a big white smile and easy laugh. My feeling for him was a little like love. We were together all the time that summer, morning to night. We rose early in the mornings to go out prowling in the mild air, breathing the aroma of honeysuckle and cut grass. Usually I rose first and called for him because of his sister.

The Reicherts lived in an attached house on Ithaca Street, and he and his older sister, Fran, shared a bedroom at the rear of the second floor. When I called for him, his mother used to send me straight up to Billy's room, and because his sister just saw us as little squirts, she went about her business without paying us any mind. Lots of times she would come out of the bathroom wearing nothing but underpants and bra or wrapped in a towel with beads of water on her tan shoulders and long thighs.

Once I remember she sat on her vanity bench wearing just a skirt and bra and slowly pulled on her nylon stockings the way women do, even when they're only fifteen as she was, so slowly and wonderfully, the leg extended out in the air and curving like heaven. Billy and I sat there pretending to play checkers. We watched her draw one all the way up to the top of her thigh. I sighed, and Billy said, in a singsong kind of way, "It's gettin' ha-ard." And she didn't get ticked off or anything. She just glanced over and smiled as she pulled on the other stocking. To this day, I don't know whether she knew what her little brother meant, whether she enjoyed us watching her as much as we enjoyed watching, or whether she was completely oblivious of us as males and was just smiling innocently, maternally at us. If I knew that, maybe I would have a better handle on women today, but all I know and knew was how happy I felt at that moment with my eyes full of her and the whole long wonderful August morning and afternoon stretched out before us.

In my memory, that was in fact the last day of that summer, the day when it all hit the fan. Probably my memory is not completely right. It seems hard to believe that so many things could have happened in one single day. But then again I was only nine then, and when you're nine, any day is full of wonders.

It was Tuesday. Indian Head Penny day at the Jackson Movie House. Every Tuesday morning the Jackson had a special offer for kids where you could get in for a can of soup or for an Indian Head Penny. I think it was to benefit charity, or maybe the owner of the movie house was a coin collector and was hoping to acquire some rare and valuable dates. Anyway, my father had a box of old pennies, and we had standing permission to help ourselves. Otherwise, we would have had to lift a can of soup from the A&P. My parents would have given us the cans of soup, too, they were generous, but we'd just as soon have lifted them.

Most Fifties movies, when I see them today, are junk. But back then, to a nine-year-old, they were magic. Wonder tales of heroes and desperadoes, love and murder, cruelty and kindness, theft and retribution. I can't recall the titles or even the stories, only a scene here and there: Jimmy Stewart in a lambskin jacket rolling in the dust cradling a pump action rifle against his chest. Gary Cooper's face glistening with sweat as he poled a raft through the Everglades. Dale Robertson on horseback, riding up a rocky hillside along the foaming Red River where, no doubt, some woman, an Indian squaw or a white woman abducted by the Indians, would be bathing her bosoms.

This particular Tuesday, we paid our Indian Head pennies to the gray-haired, white-faced matron in her white dress—the same one who would later prowl amongst the dark aisles, clutching in her white, blue-veined hand a steel-cased flashlight that she would shine and swat at our feet to make us take them down—and took our usual seats down in the front where the great blue-gray screen loomed up above us like a billboard for the gods. The film that day, all I can remember of it, included a lovely scene in some jungle somewhere, and we watched Clark Gable watch Ava Gardner take a bath in a wooden tub underneath the vines and palm trees. She lifted one creamy leg from the water. Gable's moustache stretched across his grin, and she gave him that incredible smile of hers which hinted of things whose beauty no imagination could match.

"It's gettin' ha-ard," Billy sang.

As we stumbled out of the dark moviehouse into the midday sunlight, blinking, laughing, we ate the last of the Jujubes we'd hoisted from the Cigar Store, made a horn out of the empty box, ripped the flap off one end and blew into it, and it honked like a duck. I got to thinking about a girl we knew named Sally Donnell who lived in the Hampton Apartments. She was a friend of one of the other kids in our class. I played with them one day months before in the basement of her building.

"She took her underpants down," I told Billy.

"Bull."

"She did. I dared her, and she did."

"What did it look like?"

"I'm not sure. It was kind of dark. She lives just around the corner here."

We looked at each other. "Let's go!" And we took off running.

The lobby of the apartment was dim, solemn as a church with its old dark wood and smell like the bottom of an empty fountain. We rode the wooden walled elevator up to the third floor and found the door halfway down the dim corridor. The two-noted sound of the bell was lonely in the empty hallway. Then Mrs. Donnell, a smiling, gray-eyed woman, was looking down at us.

"We're in the same class as John Brandt at Christian Brothers School," I said. "He had my reader from school and said he'd give it to Sally for me."

I was pretty nervous in case she questioned me further about it, but she just called Sally, who came out into the hall and fixed the door so it wouldn't lock before closing it behind her. I was glad she didn't invite us in. "Johnny didn't give me no book," she said.

I smiled. Billy smiled. She looked at us. She smiled.

Down in the basement was a meter room with a single window, high up on the wall, through which motes of dusty sunlight slanted down across a patch of the concrete floor. I don't remember too many details, but until the day I die I will never forget how beautiful Sally looked taking her clothes off and folding them, piece by piece, into a neat pile on an old trunk in the corner, how she looked with no clothes on in those motes of sunlight, smiling and showing herself, slender and blond, her face flushed and shining. We sat on seltzer crates and watched her turn for us in the light beneath the window.

"Gee, it's gettin' hard," Billy said, but there was a reverence to his voice, and I couldn't speak at all for the lump in my throat. I just watched. I just drank her in through my eyes, into my heart, to fill my memory with enough of her to last forever.

Somehow the moment, the meeting, found its end, I don't remember how, but next thing I know we were out in the sunlight again wearing cap pistols in holsters slung low on our thighs and tied with strips of rawhide, gunfighter style, our pockets bulging with cigarettes and pop bottles, all acquired by virtue of our special talents. We were waiting for the bus to Forest Park, to visit a secret little pond there that not many people knew about and where we could be alone to exchange our thoughts about the beauties and wonders of Sally Donnell.

Our pond was up behind the golf course, through a path that wound between the hills and back behind a wall of tangled overgrowth. You never saw grown-ups there and only rarely other kids. We had a favorite rock we sat on, a big slate-gray boulder, the kind my father had once told me was the very thing New York was built on, the same kind of rock that the Mespatches Indians and the Dutch and British colonists saw hundreds of years before. "Just think," he said, "Indians might have camped right there, hunted over across the river, in that park. Wolves and wildcats and brown bears and rattlesnakes..."

I drew my pistol. "Watch it!" I shouted. "Snake!" And fired a roll of red paper caps, smoke and the smell of gunpowder rising from the little pistol as a diamondback twitched and bounced into the air, twisting, dead. I blew the smoke from the barrel of my shooter, holstered it again, sat on the warm sunny rock, and popped the cap from my Mission orange soda.

"If this was real jungle wilderness, like in the movies about Africa or something," Billy said, "we'd take off our clothes here and dry ourselves in the sun."

"We're not even wet."

"We would be if this was the real jungle. That pond would've been a river where we had to wash ourselves, like Stewart Granger and that woman did there in *King Solomon's Mines*."

"They still had clothes on."

"That's all the movie shows. In the real life part, they were nude." He tore the cellophane off the pack of Luckies and tapped out two cigarettes for us. I dug a matchbook from my pocket and we lit up. We smoked in silence for a while. Then I said, "You want to?"

"What?"

"Take off all our clothes?"

He smiled. He was pretty. We unbuckled our capguns and doffed our clothes, admired each other for a while—he was almost as pretty as Sally, the way his tan skin rippled over his ribs and stretched tight across his belly. Then we lay back in the sun, the warm rock beneath our naked flesh, sunlight tingling in our faces and chests and bellies, as we smoked cigarettes, blew smoke rings at the sky, washed the bitter smoke from our mouths with orange soda. I twisted out my cigarette, closed my eyes, and turned my face to the sun and I guess I've never felt more content, more completely alive than I did just then.

Suddenly, we heard footsteps, voices, giggling, on the path behind the overgrowth. We hid our cigarette pack, ditched the empty soda bottles and pulled on our clothes, tied the holsters to our thighs. Someone was moving closer. We practiced drawing on each other while we waited to see whether we would have to make a run for it or stand and fight or what. Two older kids came crashing out of the overgrowth. They had funny looks on their faces, like they knew something we didn't, like maybe they had seen us. I recognized them both, but I didn't think they knew me. The one kid, William Zipler, used to be in my older brother's class at school, and the other, a Latin kid named Manuel, always hung around with him. Manuel was older, too, though small and dark-haired with big dark eyes and long black eyelashes like a girl's. Zipler was a tall skinny kid with a big nose and a mouth that made me think of an owl's beak. He drew a deck of cards from his pants pocket. "You guys want to play some poker?"

"We got no money," Billy said.

"No sweat," said Zipler. "We can just play for fun."

So we all sat on the rock, and Zipler dealt a couple of hands of stud. Billy got brave and lit up, offering the pack around. "Estunt your growth," Manuel said, but Zipler took one, and I did, too.

The Lucky wobbling between his lips, eyes squinted against the smoke, Zipler said, "Hey, I got an idea. Let's play strip poker."

Manuel giggled. "Panty ante."

Billy said, "That's no fun unless there's girls."

"Well, look," Zipler said. "You don't have to play. You can just watch."

Pretty soon, the two of them, Zipler and Manuel, were naked. Me and Billy sat where we were and watched. It was fascinating, but a little sickening, too. Zipler had a very big dark cock with hair around it. He started rubbing it between his palms, and it got bigger. Then he said, "Manuel, tell them about your dream you had." To us, he explained, "Manuel had this crazy dream about something, something he had to do to someone."

Billy flipped his cigarette into the pond. We were backing away, gun hands poised over our holstered capguns.

"Show these kids what you dreamt about, Manuel," Zipler said and lay back on the rock with his cock sticking up in the air, but we had already backed up to the tree line.

"Hey, where you going!" Zipler called out as we dashed across through the scrub and out to the path, running like hell. There were snakes all around us, hanging from tree branches, coiled at our feet, wrapped hissing around the trunks of trees, and we fired our cap pistols as we ran, killing the one after the other, but they kept on coming as we ran along the sunlight-dappled path beneath the leafy trees.

"That guy's a queer," Billy said.

"He's pretty weird," I agreed.

The bus wheezed in to the curb, and we climbed on. We sat

in the back seat, rode in silence for a time. The I said, "Hey, what was he doing that with his cock for? Rubbing it like that?"

"Who knows? The two of them are probly just queers."

"Oh, right." And, "What's a queer again?"

"A queer is just a queer guy who does queer stuff like that. That's all. My old man says if a queer takes a drink in a bar, the bartender smashes the glass with a ballbat afterwards."

"How come?"

"Cause that's what they do."

The bus pulled in along the curb at 82nd Street, and we climbed down to the pavement and started walking again. The day, which had been so perfect, so wonderfully beautifully perfect, suddenly, inexplicably was blemished. Something needed to be done. Of course, we couldn't understand that or know what had to be done. We could only sense that all the beauties of that day, all the beauties of the female body and of our own, the wildness of our freedom was in threat, the day was in danger of being lost somehow.

The sun was no longer high in the sky. Our shadows were long and slender before us as we walked. "What you want to do now?" I asked.

"I don't know. Somethin'."

We were passing by the local tavern at just that moment, and a man named Mr. Sweeney stepped out, blinking into the late afternoon sunlight. He had wild hair and a swollen red nose and white gunk in the corners of his mouth. He didn't know us at all, but he pointed at me and said, "You. What the hell you think you're doin'?"

"We're walkin'," I said.

"Where to? You walkin' to the ballfield?" His nose was bumpy and full of broken veins. His eyes were bloodshot. "You play any ball today?"

"Uh-uhn."

He leaned close to us with fierce eyes and snapped, "Why not? You a shitheel, are you? Get out and play some ball, the two of you! Little baseball. Basketball. Football. Don't be a goddamn shitheel all your goddamned worthless life!"

This was just what we needed to lift the mood. We went right into a dialogue. I turned to Billy and said, "Get your ass out and play some baseball!"

"You shitheel!" Billy said.

"Some bowling ball!"

"Damn shitheel!"

"Tennis ball!"

"Shitheel!"

"Ping pong ball!"

That one broke us up pretty good. We started giggling and staggering along the street, and old man Sweeney was yelling after us as we took off running.

"Snotnoses!" he hollered. "Idiots! You goddamned little sinners!"

We threw our stolen capguns, holsters and all, off the top of the Long Island Railroad Trestle, and decided to head over to Searsie's to hoist just one more thing, something really great, something to remember the day by, to heal its wound. As we headed on up to Roosevelt again, I watched the long weird shadows strutting out from the tips of our sneakers before us, and I couldn't help thinking about Zipler, about what Manuel's dream might have been, what they were out after, what Zipler looked like lying there with it sticking up in the air. I didn't like it. It wasn't good. It wasn't beautiful as Sally had been in the meter room, turning in the sunlight with her slender golden body. Or as Billy had looked sitting naked on the warm rock with his smiling face.

At Searsie's, we took a drink of cold water from the stainless steel water fountain and wandered around looking at the objects displayed in the glass-partitioned counterspaces: sparkplugs, fuses, batteries, headlight bulbs, flashlights... And then we saw it. A beautiful little flashlight charm on a chain. It was wondrous to behold. A yellow and white plastic oblong on a golden drainplug chain. You flipped open the top and thumbed a switch on the side, and a strong, clear, pencil beam shone forth. My heart thumped with desire to have it in my pocket, the cool plastic against my palm, to have it home with me, crawl into the depths of my closet, lighting my way into the unknown with its scalpel sharp beam, studying the secrets of floor cracks, the mysteries in the corners of upper shelves, beneath beds...

We made our move fast. Once around the counter, a glance at the guy in the white short-sleeve shirt through which you could see his strapped undershirt as he slouched up against a counter waiting for a customer, back to the end of another circuit and zip! Our pockets were thick with treasure.

The guy in the transparent white shirt glanced at us. He was chewing something very slowly with his lips closed. "What's the story with you two?" he said.

"Huh?"

"What's the story? What are you looking for?"

Billy said, "Uh, where do you have the toothbrushes and toothpaste and all?"

The man wrinkled his brow. "This look like a freakin' drug store to you, kid?"

"Sorry, mister," Billy said. "Guess we better try the drug store," he said to me. I felt his eyes on my back as we headed for the door. I felt fear in my knees, in the pit of my stomach. Is it this time? I thought. Is it now? Waiting for a hand to clutch my shoulder. Just for good measure, we took another drink of water from the fountain before exiting. Then we hit the street, spun: no eyes watched, no hands reached for us.

We ran like hell.

Maybe it's only something manufactured by my imagination, by the retrospect of memory, but there seemed something sad in the way we parted that evening. Dusk lay across the town. The streetlights had just been lit. We parted at the corner of Gleane and Baxter, I to proceed to my house through the tunnel of trees that was our street, Billy to head along beneath the El to his own house. He had chained his flashlight to one of his belt loops. Mine was secreted in my hip pocket. I don't remember what we said. I only remember, or think I remember, a melancholy yellow light from a streetlamp, a sadness of dusk, Billy's downturned face and the shadows on his yellow hair, a sharp sense of loss, though of what I could not know.

That evening as I lay on the living room floor on my belly, chin propped in my palms, watching "The Big Story" on TV, the telephone rang. My father answered, spoke quietly for a time into the black mouthpiece. Then he hung up, and he and my mother went into the kitchen and shut the door. A few minutes later, the door opened again and he invited me to join them.

They sat in the ladderback chairs at the beige metal kitchen table. My father motioned me to sit. Then he said, "I just spoke with Billy Reichert's mother on the phone. She said he came home with a little flashlight on his beltloop, and when she asked him where he got it, he finally admitted that he stole it. She said he told her you stole one, too. Is that true?"

"Yes," I said and lowered my eyes.

"Why?"

I shrugged, shook my head.

"Don't we give you enough? Do you feel cheated? Do the other boys have more than you?"

"No," I whispered. Which was true. My parents were very generous.

"Then *why?*"

I shook my head, stared at the black and white checked linoleum.

"Have you stolen other things, too?" my mother asked.

"Yes," I said. "Twice. A pack of gum and a quarter from the newspaperman's box outside the cigar shop."

"You'll have to put that quarter back," my mother said.

I nodded.

"And the flashlight, too."

"I threw it away. Down the sewer."

"Well, then, I'll have to go up to Searsie's and make amends for that," my father said. "I won't make you come with me. Unless the priest says you should. The gum I suppose we can just forget. You can put a dime in the poor box to make up for that. Out of your allowance. But you'll have to tell the priest in confession about each of the things you've stolen, and then we'll see what else there is to do about this."

I nodded, raised my eyes for a moment, swallowed, whispered, "Are you mad?"

"Not mad," my mother said. "Just disappointed."

"And puzzled," my father added. "We don't understand *why* you would steal. You have a good allowance. We don't deny you anything within reason. Why would you steal? *Why?*"

I looked into my mother's sad blue-gray eyes, my father's brown troubled ones. Their sadness pierced me as nothing could. If they had yelled, beat me, my heart could have hidden from it, but there was no escape from this. I wanted to explain to them, but the truth, the fact of it, the experience, which had never found or needed words in my consciousness, that it was beautiful to steal, already was beyond the reach of my tongue, hiding away like a shy fish beneath some deep rock of consciousness. But their eyes, their sadness, disappointment was a wound that needed comfort, an emptiness that needed filling.

I said, "William Zipler made us do it."

They leapt at my words, sat up straight and stared at me. "*Who?*"

"William Zipler."

"Who the hell is William Zipler?" my father said.

"He was in Ralph's class at school, wasn't he?" mother said. "He's much older than you."

"Promise not to tell Ralph," I pleaded. "Ralph will kill him. Promise not to tell." I knew they would honor the confidence. My mother and father were reasonable, dependable people.

"How did he *make* you do it?" my father asked.

"He just, he didn't *make* us exactly, he just showed us how, and then he said we should do it, too, or he'd give us a rap in the teeth."

"The little *creep*," my mother said.

"That makes it at least a little bit more understandable," my father said. "But still it doesn't *excuse* you. I *still* want you to tell this in confession."

"I know," I said.

"You stay away from William Zipler from now on," my mother said. "The little *creep*."

"Do you have anything else to tell now?" my father said.

I shook my head. Then I whispered, "I'm sorry."

My father placed his gentle warm hand on the back of my neck. "It's all right, son," he said. "It was an experiment. Now you've tried it once and it's *over*, and I want your promise that you won't *ever* do anything like that again."

I promised, was hugged, allowed to hug back, released, and went up to my room where, in bed, in the dark beneath the covers, I played with my plastic flashlight on a chain. I pressed it up behind my fingers, inside my fist, and saw the light glow eerie red through my flesh, limning the bones of my fingers. I realized I was going to have to ditch the flashlight, for if they saw me with it they wouldn't understand, it would bring that sadness to their eyes again, and this time they wouldn't believe me. Yet there were so many things I wanted to do with that light, so many small corners and crevices, floorcracks, to explore, the inner depths of the closet, the dim far reaches of the basement...

On Saturday, as always, I got my allowance, thirty-five cents, with instructions to return a quarter to the news stand, put a dime in the poorbox at Blessed Virgin Church, and go to confession.

I *did* put the quarter in the cigar box, reversing my talents, getting it in there without being observed. The challenge distracted me from the pain of forking over the two bits. But putting my last dime for the whole week in the poorbox, with no prospect of other means of procuring the goods I wanted, was something else again. I stood there for quite some time just inside the church doors, the little silver coin sweaty in my palm. I decided *not* to do it, was about to turn away, but saw my hand lift to the coin slot, felt the dime slip from my fingers. It clunked and echoed into the depths of the tall metal box. Then, in confession, my little flashlight in my pocket (how I would have liked to explore the dark shadows inside the confessional box!), I spoke to the dim outline of Father Walsh behind the screen, told him I had stolen gum, a quarter and a flashlight.

"Have you made retribution for these things, bub?"

"I returned the quarter, Father, and put the gum money in the poor box, and my father made retribution for the flashlight."

"And are you sorry for these sins?"

"Yes, Father," I lied—though it didn't really seem a lie so much as a formality, a concession to the social order.

"Okay, bub, then say ten Hail Marys and make a good act of contrition now."

As I prayed, "Oh my God, I am heartily sorry for having offended Thee..." I couldn't help thinking how ironic it was that, in fact, I had never stolen gum in my life. That has always seemed a funny kind of administrative irony to me.

I've often wondered about the fact that it didn't bother me, lying in confession. It was no doubt also a sin to have lied about William Zipler as I had, but I never confessed that, never really regretted it either.

That day was the end of my friendship with Billy Reichert. I *did* regret that. He was such a nice, good-looking kid, and we had shared so much joy that summer.

I still have the flashlight. It doesn't light anymore, been dead for years, but I keep it in a cigar box where I have a bunch of little doodads and souvenirs, a broken watch, an old tarnished silver miraculous medal, an Indian Head penny, things like that. From time to time, I take the flashlight out and hold it in my palm, dangle it by the little gilt chain from my finger. In all the years since, I never did steal again. I never felt real sorrow for what I did or remorse, but I never did steal again. In fact, I don't think I *ever* sinned again with such pure joy.

Baby Mansion

BY URSULA HEGI

When Karin Baum, who was in seventh grade with me, got so big that people could tell she was carrying a baby, it didn't take her parents long to discover that her grandfather had gotten her pregnant. They closed the old man's bicycle shop and sent him off to live with his unmarried brother in München, while Karin was taken to the baby mansion, a white villa with a clay tiled roof and balconies four kilometers from Bergdorf. It was a safe place where a family could store a daughter who was gaining around the middle, store her for a few months and then take her back home, slender again as though nothing had changed.

During those months of preparing for birth, the pregnant girls took care of the babies who already lived at the mansion and waited for adoption or for their mothers to finally take them home. Most of those children were in limbo: their mothers had not decided for or against adoption—they'd simply left them there. And so they stayed, growing beyond the age where people wanted to adopt them as they were moved from the nursery to the room of the one-year-olds to the two-plus dormitory.

On Sunday afternoons some of the unwed mothers visited their children. They gave them bright toys, carried them through the rose garden behind the mansion, played with

Reprinted by permission of Poseidon Press from *Floating in My Mother's Palm* by Ursula Hegi. Copyright © 1990 by Ursula Hegi.

113

them on the lawn that surrounded the marble fountain. A few of them brought their boyfriends. Occasionally a girl's parents came along. In the lobby of the baby mansion, a linen-covered table was set up with refreshments where a pregnant girl poured coffee and offered the visitors leaf-shaped cookies from a silver platter.

It rained the first Sunday of June when my mother and I drove out to see Karin. It was my idea to visit her, but once we were there, I didn't know what to say or where to look. In the three weeks since she'd left school, she'd grown even bigger; the pleats of her loose dress spread above her stomach as she led us into a visitors' room. Her straight, brown hair which used to hang down her back had been cut; it exposed her earlobes, and the center part made her look serious, older.

After sitting with us for a few minutes, my mother stood up. "I'll be back in a while," she said and left the room before I could stop her.

Karin pulled off a shred of skin next to her left thumbnail. "So—" she said, examining her thumb. "How's school?"

"All right." My neck felt stiff from the effort of not staring at her belly. "How's—you know... living here?"

She shrugged and hid with me in an embarrassed silence that folded itself around us until I felt as though my body, too, were swollen. Occasionally voices drifted in from the lobby. A young girl's laugh. The sound of a door. A few times Karin reached up in the familiar gesture of twisting a strand of hair and instead touched her shoulder.

When my mother finally returned, Karin looked as relieved as I felt. "Let us know if you need anything," my mother offered.

"Thank you, Frau Malter," Karin said.

Before starting our car in the parking lot, my mother sat with her eyes closed. The collar of her cotton shirt was turned up, catching strands of her blond hair between the blue material and her skin. She smelled of tobacco and oil paint.

"What's wrong?" I asked.

"I should have known..." She opened her eyes. Lit a cigarette. One hand on the steering wheel, she maneuvered the car out of the parking lot. She drove fast. Too fast. "I should have talked to her parents that day," she said, "not just to the old man."

All at once I remembered the white coating on the back of my doll's eyes, remembered the make-shift surgery on the dining room table, and I was seized by an odd sense of loss of the friendship that had ended the year Karin and I were seven.

Until then, the bicycle shop had been a magic place for me, filled with the fairy tales Karin's grandfather told me, warm and bright even in winter, oddly familiar with its faint smell of machine oil and black rubber that drifted up the stairs and wove itself into the apartment above, through the kitchen, even into Karin's room.

Karin was my best friend and sat next to me in Frau Behrmeier's second grade class. I liked to visit her and listen to her grandfather who knew all the fairy tales from the Brothers Grimm book: *Der Froschkönig, Hänsel Und Gretel, Schneeweisschen Und Rosenrot, Rumpelstilzchen*... He told those stories in a voice that could drop from the roar of a dragon to the whisper of a princess.

An old man with wide shoulders, he had a squat build that seemed to grow closer to the floor with each year. He lived above the shop with Karin and her parents. In the back pocket of his overalls he carried a rag for polishing the bikes on display. Oil stains spread across the backs of his hands like birthmarks, but the bicycles were spotless and gleamed under the many lightbulbs he'd rigged from the ceiling. He liked to stroke my hair and lift me on the glass counter between the cash register and the display of bicycle chains. He too smelled of oil and rubber, a dark smell that clung to his olive-colored skin and gray mustache.

Once he took Karin and me on a ferry trip to Kaiserswerth and from there on an excursion boat to the *Altstadt*, the old section of the Düsseldorf. At an outdoor cafe with round tables, he ordered *Früchtebecher*—banana ice cream with pineapple chunks and whipped cream—for us and *Berliner Weisse*—beer with raspberry syrup foaming in a goblet—for himself. Whenever flies tried to land on the checkered tablecloth, he swatted them away with his broad hands. A maple tree on the sidewalk shed some of its doublewinged seeds, and we caught them as they came drifting down like propellers and stuck them to our upper lips like mustaches.

One Monday afternoon, when I came looking for Karin at the shop, her grandfather told me her mother had taken her to Mahler's department store in Düsseldorf.

"Shopping," he said.

"Can I stay?"

He pulled a rag from his pocket and wiped his hands. "Here," he said and lifted me on the counter next to a flowerpot shaped like a duck. It was filled with real ferns and red plastic daisies.

"Will you tell me a story?"

"How old are you now, Hanna?"

"You know." I smiled at him.

He shook his head. "Come on. Tell me. How old are you?"

"Seven. Remember? You gave me a bicycle bell on my last birthday."

"Seven." He nodded as if not one bit surprised. In the ridges of his cheeks and across his neck lay a film of dust. "Big girl like you... doesn't wet her pants any more, does she?"

My neck felt hot. "Only babies wet their pants."

He brought his face close to mine and peered into my eyes. "You're sure?" His breath felt moist against my face. Hair sprouted from his ears and nose.

"I don't. I never do."

On the wall beyond his face hung shiny bike parts and black tires. Two air pumps leaned against the lower part of the wall.

"Really sure?" His hand reached under my skirt and pressed against the dry patch of cotton panties between my legs. "You're sure now you don't wet your pants?"

"I told you." Squirming away from him, I slid from the counter and ran toward the door.

"Wait." His voice sounded as if he were afraid of me. "The story. I'll tell you a—"

But I kept on running. Onto the sidewalk that shimmered white in the afternoon sun. Across the empty street. Around the corner. Past the elementary school where the Hansen bakery truck was parked. Kept running until I reached our apartment building which my great uncle Alexander had built. In the kitchen our housekeeper stood ironing my plaid dress. Her son, Rolf, who was in my class and often came to our house after school, sat at the table, drawing a black truck.

"Where's Karin?" Fine beads of sweat coated Frau Brocker's forehead as she moved the iron across the material. Her brown hair lay in new curls around her head, and she wore pink lipstick.

"I don't know." I darted past her into my room and closed the door.

"Hanna?" she called after me, but I pretended not to hear.

I sat on my bed and looked out of the window into the backyard with the chicken coop and the high iron rods over which the women from the apartments laid their carpets every Friday and beat them with long rattan paddles. The fence that closed off the backyard had several rows of chain links which didn't match the lower section. Until two years ago, when I'd been allowed out on my own, my father had drawn the fence higher every year; yet, I'd managed to climb across it on my many trips to explore the neighborhood. It had started when, at age three, I'd been found inside Emma Müller's bedroom two blocks away, sitting on her bed and playing with her dolls.

I didn't play with dolls anymore. They were boring. I liked books; yet, people kept giving me dolls. Frau Brocker had lined them up on the shelf next to my bed, from the tallest one, Inge, to a fingersized doll named Birgit.

Inge was made of celluloid and had blue glass eyes that closed as I tilted her back. Her eyelashes lay against the pink cheeks until I moved her whole body forward again and the eyes clicked open. Hard and glossy, they sat in the doll's head. When I pulled the eyelashes, the blue disappeared again, and I wondered what the doll saw inside her head.

I carried her to the open window where the light was brighter. Such a stupid looking doll—all stiff and pink. As I pushed my fingers against the eyes to test how far in they could go, they moved back from the sockets but then snapped right back into place, blue and glossy. I pushed again to see how they were held in place. Then again, a little harder . . . Suddenly the eyes disappeared into the head. Just like that. I shook the doll, her face pointing toward the floor, but the eyes wouldn't drop back into place; they only rattled inside the celluloid head.

"Frau Brocker," I shouted, then covered my mouth. I didn't want her to see the doll, didn't want anyone to see.

The door opened. I wanted to hide the doll, but I couldn't move.

"What's the matter?" My father came into my room.

The doll hung from my hand. I thought he'd get angry at me for breaking her eyes, but instead he lifted her from my hands as if she were a newborn kitten.

"How did it happen?"

I started to cry.

He brought one arm around my shoulders. "I'm sure it was an accident."

"I don't even like dolls." I wiped the back of my right hand across my eyes and nose. My stomach ached from letting him believe it was an accident.

"I think we can fix her. At least we'll try, all right?"

My father had finished with his patients for the day and took most of that afternoon to restore the blue eyes to their proper place. With a thin plier, black thread and tweezers, he sat at our dining room table, fishing through the empty sockets for the eyeballs. I sat across from him and handed him instruments as he called out their names. The light above the table made his scalp look shiny where his reddish hair had thinned; yet, his beard was full and curly as if all the growing went into the hairs there.

Around five o'clock, large rain drops began falling rapidly, splattering the windows. On the wall between the two windows hung my mother's painting of the Sternhof, the one she'd been working on the day she fell in love with my father. She'd painted the Sternhof since then, but in this picture the drawbridge was down, spanning the moat that surrounded the old farm which used to be a castle. The light in the painting kept changing: on sunny days it looked transparent while in the evenings, when we turned on the lamps, it took on an amber sheen as if warmed by the light surrounding it.

My father still had on the white jacket which he wore to drill on people's teeth. He didn't work on my or my mother's teeth but insisted we go to Dr. Beck in Düsseldorf.

"But why?" I'd asked him once after coming home from another painful visit with Dr. Beck. "I'd rather let you do it."

He'd shaken his head. "But then you would associate the pain with me."

When Frau Brocker and Rolf came into the dining room to tell us they were leaving for the day, he interrupted his operation to look at Rolf's picture of the black truck. Frau Brocker stopped by the window, frowning at the rain. Her hair was covered with a plastic scarf to protect her permanent.

I ran my fingers along the edge of the tablecloth and found the knife she'd hidden under the beige linen. Terrified of thunder storms, she believed a knife under the tablecloth kept lightning from striking.

After they left, my father bent back over the doll. From time to time he blinked. His breathing was slow, measured. When finally he pulled the blue eyes from one of the sockets, they were connected by two wire loops that formed the number eight, and I was disappointed that their backs were coated with a white substance that felt like hardened flour against my fingertips. My father glued the eyes into the sockets, holding them in slings of thread until the glue set; then he cautiously pulled the threads out and applied more glue around the seams where the glass joined the pink celluloid. Though he dabbed the corners with an old hand-kerchief, some of the glue hardened into tiny drops that looked like tears.

"Here." He handed the doll to me. "I think that's the best we can do."

The blue eyes stared at me, open although the doll lay on its back.

"She's almost like new," I tried to convince myself as I held the stiff doll in my arms. But she was not like new: she couldn't close her eyes anymore, and inside her head the backs of her eyes were blind.

Around eight, my father left to play chess at the Bergdorf chess club which met at Herr Stosick's house. When my mother tucked me in and sat on the edge of my bed, my stomach still ached from not telling her and my father how I'd broken the doll.

"Karin's grandfather forgot how old I was," I blurted out. "He even thought I still wet my pants."

She shook her head. "Why would he ... ?"

I tried to laugh away my uneasiness. "But then he checked, and now he knows I don't."

My mother sat very still. The skin around her nose became white as though all the color had drained to her neck. She laid one hand against my cheek and asked softly, "Are you all right?" And when I nodded, she gathered me into her arms and said, "Will you please tell me? Everything?"

I told her about pushing out the doll's eyes and that I was sorry, but she wanted to know about Karin's grandfather touching my underpants. As I told her, she held me, gently, and said what he'd done was wrong. "Very wrong." Then she got up and put on her raincoat and walked to the bicycle shop.

I kept the light on and lay with my arms folded under my head, counting my breathe in the empty apartment. On the shelf next to my bed sat Inge, her blue eyes wide open, opaque drops of hardened glue in the corners of the sockets.

My mother didn't tell me what she'd said to Karin's grandfather when she came back into my room, but she asked me, "Will you promise me to stay away from the bicycle shop?"

I thought of the bicycle parts reflecting the lights, thought of the cool glass counter and felt the sudden loss of a place I didn't want to return to.

"It's a filthy place," my mother said.

Yet it was also warm and bright and magic.

"Promise to stay away from there?"

I nodded, suddenly relieved that I didn't have to go back.

"Karin can play with you here. Any time." My mother bent to kiss my forehead. "I'm glad you told me what happened."

My friendship with Karin Baum straggled on through that fall and winter. We played in the schoolyard or at our house, but not in the bicycle shop. And the following spring Renate Eberhardt, who was to become my new best friend, came to our school for the first time, her polio legs like bleached out sticks under her green skirt.

Some things are too complex to name, to separate into safe units labeled good or bad, and it becomes simpler to discard them entirely. I think that's what happened to my friendship with Karin when we were seven, and it wasn't until she carried her grandfather's baby, that I came to understand the loss of our friendship during those years.

My first visit to the baby mansion was so awkward that I felt reluctant to return when my mother wrapped a box of pralines and a book for Karin the following Sunday. But something happened that second afternoon in the visitors' room, something I couldn't even remember afterwards except that Karin laughed at something I said. Somehow that moment wiped out the embarrassment between us, and when my mother suggested the two of us take a walk through the rose garden, Karin and I left her in the visitors' room and walked along the manicured paths.

The people in Bergdorf did not approve of my mother taking me to the baby mansion; they approved even less of me riding my bicycle there some days after school as if, somehow, unwed pregnancy were contagious. But the only thing that was contagious was our need to fill each other in on what had happened to us during those years we hadn't been friends. Sure, we'd seen each other in school, and a few times we'd played pranks, unhinging garden doors all over Bergdorf and carrying them around the next corner, but that was not the same.

And so we talked. For hours. In the visiting room. In the rose garden. In the nursery where Karin worked. We talked about friends and school and boys and parents. But not about her baby. And certainly not about her grandfather though I thought about the old man whenever I tried not to look at Karin's belly.

She was assigned to work each afternoon in the dormitory of the one-year-olds, a long, airy room with rows of cribs. When school closed for summer vacation, I asked Karin if I could help her with the babies, and she got permission from Frau Doktor Korten, who ran the baby mansion, that I could help two afternoons a week. The doctor had small hands and a gentle voice, but she was so heavy and tall that she could fill a door frame with her bulk. Her gray hair was parted in the middle and pulled back into a low braided knot. When she walked into the nursery—a white smock over her flowered silk dress—most of the children raised their arms toward her.

Two sixteen-year-old girls, Anita and Grete, worked with

us. We fed the babies, took off their diapers and shirts, gave them baths in high sinks shaped like miniature tubs. We laughed when they splashed us and when we sprinkled powder on their bottoms and bellies.

Anita was at the baby mansion for the second time. She'd given her first child up for adoption. One afternoon, when Anita told us she was going to keep this baby, Karin surprised me by saying she was keeping hers too. Up to then she hadn't spoken about the baby.

"Hanna is going to help me care for the baby after school." She reached for my hand, held it against her belly, and I felt the baby move under my palm like a sleeper stretching after a long rest.

For the first time we talked about names for her child. She liked Adelheid for a girl and Siegfried for a boy, though I tried to tell her that Martina and Joachim were better names. If my brother, Joachim, had lived, he'd be eleven years old. But he'd died as an infant.

A few of the babies had something wrong with them: Andrea was blind, and Franz only had a thumb and little finger on his left hand. Renate Eberhardt told me that just marrying a cousin could get you a baby with two heads or a club foot. Her mother was a midwife and had helped bring all kinds of deformed babies into the world. "A grandfather," Renate told me, "is even closer related than a cousin." She probably only said this because she was upset at me for spending so much time with Karin; yet, I couldn't help imagining the baby behind the wall of Karin's huge belly, waiting like an actor with a frightful mask behind the curtain of the stage.

But when the child was born in September, she was not horrible and ugly. She had fine black hair and blue-gray eyes and thin fingers that gripped my thumb that afternoon, I was allowed to hold her for the first time. She was two days old, and I felt a jolt of love that stunned me into silence as I stood with her in the newborn nursery. I walked with her to the French doors and lifted her close to the glass so she could see the rose garden and the fountain. I could picture myself taking her for walks in a wicker carriage. Now that Karin's grandfather didn't live above the bicycle shop anymore, I'd be allowed back to the apartment. Karin and I would play with her, give her baths, sing to her.

But Karin's parents wouldn't let her bring the baby home. They talked about adoption. At first Karin cried and refused to leave the baby mansion, but one evening, after a long talk with Frau Doktor Korten, she let her father pick her up. The first time I visited Karin at home, I felt strange walking through the bicycle shop. It had been leased to a young man without a mustache. The same old smell of tires and machine oil hung about the apartment and opened a strange sensation in my stomach.

Karin sat in her bed, a stack of closed books and magazines on her blanket. Her hair was stringy. "They wouldn't even let me name her." She started to cry.

"They can't do that." I sat on the edge of her bed. "If you don't sign the adoption papers, they can't give her to anyone."

"But then she'll just have to stay there."

"We'll visit her. And after a while—maybe your parents will change their minds."

"They won't." She shook her head. "I know they won't."

Right then I decided to name the baby Martina even if she got adopted and her new parents chose a different name for her, and the next afternoon, I rode my bike to the baby mansion and offered to help in the newborn nursery on weekends.

"Let's go for a walk in the garden," Frau Doktor Korten suggested. As she moved along the paths, soft ripples went through her body and made the flowers in her dress shiver. She told me I'd helped Karin a lot while she'd been here, but that it would be better for me if I didn't come back. "And for the baby," she said. "You've become too attached." Below her skirt her thighs made a soft, slapping sound.

"Martina can sleep in my room," I told my parents at dinner. Frau Brocker is here all day anyhow, and I'll take care of the baby after school."

"I know you like her a lot," my mother said, "but it wouldn't be good for her if she stayed in Bergdorf. For her or Karin. She'd only be reminded of her all the time."

My father laid one hand on my arm. "Try to understand. You're too young to take on that kind of responsibility."

"But Karin could visit her here. She'd help—I know she would."

My mother shook her head.

"If you adopted her... I mean, if Joachim hadn't died—"

"But he did, Hanna," my father said softly.

They both assured me that Martina would find a family of her own who really wanted her, that it would be better for her to live away from here, but I didn't want to listen: all I could think of was how unfair it was that Martina should be punished for who her father was. Though my parents didn't say so, I knew it was all about that. Martina had been banned from Karin's life, just as I had been banned from the bicycle shop. And all because of Karin's grandfather—not because either of us had done something wrong.

When Karin came back to school, the other kids didn't quite know what to say to her. Especially Renate Eberhardt. I tried to do things with them together, but since they didn't like each other, I split my time between them, riding bikes with Renate or sitting in Karin's room above the bicycle shop. Karin seemed so much older than the other kids, and when I was with her, I felt almost grown up. She was thin again and the ends of her hair touched her shoulders. Her parents hadn't taken her back to the baby mansion—not even once—and she wasn't allowed to ride her bicycle there.

"They'd find out," she said when I tried to talk her into riding out there with me one Saturday morning. "And I promised not to."

Martina was two months old when Karin's parents convinced her to sign the adoption papers. When she told me the next day in school, it struck me that, lately, entire days had gone by without me thinking of Martina, and I felt as if I'd been the one to abandon her.

"Maybe it is better for her," Karin said, "getting two parents who love her." But those words didn't sound like her own, and the skin around her eyes looked puffy.

I left her standing in the tiled hallway and ran out to the bike rack. The November sun stood low in the sky as I rode my bicycle to the baby mansion. I had to do something, but I didn't know what. When I tried to picture myself riding back, Martina in one arm, I couldn't see beyond that. My parents certainly wouldn't let me bring her home, and I couldn't just hide her in our basement. Some of the puddles along the way had glazed over with skins of ice that tore under my bicycle tires.

In back of the mansion the rose bushes had been pruned and the water to the fountain turned off. I leaned my bike against a hedge and walked up the steps to the flagstone terrace. The French doors of the newborn nursery were locked. Martina's crib stood close to the glass panes: she lay on her back, awake; her black hair had grown fuller and looked as if someone had just brushed it. A clean sheet covered her legs. Though her features hadn't changed, she looked larger, stronger than the infant I'd held in my arms. She raised her right arm as if tracing an invisible picture in the air, and I pressed my palms again the cool window squares, wishing I could feel that same love for her that I'd felt in the beginning, but all I felt was an odd sense of peace I couldn't explain to myself.

HIS MOTHER, HIS DAUGHTER

BY JOANN KOBIN

Phillip's mother hadn't actually asked him to come out to Huntsburg to hear her sing in the senior citizens choral group. Phillip was the one who thought it would be a good idea to take his children, Matina and Eric, and go. "We're only amateurs," his mother told him on the phone, "and I'm afraid the children will be bored. Besides, you'll think we're foolish." Phillip objected. "Ma, we think what you're doing is amazing." And indeed he was amazed. It was the first time he had ever known his mother to do something outside the house, although she always used to tell him how much she loved working before he was born; he had been born forty-two years ago.

Phillip expected Matina, who was seventeen, to dress normally for her grandmother's debut. Instead, an enormous silvery earring in the shape of an eight dangled from one ear; she wore pants made of zebra-striped material, a white T-shirt that looked dirty, rubbery pink plastic shoes and white socks with lacy cuffs on her feet. "What about a pair of regular jeans?" Her regular jeans, she explained, were at home. "At home" was Matina's small-to-be-counted-on jab—to let him know that Harriet's—her mother's—apartment, and not his, was home. His apartment, still rather barren, she referred to as "your place."

At his place she never unpacked the medium-sized lavender and red nylon backpack in which she transported her clothes

126

and schoolbooks. She took the backpack into the bathroom when she changed clothes. There were things in it he wasn't allowed to see—hidden objects that comprised some kind of life support system, which neither he nor his apartment could provide. The backpack, of course, would accompany her to her grandmother's concert.

"We have exactly sixteen minutes to catch the train," Eric announced. He was the child who saw to it that time moved forward, and that they all moved forward with it.

Pennsylvania Station, which was only a short distance away, was walkable if Matina could be counted on to walk fast, but Phillip couldn't count on Matina's willingness to let him set the pace for anything. Matina didn't want things to proceed happily and easily without Harriet. Out of respect for her mother, there had to be a period of limping and wounded-ness and awkwardness. He was beginning to understand that. They took a cab. "We'll make it in good time," Eric said in the cab, his eyes never lifting from his digital watch. And they did—with five minutes to spare.

On the train Matina looked squarely at her father. She had velvety gray eyes, and had recently mowed off her long, dark rather wild hair and bleached what was left of it a pale blond. "Are you going to fix up your place, Dad—or are you coming back home?" He flinched. In her eyes he was still a misguided Odysseus who had left home, and home was legendary Ithaca, golden Ithaca. She had a memory like an elephant's—the details of how it used to be with them, the blessed family of four.

"Last week, I ordered a queen-sized pull-out couch," he replied. "When it comes you'll be able to have a friend stay over." Matina turned her head towards the train window. Phillip followed her gaze. Outside there was a highway that paralleled the tracks, a marsh, a dilapidated factory. She was silent and motionless, except for one quick searching encounter with her backpack.

"I've been wondering, does Grandma really want us to come to this concert?" Eric asked five minutes before they reached Huntsburg.

"I don't think Grandma likes to ask for anything," Phillip replied after a few moments. He saw his mother's face—careful neutrality—as though expressing a preference or a wish or anything was bad manners. "It doesn't matter to me," she would say with a touch of sing-song and pride in her voice when someone asked her to choose something, even ice cream.

"But will it make her *happy* that we're coming?" Eric persisted.

"I don't know. I hope so," Phillip said, and at that second Matina broke her silence. "We're her family. Of course she wants us to come. Of course it'll make her happy." She spoke with so much authority that Phillip believed she was right. Of course his mother wanted them to hear her sing. Matina, at seventeen, was almost five years older than Eric.

Phillip's parents had sold their one-family home about seven years ago and moved into the first condominium townhouse to be built in Huntsburg, the Long Island suburb where Phillip had grown up and where he and Harriet had first lived. The concert was to be held at his old high school, a pleasant walk from the train station. Matina, Eric, and he strolled together, three abreast. It was warm, the middle of June, a day full of sunshine. Matina linked arms with her father and brother. For her, until her grandfather died a year and a half ago, Huntsburg stood for all that was whole and right in the world—her infancy and her parents as a happy couple, and her grandparents, not exactly doting, but there to be counted on. For Phillip, because adult life had been lived in Huntsburg, the town was less than idyllic.

Once in the high school, Phillip remembered precisely how to find the auditorium: through the double doors on the right, to the end of the corridor, and then a left turn. However, once he got there, he grew hesitant and stopped, reluctant it seemed, to choose seats. Eric took over. He strode down the aisle and found seats for them in a row not far from the stage. The place was filling up, mainly senior citizens, well-dressed active-looking men and women, saving seats, passing each other programs.

"You must be Belle's son, Phillip," a woman in the row behind them said, tapping him on the shoulder. "I'm Mary Sherman. Belle told me to be on the lookout for you. And this must be Eric and Matina. Your mother described them to me— 'Matina has a flair for fashion,' she said, 'and Eric is a handsome boy.' But wait till you see how beautiful your mother looks, Phil. Children, wait till you hear your grand-mother's group."

"We're really proud of grandma," Eric said, and Phillip shivered. His sentiments sounded patronizing on Eric's lips.

"Your grandmother is changing," Mrs. Sherman said, speaking to the children but looking at Phillip. "She's not so scared anymore. She's coming out of her shell."

"It certainly seems that way," Phillip replied, and he felt a tiny flapping of excitement as he waited to witness his mother on stage—out of her shell and transformed, a baby bird in surprisingly splendid plummage.

Matina turned to her father. "I didn't know Grandma liked to sing. Did she used to sing and dance around the house when you were young?"

"Sing and dance?" It had been a home where things ran smoothly but it wasn't a singing and dancing home, and of course Matina knew that. "I never even knew that Grandma liked to sing," he told Matina, and to himself he thought, *I never heard my mother hum one song.*

As the lights dimmed and the audience quieted, a sense of his high school years hit him, a faint memory of disappoint-ment. In high school he had not been as good a student as he had hoped, or as good an artist, although he had been a member of the art club which in this competitive school had been no small honor. Always there was a longing for some-thing more—of finding the art teacher who would help him uncover his hidden personal style, or the beautiful girl who would make the effort to get to know him—or better yet, seduce him, or the class that would truly activate his slumber-ing intelligence. It was because Matina was so different—so persistently curious, so bold and plaintive, and such a fine student that he loved her so much. There was something fierce about Matina—fiercely selfish, fiercely loyal, fiercely a pain in the ass. Matina understood so much about so many things but she refused to understand that her parents' divorce was probably more her mother's decision than his.

As soon as the curtain opened the audience applauded. The coral group consisted of about twenty-two people, fifteen women and seven men. "There's Grandma," Eric whispered; "second from the right in the first row." "That's a great dress she has on," Matina said. His mother was wearing a navy blue dress with a sparkling white collar and bow. "Grandma has really good taste, doesn't she?" Phillip didn't respond. "Well *I* think she does," Matina insisted.

The choral group sang a selection of known and unknown music—Cole Porter, Rodgers and Hammerstein, and songs from before his time—old standbys from the Twenties or Thirties. The audience was in heaven, and lavished their friends with frequent bursts of applause. The singers, jittery in the first couple of songs, warmed up. Their voices were sweet, but to Phillip's ear, thin; there was no resonance, no richness, and occasionally someone veered off-key. Then an elderly gentleman and a sweet-looking plump woman, who stood holding on to an aluminum walker, sang "Tea for Two." Cries of delight and more clapping. While the entire group sang "Oklahoma!" Phillip's eyes settled on his mother. A certain fading had taken place in the two months since he had last seen her, a gentle wilting—small changes. She was not able to sit up straight anymore, although it was plain to see she was trying. She was trying to sit up very straight. Seventy-two years old, growing smaller. Her head jutted forward, her back curved. Almost as if to compensate, Phillip straightened his spine, pulled back his shoulders.

His eyes remained on his mother. She was singing with all her heart, moving her eyes swiftly back and forth from the music on the stand in front of her to the baton of Bob DiFranco. She was singing and reading her music, keeping one eye on Bob DiFranco. There was an expression on her face—Phillip tried to read it—of pleasure, yes, but also...what was it? An expression he had seen so many times but had never named. His chest tightened, he turned away. He wanted to bolt.

The heavy gray curtain closed before Phillip could name the look on his mother's face. Along with everybody else he applauded, stopping finally when Matina stopped. Checking his program, he saw that the next segment was a series of folk dances put on by the senior citizens dance group, followed by a ten-minute intermission, followed by the final offering of the choral group. In the dark minute between acts, while Eric was whispering his approval of his grandmother's performance,

Phillip suppressed a yawn. Just then Mrs. Sherman touched his shoulder. "I want you to be sure to notice the beautiful dancer you're about to see: Helena Whiteley. Eighty-two years old. And don't tell me I'm lying—she *is* eighty-two."

Phillip worried that he wouldn't be able to tell Helena Whiteley from the other women on the stage. He also worried that the folk dances, usually danced by lusty youth, would seem ludicrous when performed by golden-agers. Something about being in this auditorium made him worry about everything. Indeed, when the curtain parted, he could see that the men on the stage were frail. One old man in yellow plaid trousers kept heading in the wrong direction when it was his turn to promenade his partner, and his partner had to yank him around, tactfully of course, in the opposite direction. However, it was not difficult to tell who Helena Whiteley was. He knew who she was at once. She was a tall woman with soft white hair piled high on her head, and a straight supple body. She was dancing, not performing, not pretending. Phillip could feel his whole body unwind as he watched the woman. The muscles in his legs relaxed, although minutes before he hadn't known they were tense. He slumped more comfortably in his seat.

Matina whispered, "I don't believe she's eighty-two," and a voice from behind them, Mrs. Sherman's, piped up, "She is. I saw her passport last year."

Helena Whiteley was dressed in a flowing pale blue flowered skirt and a white blouse edged with blue embroidery that looked east European. There was a white fabric belt around her waist. She had a waist. She had hips. Her breasts were round and high and quite separate from her midriff. She wore beige high-heeled shoes with narrow straps—the kind that dancers wear; "character shoes"—Phillip recalled the name for them. Each step she took counted. There was nothing shuffling about the way she moved her feet. Her legs were shapely.

"I don't believe she's eighty-two," Eric murmured.

Helena Whiteley managed the English folk dances with spirit, but she was especially fluid and stately in the Greek dance, known as *Misalu*. She shifted directions with one clean flowing movement. A section of her soft white hair came unpinned. She held her head with pride that stopped an inch away from arrogance.

"She does Yoga," Mrs. Sherman, leaning forward, whispered in Phillip's ear.

An almost inadmissable longing occurred to Phillip—to have a mother who could dance like Helena Whiteley, to have a mother who did Yoga.

In the final dance, a dance from Hungary, Helena Whiteley put one hand on her hip, the other in the air and moved it as though she were waving hello. Several people in the audience broke into applause, and Phillip was sure that it was in response to the lovely openness of Helena's gesture, which she alone had added to the dance. He found himself applauding too.

Helena Whiteley loved to dance. Harriet, his wife, his ex-wife, had also loved dancing. She liked reggae and before that, calypso. Dancing, in fact, made Harriet feel sexy. She got carried away. If she danced long enough, she'd want to make love. The connection between those two things had always made him uneasy, although he had never stopped to figure out why.

There was a clearly discernible mumble in the audience about Helena Whiteley during intermission. Phillip heard it all around him. It had mostly to do with disbelief about her age. Mrs. Sherman and Matina were also discussing it. Eric chirped, "I don't think she even looks *seventy*." "I gather she does Yoga everyday," Mrs. Sherman told them again.

"It's not a matter of age—age is never that important," Phillip said to Matina and Eric when Mrs. Sherman turned away to talk to her friends; "what's important is that Helena Whiteley knows who she is. No one tells her. She knows." He stopped. His words embarrassed him; his intensity made him open to ridicule.

"What do you mean, 'No one tells her who she is,' Dad?" Matina asked and he sighed. For Matina the possibility of understanding something tended to win out over her baser needs—like taking a jab at her father, or being sarcastic. She was a born question-asker, rarely satisfied with the first half-dozen answers. His own mind, he was convinced, had been sharpened by years of Matina's questions. "I guess I mean being yourself, doing the dance the way you truly feel it."

"How can you tell all that from watching the woman do a few folk dances for twenty minutes!" Matina said almost angrily. She had slipped out of her pink plastic shoes, and was hugging her zebra-striped knees. "You're *imagining* what she's like."

"I don't think I am," he replied.

"Of course you are. You're coloring in the lines."

Eric changed the subject. "I thought Grandma's singing group was O.K."

"I did too," Phillip agreed.

"But what didn't you like about the way Grandma looked?" Matina pressed.

"Who said I didn't like the way Grandma looked?"

Matina insisted that she could tell, and pushed him to explain, but he demurred. "I don't think you like the tailored look," Matina said after a while. "I guess I didn't care for the little white bow," Phillip finally admitted, and then regretted that his daughter had gotten him to say anything at all.

The second part of the choral group's program began with a presentation of flowers to Bob DiFranco, the young conductor, by one of the men in the group. The choral leader's energy and patience and good cheer were praised to the sky. Bob DiFranco bowed modestly to the audience, who bathed him in affectionate glances and applauded. DiFranco was perhaps twenty-five or twenty-six, and small and lithe with dark curly hair. Phillip knew that his mother was one of Bob DiFranco's most ardent fans. "His smile is a tonic for all of us," she had told him a month ago on the phone. At the time he had felt a silly little rumble of jealousy of Bob DiFranco. Now she applauded until the moment Bob lifted his arm and gave the signal to begin singing. He noticed then that his mother had dyed her hair the same color as Matina's—the color of sauterne.

He listened to the medley of old favorites, "Down in the Valley," "You Are My Sunshine," and saw delight written on

his mother's face. A woman who always took pride in not
wanting anything she didn't have, not asking for anything,
who believed that the absence of desire was her strongpoint.

He watched her closely, her hands folded in her lap, her
hands pale against the navy blue of her dress. Her eyes did
their dance, moving quickly from the music on the stand in
front of her to the figure of Bob DiFranco and back to the
music.

She had wanted to join this group, and had. That was
impressive. He gave her credit and yet as he did he allowed
himself to imagine being the other woman's son. What sort of
a man would he have been? Would he have been bolder? More
determined? More abandoned? He saw himself on the beach
with a group of friends—men and women, and he was
building sandcastles with turrets and towers and domes, a
Kremlin-like compound. Small, energetic, he was bouncing
around on the sand and laughing and speaking in foreign
languages and wearing a straw hat. Everyone was wearing a
shade hat of some sort. It was a beach in a foreign country. He
was a renowned artist. Women were enchanted by his playful-
ness and flirted with him, and he could tell simply by looking
at them which language each woman spoke. As soon as he felt
Matina's eyes on him, he stopped daydreaming and went back
to watching his mother. For a split second he saw her lose her
place in the music and stumble, look worried and frantic, and
then glance quickly at DiFranco and find her place again.

What was the expression on her face that had made him
want to bolt from the auditorium earlier in the concert? It
came to him now. Obedience. She was obedient. His mother
was in class and she was being good. She was part of the class,
waiting for what the teacher wanted her to do next. As though
she had shed flimsy layers of grown-upness to reveal this: that
at heart what she wanted was to be a good schoolgirl. Phillip
squirmed.

When the concert ended, there was a rush for the front of
the auditorium. The singers were filing off the stage. Some of
them were already waving to their families and friends, and
calling out to them. He watched his mother remove loose
pages of music from her music stand and tap them into a neat
pile.

He could barely move. Eric and Matina stood up. "That was excellent," Eric said, "they were good." "Grandma looked so happy," Matina exclaimed. "I don't think I've ever seen her look so *blissed out*. Even when Grandpa was alive and you and mom were together." Matina glanced at her father, waiting for a response. "Yes, she was having a great time," he said with some difficulty.

"What didn't you like about it, Dad?" Matina asked.

"I didn't say anything about not liking it." He paused, faltering for a second. "I loved it," he said emphatically.

Matina's face lost its ruddy color, grew clouded. "You didn't love it," she hissed. She stared at him for a moment or two, then turned away. She was side stepping her way out of the row. He could see only the back of her head, her painfully short dyed yellow hair. But he knew exactly what she was thinking: that he was a liar, and more than that—that he was a traitor.

Matina moved ahead, didn't glance around at him again. The distance she created in her wake was dry scorched earth. Eric followed her. Both children clutched their concert programs in their hands; he had let his drop to the floor long ago. The auditorium whirled and shrieked. He tried to find his program on the floor under their seats, and couldn't. Then, out of the corner of his eye, he observed Matina slip two programs into her red and lavender backpack. She was building her case against him.

He took off after her. He had absolutely no idea of what to say to her. What could he say? Within seconds he was tapping her shoulder, stretching out his arm. "I'd like my program, please," he whispered.

She pulled back, stared at him. "You threw it on the floor."

"You picked it up."

"You didn't like the concert."

He felt jittery, short of breath. "I didn't love it, that's true." He forced the words. His voice was rough, he wasn't smiling.

"You were sitting there picking everything and everyone apart. Everyone except that woman, that show-off who thought she was God's gift to dancing. You were madly in love with that woman, and I don't understand why." She stopped, then murmured, "Poor Grandma."

Phillip took a deep breath. "Why did you take my program, Matina?" He made himself wait for an answer.

She stared at him as though he was a code she were struggling to decipher. He was standing there waiting, and she didn't know what to say. She had no answers, no questions. For a few seconds there were no questions taking shape, no questions spiraling and arching, ballooning. No answers. She looked confused and young, her eyes tearing slightly, her hair pathetically shorn.

"Matina, I'd like my program." He held out his hand palm-up.

She did not put the program on his open hand, and for a moment she turned away. He didn't move. He waited. It wasn't easy for him to wait; he loved her so much. Finally she handed him the program. He folded it and slipped it into his back pocket. "Grandma is waiting for us," he said. "Come on." On the stage his mother, her cheeks flushed, her body leaning towards them, was waving. Phillip waved back.

Nobody Under the Rose

BY JELENA BULAT GILL

I.

Above the open grave, Thelma's mother grumbled: "For all the years I've known him, there was nothing he wouldn't do to make me feel miserable." Muffling her sobs, Thelma hoped for her father to push up the lid and step out of the casket. She was only five.

They sold their house with a big yard and rented a small place at the edge of the town. When the money ran out, they started looking for something more affordable. Persuaded by a good-hearted neighbor, an old lady named Renate Pirchner agreed to let them use a small one-bedroom apartment in her basement in exchange for some housework and help with shopping. In addition, Thelma's mother found a regular job at a nearby restaurant.

When Thelma was seven, her three-year-old brother got a fever and died in less than a week. Thelma spent days in a corner of the laundry room, crying. She wished she had died instead. "Come out of there," her mother yelled. "You're just like your father—doing whatever annoys me the most. Dust everywhere, dirty dishes in the sink, and she's sitting and doing nothing."

Sometimes, her mother stayed out a whole night. Next day she slept until late afternoon. Seated by the small window of what they liked calling their living room, Thelma listened to her mother's snoring and tried not to think of the events that were going on at school.

"My poor child," the old lady used to tell her on such days. "If I were younger, I would take care of you."

Thelma would fight tears. "No, Mrs. Pirchner, you don't have to worry. I'm fine," she would say, hiding her eyes. "It's only that Mommy has to work so much. But, as soon as we have enough money..."

Occasionally, after a whole weekend away from home and a good ten hours of sleep afterwards, her mother would treat her kindly. They would go to the best children's store downtown. "Which dress do you like, honey?" her mother would ask. Fascinated, Thelma would touch colorful fabrics, let the finest lace slide between her fingers, try hats with ribbons and those with bows. Together—maybe with some help from one of the clerks—they would choose a dress, a hat and a pair of shiny shoes. Thelma would wear everything immediately. Then they would go for a stroll along the main street, and even have a piece of cake at one of the outdoor tables at the square.

But, as time went by, the night excursions of Thelma's mother became more frequent and longer. Linen on her bed needed to be changed only once in two months. The old black stove in the kitchen was rarely used. Silence filled the basement apartment.

Thelma started spending most of her time with Mrs. Pirchner. At first she helped with cleaning and cooking, then even started going to a little corner shop to buy groceries. The old lady arranged for one of the neighbors to take her to school and bring her back.

Occasionally and with no apparent reason, Thelma would plunge into a fit of rage. At those times, she would yell and scream, kick the furniture, throw pots and pans, and say things that would never escape her lips otherwise. Once the fury was over, she returned to her normal self swiftly and smoothly, as if nothing unusual had ever happened. She responded with stubborn silence to Mrs. Pirchner's attempts to make her talk about the incidents. Having grown to like her and even depend on her, Mrs. Pirchner was afraid to insist. Periods of peace and those filled with rage continued following each other; the former lasted longer, the latter compensated their briefness with intensity.

However troubled, life had been merciful for Thelma until one day when, after a full week of absence, her mother was brought back unconscious. She had fallen on the street and broken her arm. Worse yet, she was unable to move her left leg. A few weeks later, her vision became distorted and her speech difficult to understand.

At the age of sixteen, Thelma had to leave school to look after her deteriorating mother. As Mrs. Pirchner, being in her upper eighties, had difficulties going even from her bedroom to the bathroom, Thelma found her days becoming reduced to hours spent with one or the other of the two women. After four years and countless trips up and down the stairs, she rearranged the furniture in Mrs. Pirchner's living room to make space for two beds, one on each side of the big window overlooking the mountains. She put the old lady in one of them, her mother in the other. From an adjacent room, she made a bedroom for herself.

Once when Thelma's mother appeared asleep, the old lady said:

"You don't deserve this kind of life, my child. Out there, people are talking, laughing, traveling..."

To make her more comfortable, Thelma put an additional pillow behind her back. "I don't mind this life, Mrs. Pirchner," she said softly.

"If you wish, I'll pay someone to look after your mother and me," the old lady proposed, "so you can have some time..."

"You...you..." came a sudden outburst from the other bed. "You teach her to betray her own blood," Thelma's mother blurted with effort. "I gave her my life, my whole life, and now...you..." Mixed with groans and interrupted by stuttering, the words rolled out heavily.

"But, she's only twenty-two..."

"It's her turn now," the woman spat out. "Her father...he left me....Now, it's her...her turn..."

Thelma closed her hands into fists. The rooms spun around. Faces chased each other. Mrs. Pirchner, her mother...Mrs. Pirchner, her mother...From the darkness of her memory, her father's blue eyes emerged, then his cheeks, his nose, his mouth...Her little brother looked frightened...They all sailed around her. Faster and faster. Then her own face joined them. Young at first, with two thin braids and red ribbons. Slowly, it grew long and tearful; shadows darkened the eyes. The hair lost its firmness, the cheeks their freshness. At one moment her face was similar to her father's, at another it resembled her mother's. With the other four, it whirled vigorously. All people she had ever really known were there, running after each other, changing their expressions and their age. Thelma wished to scream, but her throat was too tight to let a sound out. She wished to run away, but her legs refused to carry her. She wished to cry, but no tear came out of her eyes.

"Thelma," a voice came through. "Thelma, Thelma, my child..." Trying to reach her, the old lady rolled over the edge of the bed.

The spinning stopped. As if seeing them for the first time, Thelma looked at the two women. Slowly, she took a pillow, only a moment later to throw it at the one who was still yelling furiously. With immobile face, she lifted Mrs. Pirchner from the floor and placed her on the bed.

From the door, she looked back once again. A minute later, sounds of breaking furniture and smashing dishes shook the house.

Two years later, having bequeathed both her house and her savings to Thelma, Mrs. Pirchner died. But, while the house was left to her unconditionally, she was permitted to use the money only after her mother's death or after she found somebody to care for her mother and she herself started living what Mrs. Pirchner had called "a normal life."

"So, the old witch found the way, didn't she?" her mother hissed. Although she was nearly paralyzed by that time, her speech had improved. With wild strength, she shouted: "Go! Why not? Your father left me, you might as well."

For several weeks following the old lady's death, Thelma remained silent. She shopped and cooked and cleaned, washed her mother's heavy body, fed her and combed her hair, but never said a word.

"I know you're trying to kill me," her mother accused her one day. "You want all that money, that's what you want."

For the next couple of days, Thelma did not enter the living room. From the apartment downstairs she did not hear her mother's cries and scoldings, her complaints and curses. Then, as if nothing had ever happened, she resumed her everyday duties again.

When the money she had at the time of Mrs. Pirchner's

death ran out, she had to make up her mind. One whole morning she spent looking through the window, hoping to see somebody who might look willing to take away her burden. Then still examining every face that went by, she walked to the corner grocery store.

"Would you happen to know how..." she started, addressing the grocer.

Surprised, the man stared at her. Never before had he heard her say more than a couple of words at a time.

"Care...how the care..." she stumbled further. "I thought since you...Then certainly..." For years he had been able to satisfy all her needs—he had to know how to deal with this one as well.

"What is it you want?" the man asked, still staring at her.

Thelma shook her head, stood a bit longer, then left.

Back at home, she opened her mother's wardrobe, the one that had not been opened for nearly fourteen years. At first reluctantly, then feverishly, she tried on the dresses. They fit her, every one of them. After dark, dressed in one she liked particularly well, she slipped out of the house.

Next morning, she went to the grocery store again. To the grocer's question about the reason for her visit the day before, she answered with a frown. Following her orders, he filled the shopping basket.

When she stepped out, he mumbled to himself: "Not more than two words, just like before. Must be fine now."

One morning, Thelma felt tired. Her feet were swollen. Preparing breakfast for her mother and herself required an extraordinary effort. That evening she stayed home.

Days grew long and monotonous. She felt so weary that even her mother's tireless rumblings did not bother her. For hours, she would lie motionless, unaware of sounds and light. Vague and distant, one thought entered her mind: that it was her mother who, wanting to keep her home, managed to put something into her food. Then even that faded, leaving her empty and insensitive.

One day, her old strength was back. She fed her mother with a sudden enthusiasm, went to buy groceries and did some cleaning. In the evening, clad in one of her mother's dresses, she went out through the back door.

Not very interesting were those night trips of hers. All she ever saw were cobblestones of the town's most disgraceful streets. She never looked up, never wished to see houses or trees, to have a glimpse of the evening sky. Only rarely she noticed the shops or other women who, like herself, spent hours walking up and down. All she wanted was for someone to stop her, mutter an amount she never quite understood, and take her aside to one of those dark alleys with rooms by the hour. After some time, when she would emerge from one of the buildings with no street number, uncertain of the place or the way she should take, she would crouch against the wall and stay there until early passersby would start casting strange looks at her. Although her home was only blocks away, more than once it took her a good two hours to reach it.

The other girls from the district believed that the secret of Thelma's extraordinary success had to be ascribed to her unusual clothing. Some of them even asked her where she got the old-fashioned hats and dresses with low waists and well supported bosoms. Either because she did not understand their questions or because she did not know what it really was that they wished to learn, she never acknowledged their words. To retaliate, they tried to scare away the customers by telling them about an entire array of terrible diseases Thelma had. Yet, nothing really changed. Thelma always found a man before any other girl. But she never looked for a second one. Her obvious lack of desire to compete and her soft manners might have been the reasons—perhaps the only reasons—that, after some time, they accepted her as one of them. In their own way, they even liked her. Once when it rained so badly that streets were nearly deserted, one of the girls brought an old umbrella and gave it to Thelma. On another occasion, in winter, a different girl put a heavy shawl around her shoulders. Yet, Thelma never thanked them. If anything, every kind gesture made her bow her head even lower, withdraw ever further.

Although her mother grew weaker physically, her mind was as clear as ever. "This soup doesn't taste any better than dish water," she would yell. Sometimes, afraid of being poisoned, she would ask Thelma to taste the food before feeding it to her. Without either a complaint or a change in her expression, Thelma adjusted to her mother's moods. Occasionally, to please her, she stayed home for days and sometimes even slept in the living room.

After a pause of several weeks, Thelma opened the old wardrobe again. Some of the dresses she had not worn yet. Slowly, she pulled out one made of burgundy velvet. It had a wide lace collar and silk trim around the borders. It rustled with half-forgotten memories from her early childhood; it smelled of freshly baked Sunday strudel and her father's warm hands. She shook it and steamed it above a pot of boiling water. After she fixed her hair in a way that seemed appropriate for a matching hat, she lifted the dress again. With a jerk, she pulled it over her head. It passed the shoulders, then the breasts. At the hips, it stopped. She pulled it down, and pulled some more. The dress seemed to be jammed. She took it off to inspect the closure, then tried it again. It stopped at the hips. Upset, she tried the other dresses from the wardrobe. They all appeared to have changed—although comfortable enough for her shoulders and chest, they refused to pass her hips. Angry, she threw the dresses on the floor.

That night, in the bed, she felt a strange pressure inside her stomach. It moved from one place to another, intensified and almost went away, grew to the point of becoming painful and felt as gentle as the softest caressing. She pressed both palms against her abdomen, only to realize that her shape had changed. A strong blow made her twitch both hands. Another blow forced her to turn sideways. Wrapped in fear, the truth crept out of the darkness.

II.

Every day, Thelma's stomach was a bit more swollen. She widened some of her skirts and even started wearing some of Mrs. Pirchner's. Although she wished very much to eat southern fruits and seafood, all that she still had money for were bread, milk and cheap meat. Consequently, her shopping trips became infrequent. Without taking time to examine the decision, she switched from her usual grocery store to one that was ten blocks farther but where nobody knew her.

At first indifferently and then with revolt, her mother observed the changes in her daughter's figure. "While I thought you were washing and cleaning and cooking, you were out having fun," she scolded with wrath. "Selfish, always selfish, just like your father."

Another time, she yelled: "You bitch! Is that why I sacrificed my whole life for you? To put shame on my name, on our family?! I wish your father was alive to see what his blood's capable of."

Tired and hungry, Thelma went about her everyday jobs. Making the best with the money she had was the most difficult of them. By a mere accident she found out that some of Mrs. Pirchner's furniture was quite in demand. A man all the way down the street showed a great interest in the enormous lacquered mirror and a couple of ornate planters. Another liked the long serving table carved from one piece of wood. A third wanted the bed that her mother had been using for the previous twelve years. One by one, the best pieces left the house. Thelma did not feel remorse. In fact, she did not feel anything but a pressure in her stomach.

She was sure a blond man who had wished to see her again was the father of her child. She remembered the night clearly. With his eyes closed, gripping her shoulders, he came down strongly, then pushed himself up, to return with a renewed vigor. Again and again. Until the pain inside her had become unbearable. Believing that her whole body was about to split, she had screamed. Imprinted firmly between her legs, his body had twisted. His growl had changed into a moan. Then, sliding next to her, he had asked, "Did I hurt you?" Before she was able to speak, he had added, "I'm sorry." He was the only one who ever apologized for the pain she suffered, the only one with feelings. She was sure he was the father of her child.

One evening a couple of months later, dressed in her own clothing and with no hat, she went out. Several times she paced the familiar streets. Now and then, she stopped to look at this man or that. Some were of the same height as the man she was looking for, some had his hair or his shoulders, but none of them was he. They blinked with surprise, then went around her. Not able to recognize her, the girls laughed. In the morning, exhausted, she returned home.

"Still selling yourself?" her mother barked. "And leaving your mother alone?"

"No, Mother, all I want is..." Thelma wished to explain.

"I know what you want," her mother charged. "You're looking for a fool who'd take both you and your bastard. As soon as you find him, you'll let me die." Anger distorted her features. "That's your way of thanking me for everything I've done for you, for my sleepness nights, my despair and loneliness."

Many times Thelma tried to explain, to reassure her mother. Then she withdrew even further. Only rarely, at night, she would talk. To herself. Mostly about the things she wished to learn and about those she wanted to see.

She needed a dream. So, she created one. It was about the blond man. She called him Lars. "Our son will be big, just like you," she would tell him. "When you return, he'll be waiting. "We'll both be waiting. Then we'll make our own home..." Although she did not know what her future home should be like, one thing was sure—it would in no way resemble the one in which she was living. With effort she would remember some of the evenings from many years before. Seated on her father's lap, she was listening to a story. Like Lars, her father was blond; like Lars, he held her tightly. But, unlike Lars', his words were tender, soft with promises, ripe with dreams. Thinking about those distant events would bring light into her eyes. "Yes, we'll wait," she would say aloud. "Then, you'll put your son into your lap and tell him a story. The nicest you could think of..." Images would become hard to distinguish. To bridge the years of loneliness, the past would move closer. "And he'll hug you and hug you," she would extend the dream. "But don't ever hurt him...don't ever hurt either of us." A sob would shake her body. "Please, Daddy, just you and me. Let everybody go. Just you and me..." Restoring the past was all that was left.

One day, a knock on the door found her unprepared. She pulled the door ajar and, with her foot securing it from the inside, peeked out.

"Excuse me, Ma'am," the man from the corner grocery store said in a confused manner. "I didn't see you for so long...I wondered..."

At first, Thelma wanted to slam the door, but then remembered that her pantry was nearly empty. In a trembling voice, showing only her head in the opening, she thanked him for the kindness. "My mother's very sick," she uttered quietly. "So, I can't..."

"Oh, I'll be glad to bring anything you need," the man said eagerly. "I'll come once a week. If you'd just leave me a message on the front steps..."

When her stomach fell low, Thelma knew the time had come. She reduced the visits to her mother to one a day. With an absent gaze, she would enter the room, do the feeding, clean the woman's face, collect empty dishes and leave.

"As soon as you deliver him, you'll leave me," her mother repeated every day. "His life for mine. If I'd only known..."

Thelma did not listen. Slow and clumsy, she wobbled around the house. One day, she unfolded a couple of embroidered sheets and washed them. From a chest in the living room, she pulled out a pair of long scissors and a sewing supply.

"Kill me with the scissors, that's what you'll do," her mother screamed. "Then you'll go to your lover." Maliciously, with helpless rage, she snarled: "But you're too fat and too old for anybody to want you." Then she pleaded: "If you stay with your Mommy, she'll take care of you, she'll love you...your Mommy..."

Thelma found the softest pillow. Without even once glancing at her mother, she collected everything and headed toward the door.

"My blood will fall on your head!" her mother's scream caught up with her.

One night, an unusual sensation made her sit up in the bed. She was wet. Her bed as well. At first she thought it was blood. Then she understood. A wave of sharp pain made her life flat again. Another cramped her legs. She was still to learn about the suffering that the first birth carries.

Hours later, her legs spread far. Her bones seemed to be breaking. With the greatest strength, her innards pushed out. She bit the pillow, then her own arm. Her heart could not stand any more pressure, her body could not handle any more pain. Things around her lost their shapes. Her thinking became unclear. Her pelvic bone split. She felt her soul leave her body. A scream grew inside her.

Then a relief came. Without panic or fear, as if that was something she had done many times before, she reached between her legs. The small body was warm and slimy. It cried, at first weakly then loudly. Not a muscle on Thelma's face moved when she extended her hand to find the scissors.

It took her only two movements. With the first, she freed her son from herself. With the second, she ended his life.

The rest was easy. On a large, soft pillow, wrapped in the embroidered sheet whose corners were sewn together, he rested peacefully. Before throwing the first lump of soil on his miniature grave, she uttered: "The time might come... Maybe..."

Next morning she came to the living room at the usual time, but with no tray in her hands. Looking at her mother, she said slowly:

"Today I'll find somebody to look after you. Then, tomorrow, I'll leave."

Her mother stared at her. Understanding made her eyes open in horror. "Your child!" she screamed. "No, you didn't...I'll tell them! If you leave me, I'll let everybody know.... Then..."

Preparations proved more difficult than Thelma had anticipated. She felt that everything she had ever touched deserved to be told goodbye. And Mrs. Pirchner's things deserved that more than the others. So, instead of finishing the packing in a couple of hours, Thelma found herself busy even after the sunset. Looking for somebody who would agree to care for her mother had to be left for the next day.

As it turned out, her plans had to change once more. In the morning, when she entered the living room, only silence greeted her. The absence of her mother's sharp voice, of her scoldings and complaints, made her stop abruptly. Stunned, she looked at the bed. With her eyes closed, her mother lay still. The air felt cleaner.

III.

The grocer was most sympathetic. "Such a catastrophe," he nodded with understanding. "I'll be honored to help."

"I'll do it myself." Thelma shook her head. "I have a shovel..."

No, the body must not be buried behind the house, the grocer explained. After the mortician does his job and all the forms are filled, Mrs. Mason should be buried at the city cemetery. It is prohibited, strictly prohibited, he spelled it out clearly, to bury people any other place but at cemeteries. "I know it's hard for you to have your mother so far," he said, touching her elbow gently. "After all those years... But I can get you a fine spot, the finest that is."

Thelma let him organize the burial. The two of them and a priest followed the casket from the chapel to an open grave in a secluded corner above the city. Thelma had on a black dress that the grocer—Gottfried Schmidt was his name—had bought for her a day before. He held her hand during the service.

On the next day, a man who introduced himself as a lawyer came to the door. "I got word that your mother had passed away," he said compassionately. "As you probably remember, in her will Mrs. Pirchner specified that..."

Thelma listened to the lengthy explanation, signed the papers and agreed for the money to be coming in equal monthly installments. "The amount won't be much, but it's still better to have something regular," the lawyer assured her, collecting the papers.

For days, Thelma busied herself with cleaning and washing. She pushed the only remaining bed out of the living room, arranged the available furniture as best she could, cleaned dust from the old paintings, and washed the windows. Then she pulled on the drapes, locked the front door and returned to the apartment in the basement. With extraordinary meticulousness, she collected all of her mother's personal things and stuffed them in a large sack. She buried the sack in the back yard, in the corner all the way down next to the trash bin.

The little apartment needed cleaning, a lot of cleaning. Thelma spent several days scrubbing the floors, washing the windows and taking down cobwebs. Every piece of linen was carefully laundered, starched, ironed and put away again. Insensible to fatigue and unaware of time, she went after her chores with blind energy, sometimes even forgetting to eat.

After two weeks, she went to the grocery store. Gottfried Schmidt took her under the arm. "You should take better care of yourself, Ms. Mason," he said warmly. Seated on top of his fat, rosy cheeks, his small eyes smiled. "If you wish, I'll ask my mother to help you get around and find what you need."

Thelma looked down at her dress. It was old and wrinkled, even dirty along the hems. Her fingernails were cracked. The skin of her hands was dry and rough.

"She already knows about you," Gottfried confided. His short, chubby fingers were squeezing her arm. "She'll love you, I'm sure."

Thelma did not respond. Instead, she turned to the counter with fresh vegetables. Unaccustomed to being around people, she placed orders slowly, with deliberation, as if not quite sure whether the words chosen were the proper ones. Smiling continually, Gottfried packed the items she had indicated and escorted her to the street. "If you don't mind, she'll pay you a visit," he said. handing her the basket. She shook her head in a way that was difficult to interpret.

Two days later, Mrs. Mathilde Schmidt knocked on Thelma's door. All smiles and sweetness, she seemed to have a great liking for the insecure woman in her early thirties. "We'll get you some nice dresses and gloves and proper shoes and this season's hats," she rumbled with excitement. "And I'll show you how to fix your hair."

The woman who entered a stylish downtown store was dressed in a well-worn gray skirt and a faded wool shawl; her shoes were wide and shapeless, her head was bare. The one who came out wore a hat with a wide rim, a dress with a high collar and a pair of fashionable shoes. "The street doesn't hold me," she whispered, stumbling along. "With a bit of practice, you'll learn how to walk properly," Mrs. Schmidt assured her.

Kind and helpful, Mrs. Schmidt accompanied Thelma to her home. "I'll be happy to advise you about the decor of your house," she said when they reached the garden gate. "Curtains are my weakness..."

Thelma led her around, then unlocked the basement apartment.

Stunned, Mrs. Schmidt exclaimed: "But, my child, surely you don't live here!" She took the set of keys from Thelma and made her way back, to the main door. "A girl with your charm should live where she belongs," she declared firmly, starting to inspect the spacious entry hall.

"It's not good for a girl like you to live alone, my dear," Mrs. Schmidt explained in her irresistible way. "You need someone to take care of you. Someone like my Gottfried . . ." Too shy to comment, Thelma only blushed. Arrangements were made quickly and quietly.

When Gottfried Schmidt and his mother moved in, the old lady told her with a smile: "I see you like your clean little rooms downstairs. We'll understand it if you keep them for yourself." Gottfried's attempt to say something was cut short. "That'll stop people from talking, too." Still looking at Thelma, she made it clear: "It's because of you, my dear, that we came to live here before it's time. But, as soon as the mourning months are over, we'll think about the wedding."

At first Thelma went to church with Gottfried and his mother. Later they got into the habit of leaving her behind to do various jobs around the house. And jobs were plentiful indeed, especially as Mrs. Schmidt made a point of systematically avoiding any work. It was up to Thelma to cook, clean, wash, iron, work in the garden. . . . Sometimes, in the evening, too weary to do anything but sit by the window and look out, she dreamed about the life she would live once the mourning was over.

Months went by. Plans for the wedding were never mentioned again. Thelma never bought another dress either. Instead, Mrs. Schmidt asked her to wear a black skirt and a white apron, and ordered her not to go anywhere without being permitted.

Thelma's hopes turned first into resignation, then into numbness. At the beginning of the next spring, she was asked to make a vegetable and flower garden in the back yard. That meant getting up at sunrise and working until sunset. Above her son's unmarked grave she planted a rose bush. "That's ridiculous," Gottfried ruled one day when the roses were in full bloom. "The bush takes too much space, and that type of rose just doesn't sell." He took the bush out. After many years, that was the first time Thelma cried. She was afraid that the watermelon which replaced the rose bush would be too heavy for her boy.

It was not before the fourth year from her mother's death was nearly over that Thelma suffered another of her destructive rages. After breaking most of the dishes in her apartment, she climbed the stairs. Smashing fine china felt much better than finishing already cracked ceramic pieces. When Mrs. Schmidt and Gottfried entered the kitchen, the floor was covered with segments of finest plates, bowls, cups and saucers. Thelma's bare feet were bloody, her eyes shone with wild passion. "You bitch!" Mrs. Schmidt screamed. "I'll show you how to destroy what doesn't belong to you!"

For a week, Thelma was locked in the laundry room. Once a day, Mrs. Schmidt brought her a piece of bread and a cup of water. "Here's a cup," she said every time. "Break it and you'll never see water again."

When Thelma was finally permitted to leave the laundry room, she found heavy iron bars on all basement windows. A brick wall had replaced the flimsy wooden fence. "I need a key," she said slowly, pointing at the iron gate. Gottfried shook his head. "No, you don't," he said. "Your business is on this side of the wall."

Mrs. Schmidt's demands had no limits. For Thelma, days grew longer. The sun burned her hair, the hard work bent her back. Unable to endure the present, once more she chose to turn to the past. Early one morning, she rolled away a huge watermelon and started digging. By that time, her boy had to be big, much bigger than the night he was born, she thought. When her hands felt the softness of the pillow, a shiver of anticipation climbed her spine. Gently, she scooped out the remaining soil. What she saw made her shriek. Her life crumbled on top of her son's rotted body.

The sun found broken watermelons, smashed tomatoes, strewn flowers. All windows on the basement apartment were shattered into pieces. The cupboards in the upstairs kitchen were emptied on the floor. Amidst the debris sat Thelma, impassive to the things going on around her.

Only a week later, the downstairs windows were replaced with wooden boards, and a heavy padlock was installed on the door. Days went by before Thelma was brought food for the first time.

IV.

If it were not for the lawyer—the one who had taken care of Mrs. Pirchner's will—Thelma might have met her last days as a prisoner in her own home. But, as it turned out, to satisfy some new regulations, the lawyer needed another signature from Thelma. Suspecting nothing, he came to the front door. After asking him to wait in the living room upstairs, Mrs. Schmidt grabbed some of Thelma's clothing and hurried down. However, neither threats nor kind words made Thelma move. Tired from waiting, the lawyer came down himself.

Soon after this visit, Gottfried and his mother moved out. Once more, Thelma cleaned the whole house, this time to make her home upstairs. The lawyer arranged with a pastor of a nearby church to find somebody who would help her to put together her wretched life. An old couple—Mr. and Mrs. Yablonski were their names—took her to the church every Sunday. They introduced her to other people. Everybody was kind to her, everybody showed concern and willingness to help. But Thelma responded with coldness and silence. Soon, people lost interest in her or, most likely, lost desire to fight her inability to communicate. After some time, Mr. and Mrs. Yablonski were the only ones who saw her regularly. Although they had stopped insisting on taking her to church, they still came to visit her two or three times every week.

Thelma planted hundreds of roses in her walled back yard. Whenever she went around with a watering can, she talked to them. "Red, you should all be red," she used to whisper, nodding her head. "It's blood that makes you red. It makes you big, too. And strong. Strong enough to fight the wind and the cold." The spot where her son was buried did not house a rose. It did not need to, she had decided. Nobody lived under the layer of soil any more.

Slowly, she became used to Mr. and Mrs. Yablonski to the point that she expected their arrival with anticipation. Together, they would make a round through the roses, or go shopping, or stroll along the main street. Not having children, Mr. and Mrs. Yablonski came to believe that Thelma was the child that God had meant to be theirs. Love was what their hearts were rich with and starved for. They made their advances slowly. First they gained Thelma's trust, then they sat out to awaken her numb feelings, to teach her to laugh, to make her want other people. They brought books and asked her to read aloud for the two of them. They gave her good clothing and asked her to put it on whenever they came to visit. They learned what it was she wanted to do and made sure to fulfill her wishes. One day when Thelma told them that her father was from Michigan and that she herself was born there, they brought a map of the United States. "I was only two when we moved to Austria," Thelma told them, a subdued longing in her voice. "Mother wanted it that way." Bent over the map, Mr. and Mrs. Yablonski marked various towns, highlighted the points they knew something about, then started planning a trip that would acquaint Thelma with her father's homeland.

Some months later, Thelma started going to Mr. and Mrs. Yablonski's home. She would bring them a bunch of roses or a few pieces of a freshly baked cake or an invitation to spend a weekend with her. Her back was not bent any more. If not exactly fashionable, her clothing was clean and of good quality. Her lips even knew how to smile. Yet, her previous life had left its marks. In the middle of a pleasant conversation, her brow would furrow or her hands start to shake. Although rare and less intense, fits of rage still disturbed her otherwise calm days. Sporadically, she woke from a deep sleep with a scream.

One day, Mr. Yablonski asked Thelma to sit next to him. Holding her hands, he said: "If you think you could live with two old and grouchy people, we'll be happy to share our home with you." Thelma's initial surprise soon changed into a grin. He did not have to say anything more. Somewhat clumsily, Thelma hugged him. For the first time ever, her tears were those of joy.

Preparations for the change progressed slowly. Mr. and Mrs. Yablonski wanted to add a large room to their home before Thelma moved in. Also, they wanted to plant roses in their back yard. "You need a large room with a lot of light, our dear child," they told her. "We want you to have everything you never had before." They did not listen to Thelma's assurances that she would be quite happy with a small room next to the kitchen, and that roses were of no importance at all. "No, it's a garden room you need, and it's a garden room you'll have," they remained firm. "And you love roses, don't you? Yes, you do love roses."

The excitement connected with the construction project and the anticipation of living with a woman whom she considered her daughter influenced Mrs. Yablonski in a way that had been impossible to predict. First she lost sleep, then her appetite. Too eager to see the new room finished, her husband failed to register the change. Thelma's attempts to warn him produced no result. Collecting her last strength, Mrs. Yablonski went around the house making plans for the new furniture arrangement and imagining the marvelous time they were going to have with Thelma.

On the morning of the big move, Mrs. Yablonski felt too weak to get out of bed. Some time in the afternoon, her husband and Thelma helped her to the nearest chair, then carried the chair to the new part of the house. "God bless you for coming to live with us," Mrs. Yablonski whispered, holding Thelma's hand.

Thelma was glad to prepare dinner for the three of them. Now and then she peeked through the door to see what Mrs. Yablonski was doing. Her worry for the old lady was subdued by her happiness.

Although Mrs. Yablonski hardly ate, she praised the food and complimented the way Thelma had arranged the furniture in her new room. Slowly, she talked about the day when the roses would bloom, about the years they were going to spend together, about the trip to Michigan. Soon after dinner, she kissed Thelma's cheek and asked to be taken to bed.

Some two hours later, when her husband joined her, her face was serene and happy. Surprised by the smoothness of her skin, he looked at her carefully, then extended his hand. Her forehead was cold and so were her hands.

V.

They never enjoyed the roses in full bloom and never mentioned the trip to Michigan again. In fact, Mr. Yablonski and Thelma never did any of the things that the three of them had dreamed about. His anguish started with his wife's death. His break with reality as well. The first few months he waited for her to come back. Later, he started worrying that something might have happened to her. "Maybe you should see if she's at the butcher's," he would tell Thelma. Thelma would walk to the end of the street and come back to report that Mrs. Yablonski was not at the butcher's and neither was she at the grocer's or at the post office or the church.

Instead of healing it, the time made the wound even more devastating. Mr. Yablonski became nervous and harsh with Thelma. His bad appetite he attributed to her inability to cook, his deteriorating physical condition to her lack of concern for him.

With the help of some churchgoers, Thelma arranged for him to visit several physicians and even to go east, to some highly praised spas. Then she took him to a local woman who used folk remedies to cure all ailments. After that, she returned to physicians. In spite of all efforts, Mr. Yablonski grew weaker. Also, he grew more and more suspicious of anything that Thelma was doing. Eventually, he made it impossible for her to have access to his bank account. Unable to find any other solution, she sold her own house. With unchanged energy and her own money, she continued searching for a way to help the old man.

Nearly six years later, after returning from yet another physician, Mr. Yablonski died in his sleep. If it were not for the persistence of the lawyer and testimonies of the neighbors, Thelma would have been denied the right to the house and belongings of Mr. and Mrs. Yablonski. But, since nobody aspired to the couple's estate and since the judge believed the arguments presented to him, she was permitted to remain in the same place and was even awarded the little money the old couple had saved.

Once again, she set out to clean and wash. Being quite a few years older, this took her much longer than any time before. She closed the shutters on the windows, pulled the drapes, locked all rooms but the one that had been built for her. Over the yellowing map, her eyes watering and heart shrinking into a painful knot, for hours she thought about the land to which she belonged. The back yard grew wild. The paint from the facade started peeling. Yet, on those rare occasions when she went out to buy necessary things, she did not seem to notice the changes.

At first people from the street talked about her, then they abhorred her, and finally, some months later, they forgot about her existence. And she was still behind the discolored walls, spending the little money she had, hoping to find a place she could call home.

It was not until nearly twenty years later that she attracted the attention of her neighbors again. When the first shingles started sliding from the roof, they knocked on the door, then left a message in the mail box. When, during a thunderstorm, the whole chimney crashed on the sidewalk, they decided that going to the police station was the only option left.

It was the middle of the summer when a police officer, a social worker and the town attorney forced their way into the house. The air behind the closed shutters was musty; the thick darkness was still. One after another, they tiptoed their way through the long abandoned rooms.

Dressed in an old-fashioned white dress that once belonged to Mrs. Yablonski, Thelma gave them but a brief glance. Then she turned her attention to a rose bush. She did not have time for visitors—a double row of blooming roses required a lot of time, and her hands were neither strong nor fast any more.

At the end of that summer, only a day before she was to be taken to the local home for the elderly, Thelma paid her last visit to the rose garden. With a pair of large garden clippers, methodically, never pausing to look back, she slashed every bush just above the ground. From the gate, with an absent gaze she surveyed the result. "You don't deserve the loneliness," she said softly, addressing the red petals scattered along and around the narrow path. The clippers fell on the ground. Careful not to step on the petals and buds, she returned into the house.

Her belongings fit into two small suitcases: one contained her modest wardrobe, the other a faded map and about a dozen books, most of them about Michigan. At last she had a dream.

The Elevator Man

BY PAT HARRISON

"I don't know why you'd want to go there," Iris said. "You don't know a soul in the city. Why would you want to go there?" She was leaning against her kitchen counter, talking to her brother-in-law, Les, who sat at the table.

Les stared at his fingers, splayed rigid and wide in his lap, as if he were counting them. "Well," he said, drawing the word out to two syllables, "I just figure it's now or never."

Iris turned to the sink and emptied her coffee cup and rinsed it out. Les sneaked a look at her then, at her soft gray curls and small shoulders, her bottom that was wider and softer now, her thin, spindly legs. She had rounded out all over, he thought, except for those legs.

She sat down at the table. "I don't see the sense in it," she said.

"You have any more coffee?" Les asked, meeting her eyes. "I've got to be getting back to town."

She laughed. "You already had three cups." He stared at her upper teeth, that tiny space on the side that made her look snaggle-toothed and girlish. That space was a secret, revealed only when she smiled. He watched, entranced and alarmed, till her lip came down and concealed it.

"I've got to go, I'll see you later," he said, pushing his chair back, lurching toward the door.

"Wait a minute," she called, but he was already gone.

In the safety of his car, Les rubbed his hands together hard, twisting the flesh on one hand, then the other, digging his thumbs deep in his palms. She made him want to do

157

something. How could he even think it? His own brother's wife. Ed would kill him if he laid one finger on Iris. Les squeezed his hands till his fingers throbbed.

He drove slowly on the ten-mile trip back to Elgin, ignoring the red dust that followed him all the way to the highway and the bits of rock that flew up and hit the sides of his '54 Chevy, chipping its faded green paint. He took no notice of the wheat that rose on both sides of the road, swaying in the spring wind, though wheat was his business and much of the land he passed was his homeplace. He drove with his neck stuck out in front of him, shoulders hunched over the steering wheel.

He hadn't meant to stop at the farm today, he shouldn't have. And he hadn't meant to tell Iris his plan to move to the city. Now she would tell Ed and Ed would tell Smokey Atkins before he had a chance to properly resign. And they would all think he was touched. Why's old Les want to move, after all these years? Who's he think he is? Well, it was none of their business. He'd go no matter what they thought.

At the stop light on Main, Les sat through a red and a green before somebody honked and yelled at him, then passed him on the right. Startled, Les looked around to see who it was, but they were already gone. A few cars were parked in front of the drugstore and Ollie's Cafe, but nobody was out on the street. Everybody was working, as he ought to be. It was time to get ready for harvest.

At the end of Main, Les turned right and drove the short gravel road to the Elgin Co-op Grain Elevator. It gleamed in the afternoon light, drawing the sun to its tin roof and sides. A candy wrapper waved in a small wind on the scale out front. Les parked his car and went inside, suddenly tired. In his room off the office, he undid his black work boots and lay down to rest, too tired to take off his overalls and work shirt.

Standing in his stocking feet at the big front window, Les watched the Harrington kids, Henry and Amanda, take turns riding their bicycle up the little hill to the cement scale. Seeing that his car blocked their path, that they couldn't circle the scale the way they usually did, he went out and moved the Chevy.

Henry and Amanda stopped playing and watched him as he

picked his way back to the scale between rocks and sticker patches. Unlike some children in Elgin, they were not afraid of Les. They had played around his place for years: in the dirt road that led from the motel, where they lived, up to the elevator; on the scale out front; and on the boxcars out back. They had brought their wagon here before they got the bicycle.

Amanda sat down on the steps as Les settled into his metal chair, which had a seat in the shape of two large buttocks.

"Watch this!" Henry called. Stopping in front of Les and Amanda, he raised his hands from the handlebars and shrieked. His hollering grew louder and higher-pitched as the front wheel began to wobble. Just as the bike was about to fall, he grabbed the handlebars and pedaled down the hill.

"Can I borrow some paper?" Amanda asked.

Les nodded, knowing she wanted a receipt book. He went inside and got a new one, then handed it to her with a freshly sharpened pencil.

She bent over the book. He watched her fingers move to the shapes her mouth made, wanting to pull her hair back so he could see her better. But he wouldn't. He must never ever touch her, or any of the children. He leaned over and tried to tell what she wrote, but couldn't. She was too far away.

Henry stopped the bike with a jolt in front of Amanda. "We gotta go home. Can't you hear?"

Les hadn't heard it either, but now he did. The voice of Mr. Harrington, calling from behind the motel. "Henry... Mandy... Henry... Mandy."

Amanda dropped her pencil and receipt book and ran after Henry. "Coming... coming," Henry yelled.

Les picked up the receipt book. On the top page Amanda had written her name, over and over, in various combinations. "Amanda Jane Harrington, Amanda Harrington, Mandy Harrington, Jane Harrington, Mandy Jane Harrington, A.J. Harrington."

On the next page, she had written, "Les Howard," and beneath it, "Mandy Harrington." A plus sign was drawn between the names and around them a heart, with an arrow through it. "Les Howard plus Mandy Harrington," he said aloud. And again, "Les Howard plus Mandy Harrington."

He tore the pages from the book and folded them into a small square, then slid the papers into his billfold, beneath the photo of his mother, Ida.

Smokey Atkins' lips were flecked with brown spots from the cigar that always rested in the corner of his mouth, half-lit or out most of the time, chewed and wet. He rested his cowboy boots on the lower rung of a high metal stool.

The other men sat on straight-backed chairs that Les had assembled in a loose semicircle for the meeting. Their faces were yellow in the dim light of the office.

"How about we line somebody up to help you this summer?" Smokey asked. He shifted the cigar to the other side of his mouth. "Then you can think about next year after this one's over."

Les could feel their eyes on him, Smokey's and Ed's and everybody else's. He tried to look at them, but couldn't. His eyes couldn't leave the floor. And he couldn't get his breath. They were using up all the air in here. "Okay," he got out, "that'd be okay." At least he had told them. They might not believe him, but he had told them.

"What about Jimmy Earl?" Smokey said in Ed's direction. "He might have time this summer."

"We could ask him," Ed said. "It's worth a try."

Ed had been friendly all evening, Les thought, saying he was sorry he'd missed him at the farm the other day, asking him to come out again soon. Probably Iris had told him, though he had seemed as surprised as the others. Which wasn't very surprised at all, now that he thought about it. "So you wanna leave God's country," Smokey had said. "Better you than me. It's away too crowded down there for me."

Smokey flicked a dead ash onto the cement floor and ended the meeting. "It'll be a big one this year," he said. "We need all the help we can get."

Les stayed up late that night, sitting on his narrow bed in his shorts, poring over his wrinkled, dog-eared atlas. He thought he might move to California, to San Francisco, instead of Oklahoma City. Everybody went to the city. Why not go the whole way, clear out to the West Coast? He traced the journey, out to Amarillo, on to Gallup and Flagstaff, then Barstow and Bakersfield, up to San Francisco. He had been there during the service, seen the ocean and mountains, the

light colored houses built on hills. It was far nicer than
Oklahoma City. Maybe he'd go there instead.

Les had been raised to leave Elgin, chosen by his mother Ida
for a better life than farming or ranching. He was her baby,
the one she taught to play the piano, the one she taught to sing.
She had coached him from the time he was five years old to
harmonize his voice with hers. He learned so well that
eventually the members of the First Methodist Church could
barely distinguish his nasal soprano from her firm contralto.

If Ida hadn't died the winter Les turned thirteen, he might
have left Elgin directly after high school and gone to the state
university. He might have become a minister or schoolteacher
or who knows what. But as it happened, his heart seemed to
give out when hers did.

In the years since, only one event had stirred him. In 1941,
at the insistence of his father, Grover, Les had signed up for
the Army Air Force. In the islands of the South Pacific, he
woke up briefly at the threat of death. He was also accorded
new status in the eyes of his brother Ed, whose family
responsibilities kept him at home. Les was protecting their
country, fighting the Japs. If the Japs seemed to Les an
abstract, almost meaningless reason for what he did, the
proximity of death did not; he could have died a thousand
times in those islands.

Iris wrote to Les every week during the war, sending news
of Elgin and the farm, pictures of her and Ed's two children,
news of who had married and who else had had children; she
wrote of Grover's death in 1943. Les treasured her letters, the
thin blue envelopes and white tablet paper, and he carried
them in a shoe box all during the war. He had her letters still
in his room at the elevator.

Les returned to Elgin in 1945 with a tired, remote look in
his eyes and no plans for the future. He went back to the farm
and sat, in the kitchen or on the porch, and listened to Iris,
availing himself of her food and gossip. After four months, he
went to work at the elevator, a job Ed secured for him when he
saw that his brother would not work at all unless he was told
to.

Les was sitting in the office drinking his first cup of coffee,
when Jimmy Earl drove up. "Morning, Les," he said, letting
the screen door slam behind him.

Les was embarrassed to be sitting there in his overalls with no shirt or socks on, no boots.

"Smokey came by last night," Jimmy said. "I'm short on time this summer, but I always am, I'll fit it in." He adjusted his "Elgin Eagles" baseball cap and flicked his cigarette ash on the floor.

"First thing," he went on, walking over to the desk, reaching for a receipt book, "we gotta clean out that pit." He took a ballpoint pen from his shirt pocket and began making a list, holding the burning cigarette in his mouth while he wrote. "May be some water in it," he mused.

"Then we need to get them cars coopered. We may need some help with that." He made another note. "By the way, Les. I seen some kids playing out there the other night. I wouldn't allow it if I was you. I'd run 'em off. It's dangerous."

Les sipped his coffee, thinking Jimmy had his nerve, to come around here giving him orders. He could remember a time when Jimmy had played on those boxcars, and it wasn't that long ago. Now he thought he was a big shot, married to Smokey's daughter. But he didn't own a single acre; he had to rent land from Smokey to run his cattle on. Who did he think he was?

Jimmy finished the list and handed it to Les. "I'll check back with you later in the week," he said as he left, tugging on his cap.

Les crumpled the list and threw it across the office. He'd be damned if he'd take orders from Jimmy Earl Henderson. He knew how to get ready for harvest. He'd been running this place for fifteen years, when Jimmy was just a runt. He was still just a runt, an overgrown kid.

Les went in to shower and shave. Studying himself in the medicine cabinet mirror, he had an inspiration. He'd grow a beard. He was tired of shaving every morning for all these years. He'd grow a long black beard. That would surprise a few people, make them sit up and take notice. He laughed as he pulled the curtain aside and stepped into the dark shower.

Ollie served Les his iced tea. "About ready for harvest, are you?" she said.

"Just about, another week or so," he said. He slid the tea glass toward him.

"Jimmy Earl'll be helping out this year?" she said, wiping her long fingers on the tea towel she used for an apron. She was a tall, thin woman, muscular from hard work.

"Or I'll help him, one way or other," Les said with a smile. He took a long drink and waited for Ollie to leave, wondering how she had found out about Jimmy Earl.

Les watched Ollie as he ate. Soon she took an order over the telephone. "Okay, six hamburgers with everything and two chili burgers with mustard. All to go." She hung up the phone and tossed several meat patties onto the grill. "That was John Harrington down at the motel," she announced over her shoulder.

Soon the cafe had fifteen or twenty customers, and Ollie's daughter Jimmae was taking orders and serving while Ollie cooked. Les watched her finish the Harrington order, wrapping each burger in thin paper, then squeezing as many as she could into the box that the buns came in. She placed the boxes in two brown papers sacks and set them on the counter by the cash register. By the time Amanda came in to get them, the sacks were spotted with grease.

Les knew it was her without even looking, the way she moved through the door so quietly, catching it before it slammed, closing it softly. She never said any more than she had to. "Is this our order?" she asked Jimmae, nodding at the sacks.

Ollie called to her from the grill. "That's yours, honey. Six hamburgers and two chili burgers. A dollar and ninety cents. Your mother gone or something?"

Les was sure she wouldn't answer. She looked at the bag and held out the money. Jimmae took it and gave her change. Amanda hurried to the door, as if escaping, her head lowered over the sacks. Les imagined her thick brown arms, slick with grease.

By the time harvest started in mid-July, Jimmy Earl had come by the elevator three times to check on preparations. Les had completed none of the chores Jimmy had outlined for him, with the exception of spotting extra railroad cars, a job of which Les was prideful. Spotting cars was delicate work, he reasoned. The railroad agent had to trust you, to know that you wouldn't order too many and thereby tie up their business. And it was worse if you ran short: then the co-op farmers had to take their wheat to the elevator out on the Flats. You had to spot the cars exactly right. Les kept the agent's phone number on a slip of paper in his billfold and was vague when Jimmy Earl asked for it: "It's around here somewhere; I had it this morning. But I already talked to him, Jim; the cars're already spotted."

During harvest, Les sat in his chair on the front step and watched Jimmy Earl work. Jimmy climbed on the trucks and took a wheat sample, checking the dew content with a moisture gauge, then weighed the trucks, emptied the wheat, and weighed the trucks again empty.

Most farmers didn't start cutting till afternoon, when the dew count was lower, so Les had the mornings to himself. He woke early, went through the receipts from the day before so he'd know how many cars to spot, then waited for the newspaper, which he had recently asked Henry to deliver.

At six forty-five one morning, Les sat on the front steps, shirtless, in his overalls, drinking coffee. He watched the road till he saw Henry turn the corner at the Conoco and ride down toward the elevator, his newspaper sack flapping against him.

"You're early today," Les said.

Henry pulled the empty sack over his head and shoulders and tossed it into the bike basket. "I've got a job," he announced. "I've gotta get to work." He swayed back and forth on the bike, trying to make it stay upright without putting his feet on the ground.

"Where're you working?" Les asked.

"At the elevator out on the Flats. Helping my dad."

"When did you start this?"

"Today," Henry said, his voice rising on the second syllable. "Today's my very first day." He pedalled across the scale and off down the hill.

Les thumped his knee with the newspaper, wishing harvest were over. The kids didn't play at the elevator during harvest, there was too much commotion, and now Henry had a job.

Les took the rubber band off the paper and went back inside, stopping at the desk to put the rubber band in a jar, where he saved them. After he showered and dressed, he walked up town, carrying his paper.

The cafe was crowded with harvest hands: every booth and almost all the stools at the counter were taken. Jimmae gave Les his coffee and took his order, but he didn't get his eggs and hash browns till thirty minutes later, and she didn't refill his coffee cup once.

While he waited he read the classifieds carefully for the first time. Most apartments in the city were expensive, and most of the jobs required experience. Experienced short-order cook; experienced truck drivers; experienced night watchman. Maybe he'd just live on the money he got from Ed as rent for his part of the home place. But if he did that, how could he live in one of those high-priced apartments?

Les was in a sour mood by the time Ollie joined him after the rush. He closed the newspaper when she sat down with her coffee.

Ollie took off her glasses and wiped her face with a napkin, which came away greasy and stained with wheat-colored makeup. She crumpled the napkin and put it in the ashtray, then lowered her head over her coffee and blew on it. Finally she glanced at Les and spoke. "A little outa season, aren't you?" Les looked at her, uncomprehending.

"With that beard you'd make a good Santa," she said.

He felt his beard, which was several inches long by now, and untrimmed. It had grown in gray and white, not black as he had imagined. Ollie was the first person to mention it.

"I thought there for a while you'd just forgotten to shave," she said, sipping her coffee, glancing out the window.

He felt a faint satisfaction that someone had noticed his beard. Jimmy Earl had stared at it; Les had seen him, but he hadn't said anything.

"Time for a change," Les said, making another fold in his newspaper.

"Yeah, I been hearing a few things," she said. "Somebody said you're fixing to move to the city."

Les made yet another fold in the paper. "Yeah, I'm thinking about it."

"I don't know, Les. I wouldn't let anybody run me off if I was you," she said.

"Nobody's running me off."

"How's Jimmy Earl doing? He workin' out?" she asked.

"Yeah, pretty good. He can't spot cars though. That's important too. He can do everything else, but he can't spot cars."

"Well, he's new at it. He's a cattle man anyway, not a wheat man. But just remember, Les," and now she lowered her voice and spoke seriously, emphasizing her words with little waves of her long fingers. "That place is yours, like this place's mine. Jimmae helps out, but it's not the same. She's back to school as soon as it starts, and Jimmy Earl'll be back to Smokey's as soon as harvest is over, before you know it."

Les tried to follow her. She thought Jimmy was the reason he was moving. She had it all wrong. He could tell her he'd decided long before Jimmy was hired, he could set her straight. But it was too hard, he'd never get the words right. And it didn't matter anyway. She was right, Jimmy Earl would be gone before he knew it. And so would he. Harvest would be over in no time at all.

One afternoon near the end of harvest, Iris brought a load of wheat to the elevator. Les was in his chair out front when she pulled into the line of trucks waiting to be weighed. She waved to him. Self-conscious, and suddenly embarrassed to be sitting idle, he got up and went inside.

Jimmy was standing at the desk, hurriedly writing a receipt. He glanced up, frowning, as Les walked to the icebox and took out an R.C. Cola. Les opened the bottle with a church key that hung from the icebox.

"Can you get me one of those," Jimmy said. Les opened another and carried it to the desk. He sat it down in a litter of yellow receipts.

Iris stood in the doorway, wearing blue jeans and a man's white shirt, with the tails tied together in front. Her hair was covered with a red headscarf, except for a few sprigs that curled out at the sides.

"You all going to offer me one of those?" she said, smiling. It took Les a minute to know what she meant.

"Sure," he said, moving toward the icebox again.

Jimmy nodded at Iris on his way outside.

Les watched as she tipped her head back and drank. Her pink throat, dotted with freckles, pulsed as she swallowed.

His eyes moved down her body. Her shirt was unbuttoned, way too far: he could see the beginning of her breasts. He wanted to scold her then, to tell her to button up.

She wiped her hands on her jeans. "I almost didn't know you with your beard," she said.

"Oh," Les said.

"How's harvest going?"

While he searched for an answer, she went on. "Our combine's down. Ed's fixing the combine, so I'm driving the truck today. It's okay for a change, but I'd always rather drive the combine."

Les struggled to understand. His eyes kept moving back to her bosom, to the pink skin there, the soft bulges. She shouldn't come in here like this, he said to himself, closing his eyes. She didn't know what might happen.

Iris was still talking, saying something about supper. He struggled to hear.

"Come on out about six o'clock next Saturday," she said. She moved toward the icebox to put away her bottle.

"What are you saving all those papers for?" she asked. She pointed at the pile of neatly rolled newspapers that sat like a small pyramid beside the icebox.

"That's how I store them," he said. For he had saved every copy of the *Daily Oklahoman* since he had started subscribing. He had folded and rolled each one to look exactly as it did when Henry delivered it, then added each to the stack, which was growing tall and precarious.

Les stood at the back window of the elevator and watched the kids play on the boxcars. Henry and Amanda and the Jenson boys were climbing inside an empty car and seeing who could jump the farthest.

Henry seemed to be winning. He made a running start from the far side of the car and dived helter-skelter into the weeds and rocks and trash that bordered the shoulder of the train track. After every jump, he got up, shook himself off, and went back to do it again. The older Jenson boy, Joe Bill, was right behind him, landing every time with a curse. "Shit!" he would yell, or "Fuck!" Soon Henry was shouting "Son of a bitch!" when he landed.

Amanda and the younger Jenson boy took longer to jump and didn't curse when they landed. After awhile they started their own contest alongside the big kids.

Soon, Henry and Joe Bill started arguing over who was winning. Henry suggested they climb on top of the cars. "Okay," Joe Bill yelled at him, "but I'm going first." He led the way to the ladder at the end of the car and they climbed up, becoming two silhouettes, running across the top, stopping to look at something, pointing, running on. Amanda and the little boy stopped jumping and watched them.

"Come on up, you guys," Henry called.

The little Jenson boy went first, moving carefully from the first rung to the second. At the third rung he stopped and yelled at Amanda, who was right behind him on the ladder. "Get down! You can't come up here. This is for *boys*! Get down."

Amanda had reached the rung where his feet were. "Get going, Teddy. Hurry up!"

"Come on you guys," Henry called from the top.

"I'm gonna go around you, Teddy," Amanda threatened.

Teddy didn't move. Amanda grabbed one of his shoes and shook it. He screamed.

Les pushed open the door and started toward them. He would get Amanda down, then help the boy.

Teddy turned to look when he heard the door slam. "Oohh, Mandy, it's The Elevator Man. He's gonna get you. The Elevator Man's gonna get you." Still yelling his warning, but emboldened now, Teddy climbed to the top with Amanda right behind him.

The Elevator Man. Les stumbled towards the boxcar. That must be him. The boy had called him The Elevator Man. He stopped for a second and looked up. They were frightened of him, the boy had warned Amanda, they had both hurried up the side. *The Elevator Man.*

He was blinded, confused. The Elevator Man will get you. Yes, he would. He would touch their little bodies, their arms and legs, their little feet, he would touch them all over.

Les got halfway up the car before he fell, hitting the ground with a thud that the little kids heard first. They yelled for Henry and Joe Bill.

"He's just had the wind knocked out of him," Mr. Harrington said when he got there, after Henry ran down to the motel and told him to come quick. "He'll be okay." He unbuttoned Les' shirt and sent Henry into the elevator for a glass of water. When Les opened his eyes, Mr. Harrington repeated his diagnosis—"You just had the wind knocked out of you. You'll be okay"—and led him back inside.

"This was our best year in a long while," Ed said. He and Iris and Les were eating supper at the farm. "You boys had your hands full," he said to Les.

Les nodded, keeping his eyes to his plate. Ed seemed not to know that Jimmy had done most of the work. But what did it matter. Harvest was over, Jimmy was gone, at least till next year. Maybe by next year he'd be gone himself. To Gallup, New Mexico. The atlas called New Mexico "The Land of Enchantment." That sounded better than the City, and yet it was out of state, but not so far as California. Maybe he'd move to Gallup, New Mexico.

Dancing at the Holland

BY JOANNA HIGGINS

Holding the tiny face of her wristwatch with thumb and forefinger, she angles it toward the light. Bends to the task of reading the time. "Nine-thirty?"

I glance at the red digital numbers above the car radio. "Eight. Eight-thirty. We've got lots of time."

Vistas of fall-scorched woods, then Lake Huron in the distance, silver under morning light. Paper-birch along the highway. White, gold, celadon. Gold leaf-showers. Sunlight streaking through purple clouds intensifies the colors, the contrasts, the dying beauty. You can't look for too long before it starts hurting.

I ask if she needs to use a restroom.

"No."

I do. Nerves. Coffee. "I think we'll stop in Harrisville. Get out and stretch."

"You're the driver."

"But you can say whenever you want to stop."

"I don't need to."

"O.K. Look at those trees. Isn't that something?"

A brief look, vague, then inward again. "He always used to bawl me out for reading my newspapers when we went on trips. I'd have all my papers to catch up on, and he'd say, For cripe's sake, all this nice scenery and you read newspapers. How I loved to read."

"I know it."

"The fall was his favorite season. How he looked forward to the fall, that man. And then he died in the fall. No. July. I

170

don't care for it. Everything dying. I like the spring. All new life."

Driving is like carpentry, or cooking. The small sequential challenges that keep you focused. The possible victories. I drive. There's a swaying camper trailer to pass. I pass it. A detour that takes us down toward the lake for a few miles, then back up to the highway. I do that, encountering a fuming semi dragging itself through fine woods, despoiling the air. I pass it on a double-lane section that soon narrows.

"I think he'll be able to help," I say.

She looks, out of dimming eyes, at the empty highway ahead. "I don't know."

But I am hopeful, mainly because, two months ago, her ophthalmologist was; and this new doctor's brochure is so upbeat; and he, after all, said yes to this appointment.

Strung along the lake, old resort towns with their bait shops, marinas, and new McDonald's and Burger Kings alongside tacky souvenir shops and log cottage motels.

"Are you warm enough?" I ask.

"*Ja.*"

This word and a few favorite expressions are the only Polish words I hear her speak now. Once, at any gathering, there'd been long fluid exchanges, the words merging with laughter, and out of the laughter, more words, on and on until people went home.

"You be careful of your purse when we get there," she says. "Don't let me forget mine anywhere."

"I'll be careful. You want to stop and use a restroom before we get to the Interstate?"

"I don't care."

This means yes.

My mother is eighty-one and walks with great attention, her eyes on the untrustworthy pavement. She holds my arm tentatively, and in this way we negotiate curbs and heavy swing doors. Slow procession, but victorious. She doesn't fall or stumble or pull that weak muscle, which would cause excruciating pain and necessitate finding a hospital.

"Do you want anything to eat?" I ask. "They have home-made donuts and things." I know because this is my halfway point on trips up to visit her. My little routine. First fly to a downstate airport, then rent a car and drive for a few hours, then stop here. Then drive for a few more hours. The restroom is clean, the coffee strong, and they'll give you milk for it if you don't want the non-dairy creamer.

"Do you?" she says. "Get something." She works at pulling her wallet out of the crowded purse.

"No! Let me." We fight, but less than usual, and then she buys.

The walk, the restroom, the diversion of looking at things to buy and then buying something do us both good. Driving, I smell the blueberry muffins.

Beet fields, long, stretching to distant poplar windbreaks reduced by perspective. Fields striated by the fickle autumn sunlight. Dark green, lighter green. Fields once the floor of a vast sea.

"I told you I want a little service," she says.

This is a question. "Yes, you did."

"Before, I didn't want anything, but then I went to that Greco's funeral, and it was really nice for the people."

In my purse is a reminder to myself: *Just Say Yes*. This note necessary because of her volatile blood pressure and our history of argument, ineradicable differences.

"Before, you couldn't do that. Get cremated. Now you can. It's all different today. The Church understands."

Why bring this up now? We've had this hard conversation before. I suspect it's because of *today*, her conviction that it won't work out. Just another *ordeal*, and nothing but, her silences tell me. Something inside is mounting—my own blood pressure, maybe. Let's be a little *hopeful* for a change, I want to say. Let's give it a try, shall we? Anger collapses into the old depression, the old awareness: how in no time she can throw us both into the darker chasms.

"That Rosie," she says, "wants to be cremated, too."

"Look at all those sugar beets." Emerald green. Hunter green.

"Before, they wouldn't bury you in the Catholic cemetery, or give you a service. Now it's different."

Harvested sugar beets are gray-brown and lumpy, about the size of a large man's hands making double fists. I know this because I've been seeing huge piles of these beets outside fruit stands and grocery stores up north. Pyramids of sugar beets, piles of outsized carrots—high as one story houses. Sweating plastic bags of the gray beets stacked high; sweating bags of red-gold carrots. Hunters up there buy truckloads weeks before hunting season in order to lure deer to some spot. Elsewhere in the state, the beets are made into sugar. Pioneer sugar. Big Chief sugar. I'm seeing billboards advertising these companies. I don't know about the carrots.

"Rosie and I went to the undertaker's together. Everything's all set."

Pain like a burr sticks to the top of my nose, just under the bridge of my glasses. The bone there pulses with it.

"I want a little breakfast for people. Take them out somewhere afterward."

"All right."

If I go first, I'm thinking, then what? Where I live—a rural area a thousand miles away—a man forty-seven years old has just died of a heart attack. A young mother has just been killed in a head-on crash a few miles outside the village. Compared to everything else, death is easy.

"Look at those fields," I say. "Like a painting."

She humors me by pretending to look.

We are zooming through what is advertised, on another billboard, as "The breadbasket of Michigan." It is also Dow Chemical country. And the smell of natural gas, too, seeps into the car. The big thing up here is all the illegal dumping of toxic wastes, PCB's, and who knows what else. "There's so much cancer now," she has told me. "More than ever before. It makes you wonder." In restaurants I don't drink the water. Never order meat, or smoked fish, the region's specialty. We fight about this. She tells me I am anorexic, that my clothes hang on me, that I'll be wrinkled. I already am, though her eyes don't allow her to see how badly. At a Wendy's, one of her favorite places, I load up at the salad bar. "Look at this," I say. "Look how much," making a big production of it so she'll remember, but she doesn't.

"I still can't get over that Ella," she says.

"I know it." This we do agree on.

"Lose everything like that, all at once. That daughter of hers could have waited. She didn't have to sell that house right away. She must have wanted the money awfully bad."

We visited Ella, who'd suffered a minor stroke, at a place called Janet's Care Home and found her watching TV, on a brilliant Sunday afternoon, in one of three drape-drawn living rooms, each with a few silent ladies. Ella, ninety-some-years old, but with all her faculties, as they say, and able to walk with the help of one of those tubular stainless steel walkers that resemble the bow railing on a yacht. Not frail, as you'd imagine, but a woman with heft, substance—too much, it seemed, for that limbo. Her voice deep and full and pleased, as she told us her daughter had taken her out to dinner the night before. But this same daughter also had Ella's Siamese cat "put to sleep" after the house was sold, then told Ella the cat was with a neighbor. When Ella asked if she could be taken over to that neighbor's to see "Marcy," her daughter told her the truth.

"I'm still trying to get over it," Ella said that day, her deep voice striving to sound neutral, sociable.

Health, home, belongings, and then her beloved companion for over thirteen years. I'm amazed she's still upright, still able to form coherent words. Above all, go out to dinner with such a daughter.

"Put in a place like that, just waiting to die," my mother says. "But maybe she's not so bad, that daughter, if she takes her out to *dinner*—"

The driving is good. I've finally gotten the hang of this rental—a snazzy Pontiac, and work its buttons and knobs with ease. On admirable American suspension, we glide over this sea of still growing things and will be there in no time, but I'm thinking it would be nice to just keep going.

"I worry about you," she says. "All alone like that."

"I'll be O.K. Don't worry."

"I can't help it. What're you going to do?"

After, she means. After the cremation and little service and breakfast for friends. And then after that, when it's my turn.

"Manage."

"It's not so easy."

No McDonald's, Wendy's, Burger King along the truck route taking us into the city. With her, anything else is risky, but I turn into the parking lot of a steak house. Steerhorns for door handles, then we're in near-absolute dark. I could kill myself for this stupidity. A half-invisible woman greets us and says our eyes will adjust. My mother grasps my arm, as we totter after this woman.

"How come it's so dark in here" my mother asks our waitress—pretty and young and not haughty. She laughs like a farmgirl, and my mother later pronounces her "nice." The food also astonishes her—so much! so good! and so reasonable too, you'd pay almost that much at Wendy's. Two unadjusted businessmen stumble after our laughing waitress, her pearly skin gleaming in this cave.

Today, for her, I eat. Corned beef on rye. A large salty pickle. With our water from Dow Chemical land, we take aspirin.

"Why do you suppose they keep it so darn dark in here?" she asks.

"It's just a bar. A cocktail club. They have entertainment at night."

She looks around. "It seems kind of crazy."

Before leaving, we use a well-lighted ladies' room, and then stumble through bar-murk all over again.

The ophthalmologist's clinic is in a converted brownstone with steep concrete steps. Climbing them is, for her, a form of penance. Inside, the usual. A modernized reception room with cool young women working behind a high counter. Today is a "low vision" day, and we are alone in the waiting room. Her name is called almost at once. I follow her into a narrow, high-ceilinged room where the light is blue-gray and chilling.

An older woman with ash-blonde hair in a short, trendy style does not introduce herself but gets right down to business, asking questions we'd already answered on forms sent weeks earlier. The woman's voice is shallow and gritty; little girlish yet hard. Quiet tones suited for terrorizing. Her pressed lab coat, her downy, aging skin, her voice all remind me of certain nuns I'd had in various parochial schools. Cranky, volatile beings smelling of starch and a hot iron. My mother answers the questions like a school kid trying too hard. Her small hands—heavy-veined, liver-spotted—are linked together in her lap and look cold.

The woman turns off the lights and starts one of her machines. E-chart letters appear on an opposite wall.

"Can you see that?"

"No."

Her movements convey sentences of disapproval as she turns on the lights again and takes what appears to be a large sketchbook from a table. She hands my mother a black plastic object resembling an out-of-proportion mirror, and tells her to cover her left eye. Then the woman stands in the middle of the room and, holding the sketchbook in front of her, opens to its first page. A large black numeral eight.

"Can you see that? What is it?"

My mother's hand is shaking. The black disk slides off the lens of her glasses.

"Hold it straight. Keep it covered. With the—" She says a word that sounds like *occular*.

My mother does not know this means the black thing.

"Fix it for her," the woman tells me. Gently I raise the disk against the lens, then go back and sit down.

"Now. What's this?" She points again.

"Eight."

She flips a page. "And *this*."

"It looks like a five."

"It is." Another page. "And this?"

"I don't know."

"Guess."

"Guess?"

"*Guess*."

"A six."

It is a smaller eight.

And so on.

The woman turns off the overhead lights again, projects a four-inch square of light on the darkened far wall, gives my mother a piece of cardboard with a circle cut out of the center, and tells her to hold it out, both arms fully extended.

My mother holds it half-extended, her elbows bent. The woman tries to correct this, then gives up. Anxious about this new test, she is not paying careful attention to the directions.

"Look through the circle with your left eye and find the light."

My mother moves the square of cardboard up and down, and from side to side.

"Can you see it?"

"No."

"*Find* it."

The cardboard slides around on air.

"See it?"

"No."

"Try the other side." And when my mother fails to comprehend, "Your *other* eye. All right. See it?"

The woman flips on the fluorescent overheads and snatches the cardboard away. She dumps a tray of objects that look like small rouge containers out on the table. As they clatter out and spin, she gives rapid new directions. The idea, I gather, is to put related colors together, or closest colors next to each other. They're in pastel shades ranging from blues and grays to mauves and pinks. My mother leans over this task as she leans over her wristwatch to read the time. When she finishes, working too fast, too carelessly, the woman turns over the tray, and holding the containers in place, notes numbers, then lets them fall again. They rattle down, rolling everywhere.

"Again."

I want to say something. I want to slam this woman. But years of conditioning in parochial schools, I suppose, keeps me immobile and diffident. That fear of making everything worse.

The woman takes my mother's blood pressure. It is two-ten over one hundred. "You poor thing!" she says, putting a whited arm around my mother's shoulders. Sudden terror humanizes her.

My mother asks me to leave. I've made her nervous, watching, she says. All this has. Everything.

In the waiting room, a scented magazine advertisement gilds my hands with some deadly, overpowering aroma. I throw the magazine down and go outside. It feels like rain, a storm. Nice, like spring, unsettled and promising, but leaves are flying down, skidding along sidewalks and streets, gusting in swirls along strips of green lawn. In an old neighborhood off the main street, a portable sign advertises undrugged meats and oat bran. A health food store, in another brownstone. Inside, absurdly small pears are ninety-nine cents each. I buy two.

The doctor tells me he can do nothing for her. No, those special lenses won't work. Not at all. Not even closed-circuit TV magnification? No. There's been a great change in the two months since he received the letter from her ophthalmologist. He gives me a deck of cards with large, bright numerals. He gives me a two-hundred-watt lightbulb. And to make her life easier, he says, he will get the state to do some things. The telephone company. An income tax deduction. Literature from Lansing. A large-print Bible.

A perky, kind, older gentleman—"a lot of personality," she will later say. "Not like that other one, the Battle Axe. How come he has such a person working there anyway? Do you suppose it's his *wife*?" In Polish she'll call the woman a witch.

The visit costs a hundred and eighty dollars. Had the doctor been able to help, it would have been much more. She counts out nine twenty-dollar bills kept in an envelope—the clinic will not, they informed us ahead of time, fool around with insurance.

We use the restroom. Make sure we have our purses.

On the truck route, wet leaves smack the windshield. I reach in back, grab the lightbulb and throw it out the window. Somebody blares a horn.

"You're going to cause an accident!"

"How's your pressure?"

"It's still high. I can feel it."

Rain and whipping crosswinds on the expressway, the car swaying.

"I knew it," she says. "I didn't think he could help. But at least now I know for sure."

A hundred and eighty dollars to know. Plus the trip, the stress, that woman, the trouble of it all: my fault.

The driving is good—outracing the storm, other cars, fiddling with the radio, looking for something nice. The sky behind us is blue-black, fractured every so often by lightning. She's relaxed in her wide, cushioned seat, as if ready, now, for a nap. Not mad at me. I know the variables within these

silences of hers. This one is beneficent. Now she doesn't seem
to mind the storm, the traffic, everybody rushing, edging
over the new sixty-five-mph limit. I don't mind either, though
my headache won't let go. It's good, this taking off, this
zooming away. Even if homeward.

At a moribund Holiday Inn in Bay City, we're given a room
on the fourth floor, facing the Saginaw River. The corridor is
garishly lit, high up, by vertical fluorescent lights resembling
bug lights. Our room is cold and feels damp; the squally rain
has caught up with us and glazes the big window, rain like
gravel thrown at the glass, one handful after another. Rush
hour traffic crossing a bridge separates on our side and flows
to either side of the motel. Light streaming apart in the
streaming rain, flowing neon tubes, an arabesque, and we at
its darkened heart.

I start up the boxy radiator. Noisy heat gusts. I turn on all
the lamps. We claim the room with our clothes, toiletries and
pill bottles. It warms.

Three aspirin, but pain fills my head like a cold. "Are you
hungry?" I ask. As each word reverberates, so does the ache.
"Should we just call room service?" I do not want food. What
I want is a hot shower, another aspirin or two, and then, for
eight hours anyway, no more images.

"Is there a Ponderosa, maybe?" she says.

I translate: The Ponderosa in her town has shut down.
Become something else. Wouldn't it be nice if, *etc.*

"They have a salad bar," she adds.

In grade school, the nuns taught us that with certain sins,
stealing, say, or slander, or sins wreaking havoc on another's
heart, penitence alone may not be enough for forgiveness, for
Absolution. There must also be conscious acts of reparation.

I call for directions.

We dress. We make sure we have purses. In slow procession
we walk down the corridor, under the bug lights. Negotiate
elevator, heavy doors, car doors. Wind, much colder. Raw
lakeport air. Rain. Dark slashed by headlights, so many, and
then a Ponderosa's illumination and clatter, entering like
shards.

As we age, each defeat registers with more and more of a
punch, it seems, and that may be why we all wind up looking

so beaten-up at the end. Tonight I feel sore everywhere. But our table is covered with heaped plates, the aspirin is doing its work, and this waitress, too, is kind. Crazily, it begins to seem like an *outing*, some kind of a celebration.

In the morning, frost on the car. A purple mountain range of clouds rimming the land. Nearly level sunlight creates long shadows, and those striations on the beet fields. Green against green against papery standing corn. Spectacular clarity—for me. I don't say, *Look*.

Spacious farm country becomes tourist clutter along both sides of the "scenic" Northwoods Highway. Restaurants have signs in their parking lots. NO SEMI'S: But Lake Huron is a gray, shimmering expanse under autumn clouds that touch the horizon.

At a red light in one of the lakefront towns, she says, "That's The Holland. We used to have such a good time there."

"You did?"

"On trips north when we lived in Detroit. Such a good time."

A corner building a few stories high. Sandstone-colored brick. Large plate-glass windows in which fishing nets are propped. A sign—FISHING LICENSES.

"We'd stop there and dance. We had a grand time."

Miles later, the road following postcard shoreline now, I'm still thinking about that. The boat-like Chryslers and Buicks and Plymouths. The smell of lake perch frying. Of beer. Cigarettes. Sen-sen on the breath. Clove chewing gum. Men in rumpled suits, double-breasted, with flaring lapels. Hair short and gleaming; burnished cheekbones. And the young women in their high, strappy heels and short dresses with narrow waists and full, wide, confident shoulders. Their lips a deep red, with rouge to match. Fingernails, too. A certain, glistening red against powdered-pale skin. And eyebrows, eyelashes, darkened with tiny red Maybelline brushes. And those costly silk stockings, with their dark seams, and dark oblongs at the heel. Dancing, these survivors of poor farms and educations and migrations to the city, these survivors of the Depression. Survivors with no visible scars, dancing to big band music on the juke box—casually, joyously arrogant, knowing that in Detroit they'd had the real thing.

"Did they have one of those spinning ballroom globes at The Holland? Over the dancers?"

She knows what I mean, but can't remember. In Detroit, she says, they did.

The FM station fades. I turn the dial, looking. Two downstate stations, at least, are playing old rock and roll hits. My Holland Hotel. I listen for a moment, recognizing the tunes and allowing an old pain to swell again, a kind of homesickness—that remembering.

After my marriage failed, the first job I took involved a lot of car travel, and I was amazed to find several stations playing "classic" rock all day, creating the illusion that time hadn't happened. Driving, I punched buttons, going back and forth from one to the other, excising commercials and news and weather, wanting only the music. Finally I had to stop. Hazardous to mental health. Better to come back and find everything changed, everything new.

A grand time. But she did not sound regretful or sad—in the remembering.

On the radio now, something appropriate to the day, the season, the circumstances.

"That's nice," she says. "What is it?"

"Beethoven. It's called 'The Leonora Overture.'"

"It's nice. I like it."

"I'll get you the tape." I turn up the volume on that austere, noble clashing. The mournful, distant horns.

"Remember that time you took off in the Hudson," I say. "And drove us to Detroit? Just you and me?"

"You remember that? You were just a baby, only two years old."

"Mostly I remember coming back. How the house was all fixed up, modernized. And they were still working on it, Dad and Grandpa, when we walked in. Everybody seemed embarrassed."

The leafy, dull-brass chandeliers gone, and in their place, something modern, with small chimney lamps. A new dining room set. And throughout the big Victorian rooms, a clean, confection smell of new paint, varnish. Pastel colors, the old flowered wallpaper gone. And the outside world flowing in, dazzling, as if there were no glass in the windows. It might have been summer, or fall—I no longer remember the season, but the feeling in the house was of spring—spring cleaning, big projects, exhaustion, happiness, change.

"I almost killed you."

"You mean driving? An accident?"

"No."

I wait, scared now, knowing without knowing, as I probably did then.

"I was...I wanted to die. I didn't care. We gave up everything in Detroit, a nice house and good jobs, to go back there. And what? He was drunk all the time. Men from the cement plant would come and tell me they were covering for him...Here, I go back to take care of Mama when she got sick, because nobody else up there would, and then everything goes—haywire. So I wanted to die, but I worried about you, who was going to take care of you? *He* couldn't. Filthy sick, throwing up, the d.t.'s, and Pa so mad all the time, I was afraid he was going to kill him, knowing how Pa was, such a fighter. You probably don't remember, and I'm glad. He was quiet, anyway. He never raved, like some men. Or got violent. I'll say that much for him."

I drive, eyes on the no-passing line. *Me*, I'm thinking, but that falls away into some larger sorrow—for a young woman and a child in a bullet-like Hudson, flying past The Holland, heading for Detroit, and eternity, wherever that may be. Sorrow for her bitterness, still, after all these decades.

"How were you going to do it?"

"I didn't know! I thought: in the car, maybe. Run the engine. Then halfway to Detroit, I thought maybe I could get my old job back, live there again. But on the outskirts nothing was familiar. I got lost and then, after a while, just turned around. We stayed at some place near Tawas for a week. You liked the water and didn't want to leave."

I watch the clouds, where I can. Silent massive turbulence over the calm lake. Gray and blue and charcoal.

"I wasn't going to tell you. I never wanted to tell you."

All these years. What words of mine to reach that depth? Relieve the press of emotion. Hers. Mine. Her words parting curtains upon curtains of loss. Guilt. That distance between us all this time, the withholding, the way the air used to go storm-still around her, the way she would hide out in her bedroom at the top of the house, crying, alone, up there.

Trying to get away from us—the storm lasting, sometimes, several days. The exile. In contrast, I hardly remember his d.t.'s.

"But you didn't do it," I say finally. "You went back."

She broods for at least a mile. "It wasn't in me."

"If it doesn't get any worse," she says, "I'll be able to manage alone O.K."

Again, hope. A variation, inversion of the theme. I hear it in her voice, and the fragile resolve there. It touches me.

"He said it may have bottomed out," I tell her. Central vision almost totally gone, he'd said. Some peripheral remaining. But how much, and for how long, he couldn't say.

"If it does, though, I just don't know . . ."

"Do you want to come stay with me?" I would like to think this could work.

"No. That's no good."

She would die of loneliness, we both know, away from her house, alone all day, and so far from her friends, her "roots," as she says. Also, we would probably fight. Better Janet's Care Home. Which would kill me.

"Then I'll try to come up more often."

"You got your job. Your life. You can't be spending so much money . . . . It's only the holidays that're bad."

"I know it." For me, too. Terrible, in fact.

"Still, what can a person do but keep going? You can't expect things to be easy when you're old. I had my fun."

Gloomy tonalities now, smudged with regret. The old ominous stuff, vaguely wrathful, and conveying, like that woman's in the doctor's office, unspoken, angry sentences, the nutrients of guilt. Mine.

But miles later she wakes from a doze and says, "You know, that Ella doesn't have it so bad there, such a nice warm place. All those people to visit with. She's got it pretty good."

I drive, but want to keep watching those big shifting veils out over the lake, dark-promising, light-promising. I'm looking, looking, as the road curves along the shore, then away again into woods.

She wakes again. "Where are we?"

"Almost home."

"Can we stop at the store?"

"I'll go. What do you need?" When I visit, food shopping—in the luxury of a car, with a "chauffeur"—is a big thing for her. We've already done a lot this time, so I'm curious.

"A few heavy things I forgot. I can't carry them on the Dial-a-Ride. I made another list."

"All right." Once, we'd fight at this point. That is, I—driven to the end of endurance—would say something finally wounding and irrevocable, the truth probably, and she would respond with the worst silence in her arsenal.

"Wasn't that corned beef good," she says, "at that place?"

"It was."

"Where do they find good corned beef like that, I wonder. What do you want for supper? I have a little of that chop suey left I could warm up."

"That sounds fine." I will eat the over-cooked vegetables. The leftover white rice that has been frozen. So what? How can it seem—given all this—a big deal?

"Or should we go out and get something? No, let's stay in. We had enough eating out."

"If you're not too tired."

"I'm not tired at all—just sitting! We'll have a nice supper at home."

I translate, zooming northward, again, the two of us once again. She will see this through. We will.

Is It Sexual Harassment Yet?

BY CRIS MAZZA

Even before the Imperial Penthouse switched from a staff of exclusively male writers and food handlers to a crew of fifteen waitresses, Terence Lovell was the floor captain. Wearing a starched ruffled shirt and black tails, he embodied continental grace and elegance as he seated guests and, with a toreador's flourish, produced menus out of thin air. He took all orders but did not serve—except in the case of a flaming meal or dessert, and this duty, for over ten years, was his alone. One of his trademarks was to never be seen striking the match— either the flaming platter was swiftly paraded from the kitchen or the dish would seemingly ignite spontaneously on its cart beside the table, a quiet explosion, then a four-foot

column of flame, like a
fountain with floodlights of
changing colors.

There'd been many rea-
sons for small celebrations at
the Lovell home during the
past several years: Terence's
wife, Maggie, was able to
quit her job as a keypunch
operator when she finished
courses and was hired as a
part-time legal secretary.
His son was tested into the
gifted program at school.
His daughter learned to
swim before she could walk.
The newspaper did a feature
on the Imperial Penthouse
with a half-page photo of
Terence holding a flaming
shish-kebab.

Then one day on his way
to work, dressed as usual in
white tie and tails, Terence
Lovell found himself stopping off at a gun store. For
that moment, as he ap-
proached the glass-topped
counter, Terence said, his
biggest fear was that he
might somehow, despite his
professional elegant man-
ners, appear to the rest of
the world like a cowboy
swaggering his way up to
the bar to order a double.
Terence purchased a small
hand gun—the style that
many cigarette lighters
resemble—and tucked it into
his red cummerbund.

It was six to eight months prior to Terence's purchase of the gun that the restaurant began to integrate waitresses into the personnel. Over the next year or so, the floor staff was supposed to eventually evolve into one made up of all women with the exception of the floor captain. It was still during the early weeks of the new staff, however, when Terence began finding gifts in his locker. First there was a black lace and red satin garter. Terence pinned it to the bulletin board in case it had been put into the wrong locker, so the owner could claim it. But the flowers he found in his locker were more of a problem—they were taken from the vases on the tables. Each time that he found a single red rosebud threaded through the vents in his locker door, he found a table on the floor with an empty vase, so he always put the flower back where it belonged. Terence spread the word through the busboys that the waitresses could take the roses off the tables each night *after* the restaurent was closed, but not before. But on the whole, he thought—admittedly in retrospect—the atmosphere

I know they're going to ask about my previous sexual experiences. What counts as sexual? Holding hands? Wet kisses? A finger up my ass? Staring at a man's bulge? He wore incredibly tight pants. But before all this happened, I wasn't a virgin, and I wasn't a virgin in so many ways. I never had an abortion, I never had VD, never went into a toilet stall with a woman, never castrated a guy at the moment of climax. But I know enough to know. As soon as you feel like *some*one, you're no one. Why am I doing this? *Why?*

So, you'll ask about my sexual history but won't think to inquire about the previous encounters I *almost* had, or *never* had: it wasn't the old ships-in-the-night tragedy, but let's say I had a ship, three or four years ago, the ship of love, okay? So once when I had a lot of wind in my sails (is this a previous sexual experience yet?), the captain sank the vessel when he started saying stuff like, "You're not ever going to be the most important thing in someone else's life unless it's something like he kills you—and then only if he hasn't killed anyone else yet nor knocked

with the new waitresses seemed, for the first several weeks, amiable and unstressed.

Then one of the waitresses, Michelle Rae, reported to management that Terence had made inappropriate comments to her during her shift at work. Terence said he didn't know which of the waitresses had made the complaint, but also couldn't remember if management had withheld the name of the accuser, or if, when told the name at this point, he just didn't know which waitress she was. He said naturally there was a shift in decorum behind the door to the kitchen, but he wasn't aware that anything he said or did could have possibly been so misunderstood. He explained that his admonishments were never more than half-serious, to the waitresses as well as the waiters or busboys: "Move your butt," or "One more mix-up and you'll be looking at the happy end of a skewer." While he felt a food server should appear unruffled, even languid, on the floor, he pointed out that movement was brisk in the kitchen area, communication had to get the point across quickly, leaving no room for

people off for a living—otherwise no one's the biggest deal in anyone's life but their own." Think about that. He may've been running my ship, but it turns out he was navigating by remote control. When the whole thing blew up, *he* was unscathed. Well, now I try to live as though I wrote that rule, as though it's *mine*. But that hasn't made me like it any better.

There are so many ways to humiliate someone. Make someone so low they leave a snail-trail. Someone makes a joke, you don't laugh. Someone tells a story—a personal story, something that mattered—you don't listen, you aren't moved. Someone wears a dance leotard to work, you don't notice. But underneath it all, you're planning the real humiliation. The symbolic humiliation. The humiliation of humiliations. Like I told you, I learned this before, I already know the *type*: he'll be remote, cool, distant—*seeming* to be gentle and tolerant but actually cruelly indifferent. It'll be great fun for him to be aloof or preoccupied when someone is in love with him, genuflecting, practically prostrating herself. If he

confusion or discussion. And while talking and joking on a personal level was not uncommon, Terence believed the waitresses had not been working there long enough for any conversations other than work-related, but these included lighthearted observations: a customer's disgusting eating habits, vacated tables that appeared more like battlegrounds than the remains of a fine dinner, untouched expensive meals, guessing games as to which couples were first dates and which were growing tired of each other, whose business was legitimate and whose probably dirty, who were wives and which were the mistresses, and, of course, the rude customers. Everyone always had rude-customer stories to trade. Terence had devised a weekly contest where each food server produced their best rude-customer story on a 3 × 5 card and submitted it each Friday. Terence then judged them and awarded the winner a specially made shish-kebab prepared after the restaurant had closed, with all of the other waiters and waitresses providing parodied royal table service, even to the point of spreading the napkin across the

doesn't respond, she can't say he hurt her, she never got close enough. He'll go on a weekend ski trip with his friends. She'll do calisthenics, wash her hair, shave her legs, and wait for Monday. Well, not *this* time, no sir. Terence Lovell is messing with a sadder-but-wiser chick.

winner's lap and dabbing the
corners of his or her mouth
after each bite.

The rude-customer con-
test was suspended after the
complaint to management.
However, the gifts in his
locker multiplied during this
time. He continued to tack
the gifts to the bulletin
board, whenever possible:
the key chain with a tiny
woman's high-heeled shoe,
the 4 × 6 plaque with a
poem printed over a misty
photograph of a dense green
moss-covered forest, the single black fishnet stocking.
When he found a pair of
women's underwear in his
locker, instead of tacking
them to the bulletin board,
he hung them on the inside
doorknob of the woman's
restroom. That was the last
gift he found in his locker
for a while. Within a week
he received in the mail the
same pair of women's
underwear.

Since the beginning of the
new staff, the restaurant
manager had been talking
about having a staff party to
help the new employees to
feel welcome and at ease
with the previous staff. But
in the confusion of settling
in, a date had never been
set. Four or five months af-

Yes, I was one of the first
five women to come in as
food servers, and I expected
the usual resistance—the
dirty glasses and ash-strewn
linen on our tables (before
the customer was seated),
planting long hairs in the
salads, cold soup, busboys
delivering tips that appeared

ter the waitresses began work, the party had a new purpose: to ease the tension caused by the complaint against Terence. So far, nothing official had been done or said about Ms. Rae's allegations.

During the week before the party, which was to be held in an uptown nightclub with live music on a night the Imperial Penthouse was closed, Terence asked around to find out if Michelle Rae would be attending. All he discovered about her, however, was that she didn't seem to have any close friends on the floor staff.

Michelle did come to the party. She wore a green strapless dress which, Terence remembered, was unbecomingly tight and, as he put it, made her rump appear too ample. Her hair was in a style Terence described as finger-in-a-light-socket. Terence believed he probably would not have noticed Michelle at all that night if he were not aware of the complaint she had made. He recalled that her lipstick was the same shade of red as her hair and there were red tints in her eye shadow.

Terence planned to make it an early evening. He'd brought his wife, and, since to have been left on greasy plates or in puddles of gravy on the tablecloth. I could stand those things. It was like them saying, "We know you're here!" But no, not *him*. *He* didn't want to return to the days of his all-male staff. Why would he want that? Eventually he was going to be in charge of an all-woman floor. Sound familiar? A harem? A pimp's stable? He thought it was so hilarious, he started saying it everynight: "Line up, girls, and pay the pimp." Time to split tips. See what I mean? But he only flirted a little with them to cover up the obviousness of what he was doing to me. Just a few weeks after I started, I put a card on the bulletin board announcing that I'm a qualified aerobic dance instructor and if anyone was interested, I would lead an exercise group before work. My card wasn't there three hours before someone (and I don't need a detective) had crossed out "aerobic" and wrote "erotic," and he added a price per session! I had no intention of charging anything for it since I go through my routine everyday anyway, and the more the merrier is an aerobic dance motto—we like to

this was the first formal staff party held by the Imperial Penthouse, had to spend most of the evening's conversation in introducing Maggie to his fellow employees. Like any ordinary party, however, he was unable to remember afterwards exactly what he did, who he talked to, or what they spoke about, but he knew that he did not introduce his wife to Michelle Rae.

Terence didn't see Maggie go into the restroom. It was down the hall, toward the kitchen. And he didn't see Michelle Rae follow her. In fact, no one did. Maggie returned to the dance area with her face flushed, breathing heavily, her eyes filled with tears, tugged at his arm and, with her voice shaking, begged Terence to take her home. It wasn't until they arrived home that Maggie told Terence how Michelle Rae had come into the restroom and threatened her. Michelle had warned Mrs. Lovell to stay away from Terence and informed her that she had a gun in her purse to help *keep* her away from Terence.

Terence repeated his wife's story to the restaurant manager. The manager thanked him. But, a week later, after share the pain. My phone number was clear as day on that card—if he was at all intrigued, he could've called and found out what I was offering. I've spent ten years exercising my brains out. Gyms, spas, classes, health clubs... no bars. He could've just once picked up the phone, I was always available, willing to talk this out, come to a settlement. He never even tried. Why should he? He was already king of Nob Hill. You know that lowlife bar he goes to? If anyone says how he was such an amiable and genial supervisor... you bet he was genial, he was halfway drunk. It's crap about him being a big family man. Unless his living room had a pool table, those beer mirrors on the wall, and the sticky brown bar itself—the wood doesn't even show through anymore, it's grime from people's hands, the kind of people who go there, the same way a car's steering wheel builds up that thick, hard, black layer which gets sticky when it rains and you can cut it with a knife. No, his house isn't like that, but he doesn't spend a lot of time at his house. I know what I'm talking about. He'll say he doesn't remem-

Terence had heard of no further developments, he asked the manager what was going to be done about it. The manager said he'd spoken with both Ms. Rae and Mrs. Lovell, separately, but Ms. Rae denied the incident, and, as Mrs. Lovell did not actually see any gun, he couldn't fire an employee simply on the basis of what another employee's wife said about her, especially with the complaint already on file, how would that look? Terence asked, "But isn't there some law against this?" The manager gave Terence a few days off to cool down.

The Imperial Penthouse was closed on Mondays, and most Monday evenings Terence went out with a group of friends to a local sports bar. Maggie Lovell taught piano lessons at home in the evenings, so it was their mutual agreement that Terence go out to a movie or, more often, to see a football game on television. On one such evening, Maggie received a phone call from a woman who said she was calling from the restaurant— there'd been a small fire in one of the storage rooms and the manager was requesting

ber, but I wasn't ten feet away while he was flashing his healthy salary (imported beer), and he looked right through me—no, not like I wasn't there. When a man looks at you the way he did at me, he's either ignoring you or undressing you with his eyes, but probably *both*. And that's just what he did and didn't stop there. He's not going to get away with it.

Wasn't it his idea to hire us in the first place? No, he wasn't there at the interview, but looked right at me my first day, just at me while he said, "You girls probably all want to be models or actresses. You don't give *this* profession enough respect. Well," he continued, "you will." Didn't look at anyone else. He meant me. I didn't fail to notice, either, I was the only one with red hair. Not dull auburn...flaming red. They always assume, don't they? You know, the employee restrooms were one toilet each for men and

that Terence come to the restaurant and help survey the damage. Mrs. Lovell told the caller where Terence was.

The Imperial Penthouse never experienced any sort of fire, and Terence could only guess afterwards whether or not that was the same Monday evening that Michelle Rae came to the sports bar. At first he had considered speaking to her, to try to straighten out what was becoming an out-of-proportion misunderstanding. But he'd already been there for several hours—the game was almost over—and he'd had three or four beers. Because he was, therefore, not absolutely certain what the outcome would be if he talked to her, he checked his impulse to confront Ms. Rae, and, in fact, did not acknowledge her presence.

When a second complaint was made, again charging Terence with inappropriate behavior and, this time, humiliation, Terence offered to produce character witnesses, but before anything came of it, a rape charge was filed with the district attorney and Terence was brought in for questioning. The restaurant suspended Terence without pay for two weeks. All the waitresses, except

women, all the customary holes drilled in the walls, stuffed with paper, but if one restroom was occupied, we could use the other, so the graffiti was heterosexual, a dialogue, it could've been healthy, but he never missed an opportunity. I'd just added my thoughts to an ongoing discussion of the growing trend toward androgyny in male rock singers—they haven't yet added breasts and aren't quite at the point of cutting off their dicks—and an hour later, there it was, the thick black ink pen, the block letters: "Let's get one thing clear—do you women want it or *not*? Just what is the *thrust* of this conversation?" What do you *call* an attitude like that? And he gets *paid* for it! You know, after you split a tip with a busboy, bartender and floor captain, there's not much left. *He* had an easy answer: earn bigger tips. *Earn* it, work your *ass* off for it, you know. But who's going to tip more than fifteen percent unless... well, unless the waitress wears no underwear. He even said that the best thing about taking part of our tip money was it made us move our asses that much prettier. There was

Ms. Rae, were interviewed, as well as several ex-waitresses—by this time the restaurant was already experiencing some turnover of the new staff. Many of those interviewed reported that Michelle Rae had been asking them if they'd slept with Terence. In one case Ms. Rae was said to have told one of her colleagues that she, Michelle, knew all about her co-worker's affair with the floor captain. Some of the waitresses said that they'd received phone calls on Mondays; an unidentified female demanded to know if Terence Lovell was, at that moment, visiting them. A few of those waitresses assumed it was Michelle Rae, while others said they'd thought the caller had been Mrs. Lovell.

another thing he liked about how I had to earn bigger tips—reaching or bending. And then my skirt was "mysteriously," "accidentally" lifted from behind, baring my butt in front of the whole kitchen staff. He pretended he hadn't noticed. Then winked and smiled at me later when I gave him his share of my tips. Told me to keep up the good work. Used the word *ass* every chance he got in my presence for weeks afterward. Isn't this sexual harassment yet?

When the district attorney dropped the rape charge for lack of evidence, Michelle Rae filed suit claiming harassment, naming the restaurant owner, manager and floor captain. Meanwhile, Terence began getting a series of phone calls where the caller immediately hung up. Some days the phone seemed to ring incessantly. So once, in a rage of frustration, Terence

Of course I was scared. He knew my work schedule, and don't think he didn't know where I live. Knew my days off, when I'd be asleep, when I do my aerobic dance routine every day. I don't mind *who*ever wants to do aerobic dance with me—but it has to be at my place where I've got the proper flooring and music. It was just an idle, general invitation—an announce-

grabbed the receiver and made a list of threats—the worst being, as he remembered it, "kicking her lying ass clear out of the state"—before realizing the caller hadn't hung up that time. Believing the caller might be legitimate—a friend or a business call—Terence quickly apologized and began to explain, but the caller, who never gave her name, said, "Then I guess you're not ready." When Terence asked her to clarify, ready for what, she said, "To meet somewhere and work this out. To make my lawsuit obsolete garbage. To do what you really want to do to me. To finish all this."

Terence began refusing to answer the phone himself, relying on Maggie to screen calls, then purchasing an answering machine. As the caller left a message, Terence could hear who it was over a speaker, then he could decide whether or not to pick up the phone and speak to the party directly. He couldn't disconnect the phone completely because he had to stay in touch with his lawyer. The Imperial Penthouse was claiming Terence was not covered on their lawsuit insurance because he

ment—I wasn't *begging . . . any*one, him included, could come once or keep coming, that's all I meant, just harmless, healthy exercise. Does it mean I was looking to start my dancing career in that palace of high-class entertainment *he* frequents? Two pool tables, a juke box and big-screen TV. What a lousy front—looks exactly like what it really *is*, his lair, puts on his favorite funky music, his undulating blue and green lights, snorts his coke, dazzles his partner— his doped-up victim—with his moves and gyrations, dances her into a corner and rapes her before the song's over, up against the wall— that song's in the juke box too. You think I don't *know?* I was having a hassle with a customer who ordered rare, complained it was overdone, wanted it *rare*, the cook was busy, so Terence grabs another steak and throws it on the grill—tsss on one side, flips it, tsss on the other— slams it on a plate. "Here, young lady, you just dance this raw meat right out to that john." I said I don't know how to dance. "My dear," he said, "*every*one knows how to dance, it's all

was on suspension at the time the suit was filed.

When he returned to work, there was one more gift in Terence's locker: what looked like a small stiletto switchblade, but, when clicked open, turned out to be a comb. A note was attached, unsigned, which said, "I'd advise you to get a gun."

Terence purchased the miniature single-cartridge hand gun the following day. After keeping it at work in his locker for a week, he kept it, unloaded, in a dresser drawer at home, unable to carry it to work every day, he said, because the outline of the gun was clearly recognizable in the pocket of his tux pants.

a matter of moving your ass." Of course the gun was necessary! I tried to be reasonable. I tried everything!

One Monday evening as Terence was leaving the sports bar—not drunk, but admittedly not with his sharpest wits either—three men stopped him. Terence was in a group with another man and three women, but, according to the others, the culprits ignored them, singling out Terence immediately. It was difficult for Terence to recall what happened that night. He believed the men might've

Most people—you just don't know what goes on back there. You see this stylish, practically regal man in white tie and tails, like an old fashioned prince... or Vegas magician... but back there in the hot, steamy kitchen, what's *wrong* with him? Drunk? Drugs? He played sword fight with one of the undercooks, using the longest skewers, kept trying to jab each other in the crotch. The chef yelled at

asked him for his wallet, but two of the others with him said the men didn't ask for anything but were just belligerent drunks looking for a fight. Only one member of Terence's party remembered anything specific that was said, addressed to Terence: "Think you're special?" If the men had been attempting a robbery, Terence decided to refuse, he said, partly because he wasn't fully sober, and partly because it appeared the attackers had no weapons. In the ensuing fight— which, Terence said, happened as he was running down the street, but was unsure whether he was chasing or being chased—Terence was kicked several times in the groin, and also sustained several broken ribs. He was hospitalized for two days.

Maggie Lovell visited Terence in the hospital once, informing him that she was asking her parents to stay with the kids until he was discharged because she was moving into a motel. She wouldn't tell Terence the name of the motel, insisting she didn't want anyone to know where she was, not even her parents, and besides, she informed him, there probably wouldn't

the undercook, but Terence didn't say a word, went to the freezer, got the meatballs out, thawed them halfway in the microwave, then started threading them onto the skewer. Said it was an ancient custom, like the Indians did with scalps, to keep trophies from your victims on your weapon. He added vegetables in between the meatballs—whole bell peppers, whole onions, even whole eggplant, started dousing the whole thing with brandy. His private bottle? Maybe. He said we should put it on the menu, he wanted someone to order it, his deluxe kebab. He would turn off all the chandeliers and light the dining room with the burning food. Then he stopped. He and I were alone! He said, "The only thing my deluxe kebab needs is a fresh, ripe tomato." Isn't this incredible! He wanted to know how I would like to be the next juicy morsel to be poked onto the end of that thing. He was still pouring brandy all over it. Must've been a gallon bottle, still half full when he put it on the counter, twirled the huge shish-kebab again, struck his sword fighting pose and cut the bottle right in half. I

even be a phone in her room. Terence, drowsy from pain killers, couldn't remember much about his wife's visit. He had vague recollections of her leaving through the window, or leaning out the window to pick flowers, or slamming the window shut, but when he woke the next day and checked, he saw that the window could not be opened. Terence never saw his wife again. Later he discovered that on the night of his accident there had been an incident at home. Although Terence had instructed his eight-year-old son not to answer the phone, the boy had forgotten, and, while his mother was giving a piano lesson, he picked up the receiver just after the machine had clicked on. The entire conversation was therefore recorded. The caller, a female, asked the boy who he was, so he replied that he was Andy Lovell. "The heir apparent," the voice said softly, to which Andy responded, "What? I mean, pardon?" There was a brief pause, then the caller said, "I'd really like to get rid of your mom so your dad could fuck me. If you're halfway like him, maybe I'll let you fuck me too." There is an-

can hardly believe it either. When the bottle cracked open, the force of the blow made the brandy shoot out, like the bottle had opened up and spit—it splattered the front of my skirt. In the next second, his kebab was in flames—maybe he'd passed it over a burner, I don't know, he was probably *breathing* flames by then—so naturally as soon as he pointed the thing at me again, my skirt ignited, scorched the hair off my legs before I managed to drop it around my feet and kick it away. What *wouldn't* he do? Looks like he'd finally gotten me undressed. It's ironic, isn't it, when you see that news article about him—I taped it to my mirror—and how about that headline, "Pomp and Circumstance Part of the Meal." There sure were some circumstances to consider, all right. Like he could rape me at gunpoint any time he wanted, using that cigarette lighter which looks like a fancy pistol. I wanted something to always remind me what to watch out for, but I didn't take the lighter. Why not? I'll kick myself forever for that. There was so much to choose from. Now one of his red satin

other pause on the tape. Investigators disagree as to whether it is the caller's breathing or the boy's that can be heard. The boy's voice, obviously trembling, then said, "What?" The female caller snapped, "Tell your dad someone's going to be killed."

During Terence's convalescence, the Imperial Penthouse changed its format and operated without a floor captain, using the standard practice of a hostess who seated the guests and waitresses assigned to tables to take orders and serve meals. The restaurant's menu was also changed and now no longer offered flaming meals. When Terence returned to work, he was given a position as a regular waiter, even though by this time most of the male food servers had left the restaurent and were replaced with women. Michelle Rae was given a lunch schedule, ten to three, Wednesday through Sunday. Terence would call the restaurant to make sure she'd clocked out before he arrived for the dinner shift.

During the first week he was back at work, Terence came home and found that his wife had returned to get the children. In a few days,

cummerbunds hangs over my bed while he still has the lighter and can still use it!

When he said "staff meeting," he didn't mean what he was supposed to mean by it. You know, there was a cartoon on the bulletin board, *staff meeting*, two sticks shaking hands, very funny, right? But long ago someone had changed the drawing, made the two sticks flaming shish-kebabs on skewers. So the announcement of the big meeting was a xerox of that cartoon, but enlarged, tacked to the women's restroom door. *Be There or Be Square! Yes, You'll Be Paid for Attending!* You bet! It was held at that tavern. Everyone may've been invited, but I'm the one he wanted there. There's no doubt in my mind. What good was I to him merely as an employee? I had to see the real Terence Lovell, had to join the innermost core of his life. Know what? It was a biker hangout, that bar, a biker gang's headquarters. One or two of

she sent a truck for the furniture, and the next communication he had with her was the divorce suit—on grounds of cruel and unusual adultery.

them were always there with their leather jackets, chains, black grease under their fingernails (or dried blood), knives eight inches long. They took so many drugs you could get high just lying on the reeking urine-soaked mattress in the back. That's where the initiations were. No one just *lets* you in. Know what he said the first day we started working? The first day of the women food servers, he said, "You don't just work here to earn a salary, you have to *earn* the right to work here!" So maybe I was naïve to trust him. To ever set one foot in that bar without a suspicion of what could happen to me. That same ordinary old beer party going on in front— same music, same dancing, same clack of pool balls and whooping laughter—you'd never believe the scene in the back room. It may've looked like a typical orgy at first—sweating bodies moving in rhythm, groaning, changing to new contorted positions, shouts of encouragements, music blaring in the background. But wait, nothing ordinary or healthy like that for the girl who was chosen to be the center of his dark side—she'll have to be both the cause and cure for his violent ache, that's why he's been so relentless, so obsessed, so insane, he was driven to it, to the point where he had to paint the tip of his hard-on with 150 proof whiskey then use the fancy revolver to ignite it, screaming—not like any sound he ever made before—until he extinguished it in the girl of his unrequited dreams. Tssss.

The only thing left in Terence's living room was the telephone and answering machine. When the phone rang one Monday afternoon, Terence answered and, as instructed by his attorney, turned on the tape recorder:

caller: It's me, baby.
Lovell: Okay...
caller: You've been ignoring me lately.
Lovell: What do you want now?
caller: Come on, now, Terry!
Lovell: Look, let's level with each other. How can we end this? What do I have to do?
caller: If its' going to end, the ending has to be *better* than if it continued.
Lovell: Pardon?

caller: A bigger deal. A
          big bang. You ever
          heard of the big
          bang theory?

Lovell: The beginning of
          the universe?

caller: Yeah, but the big
          bang, if it started
          the whole universe,
          it also *ended* some-
          thing. It may've
          started the
          universe, but what
          did it end? What
          did it *obliterate*?

Lovell: I still don't know
          what you want.

caller: What do *you* want,
          Terry?

Lovell: I just want my life
          to get back to
          normal.

caller: Too late. I've
          changed your life,
          haven't I? Good.

Lovell: Let's get to the
          point.

caller: You sound anxious.
          I love it. You
          ready?

Lovell: Ready for what?

caller: To see me. To end
          it. That's what you
          wanted, wasn't it?
          Let's create the rest
          of your life out of
          our final meeting.

Lovell: If I agree to meet,
          it's to talk, not get
          married.

caller: Once is all it takes,

	baby. *Bang.* The rest of your life will start. But guess who'll still be there at the center of everything you do. Weren't you going to hang out at the bar tonight?
Lovell:	Is that where you want to meet?
caller:	Yeah, your turf.

Terence estimated he sat in his empty living room another hour or so, as twilight darkened the windows, holding the elegant cigarette lighter look-alike gun; and when he tested the trigger once, he half expected to see a little flame pop from the end.

Elvis

BY MARK NIEKER

The fall that I turned fourteen was the fall of Elvis' comeback special and the fall that my father, whom I had seen only on and off as I was growing up, came to stay with us to get better. My father was an alcoholic, and that summer he had just gotten himself discharged from a de-tox center up near Detroit, where he had lived and worked since his separation from my mother the year after I was born. I had seen my father maybe seven or eight times before that fall, but never for very long and always in my mother's presence. The last time, when I was twelve, he had driven down from Michigan to take my mother and me to Cincinnati for a weekend "holiday." "It's not a vacation," he told me over and over again, leaning over the front seat to look at me as we drove through central Indiana on the way to King's Island, the only amusement park I have ever been to. "It's a holiday. Like boys who are good have in England. Because even though you haven't had a full-time father, you've been a very good boy. You deserve to go to a holiday park like King's Island. If the British deserve one, then we deserve a holiday too."

I know now that my father had been planning that trip for weeks, even before he began calling my mother and asking her to let him take us to Cincinnati, where neither of them had been before. He had reserved two rooms at a nice downtown hotel for us, and was hoping to show my mother that weekend that he still loved her and me, and that he was through drinking for good and could at last be trusted.

I didn't know any of this at the time, of course. I didn't
know it for certain until much later. But that weekend was the
only time I had seen my father for any extended time before
the fall that he came to live with us. I liked him then. He was
tall and lean and seemed like a kind, patient man who could
look out for me and my mother and buy things for us that we
didn't have or wouldn't even think to ask for. He took me to
King's Island, and I sat in front with him, my mother alone in
the back seat, her hair blowing from the wind of the open
windows, all the way back from Ohio. He taught me how to
play "slap" on that ride back, and after awhile let me win
almost every time all the way through Indianapolis. The last
hour he began to ask me questions about myself, strange
questions that I had never been asked before by anyone: What
was my favorite sport? What did I want to be when I grew up?
What were the names of the boys I played with at school?

When we pulled up to our house, I wanted him to stay and
to invite him in but I knew that it wasn't my place for that. He
dropped our bags at the door, I walked him to the car, and I
remember the cigarette smell on his shirt as he hugged me and
kissed the top and the back of my head. He smelled to me like
a man, like what I would become, and he held my head in his
hands and looked at me as though we were the strangers to
each other that we were.

"Goodbye, bud," he said. "I'll call you soon and maybe we
can plan another holiday together. How would that be?"

I didn't want to cry in front of him, and to check myself I
pushed at the gap between my front teeth with my tongue as
he looked at me. He kissed my forehead, then he stopped the
car once midway down the street, turned around in his seat
and waved, and I didn't see him or hear from him again until
my mother told me that September that he was coming to rest
and to stay with us and that he would sleep with me in my
room.

My father wound up, in fact, sleeping most of the time out
on the couch in the front room. I was at school the day he
arrived and my mother picked him up at the bus station. He
told us that he didn't want to upset things more than he had
to, that he didn't want to keep me from having the privacy that
I had become accustomed to. My mother told me to bring his

bags—two leather, heavy traveling bags—into my room. "I'm very happy to have this opportunity," he said to her at dinner. "There were times, Claire, when I swear that I never thought I'd see you or our son again."

This kind of talk, and there was a lot of it in the house the first few days of my father's stay that fall, changed things irretrievably for my mother and me. We were, I think, both terribly frightened to be putting my father up. I didn't know then what had caused my mother to divorce him, but I was certain that it was related to his drinking, and that for some time it had been difficult for her to maintain whatever strength she had needed to separate herself from him. Whatever had happened between them that weekend in Cincinnati had resigned her, though, to making a life without him. There was little discussion of him in our house as time went by. I don't know how often my mother heard from him, and though she must have missed him, she was, I think, happy at the time he arrived to feel that part of her life completed. From the moment, though, that my father arrived that fall, the house became all at once tense and uncomfortable and crowded.

We talked, at least, about being crowded, that first night when I came home from school. I came in the kitchen door and there was my father, thinner than when I had seen him last, in a short-sleeved cotton dress shirt and a dark pair of jeans. His back was to the door, and when I came in he didn't get up but turned around and opened up his arms as if to hug me. He put his cigarette down and smiled.

"Hello, Martin," he said, and waited for me to come to him.

I set my books down on the kitchen table, which was empty except for his cigarettes and a yellow glass ashtray I had never seen before. Though it was hot, he had on an undershirt and was deeply tanned. He seemed to me much older than I had remembered him. I walked over to him, not knowing what to do but feeling that something was certain to change for the worse because he was there, though I could not have imagined then what that change might be. He had a day-old beard with spots of light gray in it, and his arms looked thin, the veins sticking out inside his elbows and in his hands like an old man's. I remember him holding me and that smell of the cigarettes and the sad expression on my mother's face when I looked at her. My father still held me even when my mother came in from the other room and stood, as she never had to do before, waiting to kiss me.

From the beginning of his stay with us, my father, more than my mother or myself, was the most direct about the discomfort we now found ourselves in. He had, I knew, no job or car and very little money, and he had never lived near us even when he could have chosen to do so. He wasn't hostile, but he seemed to us drained and physically weak from going through de-tox, and he was not afraid to show us that he was thankful but also unhappy to be with us in my mother's house. We all let that be. My mother felt, I think, that we should perhaps indulge him in this remaining bit of pride because, though no one said it, we didn't know then when or even how he was going to leave.

He was not unkind to us, but for the first few weeks of his stay that fall, my father and I both kept largely to ourselves. One night when he was still in my room, I got up from bed and sat and looked at him, imagining what would happen while he was there and hoping that he would awaken and want to talk to me and explain what he had been doing all those years and what he was doing there now sleeping on the bottom mattress of my bed. He never woke up or tried to talk to me though, and as this distance remained, my mother silently became the leader for both my father and me, principally because we both recognized that she was the only person in that situation that fall by choice. She was the one, for example, who somehow became responsible for fixing us all dinner, though I had begun cooking for myself some time before my father's arrival. We both knew that she was a link between us and in exchange we each felt more obliged to look out for her than we might have otherwise. He and I both knew that we were only together because she had allowed him kindness and somewhere to stay. Whatever brought him there, my father recognized that just by taking him in she had already made her sacrifice. We both expected that acts of kindness and sacrifice were in return due back, especially toward her, but between each other we didn't know what was required or what, for ourselves, each act of kindness was to be.

The first thing my father did that fall that made me think we might be friends was to show me, one night while my mother was out, his Elvis Presley record albums. In de-tox he had roomed with a man who had all the early, pre-army Elvis records. My father told me that they listened to them all, all the way through, each afternoon as they sat on the porch with the other men of their living area, playing cards for cigarettes.

He had brought the records with him from Detroit in his travel bag and as he showed them to me for the first time, my father told me that he had gotten them from his roommate, an older black man whose name was Dwayne. He told me that Dwayne had become a drunk when in the same month his wife died of cancer and his son was killed by friendly fire in Vietnam. After he buried his son, Dwayne sat in his house for six weeks before his daughter, who was married and had moved away long before his wife got sick, came back to town to check on him. As my father told it, the daughter sat in this man's kitchen and cried, saying over and over, "Daddy, Daddy, Daddy," until Dwayne admitted to himself that he was drinking not because he wanted to die himself but because he didn't know what else to do.

The albums had plastic wrapped around them, and as he told me this my father smoothed out the wrinkles in the plastic of the record he was holding. "You're young yet and I hope you never have to feel that, Martin. That's the shits, to not even have any fucking family left to care for you."

When he said this, I wasn't certain if he was saying something to me about myself, or about me and my mother, or something only about himself. I guessed that Dwayne had left him the records, maybe as a gift when it was his turn to check out of the de-tox, but I felt that whatever this sadness was, it was more than I knew. Out of respect, I felt I shouldn't ask my father any more than he was telling on his own.

My father's favorite album was of the Sun Session recordings, the first recording, he told me, that Elvis had ever made. That night my mother was out with some friends and I was alone in the kitchen studying. The heat and quiet of the night must have made him want to do something, but I think he felt somehow that he had to have my permission to play the records. I brought my record player, a big black turntable in a case with speakers hinged to each side and a handle on the top, out to the kitchen while my father cleared my school books from the table.

"You ever hear real Elvis Presley before?"

I had seen his last two movies in the theater but didn't know, really, what my father meant. I didn't want to disappoint him though, so I didn't say anything until he had put the Sun Sessions album on the turntable.

"I've heard some," I said, but he cut me off before I began.

"Shit, this is something to hear, Marty. This boy was in his prime. Not much older than you are now and already doing something good with himself in his life, something that would last."

That night, before it got late and near the time my mother was due home, we listened to all of the Sun album, my father rocking almost silently, sitting sideways on the kitchen chair with his elbows up on his knees. I sat on the floor beside him and watched him and tried to listen for whatever it was I was supposed to be hearing. As I listened, I began to become afraid that my father would ask me to explain to him what I thought of the music. I hoped that my mother would return before then, but at the same time I also hoped that she would be late in returning or that she wouldn't come home that night at all. Sitting there in the kitchen, I imagined my mother in some kind of car accident, that my father and I would go to visit her and she would be happy to see us and to have us both as part of her family.

Two nights later, my father began drinking again. In his defense, he had been with us for almost three weeks at that point, and as I said before, for all of us it was difficult for him to be in the house. My mother, in particular, was beginning to suffer because of his presence. My father would sit home all day while she was at work and I was at school, and all he had was himself and the TV and, as I imagine it now, the feeling that his life was withering into something difficult to stand. He must have felt trapped and unable to help himself as long as he was there, but he had no job and very little money to begin anything new and he couldn't ask my mother, the only person who would help him, for any more than she had already given.

When he drank, I would come home from school and find him sitting in his shirt and shorts on the couch with the daily newspaper spread out or scattered across the front-room floor, listening to one of those early Elvis records, the volume turned up loud. It was time, my parents had agreed, that he begin to look for work again, but as far as I know, he was home all day. He would lie on the couch, with nothing to do until I came home, and after awhile I would try to stay out longer, until after the time that my mother came home, to avoid having to be with him alone.

He seemed to look forward to seeing her, and when she came home, he would get up then to talk to her and to ask her about her day. My mother was still a waitress at this time, and had come to depend on this time for herself. Though she never said this to him, it grew increasingly difficult for her to speak to him and to recognize that her return home and her conversation were so important. She still said nothing, though, even after the night, about a week after he began drinking again, that he pushed her up against the sink and began to unbutton his shirt and to kiss her neck and shoulders. He ran his hand roughly across her face and up the front of her blouse. She held back his chin until she managed finally to push him away. I thought he would hit her then, and though he began to swing at her, he stopped himself and instead hit the side of refrigerator hard near her head.

Hours later, my mother left the house in tears, but she said nothing much to him about what happened. A friend met her at the curb and she left me a phone number and told me to leave the house if things got out of hand with my father. I went to my room. I didn't know what would happen next, but I felt then that something had happened that was bigger than his going after my mother, that that night had somehow demanded something of me in a way that changed things.

It was just about dusk and it was too early to sleep but I was afraid to leave my room. My father didn't come to get me though. Instead, he put on the Sun Sessions and played over and over "Milkcow Blues Boogie," singing loudly and drunkenly over the record. I waited for some time until the music stopped and then went to the kitchen where the turntable was still set up on the table. He was sitting on the floor against the stove in a T-shirt and jean, rocking back and forth with his arms locked up around his knees. The turntable arm was stuck in the groove at the end of the record, and though I stood there in the kitchen doorway for some time, neither of us spoke.

I wanted to say something to him then, something that would straighten things out once and for all, but I didn't know what that would be. I just looked at him, hoping that he would be the one to say it. We both listened to the jumps on the record, and after a time he put his right leg down and slid it underneath his left. He pointed to the table with his cigarette fingers and told me to put on the album's other side.

My father and I listened silently to all of the album's first side. I slid down after a time against the wall in the doorjamb and waited, but he just sat. He looked straight ahead at the cabinets under the sink as though I wasn't there in the room with him. I was afraid to leave because I thought that might suggest something bad to him. I wanted, I guess, for him to be better because of my presence. I wanted for him to do something, or to give me a clue as to what I was to do, but he did nothing.

When the record ended, he finished his cigarette and went over to the table, using the top of the stove and the sink for support as he walked. After he flipped the record over, he turned the volume up all the way until the bass on the speakers distorted all of the sound but a loud and persistent crackling. He told me then to turn on all the ceiling lights in the house and to meet him out front on the porch.

It was the middle of October and the air had the crisp, moist smell of the first days of winter. The night was clear and black and as I stood on the sidewalk in front of my mother's house with my father, he pointed out to me the outlines of all the furniture in our front room. Then, he put his hand on my shoulder and walked me all around the side of the house, pointing as he had done before to the elements of the house strangely shadowed by the night. I still remember that "That's All Right" was playing when we got to my room and when my father turned to me, and for the first time since he had arrived that fall, kissed me. He kissed me right on the lips and his beard, which was a few days old, hurt my skin.

"This is your house, Martin," he said to me. "This is where you live. This isn't my home but it's your home and you're lucky to have a mother good enough to keep it for you."

He stopped until his voice came back and I waited for him. I could tell he was pushing toward something, and I thought that if he knew me better he would cry.

"You could be out here, Martin," he said after awhile. "You could live your life out here and this house would just be another fucking house that you pass, no more yours than any other. Do you understand me, son?" Then he said, "You need to learn this, Martin, before you become a man. Otherwise you learn it only when it's too late to do you good."

The music had stopped then and my father was crying. I tried to breathe in the air in a way that would make me feel more of the loneliness I could see in him. In the light from the house, I could see lines around his eyes and bumps on his face that looked like moles underneath the skin.

"Go on inside before your mother gets home," my father said. When I didn't move he said, "Go on, boy. I'll be in in awhile."

There was no wind but suddenly I was cold. I went inside, and when he didn't come in I cleaned up in the kitchen. I waited up for him but fell asleep before he returned. When I woke up in the morning, he was asleep on the couch in his T-shirt. When I came home from school, my mother was in the kitchen with two uniformed policemen and my father was dead.

It was years before I was able to let this feeling go, but when I saw the patrol car in front of my house that day, I somehow knew that he was dead, and as I walked to the house, before everything else started up again, I felt in some way relieved. I listened at the door for a moment and could see the policemen, both their hats on the table in front of them, but because of the refrigerator, I couldn't see my mother. For a moment then, I thought that maybe it was her, that she was the reason that they were there, but then I remembered her car out in front. When I walked in, they all looked at me. There was a moment before my mother looked at the policemen in a

way that made them the ones who would have to tell me. My
mother had been crying, and suddenly I was firmly and
completely scared.

The policeman closest to the door fingered the brim of his
hat. My father had been drinking. He had gone in to a liquor
store downtown to get some more to drink. He wasn't
stealing, the policeman said, but he didn't have enough money
to pay for what he wanted, and when the owner refused, my
father hit him and came around the counter after him. The
owner had a gun, and when he couldn't get my father off of
him, he got scared and shot him once in the stomach. My
father was dead before the ambulance reached the hospital.

I wasn't mad when I heard this, which, looking back, still
surprises me. Instead I felt the return of a sadness that I had
never really understood or recognized before. I looked at the
hands of the policeman on the table. Then I looked at my
mother. She was crying, her face and eyes were red. The other
policeman said to me, as if in explanation, "He had been in
trouble before, Martin, but he was not a thief. He was not
trying to rob the store, something just got out of hand was
all." When he said this, I knew somehow to go to my mother
and to hold her, and it wasn't until I could feel her tears on the
inside of my shirt that I wondered how the policeman had
learned my name.

We straightened up the house, of course, and buried my
father where we were in western Indiana, over three hundred
miles from Detroit, where he had lived all my life. His
parents were dead, and we didn't know anyone he knew. My
mother and I went through his things and found phone
numbers written on small scraps of paper but there were no
names on most of them. We guessed that they belonged to a
Michigan area code, but when my mother called, no one knew
my father. The hospital where he had been before he came to
us told us that my mother was listed as the person to contact in
case of emergency. We put all of his things back in his bags
and, because we didn't know what more to do with them, left
them on the floor in my closet.

I had fears at first that my mother would take to drinking. I
thought somehow that my father's drinking had been caused
by the sadness he brought with him, and that he had left that

with us even though he was dead. I began to realize, though, that, growing up, I had seen in my mother times when she was feeling what we both felt almost all the time the first months after my father's death. She didn't drink, of course. In fact, I don't remember ever seeing her have too much. We began to grow apart, then, probably just as all children grow apart from their parents. The distance felt severe to me, though, and to my mother, too, I'm sure, and we both watched ourselves in a way that made things more difficult. We were sad, and I didn't know then that the sadness could dissipate. My mother, I think, felt that the sadness she knew before had come back to reclaim her.

One night, it must have been a year or so after my father's death, my mother took out a picture of her and my father leaning up against the front of a dark, polished Chrysler. They were standing with their arms around each other, on a street with no gutters or sidewalks in what looked like early winter. She gave the picture to me to hold, and then with my help, she put it beside the pictures of herself and of me under the glass top of her dresser. I remember that it was hot that night and that my mother's hair, which was beginning to thin then, was matted on the side of her forehead from the heat. Later, she asked me if I'd like to see other pictures of her and my father, which she then brought down out of the attic. These moments are what has most remained, but then they were not enough, of course, to help to resolve things without me getting away.

That next summer, about a year and a half or so before I left my mother's house and moved to Ohio, my mother woke me up in the middle of the night. It was the middle of summer, and I had been out with my friends and had come in to sleep, a little drunk and hungover. When I woke up, she was holding my wrist and my elbow inside my arm. "Please come talk to me, Martin," she said. She rubbed my back and my shoulders. "I know that you're tired, honey, just sit up with me a little while, will you please."

I put on a T-shirt, went to the bathroom, then came into the front room, where it was dark but where I could see that my mother had been sitting. She had a glass on the table and the light was on in the kitchen. I was probably fifteen, maybe sixteen then. My mother was in her late thirties and, though she was tired and in her robe, was still an attractive woman. I remember thinking this as I stood in the hallway and looked at her in the half-light from the kitchen. She had been crying, and seeing her like that made me think of her, for a moment at least, as someone other than who she was.

"Jesus, you look so big in the dark, Marty," she said to me. "Come here and sit with me please."

She tucked her feet up under her legs and made room for me next to her on the sofa. For some reason I can't explain, though, I sat instead on the floor, with my back against the frame of the couch. I folded my arms across my knees and, before she began to talk, listened to traffic from the intersection down the block.

"I'm sorry I woke you, Marty," my mother said to me. "I'm just too sad to sit by myself tonight before I sleep. I can't sleep at all any more and I'm bone tired all during the day."

I didn't turn around but I could hear that she was straightening herself, fixing her hair and wiping her face as she said this.

"I was thinking about your father, Marty," she said after a while. "He was such a good man when he was your age."

"I don't miss him," I said. I wasn't sure really what she wanted me to do there. "Don't be sad about that, Mom," I said.

"I do. I miss him," my mother said. "I'm going to miss you too when you're a full man with all your own things to do."

I didn't know why she was saying this, but I wasn't surprised by it, really. I hadn't even thought at that time about leaving, yet I knew enough to recognize some of what she meant. My mother had never really talked to me about my father or about myself in this way, but for some time now, not talking about him had had pretty much the same effect. I wished then that I was up on the couch so that I could hold or comfort her. I just listened, and after she was quiet for a while, I put my hand on her ankle, which was cold and felt less like an ankle than something that had been pulled from a cool stream.

"You remind me, Martin, so much of what it was like then," she said. "You know what it was about your father? I've thought about this, Marty." She had stopped crying and was looking intently at the landscape picture on the opposite wall.

"It was that he looked at all the wrong things. He used to sit and stare. I asked him, over and over I'd ask him, what he was looking at. He'd say nothing, but there was something there that only he could see—something that was the wrong thing. Yes," she said after a while, "that's true. Because it was the wrong thing it brought him sadness, Marty. That's what drinking did for him. His drinking—at first at least—came to be a way to have some real wrong there, something he could point to."

When her voice trailed off, I turned all the way around to face her. I cradled my head at her feet in a way that I hoped would comfort her.

"I have to tell you this, Marty. The night before he died, when you were asleep, we were talking and I asked him about that and he said that it was so, and I asked him too what it was when we were younger that he was looking at. I didn't ask him out of spite, Marty, but I thought that if I could get him to tell me that then I could help him or make him somehow stop drinking again. I asked him, anyway, and he said it was all the wrong things in life. That it was getting bigger and that he couldn't tell himself now how to keep himself out of that hole.

"That's what a drunk was, he said. I remember his voice then. He said that that was his future and that any way he thought of it he was in that hole."

My mother wasn't crying hard, but I thought that she might, or that she had stopped crying hard only just before she came to waken me. "I just don't know what I could have done," she said to me.

"I loved your father once, Marty, you know that, don't you. At that moment I wanted to take him and to kiss him, but I couldn't. You understand. I couldn't do that. I did nothing, and then—I shouldn't say this to you but it's the truth, Martin, please don't take it as spiteful—I thought that I would let him have me then. That maybe that was what he needed to turn himself good again.

"Do you understand me, Martin. I didn't want him except in some sad way and I knew it was wrong, but I undid my own blouse then."

The room was dark, and the light from the kitchen and the sky outside made my mother's face almost a silhouette to me. I imagined then my mother doing this, tried to imagine her pale skin which I had seen often, shining in the light from the television. I have never asked, of course, but I imagine that the television must have been on then, the volume low and them more whispering to each other than anything else, both out of awkwardness and sadness.

My mother's eyes began to glass. "Go get me some tissue, will you, honey," she said.

She touched her hand down to my leg and then pushed me gently away from her and toward the hallway. When I came back she wiped her nose. She said, "I'm sorry, honey," as she took the tissue.

We sat together for a few minutes without speaking. I watched her hands and her arms, which were growing thinner, as she deliberately tore up the wet Kleenex into thin strips on her lap. "I'm sorry, Marty, I have to say this out loud to someone," she said. "Come here, honey, will you please. Come, sit here next to me."

I sat up on the couch with her, half afraid of what she might tell me then. I could not imagine what my father or what my mother might have done.

"I know I'm no longer a young woman, Marty. I know that. And maybe that I really didn't want him was something your father could tell in me." She looked at me. "I didn't mean it to be mean or selfish, Marty. I've thought about that. I swear I didn't mean for that. But your father, he must have taken it that way. I was there holding open each side of my shirt and he just looked at me then, like he was seeing something clear that was bad."

My mother made a fist and pounded it up and down on her lap as she spoke.

"Do you understand me, Marty? I waited for him but he just kept looking at me. I took his hand and I rubbed it, and then I put it on my breast for him, even though I knew that then it was too late. That I was too old or we both were too far gone—something. I'm not sure that it even was just me anymore. After a time, Marty, he took his hand away. Then we just sat there without talking, until I knew it was past the time, and that it was right for me to button myself together."

I looked at my mother then. I was trying as best I could to understand what she wanted me to learn from this. I was certain that I wasn't getting all of it, but I recognized that she had cried over this a lot already, and that she knew how to stop herself when she needed to. I pulled myself around on the couch and my mother leaned over toward me. I waited for what I thought was to come, maybe that he had hit her, or left the house, but she didn't say anything more.

"The next night he was dead, Martin. He's dead. And I believe, I really believe, that I'm to blame for it, but I can't help thinking too that I'm looking at wrong things. That your father's spirit is here with us. And that he's pointing out all the wrong things to me."

She quieted down, then all at once began to cry again.

"I can't help myself, Marty," she said.

"He's dead, Mom," I said, though I knew then that this was not what she meant. As I touched her hair and shoulders, I imagined what this must have looked like to anyone who could have walked by then and seen us through the front room window, where the shade had not been drawn.

I held my mother until she sat back up, then got her more tissue, but when I came back from the bathroom, I recognized somehow that she had composed herself and now was through talking. She set her glass down and when I gave her the tissue, she wiped her face and then fingered the tie to her robe. In time, she got up and without saying a word walked over to me, put her fingers to her mouth, and then touched her hand to the right side of my forehead in a kiss.

Her fingers were warm and her hand slid down the side of my face—tensely but comfortingly too. "I love you, you know, Martin," she said.

She went to bed then. She did whatever she needed to in the bathroom and then closed her door though the night was hot and I thought that she would have kept it open for the breeze.

I stayed there on the floor thinking. The house was hot, and I remember listening to the motor of the clock from the stove. As I said, I was fifteen then, maybe just sixteen. I cannot imagine all the things I thought about. There on the floor, though, with my mother alone in her bed in the next room and my father dead, for the first time I felt filled with a sense of myself, of my own power. I felt that this was the circumstance of my life but that it could change, that my mother and I both could change in some other way that would bring us back to each other and close together. I listened, as I had only learned to listen when my father and mother were up in the other room that fall before, for some sign that my mother wanted me to come in there to comfort her, and though, of course, there was no sign, it didn't sadden me then.

After a time, I went outside. The concrete step in the front of the house was already a little damp, and I sat on the edge of the step and pushed my feet in and out of the spaces within the welcome mat on the sidewalk below. The coolness of moisture settled evenly around the bottoms of my feet, and I thought then about taking my mother's car, or about walking barefoot anywhere I wanted to, though there was nowhere I could think of to go. I wanted to do something, though, anything other than what I could do. I wanted then to live in a world only of possibility, where, like the night, your future would always surround you, and could make you feel alone and fresh and unafraid.

The Eelskin Jumpsuit

BY DAVID MORSE

"You want girl?" Young Sam smiled across the small low table that held their empty teacups. Gold tooth glittering.

"No." Austin shook his head. He tried to say it firmly this time; he wanted it to sound decisive. Or did he? Fatigue burned in Austin's brain like a fever, indistinguishable from doubt. "I'm tired. I must go." What time was it, anyway? He would have pushed up his sleeve to consult his watch, but it would mean exposing his Rolex to the other man's scrutiny.

Sitting cross-legged on straw mats, in a room on a raised wooden platform, they were surrounded on two sides by an L-shaped courtyard, enclosed by a bamboo wall, beyond which lay the sleeping city. Austin was wearing the jumpsuit. *He'd done it.* That was the main thing. Everything else—the teacups; the innkeeper's face propped on her elbows, watching them languidly; even his own sense of foreboding—was part of the lethargy that weighed on him and kept him rooted to the straw mat.

Austin let the back of his hand caress the soft eelskin where it wrinkled at the knee; stole a glimpse of the sleeve where it covered his watch.

"So." Young Sam sat back. "So, so. You no like girls?"

Austin sighed. They'd had this argument before. Five minutes ago? Half an hour? He'd responded with something like, "Only for love. Not money." Now it occurred to him: Should he lie? Tell Young Sam that he was married? Would that get Young Sam off his case? But he knew the answer, or thought he did. The only thing that might conceivably deter

Young Sam from his single-minded pursuit would be if Austin could say *no* with conviction. But—Austin tried to think—had he ever said *no* to anything with conviction?

What would it be like, he wondered, to be married to Dency? He'd pretty much stopped seeing other women. Pretty much. And it was not something Dency had asked for. Not exactly. Sometimes Austin felt trapped in his own vagueness.

"I have beautiful girls. You choose." Young Sam nodded emphatically. "You choose!" He had a wide, fleshy face— almost handsome, but with an edge of cruelty about the lips. It was, Austin had decided earlier, a criminal face.

Austin's back ached, unused to sitting in this position. Why could he not just make his apologies, stand up and walk out of this place? Was it politeness that held him prisoner, or fear?

The trip to Korea had come out of a rebirthing session in Dency's jacuzzi, when Austin had a vision of himself swaddled in what started out as his mechanic's coveralls but which became a kind of living second skin. A few days earlier one of his BMW clients—Edmund, the coke dealer with the black 633CSI turbo coupe who'd just returned from what he called "missionary work" in Korea—showed him an eelskin wallet he'd brought back from Seoul. "Feel it, man."

Austin wiped his hands on a clean rag before touching it. It was soft as velvet. Austin gave a low whistle.

"If you go," Edmund said, "bring some cheap trinkets. You know? Think of yourself as Columbus. I took along a bunch of calculator-pens. They dig that shit, man. And wear some hip vines. In China I had a dude try to buy a shirt off my back. To copy it, I guess."

If you go. Edmund made it sound so easy. Edmund had grace; he had the gift of a glad hand, spreading charm wherever he went; women hanging around him. Austin was flattered by the advice—almost touched. He'd never been out of the country, except once to the Bahamas.

Austin lacked that kind of self-assurance. He was always being told that he could be a men's fashion model, and yet the face that turned women's heads was a problem for him. It was as though God, leafing through the pages of some slick magazine, had tapped a long lacquered fingernail at random. Austin's build was not quite perfect: he was a bit long in the waist, and he was six-two; he would have preferred another inch. Still, with his jutting chin, pensive brow, dark lashes, he could have been modeling shampoos for Calvin Klein—if not for a puritanical streak he'd inherited from his father.

Fortunately, he'd found a calling both useful and lucrative. Carrying out his operations in a tiny garage off Canal Street, he was the BMW Doctor. He wore custom-tailored jumpsuits and cotton gloves, and anxious owners could watch, if they wanted to, from an observation window. Sometimes, aware of an attractive woman's gaze, he found himself striking poses: torquing down a headbolt, he'd gaze hard-eyed into distances known only to his ophthalmologist; or he'd pause in a graceful half-turn, before plucking a wrench from the rack. But these were distraction, with the power to corrupt. He liked it best when he could lose himself in the intricacies of German engineering.

For similar reasons he liked spending time with Dency. She was his therapist and he was sleeping with her, but at least she didn't own a BMW, and in the rebirthing sessions he could lose himself in the intricacies of his own psyche.

It was the randomness that troubled him, the sense of having been plucked from a magazine ad—the feeling that success had come too easily, perhaps as a result of his looks. At age twenty-nine, he felt secretly unformed. The occasional asthma attacks he suffered represented a movement backwards into the amorphousness of adolescence. At night sometimes he woke up in terror, heart pounding, as if he'd experienced some terrible loss, the emptiness resounding like the silence following the rattle of an impact-wrench.

Once it happened while he was sleeping at Dency's.

"What's wrong?" Dency's voice behind him, thick with sleep.

"I lost something." He was gulping for air. He felt like crying.

"What was it?"

"I can't remember."

Dency's fingers smoothing the dark curls at the back of his neck. "It's okay. We'll work on it. Tomorrow. I'll cancel someone. It's okay." Her voice trailing off sleepily.

He waited for his heartbeat to return to normal and her fingers to fall still on the back of his neck. It always seemed to be the same dream, but he could never be sure; all that was left was that terrible sense of loss.

"It's gone," he told her the next day, in the jacuzzi—vocal cords relaxed, body dissolving in the swirling warmth. "Whatever it is, it's gone."

"How do you feel?" she asked.

"Sad."

"Let yourself experience the sadness. Where do you feel it?"

"My throat."

Dency touched his throat, and he began sobbing. Why was it he could cry in front of Dency only when he was paying her? His breath was coming in waves now, faster; mouth and fingertips beginning to tingle.

"Let it go through you," she said, cradling him. "Let it come in through the top of your head; let it out through the soles of your feet." She repeated it, a kind of mantra. "All the love in the Universe." She was breathing next to him, following the rhythm of his breathing like a slalom skier, an expert following a novice. "Breathe," he heard her saying. "Go into your heart-space."

He felt himself wrapped in a long hammock or pod, slick like the inside of a pea pod, but clinging and warm; then it was his coveralls, but thicker and somehow radiantly alive, an extension of himself. He felt powerful and protected and self-assured.

"What do you *want?*" Dency asked him afterwards, massaging his shoulders, straddling him. He was lying on his stomach on the warm redwood deck. He tried to listen to his inner voice.

"I want an eelskin jumpsuit." The words just fell out.

Dency leaned back triumphantly, her pubic hair tickled the backs of his legs. "Go for it."

Of course it wasn't that easy. It took several sessions for him to give himself permission to go—which meant overcoming his guilt about money; fear of risk; old business with his father. Austin had to convince himself that it was not a frivolous errand; he had to own his own vanity. He had to do abundance, not scarcity. He *deserved* an eelskin jumpsuit.

When Austin arrived in Seoul, the city was flaring into prominence on the television screens of the world: police with fiberglass shields were battling students; two-dollar-an hour auto workers had taken executives hostage at Hyundai Motors; demonstrators were picketing outside the American embassy; tear-gas wafted past the city's ancient gates. All of this went largely unnoticed by Austin, who walked alongside the unmarked buses without seeing the riot troops inside. He was not a political person.

After he'd found a hotel and checked in, he stuffed a change of clothes in his camera bag along with his Leica, and wearing the jumpsuit that would serve as a prototype, he took a cab to the Myong-dong market, which Edmund had suggested as the place to start.

Finally, he located a tailor whose competence was attested to by an eelskin merchant—the two danced around each other with excitement, displaying eelskin vests which the tailor had apparently made, for the merchant kept rapping on the other fellow's chest for emphasis and calling attention to the fine stitching: "Cannot see! No visible!"—and Austin allowed himself to be measured. He felt like the emperor being fitted for his new clothes.

Over ginseng tea, which the tailor provided in little cups, they discussed the direction in which the narrow strips of leather should be sewn. Austin made a pencil drawing showing how the strips should run vertically on the legs and sleeves and upper chest; horizontally around the torso. The tailor pointed out certain problems; Austin answered with pencil, until they arrived at a final sketch.

The eelskin merchant, dropping by to kibbitz, took one look at the pencil drawing and became very excited. He disappeared and returned a few minutes later in the company of an old man with a wispy beard who examined the drawing and then summoned them to his stall, where he unrolled a scroll to a sort of schematic diagram of a human body. "You see?" the merchant exclaimed, pointing excitedly between the two drawings. "You see?"

Austin saw that indeed his sketch bore a striking resemblance to the diagram on the scroll.

Beaming at Austin, the eelskin merchant tapped the scroll gently. "This very, very old."

The old man spoke, with the tailor translating. As far as Austin could tell, the diagram represented "energy-paths" associated with some internal organ. But which organ? The spleen? The liver? Their sense of its location seemed so uncertain that Austin wondered if it might not be a specific organ at all, but rather a function or spiritual property. The eelskin merchant put forth his own theory very volubly in Korean, which the tailor summarized. "He say this organ very, very old. He say may be no more exist."

The eelskin merchant made a sad little shrug. The pencil drawing was passed around again, reverently. Austin departed amidst much bowing, with the assurance the jumpsuit would be ready for a fitting at ten the following morning.

Austin took a cab—a bright green Hyundai Pony—back to the hotel. When he paid, the driver scooped change from a square indentation over the transmission. The coins were hot. The crudeness of this amused Austin. He held the coins in his hands as he walked into the lobby, savoring their heat. Maybe the Koreans would never produce a sixteen-valve engine capable of doing zero to sixty in seven seconds; but there was a vitality in those hot little coins—a future.

He stretched out on the bed. Outside it was dusk. The jet lag that had caught up with him during his stopover in Tokyo seemed to have settled behind his eyeballs. He slept fitfully. The mercury vapor floodlights outside his window cast eerie shadows of barbed wire from the American military compound next door. A siren went off, further confusing night and day. The numbers on his Rolex only confused him more. All he could think about were the dozens of little fingers somewhere in Seoul, doing his bidding, stitching eelskins together. In some sweatshop overseen by the tailor, a sleeve was being sewn together, a leg being created. Again and again Austin examined the stitching: the eelskin puckered in delicate folds which would tarnish with wear like the knees of a baby rhino. Again and again he turned the pages of an imaginary fashion magazine, read about the asymmetrical bellows cargo-pockets supplying bulk to the mid thighs, noted the tucks and pleats and richly sensuous openings. He saw himself photographed at the edge of an Amazon rain forest, lounging on a massive vine-encrusted log, head turned to gaze into the green mists.

Incredibly, he thought, when his mind drifted into wakefulness, the fruit of all that labor was costing him only five hundred dollars—most of which was going for materials, he was pretty sure. Boatloads of eels; fishermen grinning without teeth. So maybe a hundred dollars, total, for tonight's labor. That would buy barely two hours of his own time on Canal Street. For a job that would have taken his tailor in SoHo at least a week. What he was saving by having the jumpsuit made here would pay for nearly half the trip.

"Those Koreans," his father used to say, shaking his head in admiration. "Do you know, Hyundai was just a little construction company when the Korean War began. They got a contract building barracks for the U.S. Army, and now they're one of the ten biggest corporations on the face of the earth." His father had been stationed near Pusan, part of a construction battalion. "Those Koreans are tough little bastards. Fighters."

Finally, Austin gave up trying to sleep. He slipped out of the deserted lobby. Walking, he found the streets still dark— empty except for streetcleaners, an armored personnel carrier rumbling past. A pair of policemen asked him if he was lost, checked his identification, told him to be careful. Finally, as the sky was lightening, he happened upon an eating place crowded with workers sitting at benches and rough tables, slurping soup, the air spicy with the smell of *kimch'i*, everyone staring at him with a special intensity which he was beginning to recognize but could not begin to name. Using gestures, he ordered what everybody seemed to be having—a garlicky soup which, as he picked at it, seemed to be made from entrails. Trust the Universe, he reminded himself. He sampled the *kimch'i* and nearly gagged.

A man sitting across the table glowered, said something to his companions in Korean loud enough for everyone to hear. Laughter.

The man pointed at Austin and unleashed a torrent of words. Austin thought he heard the word "American." Then the man came around the table and shook his fist in Austin's face. Fear rose cold in Austin's belly. The man was probably a foot shorter than Austin; but his face was full of rage, his movements light and quick. The fist darting close to Austin's face was heavily calloused, knuckles encapsulated with thick calloused skin full of little cracks. Austin was afraid to raise his guard, lest it trigger an attack. Then other hands appeared; the man's companions coaxing him, restraining him, leading him away. Austin's knees were shaking. He felt nauseated.

One of the other men apologized, twirling his finger at his temple. "Him crazy. Box. Him boxer. Crazy. You no worry."

But faces hardened at Austin's glance, or avoided him. Austin paid with the large unfamiliar bills, and left.

By eight o'clock, the rumbling in his stomach had given way to hunger. The sidewalks and streets were filled with people hurrying. Construction workers peddled past on bicycles, wearing cement-bleached canvas gaitors; some obviously late, pumping furiously, joined by those who were already laden with shovels, whole sheets of plywood improbably balanced across handlebars, five bags of cement stacked up behind one rider. Austin thought of the boxer's fist in his face; the thickened leathery carapace over ligament and bone, the little cracks fanning out like river deltas. Arms so muscular under his shirt that his companions' fingers scarcely made indentations.

He'd been terrified, and he was ashamed of his terror. But Korea was a police state. What would happen to a Korean who attacked an American? It made the man's fury all the more incomprehensible.

Everywhere in Seoul was the sour, uriny smell of wet concrete—patching the sidewalks, towering into the sky, tunneling into the earth, oozing fecundity and flux—giving the impression that Seoul was being constantly constructed, deconstructed, like a termite colony; mucilaginous and urgent. Compared to this evidence, Austin supposed, of the economic miracle the guidebooks talked about—lower Manhattan was like a dusty window display.

The tailor arrived promptly at ten o'clock, carrying a packet under his arm, and unlocked the metal door to his shop. Austin followed him inside and watched him unwrap the paper and unfold the jumpsuit.

The eelskin was as lustrious as Austin had imagined, beautifully matched, soft and silvery as a pussy willow. He stepped onto a little platform behind a curtain and tried it on carefully; some of the seams were still pinned, the cuffs not yet attached and the pockets yet to be positioned. Even so, it was gorgeous.

"You movie star, Mister Austin?" the tailor asked, pinning the pockets.

Austin felt his ears get warm. "No," he said softly. He could not take his eyes off his reflection.

"You sports man?"

Austin shook his head.

It was perfect. *Breathe*, he reminded himself.

"You come back two o'clock," the tailor said. "It be finish."

When Austin came back at two, after visiting museums, the tailor was a few minutes late. The eelskin merchant invited him over to his stall to sit down, and poured him a small glass of rice wine.

"Where do the skins come from?" Austin asked.

"Eel." The merchant wiggled a hand sinuously.

"But where do the eels come from?"

"From water."

"But what water? Korea? Does Korea have many eels?"

"Yes, yes. Everywhere eel. Eel come from all over. United States have many eel, but no use. Sell Korea."

Austin was incredulous. "The eelskins come from the United States?"

The man nodded. "No use. Sell cheap."

The tailor appeared, unlocked his door, and unfolded the finished suit. Austin tried it on. The red silk lining followed his body perfectly. One seam had to be taken in. While Austin waited, the eelskin merchant poured him another glass of rice wine. When Austin zipped up the completed jumpsuit and stood in front of the mirror, the merchant applauded.

"You rock and roll star, Mister Austin?"

Austin smiled what he hoped was an enigmatic smile, transfering items into the jumpsuit pockets from his old clothes, which he stuffed into his camera bag.

The tailor smiled. "You wear it?"

Austin nodded, counting out the bills.

"Be careful," the eelskin merchant warned.

Walking from Myong-dong to another market, Austin felt the cosmic energy swirl around him, with the odor of *kimch'i* and charcoal-grilled octopus, the sound of pop music from boom boxes and the hambone rhythm of vendors slapping their palms against upturned cartons, seated up high under

the orange plastic tarps that covered mountains of goods—
famous-name running shoes; baseball gloves endorsed by Dave
Winfield; doubleknit leisure suits, women's underwear, pots
and pans—chanting their wares with a blood tempo bordering
on frenzy, one island of sounds and smells competing with the
next; an archipelago of lunatic consumerism.

Stealing occasional reflections of himself in windows,
Austin walked until the crowds thinned, until the strings of
bare lightbulbs gave way to propane lanterns, and the propane
to darkness. He was suddenly exhausted. How far had he
walked? He began looking for landmarks, not knowing
whether to walk or take a cab back to his hotel.

The man in a doorway whom he approached for directions
offered to show him the way back to his hotel. The man
introduced himself as Young Sam. He was a head shorter than
Austin, about the same age; squarely built. His breath
smelled of *kimch'i*. Wearing a dark suit with no tie, he walked
with a blustery stride, guiding Austin past patches of wet
cement. Following him through the narrow broken streets,
Austin lost all sense of direction.

"Please. You have tea with me," Young Sam insisted. They
were standing in an alley in front of a bamboo gate. A woman
slid the gate open for them. Austin recalled the eelskin
merchant's warning to be careful. Careful of what? Again, it
seemed to him that as an American he had little to fear. He
thought of the marketplace: the brassieres, the boom boxes,
the famous-name jogging shoes. It was his last night in Seoul.

"Please." Young Sam urged him into the courtyard.

They removed their shoes to step onto the wooden platform, which Austin took to be a sort of dining area, although
they were alone in the place; and the woman, who seemed to
be the innkeeper, served them lukewarm tea. But if Young
Sam was interested in talking, he showed no sign of it. He
seemed to be waiting for something, some protocol.

Finally, when they had finished their tea and it became
clear that this was a hustle, Austin was somehow reluctant to
offend his host. It didn't help to realize that he'd put these
forces into motion himself, to hear Dency's voice reminding
him: *You chose this situation.* And it didn't help that, despite this
choosing, or because of it, he was trying to keep his heart-
space open.

Throughout all this, the innkeeper, a middle-aged woman who hovered at the edge of their conversation, was sitting on the courtyard side of the low sill that defined the room, elbows propped on the sill, drinking her own tea. She had bony forearms, a long face with a jaded expression; and although Austin knew she couldn't possibly have understood their English, which was partly beyond his own comprehension, she nevertheless followed the exchanges intently, like a cat.

Young Sam said something to her in Korean. She called to a girl who looked to be nine or ten—probably her daughter—who trotted out with a couple of bottles of beer which the innkeeper placed on the little table, along with two glasses and a package of something like potato chips. Young Sam filled one of the glasses and pushed it toward Austin.

"Korean always pour beer for friend. Never pour for self."

Austin poured the other beer for Young Sam, who tore open the gold mylar bag with a practiced twist and offered the contents. Aerospace spinoff, Austin thought despondently, spinning into Korean junkfood. He tried one of the tidbits offered. It was puffy and crisp.

"What is it?"

"Eel," Young Sam said. "Salt. How you say? Salt eel."

Jesus. Was this what the Korean economy was based on? The savory taste was strange but appealing.

"You want girl?"

"No. No girl." But why was he drinking the beer? Everything was swirling around him as in a dream. He tried to listen to his inner voice, but the fatigue roared in his ears. Finally he heard himself ask the question. "How much?"

"Twenty-five, thirty thousand Won."

Austin tried to make the calculation into dollars, but it came out hazy. Sixty dollars? "Oh no. No, no. Too much." He was aware he was doing scarcity. He tried to go into his heart-space. Tried explaining to Young Sam why he'd come to Korea, how he'd come to realize it had to do with locating himself *on the planet*. "I had a vision. A picture." He thought if he let the words tumble out then the language barrier would melt away, as it had with the Japanese businessmen on the plane, eating their intricate little dinners from plastic trays and drinking Suntory whiskey. But none of it made sense without the one crucial element which he was reluctant to mention, which he was wearing. He ended by presenting Young Sam with a small token of friendship.

Young Sam studied the calculator-pen and heaved a great sigh. "I'm very tired."

"Listen," said Austin. He was feeling a sudden rush of energy. "Take a cab home. Please. You walked me this far. Be my guest." He opened his wallet, removed a 2,000 Won bill. "And here's for the beer." He peeled off another 1,000 Won. And he gave Young Sam one of his cards. Now, he told himself, while you have some momentum, *leave*.

Young Sam accepted the money indifferently, studied the card. "BMW Doctor." Then he fished in the pocket of his white polyester shirt, and handed over a card that resembled a plastic credit card. "This what I do."

Imprinted on the plastic were raised letters: NEW AGE LEISURE CLUB. All Major Credit Cards Welcome.

Austin stared at the card. He could feel his energy drain away. The whole thing seemed to him like the decision to pull an engine. Once you had pulled the engine, in order to change the flywheel, then maybe you needed a new clutch. Or a whole new drive train. But where did it stop? He'd only come here for tea. Or had he? At what point had Young Sam pulled his engine?

He returned the card to Young Sam.

Young Sam tapped the card on the table rhythmically. "You Americans no understand money. Money all around you; eat money, shit money. No understand money. Japan, same; money everywhere. Korea, different. Korean, only a little money. But Korean understand money."

"Interesting."

"Is true?"

Austin shrugged. "I suppose so."

"You agree?"

Austin nodded.

Young Sam laughed. An abrupt, harsh sound. He leaned forward, centered the corner of the credit card just above Austin's solar plexus, in the V of his sternum, and jabbed sharply.

Austin gasped—more from surprise than pain.

Young Sam laughed and returned the card to his shirt pocket. "Easy to agree. Difficult to understand."

The innkeeper's eyes twinkled. For the first time Austin realized that she understood the conversation far better than he did. He looked at the bamboo wall and saw that the gate was closed. He wondered if it was locked. What would happen if he tried to leave? Young Sam had stopped smiling.

Austin's breath was wheezing now. He patted his breast pocket for his inhailer, but he didn't use it. *Breathe*, he told himself. Relax. Gradually the weight lifted from his chest.

Two new beers appeared. Austin poured for Young Sam; Young Sam poured for him.

"I'm tired," Young Sam complained. "I'm very tired." He looked at his watch.

The game was drawing to a close. Under Austin's inertia was an animal alertness that told him he was not going to get out of the place without paying the price. But what was the price?

The woman was beautiful. Tall for a Korean; taller than most American women. So carefully goomed, with such perfect almond eyes and radiant skin, flawless white teeth, and the bearing of a princess—that when she appeared at the table and Young Sam introduced her, Austin told himself she couldn't possibly be a prostitute. Maybe she was just one of those women who are drawn to Westerners, who wanted to practice her English, to charm and be charmed. Young Sam had told him her name, but Austin wasn't sure he'd gotten it right.

She spoke no English at all, as it turned out. Young Sam translated, and the conversation dallied around tea, with occasional laughter. Finally, Young Sam looked at Austin questioningly. "This girl, thirty."

"Years old?" She seemed much younger.

"Thousand Won." Young Sam leaned forward. "That how much this girl cost. You like this? You like to fuck this?

The words grated. But Austin nodded.

The money changed hands, with everybody looking on—

the woman, the innkeeper and her daughter. Young Sam said something to the woman and she produced a package of condoms from her purse.

"What is the lady's name?" Austin asked Young Sam.

Young Sam said something to her in Korean. She responded with a name, which Austin didn't get clearly.

"Could you write it out?" Austin pointed to the calculator pen which Young Sam had put in his shirt pocket.

Young Sam seized the woman's forearm and wrote on it: ECONOMIC MIRACLE. He pulled the arm close for Austin to read; the woman winced, in obvious pain. "This it!" Young Sam yelled. "This Economic Miracle!" Then he laughed uproariously, let go of the arm, and pushed the woman at Austin, who caught her.

The woman looked at her arm, confused. Young Sam swaggered off, still laughing. The innkeeper and her daughter were preparing the room; the bamboo shades were unrolled and the low table was replaced by a futon, transforming the dining room into a bedroom. The lights dimmed in the courtyard. There was some last-minute scurrying: Austin caught a glimpse of Young Sam leading a brown-haired woman past, into a room further back from the courtyard. She was dumpy, carried a pair of white high-heeled shoes, looked as if she'd been awakened out of a sound sleep; she was protesting bitterly while Young Sam dragged her by the wrist. Later it would occur to Austin that she was speaking English.

Looking for a bathroom, Austin tried a door and found a sort of shrine to Western-style kitsch: shiny ceramic tiles; new cheap fixtures; a poster of Big Sur that said "California Dreaming." What made it more surreal was the bathtub was half-full of cold water, the floor partly flooded, the water in the toilet bowl precariously high. Austin decided not to risk flushing.

When the courtyard was quiet, Austin smiled at the woman, who was brushing her long hair. "You can go." He pointed toward the door, waved both hands as if to shoo her out. But she began taking off her clothes.

Naked, with small firm breasts, Economic Miracle had the build and grace of a dancer. Slowly, she unzipped the jumpsuit to his navel, caressing his chest. Austin unpeeled the rest. Spreading the jumpsuit flat on the futon, he rolled it up firmly, his heart thumping. Rolled tightly, the eelskin felt somehow ripe with desire. Where to put it? She was crouched behind him, surrounding him with her open thighs. He felt giddy. He stuffed the jumpsuit under the edge of the futon, and turned into her slowly, tenderly.

It was the tenderness that was difficult. The fact that it wasn't returned shouldn't have surprised Austin. He was the one faking it, the one trying to turn it into something it wasn't. Why did he have such a need? He wasn't the one being paid, after all. Her fingers playing with his nipples were brusque; she could have been cleaning grease-fittings. Did she have a lover? Would it be any different if he weren't so exhausted?

When it was over, Economic Miracle was cheerful. They had no language to fill the silence, though; and while sleep pressed in on him with new urgency, Austin needed the pretense of tenderness even more. So he sang to her, softly. "The Banks of the Ohio." She sang a Korean song. She had a pretty soprano voice. He wished he understood the words. Listening to the melody, he thought of white porcelain and azaleas.

He asked her name, using sign language, saying his own name and writing it, and getting her to write hers—first in Korean characters, then in Roman letters. It was Seong Wu.

Before they fell asleep, they heard sounds from the room where Young Sam had taken the woman carrying the white shoes—the woman moaning, her cries growing sharper. Nothing erotic about it: only grinding pain, the rhythm forced on her. The thrusting seemed to stop; then it resumed. The woman was crying miserably. It went on like that.

Austin exchanged looks with Seong Wu. She too appeared troubled. She brushed her long hair as if to block the sound, and resumed her cheerfulness. Finally the cries ended.

Seong Wu was asleep with her head on his arm, and Austin was slipping into sleep. He thought of azaleas in every shade of crimson and lavendar and pink, until sleep descended like a wad of dark wool on his eyelids.

Sometime later the sounds began again, welling out of his sleep: the thrusts, the woman's tortured cries; an evil tide rising, lapping into his consciousness, and then ebbing finally out of hearing.

He awoke finally to the deep silence before dawn. A chill in the air. Sky faintly tinged with light, blue dawn suffusing the room through the bamboo slats; the woman lying beside him, her hair spreading across the pillow like ink; the word MIRACLE showing. Somewhere, a cricket chirping.

The jumpsuit. His fingers searching under the futon located its softness.

Now was the time to leave. He didn't want to see Young Sam again, or the innkeeper—who would find some pretext for getting more money from him. He had to find his shoes without waking anybody up. Dawn was bringing the sound of birds. Silently, moving at a crouch, Austin pulled together his clothing and camera bag. He thought he remembered the innkeeper moving all the shoes to another location on the wooden platform. But if it came down to a choice between getting out of here safely and retrieving his shoes, he'd leave the shoes. That realization sharpened his senses. Pulling on his underwear, he crawled to the edge of the platform and leaned out. He spotted the shoes a few yards away. But as he crept forward he noticed a movement in the innkeeper's quarters next to the gate. A voice called out. It was the innkeeper. She uttered a high-pitched scream.

"Yiiiiii!"

The courtyard lights came on. Austin dashed forward, grabbed his shoes, and returned to struggle into his jumpsuit, pulled on his shoes. Seong Wu was still asleep, but there was a vague commotion from Young Sam's room.

Austin took off across the courtyard clutching his camera bag, the jumpsuit half-zipped, a sleeve flapping. He was relieved to see the heavy bamboo gate was open. But the innkeeper ran from her door in time to seize hold of the gate and slide it shut with all her might, her face fierce with determination—pinning Austin in it. She was trying to spike it shut. With a fury that surprised him, Austin hurled back the gate. He recovered the camera bag and stepped through. But she managed to catch hold of the trailing sleeve and slammed the gate shut, this time succeeding in pegging it fast. Austin tried to pull free, but the sleeve was caught solidly between the heavy pieces of bamboo. He inserted his fingers in the crack and tried with all his force to widen it.

He felt the knife an instant before he saw the blade flash through the crack. He snatched his fingers away. Young Sam's face appeared behind the slats, yelling to the innkeeper. Austin gathered the half-severed sleeve in both hands and pulled ferociously. The leather parted. Austin scooped up the camera bag and ran down the alley. Looking over his shoulder he saw Young Sam emerge from the gate in pursuit, but Austin outdistanced him easily.

On the avenue, under a streetlight, he stopped to examine his fingers. He wrapped a handkerchief around them. Then he slipped his arm into the twisted bloody sleeve, and zipped up the front.

He could file a complaint, he supposed. But there was no time to pursue it before he left for the airport. The cuts were superficial, and he didn't want to spoil his elation. He'd repair the sleeve himself; it couldn't be that difficult. Continuing to walk, looking down at the ragged sleeve, he found himself laughing. He thought of the innkeeper's furious face, and his own ferocity, and the hot little coins.

By Indian Time

BY MARIA NOELL GOLDBERG

When the jeep's lights cut across the living room wall, Henry rolls off the couch to the floor. His elbows and knees crack, and hurt a little deep inside the joints. Henry hasn't slept in his marriage bed since last winter when his wife died. He wakes each dawn in exactly the same position in which he dropped into sleep—face down, hands cupped over his crotch, his toes tucked into the crack between the cushion and the end of the couch.

Outside, his son taps the horn twice, then Henry begins to creep across the floor. He squeezes past the coffee table littered with empty boxes of saltines, and stays low beneath the picture window so Paulie won't see him.

He crawls across the room, over sour piles of flannel shirts, boxer shorts and socks, and his wife's hairpins clustered like pine needles on the floor. Claire was a Haida Indian with hair so thick and rebellious it seemed to throw off the pins as fast she pushed them in. The thin curves of wire bite into his knees as he picks his way toward the kitchen.

Outside, a car door slams just as Henry makes it to the basement stairs. He slips into the darkness and the basement air, soft and hushed as a blanket, swallows every noise—his breath, the click of the light switch, the hollow sound of his feet sliding carefully down each wooden stair. Maybe if he stays hidden, his son will go away and forget about dragging him to the potlatch. Henry hates being the lone white in a family full of Indians.

He'd come to this remote part of the island, where few

whites live, looking for work during the war. On the main-
land, gas stations, factories, and the Boeing plant in Seattle
were frantic for men like Henry, whose deafness in one ear
disqualified him for the service but not for hard work. But the
sudden, loud noises of these places unnerved him as he spun
around trying to locate the source of each sound. The chaos of
half-heard noise was paralyzing.

Henry points his good ear at the basement door, then the
window above his workbench, but hears nothing. He can
picture Paulie circling the house with his wife and son,
peering through the windows looking for him, and the sky
just beginning to lighten. He shivers, then pulls his old
oilskin jacket off one of the hooks along the wall and slips it
over his flannel shirt and overalls, surprised to find that after
such a long time, it still smells of fish.

His first day on the island, Henry got a job unloading
fishing boats at the Haida cannery. With the war on, there
weren't enough men around to manage the logging and fishing
that kept the clans going. Wherever he turned, there was a job
waiting, a place he could fill. It was a good time to be a man.

He'd met Claire at a CYO dance one weekend off from the
cannery. He walked into the school auditorium and saw her
standing in front of a mirror, battling with her heavy black
hair, and trying to push it into the kind of French twist all the
white girls were wearing then. Henry watched in fascination.
She was tiny and had to stand on her toes to see her whole face
in the mirror, but she went at her hair with the most
extravagently large hands he'd ever seen. They swooped
among the ropes of hair, grabbing and pushing them into
submission, fierce and graceful as a pair of hawks.

She'd died ten months ago while tying Henry's necktie for
him. The tie, a gift from Paulie, was decorated with a flock of
embroidered geese flying across a maroon sky. It was meant as
a joke—a reference to the crowd of Canadian geese who
jockeyed for position in the backyard every morning, waiting
for Henry to throw his breakfast scraps out the door—but
Henry loved the tie. He wore it every day to the liquor store
he'd bought after five good seasons at the cannery, and a year
on a logging crew.

"Hold still, Henry." Claire had pushed Henry's chin out of
her way with the knuckle of her forefinger. He was trying to

pull his chin in close to his neck and tilt his head to the side so he could see her fingers working with the silk. After all these years, the simple movements of her hands still aroused in him a kind of vague and sleepy desire.

"You're going to be late for work if I don't get this thing tied soon, Henry. Now stop fidgeting."

"My dear woman..." Henry leaned back so he could see her face, "as I've told you many times, that's one of the advantages of owning your own business, even if it's just a dinky, one-aisle liquor store. You can be late."

"All the same..." Claire stopped talking suddenly, just as she flipped the long end of the tie over the first part of the knot. Her face turned gray and her legs crumpled beneath her. She fell at Henry's feet with her arms held out in front of her, fingers fluttering in the air as if tying and retying the same knot.

"Here he is, Dad." Henry's grandson pokes his head inside the tiny basement window. "I found you, Chinny Henry."

"So you did, Jeremy, so you did." Henry stands beneath the window and looks up. "But did you have to squeal on your grandpa, and tell your dad?" he whispers.

Henry has always wished Jeremy would call him grandpa, and not Chinny, the Haida name for grandfather. After all, Jeremy is only part Indian. He'll never look white, not with that wild black hair sticking out from his head at such odd angles, and skin the color of toast, but at least he could talk white.

Paulie's booted feet appear outside the window as he gets down on his hands and knees and glares at Henry.

"Jesus, Dad. I swear, if you don't get upstairs and open the goddamn door, I'm going to break it down."

Dark like Claire, Paulie's face is flat and broad, as sharply defined as a carved wooden mask.

"And change your clothes, Dad. Please? Something clean. Maybe one of your good shirts? There must be one somewhere in this rat's nest you call a house."

They turn off the main highway and the jeep bounces along the muddy road to the clan house. The woods are deep at this end of the island. Branches of cedar and hemlock reach out over the roadway, enclosing it like a tunnel.

Jeremy and Henry sit in back while Paulie drives. His wife, Rose, bends over her lap, fingers flying as she crochets a blue tatting-edge around a pale yellow handkerchief.

"You like my new button blanket?" Jeremy asks, showing his back so Henry can get the whole effect. The motion of the jeep rocks him from side to side as he holds out the cloth with his arms.

The ceremonial blanket is trimmed all around with a wide band of black. The stylized face of a wolf, also cut from black felt, is stitched onto the red cloth. White buttons, carefully spaced a thumb's width apart, outline the ears, brow, muzzle and teeth of the large wolf's head.

"Fine, Jeremy. That's a fine blanket." Henry pulls on Jeremy's shoulders and the child's back comes to rest against him. "You'll dance in that today?"

"It's my naming day, Chinny Henry." Jeremy climbs into his grandfather's lap, settling against his chest just as he does at Henry's house. Even when his grandfather is feeling low, Jeremy likes to visit. He sings in Henry's good ear or drags him outside, no matter how cold, to feed the geese who scramble and grab at the bread crusts he brings in a paper bag. "All the boys born during Earth Renewal moon get to dance."

"January birthdays, Dad. Remember? It's not like the old days, when you got your tribal name in the first year." Paulie's arm rests along the back of the seat, his fingers playing with the collar of Rose's blouse. "You scared me half to death back there, Dad. I pounded and knocked at both doors, then ran around the house banging on windows. Nothing. I thought you'd had a stroke or something."

"Don't worry. I'm not so decrepit I'm going to drop dead anytime soon." Henry looks out the window at devil's club spilling onto the road and slapping the sides of the jeep as they pass. "I told you I wasn't going to any potlatch."

"No one calls it a potlatch anymore, Dad. They call it a 'giving.'"

"Well, whatever they call it, I wish they'd do it without me. I never liked these things when your mother was alive and I don't expect to like them now. At least she had the decency to let me be, not like some people I know."

When they were first married, Claire tried coaxing Henry into tribal ways. He followed her into the woods for a while, gathering soapberries in November and huckleberries in July, and she taught him to smoke salmon over drying racks in the backyard. He even drank a putrid concoction of ground bunchberries and a little pipsissewa tea every evening for a year, to help her get pregnant. She managed to drag Henry to a potlatch once.

When Paulie was a year old, Claire's parents gave a potlatch to celebrate his naming as a member of his mother's Raven Clan. Claire had family, lots of family, and though things were strained because of her marriage to a white, she never broke with them. The Raven and Eagle Clans gathered in the clan house, feasting and dancing for three days while Henry sat in a corner and smoked cigarettes. Claire brought him plates of ceremonial food—deer meat and mushrooms, a bowl of soapberries the women had whipped and sweetened with sugar—but Henry couldn't eat.

Claire's father made long speeches and gave presents to everyone who'd come to act as witnesses to the child's first initiation. Henry had always suspected his in-laws would never forgive him for being white. He watched the whole clan gather in a circle around his tiny son, exchanging gifts over his head, and he seemed not to matter; to the Haida, Paulie was his mother's child.

Henry had no traditions of giving, or naming; he had no people. Even his name was borrowed from the railway station where he'd been left as an infant, his basket perched on top of a crate of oysters on their way to the Pike Place Market. There was no way for him to claim his own son.

"Take it easy, Paulie." Rose now talks around a strand of tatting yarn which hangs from between her teeth while Paulie swerves the jeep from side to side, trying to avoid the deepest ruts. "How'd you expect me to finish this, with you bobbing and weaving?"

"Won't be much longer now," he says, pulling off the road and stopping at a tiny cinder block gas station. The station is deserted but a sign taped to a coffee can on top of the single pump announces, "Gone to giving. Please pay here."

While Paulie fills the tank and Jeremy and Rose wash the windows, Henry climbs out of the car and disappears behind the garage. He pushes his way through the salal bushes and circles back to the road. A logging truck roars through the trees along one of the crude tracks that crisscross this part of the island. It swerves onto the road beside the station, traveling in the direction of town. Henry scrambles through the brush with his thumb extended and tries to hitch a ride on the huge truck.

"Need some help, Henry?" Rose asks, coming up behind him as the truck flies past. She's Haida too, sturdy and built like a box.

"Can't a man take a leak without being followed, for crissakes?" Henry drops his arm and fumbles with his fly. "I'll be there in a minute. Just you run along."

Rose turns away, but stays close, picking at a bare branch while Henry pees onto the road.

When they're all back in the car, Jeremy sits in Henry's lap again and Rose picks up her tatting. Claire taught her to do handwork like this and Rose has tatted edges around dozens of handkerchiefs for the potlatch today. She and Paulie and all their uncles and aunts have been making sweaters, drums, lace-edged towels and potholders, silver bracelets and ceremonial button blankets for months, gifts for everyone who comes to witness their child's naming.

These presents have been piling up in cardboard boxes inside Paulie's garage. But it's not, as he says, like the old days. People used to give away everything they owned just to impress the rest of the tribe. Now, they give what they can.

When Paulie reaches the end of the road, Jeremy scrambles off his grandfather's lap and leans forward into the space between his parents. "Josh and Petey are here already, Dad. Look. Are we late? Did we miss the Bear Dance?"

"We're fine, Jeremy. Just fine. They can't start without us." He reaches over and takes a small flat drum from the box at Rose's feet, gently bouncing the tightly stretched deerskin on top of Jeremy's head and producing a hum which hangs in the air. "We're the chiefs today. Anyway, we're holding all the good stuff."

The woods open onto a clearing where a pack of children chase each other across ground covered with low grass and banks of fern. The clan house sits at the crest of a small hill, backed up against a dense stand of evergreens. There's a slight chop on the waters of the inlet, visible at the base of the incline.

"The aunts are here," Jeremy shouts, pointing to the old

Dodge pickup Claire's sisters take turns driving. There are already several jeeps, cars and pickup trucks beside the building. Jeremy bounces up and down on the seat while Paulie parks.

"Don't get your blanket dirty," Rose calls as he opens the door and tumbles out. He reaches into the front seat and grabs the drum, then runs to catch up with his friends. "And stay away from the water," she shouts.

Paulie comes around from the rear of the jeep and holds the door wide so Henry can climb out. He offers his hand to his father.

"Come see what we've done, Dad. We just finished the new portal pole last night. Rose and I were here with flashlights till after eleven, painting and tripping over each other in the dark."

Henry takes Paulie's hand and allows himself to be pulled from the car, but as soon as he's standing, he draws back. Silently, the two bow and gesture, each encouraging the other to be first up the gravel path to the clan house.

"Come on, Dad. I'll show you around." Paulie sidesteps his father and leads him toward the clan house, a low building made of cedar, while Rose struggles to pull a large cardboard box from the rear of the jeep. As she rests the box against her belly, Henry sees it's filled with thick, earth-colored sweaters like Claire used to knit. She carries it across the grass to a blanket where several women are sitting above the high tide line, shucking peas into a big pot, and settles among them.

The air is filled with the scent of the cedar clan house and a fishy smell from the inlet where the tide is low. Jeremy runs with three other boys, and they startle Henry every time they swoop past his deaf side. They chase each other into the hall with their new button blankets trailing behind like large expansive wings, and Henry and Paulie follow, looking up as they pass beneath the huge wooden portal pole. The pole is carved with the design of the Wolf Clan crest, the Wolf's fierce face looking down over its claws, its chin resting on the carved head of the Raven.

Inside, conversations hum around the room. Henry's eyes adjust to the light and he sees faces that look distantly familiar. He tries to recall their names, the complicated relationships between the Raven and Eagle Clans that Claire had tried endlessly to explain to him, but he never listened well enough to remember. He can't match a single face with any of the names that skitter through his mind like leaves.

Paulie now takes Henry by the arm and leads him into the room. Benches and chairs are arranged around the periphery of the hall and, in the middle, a pit lines with stones is filled with driftwood and branches for the fire. Looking up, Henry sees the round smoke hole cut through the building's roof. A huge screen stretches from floor to ceiling at the far end of the room. It is painted with enormous stylized images of Eagle on one side and Raven on the other. Two carved totem poles flank the screen and a low table stands between them.

Paulie guides Henry toward the back of the room, greeting people as they pass and stopping at the table. "I wish Mom could have been here," he says, leaning down and fingering a short staff collared with tiny beads, the talking stick he will carry as giver of the potlatch. Bending toward the beads, knotted carefully onto long strands of thread, Henry looks for the silver drops Claire had used when she repaired the talking stick before Paulie's naming.

"She would have loved everyone coming together like this again. And seeing you here would have made her very happy." Paulie places the talking stick in front of a basket of sage. The stick is very old, carved with the faces of many animal spirits, the wood polished and smooth from generations of hands. Henry remembers it in Claire's father's fist, how he had broken with tradition and handed her the talking stick when it came time to declare Paulie's tribal name, and not to Henry, the child's father.

"She was wrong to let you stay home every time the clans gathered. I always felt that. I wanted you here, wanted you to take part, but you know she didn't like to push. Always said you'd come around, by Indian time."

"What?" Henry asks. He tries to imagine what Claire said about him and realizes even Paulie knows her in ways that fall outside his own memories. All those years. The chasm between him and Claire suddenly seems wider than death.

"What?" he asks again.

"She meant when you were damn good and ready. You know, when you were ripe, by Indian time."

An old man wearing an elaborate button blanket trimmed

with feathers and rows of beads comes up behind them. "Hello there, Paul."

Henry turns. The man looks ancient, his skin folded and grooved like an old root washed up on the beach. A scar on his cheek has fallen in; his cheekbone hangs like a cliff over the left side of his face.

"Dad, you remember Jake Summer-Elk? Since last year, he's head of the Raven Clan. He and his people, they're the ones who carved the portal pole."

As the two men shake hands, Henry realizes they're about the same age. This is the man Claire once said she'd wanted to marry, the scar on his cheek from her first and, she said, last wildly cast salmon hook. Henry feels as awkward as a child beside him.

"We'll start the smudging soon, Paulie." Jakes carries the blanket of sage to the pit in the middle of the room. "Clean the air, get rid of all the negative spirits." He winks and Henry wonders if this is magic he really believes in. "Then we'll begin."

Looking past Paulie's shoulder, through the window on the other side of the room, Henry sees a crowd of teenage boys running back and forth outside. They might be playing football or soccer, and he steps across the room to watch.

A couple of boys chase Jeremy and his friends around the parking lot. Henry recognizes one or two, boys who used to pitch pennies on the steps of his liquor store. He wouldn't sell them beer so they hung around, trying to talk whoever passed into buying them a six-pack. Henry called them the "Hanging Around Boys."

Jeremy tumbles in and out of the muddy ruts in the road, trying to outrun the older boys. He holds the flat drum high over his head and Henry thinks they're playing a game until a thick muscular fellow reaches out and grabs the drum away.

Henry raps on the window with the knuckles of his hand. "Cut that out, you boys. Leave those kids alone."

One teenager close to the window glances at Henry, but the rest ignore him. He hurries through the hall and out the door.

"Give that drum back," he says, coming around the side of the clan house. Jeremy runs up beside him and hangs onto his leg. All the young boys gather behind these two, clutching the hems of each other's button blankets.

"Who's going to make me?" the boy asks, taking a step backwards.

"No one," Henry says. "You're just going to do it."

Jeremy reaches up and silently tugs the starched white sleeve of the liquor store shirt Paulie made Henry put on this morning. The shirt is scratchy and hot and makes him sweat. He unbuttons the cuff and folds his sleeve for more air.

The tough boys all take a step back and Henry looks up. Their faces are fearful and Henry has an uncomfortable realization; they think he's ready to fight.

He rolls up his sleeve with great care, glancing back and forth from his arm to the boy. "You heard me. Give him back the drum." He smooths the roll of fabric with his fingers then starts on the other sleeve. "Now."

"I'm doing it, I'm doing it." The boy tosses the drum like a Frisbee. It glides upward in a clean arc and he turns, sticking his thumbs into his belt loops and walking off, laughing with the others. Jeremy runs, his eyes on the drum. As it floats down, he reaches into the air and stops it in flight.

"Got it," he shouts and circles back to Henry's side.

Henry walks down the incline toward the beach and Jeremy follows, leaving his friends to mimic the older boys. They march up the stairs of the clan house with their fingers hooked in their belt loops, swaggering from side to side and jabbing each other with their elbows.

When they get to the beach, Henry and his grandson sit on the trunk of a fallen cedar lying in the grass above the high tide line. Jeremy lays his drum on a patch of ferns growing from a break in the bark.

"Are those our geese?" he asks in a whisper, pointing toward the flock of geese pecking at seaweed along the water's edge. They are elegant-looking birds with their long black necks and sleek bodies.

"I don't know. Maybe. See that one there?" Henry gestures at a large bird whose right eye is milky and sightless. "I'm sure that one came for breakfast last week. Remember? The day you came over with raisin bread and they all liked it so much?"

Jeremy's friends rush out of the clan house banging on drums and shouting. They chase each other, running around to the back of the building and making so much noise the startled birds begin to take flight.

The geese, regal just moments ago, look awkward and ungainly as they take the first steps of a running start. They pitch forward, gaining momentum until the impossible weight of their bodies leaves the ground. They sail out over the water, honking and falling into line in a deep and perfect V, then disappearing over the tops of the trees.

"How do they do that?" Jeremy asks, making a V with his thumb and forefinger.

"It's a puzzle," Henry says. He's studied the flight of geese since he first came to the island but is still awed by what happens when one occasionally drifts out of line. The others, still in formation, call out and answer, then open their ranks so the bird finds a new place inside their flying pattern.

Jeremy leans against his grandfather's arm. "Must be magic, I'll bet."

As the honking of the geese fades away, Henry thinks it probably is some bit of magic that keeps them in fearless suspension above the earth, some state of grace offered up to them out of their faithful willingness to fly.

He rises and pulls Jeremy to his feet. "Let's go in now."

He brushes the back of the child's button blanket where bits of moss and bark cling to the felt and the two walk up the hill to the clan house. The faint thump of drums floats in the air as they approach the doorway and Henry turns his good ear toward the sound.

The room is dim and slightly smoky with the smell of burning sage from the small fire in the pit. Women and girls sit in a wide circle along the walls. Henry looks down on their shoulders, past the tops of their heads to the men and boys stepping high and carefully around the fire as if the coals have scattered across the floor. Even the "Hanging Around Boys" now wear button blankets and dance inside the ring of women.

Jake and the other old men hold the flat drums and tap them gently with sticks. Paulie's face is covered by the carved wooden mask of the Wolf as he dances beside Jake, slow steps of toe-heel, toe-heel. He holds the ancient talking stick close to his chest.

Henry and his grandson slip past the seated women. They watch the swirling dancers follow the rhythm of Jake's drum then Jeremy takes Henry's hand. Startled by the child's touch,

Henry looks down at the hand in his. It is so large for a boy his age, the palm like a saucer, the fingers long and brown and slender. They are hands like Claire's with soft, waxy skin. Henry raises the palm to his cheek for a moment. It even smells familiar, like ferns and seawater, something so well known yet forever holding the possibility of surprise.

Jeremy smiles up at his grandfather and then lets go, moving into the dance between Paulie and Jake. Their circling makes Henry dizzy but he keeps his eye on Jeremy, holding out the edges of his button blanket, his feet falling into step with the other dancers. Jeremy's body dips and rises, swaying from side to side with each step, the blanket spread wide from his outstretched arms as he glides around the room.

Henry watches the child circle the fire and disappear behind smoke and flame, then move toward him again. Jeremy drops one side of the blanket and reaches out to his grandfather.

"Chinny," he mouths, his voice lost in the sound of the drums.

He leans into the stillness between the two circles of men and women and Henry grabs his hand, stepping into the ring of dancers. The men begin to sing a slow, rhythmical chanting song. It is a song without words, a rhythm of heartbeats and waves.

Jeremy looks at Henry and exaggerates the beat of the chant with his shoulders and head, urging his grandfather forward. Henry opens his mouth to join the others, not knowing the song but believing he can learn. The sound that comes from the back of his throat is stifled and choked but when he opens his mouth wider, his throat expands. Jeremy smiles up at him and sings out, too. As Henry dances with the other men, their steps quicken and their song grows louder, more purposeful. He follows close behind Jeremy, letting his voice climb with the child's. He pulls the sound from his chest and then reaches deeper. A clear, pure note rises from his belly. It carries out into the room, blending with the other voices and finding its own place. It is the sound of a man singing.

Jet Pilot for the Sandinistas

BY ROBIN LEWIS

It's Friday night and we're sitting at our regular booth down at the Purple Heart. Joe's telling me about *Top Gun*, the movie with Tom Cruise as a hotshot jet pilot and a good-looking blond aerospace engineer as his girlfriend.

"First of all," Joe says, his hands up in front of him, "this lady doctor dresses like no doc you've ever seen." He laughs and puts his hands down flat on the table. When he looks up at me, I laugh, too. Then his eyes shift to the side like he sees something behind me and he smiles.

"What?" I ask him.

"Miller time," he says, sitting up. I turn and see Dory coming our way.

"Hey, guys," she says and sets our beers on the table. Then she messes up my hair like she's been doing lately. "Thanks," I say, staring down at my glass, feeling myself turn red.

She leans over, her dark hair almost in her eyes, and tries to look up at my face. I turn away to hide it, but she sees and laughs. "I love it when you blush," she says, and I can't help but smile and turn even redder. She heads off to get a beer for someone else, and I watch her out of the corner of my eye.

"I don't blush," I say, looking across the table to Joe, but he's eyeing Dory, too, and doesn't hear. "Joe," I say, and then he nods his head at me as he pulls a Camel Light out of a new pack.

"Sure, okay," he says, sticking the cigarette in his teeth. He lights it as I turn to watch Dory some more. "Hey, Moon-eyes," he says, taking a drag, "do you want to hear about this video, or not?"

"Yeah, I want to hear about it," I say. "I've been wanting to see that movie."

"Why?"

"For the jets. See how real it is."

Joe scrunches up his face. "How would you know how real it is?"

I check around the bar. There aren't many people here yet, just a road crew in yellow rainslickers across the room hoisting Bud Lights. Mike, the owner, is cleaning beer glasses. He's got reddish-silver hair and everyone calls him "Tracer" because he flew an old F-86 in the Korean War, way back when I was still in the crib, way before Vietnam. The joint is full of pictures of him and his plane shooting tracer bullets all over the place like you see in war movies. Tracer starts in on cleaning shot glasses, and I remember something I read at work in *Time* magazine.

"Don't tell nobody," I say, leaning toward Joe, "but remember how I told you I broke my shoulder two summers ago down in Seattle?"

"Sure. You fell off some house you were building with your cousin."

I shake my head. "Well, I was telling you a story. It wasn't building a house, and it wasn't in Seattle." Joe's from Delta, I think, so he'll probably believe anything. I look around and lean even closer to him, so close I can look down inside his beer mug, and say: "I was flying jets for the Sandinistas."

I pull back as Joe's eyes get wide and he cracks up laughing. "Those guys in whozzit?!" he says, slapping the top of the table. "*Nicaragua?*" Everybody in the place turns toward us.

I lower my head. "Jeezus, Joe, will you put a sock in it?"

Joe wags his head around some more as he laughs. I look around the place. The road crew starts drinking again, but Tracer's eyeing me suspiciously, like he'd better not be serving Rainier on tap to some Communist. I smile at him like nothing's wrong and turn back to Joe. He finally stops laughing and winks toward the bar behind me, and the shot glasses clomp one after another as Tracer goes back to cleaning. Joe jabs his cigarette out in the ash tray.

"I'll bet your brother Bobby from Vietnam helped in all this, too," he says.

I roll my eyes at the ceiling. "You dink, Bobby wasn't *from* Vietnam, he was *in* Vietnam. Do I look like my brother's a damn gook?"

Joe drinks some more beer. "Jimbo," he says when his eyes come back to me, "I'm starting to wonder about you." He sets down his glass. "Besides which, I remember hearing that there aren't any jets down there in Nicaragua. Just choppers and Cessnas."

My head snaps back.

"Well, sure," I say, "... now."

"What do you mean, 'now'?"

I take a few pretzels out of the bowl on the table. "I crashed their only jet. One of them F-4 Phantoms left over from before the revolution. I was teaching them how to fly it." I crunch down on the pretzels and spin my beer mug on its coaster thing. Joe gets a small grin around the edge of his glass as he swallows his last chug. He waves at Dory for another beer and lights a new cigarette.

"Rowing against the tide tonight, Dory?" Joe asks when she shows up with his beer. He laughs at his joke about her nickname. She's from somewhere in Canada, and her real name's Dorothy.

"You know, it's been almost two hours since you asked me that," she says as she sets down his beer, and keeps looking at him. He gets the serious face back again. She leans against me. "And I suppose it's another one for you, too, eh?" She's got a great Canadian accent, and I love it when she says "eh."

"Another one for me," I say. I try to look her in the eyes, but can only make it up to the heart made out of purple felt on the front of her blouse.

"Yeah," Joe says, blowing smoke out in a stream, "Mr. Jet Pilot For The Sandinistas here needs another brew."

Dory laughs, and I barely look up at Joe, feeling a shiver in my back at Dory hearing about this. "All right, another Rainier coming up," she says and goes off.

I lift my head up and give Joe the major evil eye. "You've got a big trap," I say. "You can't just tell everybody about this." I finish off my beer and put the glass on the edge of the table for Dory. "I'm not telling you anything more, forget it."

"Oh, come on, Jimbo," he says, looking disappointed. I don't say anything. He smiles and takes another drag, leaning his head back against the seat, looking at me out of the bottom of his eyes. "Well," he asks, "can you tell me when you and Dory are going to get down to serious business? That's a story I'd like to hear."

I push my hand at him to get away, trying not to let him see me turning red again. "Forget that, too," I say. "You're the last person I'd tell about that."

The next morning I'm sitting on my bed looking at one of those *LIFE* magazine picture-books about Vietnam that I found at work and checked out. I used to drive a heating-oil truck for the same place Joe still does, making home deliveries. But then everybody started moving back to the Lower 48 because of the price of oil—not heating oil, real oil like from the gas companies—so there wasn't enough people left for two drivers to deliver to. Joe'd been there longer, so you know who got the can. Since then, I've been keeping an eye peeled on the "help wanted" ads, but nothing too hot has shown up yet.

For now, I'm working at a strange job I got at the library. It's called a "page," which is a pretty funny name for a job in a library if you ask me. All I do is put books on the shelves after people bring them back. It's okay for being someplace I wouldn't usually be. And you do find some interesting books that you'd probably never know about otherwise, like this Vietnam book I've got right now. Or another one I saw called *Jane's Airplanes*, or something like that, which has a whole lot of jet pictures in it and everything you'd want to know about them. I think it's pretty funny that a woman would write a book about jets, but the pictures are good.

The bed and everything in the place is crammed into the corners on account I live in an "efficiency" apartment, which Joe says is just another name for a big closet with a bathroom. I've got water on for instant coffee about two feet away, and while I'm going through the book, I scratch my cat Gaydem. Gaydem's life consists mostly of following me around like a cow that wants milking until I feed her. She's named after my brother Bobby's girlfriend in Saigon. He told her about her after he got back and before he got run over and killed in the

parking lot of some roadhouse between here and Anchorage.
He was drunk and fell down, and his head got squashed under
a semi-truck tire like one of them cantaloupes in supermarkets
that no one knows where they come from. That's what I
heard. I didn't see it because I was here at home, not on the
road with him, and I sure didn't want to look afterward to see
for myself.

Gaydem lies against me now, purring away as I turn the
pages. The book has a lot of black-and-white pictures in it, big
ones. The soldiers' faces are streaked with black, camouflage,
I guess, that's running because of sweat. The streaks look like
the scar that Bobby came back with. It started just below his
right eye, ran down to his jaw, skipped over his neck, and
started up again on his chest for about six inches. He told me
he got slashed with a knife while trying to protect Gaydem
from the gooks.

Bobby was a big hero when he got drafted, and from what I
remember, he was an even bigger one when he came back. He
did a lot of telling stories out at bars so army guys from Ft.
Wainwright would buy him drinks. At first he told me all
sorts of stories, too, about being on leave in Saigon and how
stupid his lieutenant was. "He was from West Point," Bobby
said, "but he might as well have been from East Point. The
doofus couldn't find his way across a rice paddy."

After a few months, though, after he'd started really
boozing he stopped telling me anything. But he kept up the
stories at the bars and letting GI's buy rounds for him. He
drank so many beers and shots that he ended up having to go
to Alcoholics Anonymous. But he still wouldn't stop smiling
for folks, wouldn't say no, I guess.

Then he got run over by a guy who'd just bought him a
beer.

That evening, I feed Gaydem and head out to meet Joe at
the Purple Heart.

"I'm a few ahead of you," he tells me when I sit down.

"No way, José," I tell him. "I had a couple at home before I
left." I slide into the booth. "That's what they say down in
Nicaragua: 'No way, José.'" Joe laughs and says "Is that so?" as
Dory comes over. She puts her hand on my shoulder, and her
perfume makes her smell like a big rose.

"How's it going, guys?" she asks. "Two, eh?" She looks me in the eyes and rubs the back of my shoulder, and all of a sudden my body feels like I'm laying in a bathtub full of warm water.

"Yeah, two," Joe says, smoking his cigarette with his eyebrows close together at Dory.

"All right," she says, taking her hand off my shoulder, and then does this walk like dancing away from us. Joe looks at me and grins, fooling around with his red baseball cap from summer-league softball. His eyes go sideways at Dory and back through the smoke to me. "Tonight may be the night, buddy."

I smile at him and try to think of something to say before I get all red thinking about what he means. "Time to relax," I say, and we stretch across opposite sides of the booth, backs against the paneling, making sure the Tracerman doesn't see our boots on his seats. Dory brings our beers, and we drink up. Then I feel Joe watching me.

"What?" I ask. "What?"

He grins, leaning forward. "I was just wondering. Did you fly that jet in Nicaragua before or after you climbed Andy's Mountains."

I smack my forehead. He does this all the time—never gets the name right. "You know, if I keep talking to you I'm going to have a big flat spot up here," I say, pointing up there. "The *Andes* Mountains, not *Andy's* Mountains. What do you think, that some guy named Andy owns them?" I sit back and sip my beer, shaking my head like "these folks from Delta."

"Oh, yeah," he says, still grinning. "The Andes." He sips his beer, watching me. "So?" he says. "When was it?"

I look in my beer at the dark reflection of my face and the light over my head. "After," I tell him, "a couple years ago. How do you think I paid for the climb? Out of my take." Joe nods, and I'm glad he's got a few beers down already. Hopefully he won't ask any more questions; I want to relax, not think.

He keeps quiet, and we watch people coming and going, don't talk about anything else important, which is just what I like to do sometimes. Dory brings us more beers, and pretty soon all the voices and clinking glasses run together, which I like, too. I punch up a few good tunes on the jukebox, ones I know the words to, like that cowboy song by Willie Nelson, and sit back down and think about Dory. Maybe, I think. I watch her walk around the room. Her hair is long and permed into waves and floats up and down behind her. She brings four mugs of beer to a booth down the way and stays there for a few minutes laughing with all the guys. Well, maybe not. It seems she could like one of them, too, and I can't figure out if she likes me or if she's just being nice like she is to everybody.

A few minutes later, after Joe gets up and goes to the men's room, Dory shows up with new beers without even being asked. "Thought I'd sneak these over here while Joe was in the john," she says.

"Well, he'll be glad you did."

She laughs. As she leans over to put my beer down, she looks at me from real close and says, "I get off at eleven tonight."

"Really?" I sip my beer. "Well, that's pretty nice of Tracer."

She stays there staring at me for a second, and I can feel myself starting to turn red again. What? I wonder. Then she straightens back up.

"I was thinking we could go to someplace for coffee," she says.

"Us?"

Dory's eyes crinkle up as she laughs. "Yes, us. You and me. Why do you think I said, 'we,' eh?" She smiles, actually no way I've really seen her smile before. I feel like I'm staring into headlights and realize it's because I'm looking her in the eyes.

"That sounds great," I say. "I'll wait for you."

She keeps grinning. "Good. Denny's?"

"They have good coffee," I say, "but wherever you want."

"Eleven o'clock."

"I'll be here," I say and tap the table. She messes up my hair again and goes back to work.

Dory holds my arm as we walk into Denny's, and the waitress takes us to a booth. Dory surprises me again, this time by sitting down next to me instead of across from me. She scoots along the orange seat so her leg almost touches mine, and we order coffee. "Better make it decaf," Dory tells the waitress, and I nod. "Same for me." Out the window, on the other side of our faces looking back in the glass, I see the first snowfall of the year under the streetlight, big flakes. I make a fake shiver like it's already thirty-below, and my leg rubs against Dory's a couple times. "Well, first snow's down," I say, looking back at her, "I guess winter's here for sure."

She stares at me, smiling. "Well, might not be so bad," she says. "You can stay warm somehow." She looks down fast, blushes and then looks back up.

"That came out a little strange, eh?" she says. "Sorry."

"Nothing to be sorry about," I say to make her feel better. When our coffee gets here, I ask her where she's from in Canada, and she says a town called Smithers in B.C. We start talking about me being born in Alaska, from around Fairbanks mostly, and comparing the two places. I try not to watch her lips as she talks, but it's not too easy. Her eyes are big, and I realize this is the first time we've been together but not in the Heart with Joe sitting across from us smoking away. "It gets almost as cold down there," she says, "but there's more wind. There's a ski resort near there, but I never was one for skiing and I like having no wind here."

I nod my head, trying hard to think of something to say. Dory looks down at her coffee, and her chin is near the purple heart on her blouse. She runs her lips together like she wants to say something and then flashes those eyes back up at me. They scare me, the way they jump out from behind a few strands of her hair. Then she says, "Well, you know what I'm curious about is who is your brother, Bobby from Vietnam?"

The way she uses the same name as Joe makes me wince. How'd she hear about that?

I look at myself in the window, remembering about Bobby. I can see Dory behind me lean even closer, waiting. "Well, he was my brother," I tell her, turning back. "Even though he was twenty-one, he lived with me and my mom for a while after he got back. He was a pretty good guy, I guess. He told me he hated it over there in Vietnam, but you should've seen the way he pretended for everyone else, especially my mom." I kind of grunt, thinking about it. "There was this time all three of us were in the living room, and Momma was thanking the Lord for Bobby's safe return, acting like she was in church, telling me how he'd fought his way back from the brink of Hell, 'the Devil a-scratching and a-pulling to reclaim his soul the whole way.'" I smile at Dory, sipping my coffee with both hands. My elbow accidently slides over and hits hers, but she doesn't move, so I don't either.

"'Your brother Bobby's a new man,' Momma told me, 'brighter now because he's seen the darkness.'" I grin and shake my head. "Well, Bobby had a hangover, but he was still sitting there all puffed up like a rooster that's busted into a big sack of cornmeal. You know..." I bulge out my cheeks and bug my eyes at Dory, and she laughs. "I was a little mad about his drinking then, so just to be a smartass, I asked Momma if the 'brink of Hell' was that bar I'd seen Bobby stumbling out of a couple times on my way home from school."

"Jimbo!" Dory says.

"When I said that, Momma started hacking and coughing, looking at me like the devil's coming to get her. Bobby jumped up and ran into the kitchen and got her some water, and Momma kept coughing and staring away from me at the pictures on the fireplace. When Bobby came back, I got up to leave, but in the hall a hand caught me right here near the neck and turned me around. It was Bobby. He said, 'One more remark like that, you little shit, and I'll show you the brink of Hell.' I thought he was going to hit me, the way he was holding the collar of my shirt."

Dory moves over a little so our legs are up against each other for sure. Elbows and legs. She looks over the top of my coffee mug at me as I'm about to take a sip, and asks:

"Did Bobby tell stories, too?"

I pull the cup away from my mouth fast. Some of the coffee comes back over the rim and falls on the white placemat. I pretend I burned my lips and say "Ow." Rubbing my mouth, I look straight into the shiny side of the cup.

"Stories?" I ask.

"You know, like you tell." She tries to snuggle even closer to me. "We all think they're funny," she says. "Even Tracer liked that jet story you told Joe, and he really did fly jets."

I set my coffee down and act like nothing's wrong. Great, just great. So that's how Dory knows about Bobby from Vietnam. I think about everybody down at the Heart laughing behind my back and all those pictures of Tracer around the joint, and his real Purple Heart from when he got shot down hanging behind the till. I can feel Dory looking at me, so I keep grinning a little, trying not to sweat.

I think about Bobby telling me how he used to get in fights with Marines when he was on leave, how he killed five guys at once one time, and how he carried the head of a gook around on the end of a big stick for three days before his lieutenant told him to lose it. "It was a decoy," Bobby told me.

I pull my elbow away from Dory. "Yeah, Bobby told stories," I tell her. But I don't say "too."

"Oh," Dory says, and I can feel her watching me. Then she finishes up the last of her decaf and yawns.

"Well, I need to get some sleep," she says. "How about taking a lady home?"

"Okay, sure."

We drive to her place through the snow. "Here it is," she says, "right here." I pull to the curb in front of an apartment building. Looking up, I see the number 3169 and hope I'll be able to remember it. Then I turn toward her. The curls in her hair are shiny from the streetlight. I'm hoping she'll ask me to come in, but then I think about her bringing up stories and wonder if that would be smart. In my head, though, I can see Joe pointing at me with the lit end of his drooping Camel Light, telling me, "Go for it, guy, go for it." I look around at some of the houses on the street and then back at her.

"Well, I had a great time talking," she says. Then she comes at me and kisses me on the cheek.

"How about breakfast tomorrow?" I ask her, and I'm glad it's dark because I can feel the blood going to my face again. "We could . . . talk some more."

She smiles. "Pick me up at nine-thirty," she says. "I go on at eleven at Tracer's and we can go somewhere to eat before."

"Okay," I say and then lean over and kiss her on the cheek, too. She laughs, but it's a nice laugh, like she's glad I kissed her. "Okay," she says in a man's voice, pretending she's me, and opens the car door.

It's Sunday afternoon back at the Heart. The jukebox's turned down and there aren't many people here. Dory's working, but she's sitting next to me in the booth waiting for an order. I see Joe come through the door and then cross the room to sit down. His eyes look at me and Dory like he's trying to figure something out.

"Well, hello, you two," he says, taking a seat. "Been calling you all day, bud," he says to me.

Dory cuddles over and slips her arm around my knee. "Jimbo and I went out to brunch this morning." I squeeze her hand under the table.

"'Brunch,' huh?" says Joe, grinning, reaching into his shirt pocket for his cigarettes. "What was for breakfast?" he asks and laughs.

"Not what you're thinking," Dory says. While Joe's lighting his cigarette, he looks at her with his eyes real narrow. Then he sees me watching him, and they get wide like I caught him doing something. Then he grins, and one eye closes slowly and opens back up. I don't know why, but I try not to smile back at him.

Somebody yells for a beer, and Dory kisses me on the cheek. "Gotta go," she says and jumps up, almost taking my leg with her. Joe says, "I won't need one for a while yet, Dory, so take your time."

He watches her head for the tap and then turns back to me. He sits against the seat, running his finger along the groove in the paneling, smiling, looking at me with his cigarette hanging out of his mouth like he's James Dean.

"So," he says, "what's the story?"

I look after Dory. She's carrying a full tray of glasses across the room. "No story," I say and sip my beer.

Joe sits up, looking hurt. "Jesus, buddy, don't clam up on me now," he says. "Don't jet pilots stay up longer? That's what Tracer says."

I try not to smile, but he sees it.

"Come on, you can tell me," Joe says. "Did you get it up higher than the Andes?"

I stop smiling. "Joe, I'm not telling you a story, okay? Forget it."

His eye's open up like he's just snagged a trophy-sized King and he's reeling it in. He leans forward. "So *don't*," he says, "just tell me the truth."

"The truth is..." I say, and then I see Joe lean forward even more, waiting.

"Yeah?" he says. "Come on, you can tell ol' Joe." He winks.

Jimbo, I think, don't do it. But Joe's grinning at me so wide and he's been like a brother to me so long that I've got to tell him something. What can it hurt if no one else hears it? "Okay," I say, "but don't tell nobody." He nods, taking a long drag as he gets ready to listen, and then, looking to make sure Dory isn't around, I paint a pretty wild picture about me and her and last night after Denny's.

I'm squinting at the edge of another book at work, reading those little letters and numbers so I can put it away, when Mrs. Nielson, the head librarian, finds me. "There's a phone call for you, Jim," she says. "It's a woman."

"Really?" Mrs. Nielson smiles and nods. This is a surprise. Not many people know I work here. I walk quietly in my workboots behind the front desk and pick up the phone. "Hello?"

"You goddamn, bloody bastard," a voice says. It's Dory, and she's sobbing.

"What's wrong?" I ask her, but I know. I brace my shoulder against the wall and close my eyes.

"You told Joe a big story about us," she says, "and he told everybody and their bloody dog. It's only four o'clock, but all the regs are pinching my butt to see if they can get some." She cries a little more. "I'm going to grab a beer mug here pretty soon and crack a few cheekbones."

I open my eyes and stare out the front door of the library, watching the cars drive by.

"Well?" she asks.

I feel her waiting and turn my back against the wall. "I'm sorry, Dory," I say. "I told him not to tell anyone. I didn't know he'd go and do that." I don't know what else to say to her. "I'm real, real sorry."

There's a silence and then Dory tries to laugh. It sounds more like a gasp. "You seemed so nice," she says. "But you're actually just another asshole in a long line of assholes." And then she hangs up.

I stand there for a few seconds until I see Mrs. Nielson watching me all concerned. The last thing I need is to spill my guts to somebody with silvery-blue hair who looks like the Librarian from Mars, so I hang up the phone and head back toward my bookcart. I stop and sit down on one of the couches

they have here, next to some kid reading a computer magazine. In my head, I can still hear Dory crying on the phone
and think about her in her purple skirt huddled up alone in the
hallway at the bar. That son-of-a-bitch Joe, I think.

I get up and grab the book I had and push the cart alongside
the shelves with the encyclopedias. Then I look up and see
another book that I've never seen before. It's big, with a brown
cover that says it's a Vietnamese-English dictionary. I think of
my cat Gaydem and wonder if her name's in there. Still
thinking about Dory, I pull the book out and open it up. I try
to read the little words, but I can't make heads or tails of the
thing.

"Mrs. Nielson," I call.

"Yes, Jim?" she says and looks up from behind her desk.
When she sees me standing there with a book, she comes
bustling over like she's finally got her mission in life. "Can I
help you with something?"

"Yeah," I tell her, "I need to look something up. My cat's
name's Gaydem. It's Vietnamese for something, but I can't
figure this book out." I hold the dictionary out to her.

"Let me have a look," she says. It takes her a minute, but she
licks her thumb, flips a few pages and finds the word in there.
"Here it is," she says, pointing. "Gai-diem." Then she sucks
in her breath and goes, "Oh, my." She holds the book out to
me, and I look down to see what it means. At the white tip of
her fingernail is the word "whore."

I take the book from her and slam it closed. "Uh, thanks," I
say as I put the book back in its slot, and she moves away and
then turns and heads toward her desk. I think about Bobby
and all his stories about his girlfriend Gaydem and how he
said he got his scar. I look up at the books and have this
strange memory that's only one second long. I'm stepping off
the porch back home. I think I'm on my way to American
Legion baseball practice, got my mitt in one hand, and all of a
sudden, I hear loud laughing from the other end of the porch.
I whirl my head toward it as I jump from the steps to the
ground and see Bobby talking with a bunch of his friends
from the pipeline. He's got his shirt collar pulled down and
he's pointing out the rest of the scar to them. That's what I
remember: me in the air with my feet not touching either the

steps or the ground, and Bobby with that goddamn grin of his, looking at his friends as they all laugh.

I think about Joe blabbing off, and about Dory working now with all those jerks bugging her. I really messed things up. Well, Bobby, I'm going to take care of *my* trouble. No jerk like Joe smiling and patting me on the back, like they used to do to you, is going to screw up my life.

Later in the evening, I try calling Joe again, but he's not at the Heart or at home, which is lucky for him. I've had a few beers and have been laying on my bed inventing new ways to pound him. I've got a pretty good buzz going when I think that a cold walk will be good for the noggin. Maybe cool me down a little. I get out my coat and bundle up. Outside, there's still a couple inches of snow on the ground from the other night with Dory, and I start across the lawn to the sidewalk, crunching along.

It's quiet out, and I head down toward the park. It's nice to see an open space of white when it snows, big and smooth where the grass is, especially at night under the streetlights. As I get close to the park, I see the lights are on in the basement of the church on the corner. I get curious because it's kind of strange to see a whole church dark like that with light coming from only the ground. I walk across the snow, past a spruce tree, to the windows and look down into the light to see what's going on.

What it looks like is an Alcoholics Anonymous meeting that I went to once with Bobby. There's all sorts of people in there, people in suits, guys in wool hats, and some women who look like they couldn't have anything wrong with them. The room is painted a pea-green color that nobody but churches and the Army would want to buy, and a woman who looks like she lost a fight with her hairdryer is moving her arms around as she tells her story to everybody. I stand there in the snow that's white from the light and think about what's going on with me: about Bobby and Gaydem, about Joe, and most of all about Dory. All them damn stories. And it gives me an idea. What we need, I think as a joke, is a goddamn AA for storytellers. I grin at that, watching the people listen to the woman talk. Then I hear footsteps behind me.

"Hey, you okay?"

I turn and there's a guy standing by the tree. His face is lit by the basement windows. He has a blond beard and his coat's buttoned all the way up to his chin. He steps from foot to foot trying to stay warm in tennis shoes. "You want to come on in?" he asks, moving his head sideways toward the door.

"Well, I don't think so..." I say.

He takes my arm. "Come on, it's no big deal. Really. Just listen if you want."

"Uh, well..." I say, too surprised to do anything, thinking about Bobby being the alcoholic, not me, and meantime the guy just takes me right inside the church. The warm air rushes at me as he closes the door. I hear the woman's voice now, loud like she looks, but I still can't make out what she's saying. The place smells like wet dust, and I unbutton my coat and walk through the inside door into the room where the meeting is. The woman finishes and sits down. Some guy smoking a pipe like he thinks he's a shrink or something gets up front.

"Well," he says, "how about a break for a couple minutes? Sandy brought some cookies tonight." There's a lot of noise of chairs moving, and people get up and walk around. The cookies are right next to me, and the people all turn in my direction. Seeing all those faces makes me step back a little. A woman comes up from my side, grabs a few cookies and a cup of coffee, and starts talking to the guy who brought me in here.

"Hi, I'm Martin," somebody says to me, and I turn. It's the guy with the pipe, smiling at me, reaching to shake my hand, probably trying to figure out how many brewskies I've had today. But I don't pay any attention to him, just look straight ahead and go find a chair to get out of the crowd. I sit down next to another guy who smells like he lives behind a toilet and gets hit back there all the time. I want to get the heck out of there, but don't dare move. I just fold my arms and look around at the different kinds of people, making sure no one's going to grab me.

After the cookie break, everyone sits down, and I feel a little better. Another one of the anonymous alcoholics gets up in front. He says his name is Steve and everyone says, "Hello, Steve." He holds his hand up wrapped in a big white mitt of red-cross tape and starts in on how he blowtorched it three days ago trying to light a cigarette at work.

"I'd been drinking up from my thermos at lunch because it kind of felt good," he tells the others. He waves his mitt around like one of those mummies on the late show. "Well, this didn't feel too good, let me tell you."

The people in the room laugh and then start clapping as he heads back to his seat. When no one else gets up right away, Martin stands up. "Well, is there anyone else?" he asks, and then looks at me. The guy I met outside and everyone else looks at me too, and I think about Dory and her purple heart. I look down at my shoes and hunch my shoulders. It doesn't help—I still feel all those eyes on me. But then I think, well, you know, Jimbo, it's sort of now or never. I sit there a few more seconds, and then, slowly, I raise my hand.

"Okay, welcome," says Martin and sits down.

I get up in front and look around. Everyone's staring right back at me, and I feel my stomach twisting up inside. I try to tell what they think of me by their faces, but I can't. Most look okay, but some have these sad-like eyes and look like them Hush Puppy dogs sitting on chairs.

"My name's Jim," I tell them.

"Hello, Jim," everybody says.

I smile, but they all just sit there, still looking at me. Then I remember from watching the guy before me that I'm supposed to say that I'm an alcoholic. Bobby never did it, he told me, which is probably why he never quit. But for me, it's true. I look down at my feet and say:

"And I'm not an alcoholic."

There's some rustling at this, and the hair-dryer woman gives me a dirty look. So does a man with a mustache in a fancy suit with a tie. I look at Martin who's just watching me, smoking his pipe. I can tell that none of them thinks I'm telling the truth.

"I do have a problem, though," I say, trying to make them stop looking at me like that, and, believe it or not, it actually feels good to say that out loud. I feel a little lighter. But they don't look too convinced, and I can't think how to start explaining it all to them. Then I can tell they think I'm holding back a good story, maybe even worse than theirs, and they all look tired of hearing about people blowtorching their hands. They want something good. Then I think about Dory and the Sandinistas and Tracer getting shot down, and before I can stop myself...

I tell them her name was Maria. "She did the tightest barrel rolls in an F-4 Phantom you ever saw," I say. "We met two years ago while I was training the Sandinistas in Nicaragua to fly jets." I look at my boots, breathing in. "Maria was one of them."

She had the world's greatest smile, I say, beautiful red lips, and she was gorgeous and smart. "Shiny-black hair, real curly, cut short. When she was decked out to fly, you'd think you might just be looking at a guy until she turned around and you saw those big, brown eyes." I shake my head, thinking about Dory looking at me in the car Saturday night before she kissed me. "Man, those eyes."

I tell them about how we were on a training flight and got off course and ended up over the Andes Mountains. "Phantoms come with two engines, called J79GE15's," I say, and it was while we were out there over those mountains, I tell them, that both those engines blew. "Well, the Phantom started to go down. I yelled at Maria to bail out and then pulled one of the three release levers around my chair to eject. But as I was shooting out of there, I broke my shoulder on the edge of the cockpit." I tell them about looking up before pulling the ripcord, my arm feeling like it was falling off, and not seeing Maria anywhere, and about watching the jet scream off toward the mountains as I landed in a small, green valley. Then how I heard the explosion and saw the smoke rising into the sky from a snowfield way up in the Andes and miles away.

I hear someone sniffling and look up to see the hair-dryer woman putting a box of kleenex out of its misery. Next to her, the man in the suit is leaning forward on his chair, his eyes wide, listening with a smile. I check around the room— everyone is looking at me like I'm a war hero.

"Well, when I saw her going down in that jet," I say, "and thought about those eyes, I didn't care what happened to me anymore. After I was rescued, I drank straight shots of tequila, and when they found me passed out, they had to pump my stomach so I wouldn't die."

Then I tell them about how it rained at Maria's funeral, how you couldn't tell the rain from my tears, like maybe God was crying, too, and about how the Sandinista honor guard fired a twenty-one gun salute. Then I tell about how the beautiful great-grandaughter of that soldier-guy Sandino, whose picture I saw at work, the great-grandaughter of the man they all fought for to get the jet, how she stood next to me, and how I cried on her shoulder as they lowered Maria's casket into the ground.

"Maria was the one," I say.

By now, even I've got tears in my eyes, but then I think about Dory and standing by the window before I came in here, and I tell myself that maybe I should just leave it at that, really leave it at that, and not go too far. Then I look up and see everybody staring again, wanting me to go on, and I think, Jimbo, old buddy, you already did go too far.

I feel like I'm in the middle of a river and can't get to shore, can't even find an eddy to slow down in. Dory comes into my head, looking even more disappointed, but I shake it to get her out of there. Then I close my eyes and try to picture what could have happened after the funeral. Maybe I went crazy and climbed the Andes to look for the wrecked jet, hoping to be closer to Maria, to be together again like in true love. Or, maybe, after I got over Maria, I fell in love with Sandino's beautiful great-grandaughter, and we got married. Or, maybe I stole a new jet—like an F-16—from the Air Force and flew it back to Nicaragua to make up for the one I crashed. Or, maybe . . .

Or, maybe I did all of it. I stand there for a second thinking, feeling myself swirling along, trying to remember what I know about mountain climbing—what'd it take to go look for Maria. When I get that in my head, I breathe in and slowly open my eyes.

"But that's just the beginning," I say.

The Gambler's Daughter

BY BARBARA UNGER

Sister Margaret came to fetch me promptly at four. She led me to the parlor where she unlocked the door with a key from her long chain. The practice piano stood against the wall and I had an hour to myself before I heard the patter of her feet on the stone floor again. The room was kept locked when the piano wasn't in use. After a time I began to realize that I was probably her only pupil.

The convent was a cross between Spanish hacienda and medieval cloister. Church bells echoed through the halls and harmonized with the voices of the nuns making their devotions. In the gardens grew a profusion of bougainvillea and hibiscus beneath huge banyan trees whose tangled roots bumped up through the ground. The odor of jasmine was everywhere.

After awhile, the parlor door was left unlocked and the other nuns seemed to recognize me as the little Jewish girl that had been given special permission to practice freely on the convent piano since I had no piano of my own. They'd smile at me as I walked around the bordered gardens carrying my music books and metronome.

When my father discovered that my mother had arranged for piano lessons at a Roman Catholic convent, he was angry yet amused. "Why not buy her an upright? It can't cost much," he said.

"It's the only place in this godforsaken city that offers piano lessons," countered my mother. She added that she had dutifully searched for a proper piano school but it turned out that Miami Beach was in short supply of classical pianists back in the 1940s.

We lived in a rented furnished apartment in a hotel that posted restrictions against animals, children (I was an exception), bathing suits, wet feet and musical ins ruments such as ukuleles or banjos. Mother interpreted the restrictions to mean no pianos as well. Actually, Mother took the attitude that we were lucky to be there at all. Before the war, the restrictions had included Jews, in addition to dogs, cats and banjos.

The move to a warm climate was occasioned by my young father's two near-fatal heart attacks. In search of an easier regimen, he had left behind a flourishing button business he didn't like back in New York's garment center, with his two brothers at the helm. Anyone could see that my father was better suited to a more intellectual calling. In some ways he was absolutely wonderful, never using the Southern expression "nigra" and speaking out against small-town crackers who shot black people for no cause. In other ways, he had grown distant and unpredictable.

We rented the furnished apartment for the season, which ran from October to May. We kept the lease on our West Bronx apartment where we lived during part of the off-season. The residents of Everglades Crest Apartments were flabby pale people from places like Idaho and North Dakota who never sat in the sun. They sat under the canopy in the patio on rattan chairs and never spoke to us. The apartment had a Murphy bed that came out of the wall. I slept fitfully on it, and listened to the buzz of insects all night through the screens. The windows overlooked a mosaic fish pond and a stand of royal palms. My parents crammed their closets with tropical suits, sequinned cocktail gowns and my mother's new furs. Rows of reptile shoes, each with a handbag to match, lined the closet shelves. I thought it all very grand, especially the swirling lobby fan, the central switchboard and daily maid service.

Occasionally, my father inquired about my piano lessons at the convent. Then, at a loss for words, he grabbed me and waltzed me around the room while he sang "Sweet Rosie O'Grady" or else we fox-trotted to "Second-Hand Rose." Then he dressed in his robin's egg blue gabardine jacket and knotted his thick silk hand-painted tie and left. He was off to carouse with The Boys, transplanted New York gambling cronies who had become his constant new companions.

The Boys were a suntanned group of balding males with paunches who had made it big in wartime Miami Beach with its flourishing real estate, gambling and black market trades. The leader of The Boys was named Broadway Bennie.

My father never referred to what he did in Miami as "work" or "business." My mother called it "establishing himself in The South." She lightened her hair and wore loud tropical-print playsuits covered with cherries, bananas and pineapples. On weekends, my parents disappeared on scheduled gambling junkets to Havana, Cuba and returned too tipsy to talk, throwing themselves into bed fully dressed during the early hours of the morning.

"It makes your father happy. What does it cost?" she said irritably when I asked her why they went to Havana so often. I began to look forward to those rare days when she remained at home. Sometimes, after school, she and I took beach chairs down to the ocean where I paddled in the waves and my mother tilted her face into the sun to try to burn the poor crust of the Bronx off her face. Richly leatheretted from his afternoons at Hialeah Racetrack, my father looked every bit the prosperous playboy.

When I asked my father how he spent his days, he told me it all had to do with the care, breeding and training of beautiful horses called thoroughbreds. He loved everything about sleek, beautiful horses. They had, in fact, become his true calling. When he wasn't with The Boys, he hung around with Florida natives or crackers who worked with the horses. They provided him with something called "tips." They weren't the only "tips." There were the hundred-dollar bills he had to give headwaiters who found us good restaurant tables and smaller bills for the waiters and busboys who fawned over us as we dined. "Tips" also went to the maids and butlers at The Everglades Crest and various other mysterious characters who helped charter fishing boats and guided tours deep into the heart of alligator country.

We ate dinners in exclusive restaurants. My father drove in the new Cadillac out along the waterways in search of ever more exclusive clubs where we could dine. One night, my mother took me aside while my father and his cronies drank at the circular bar. Her face was arranged in a particularly desperate expression.

"Look at your father," she said in a conspiratorial whisper. I did and looked up questioningly at her. "See how he acts. Look at him kidding around and telling jokes. You wouldn't believe he lost nearly a thousand dollars at the track today, would you?"

I shook my head.

"It makes him feel like a big shot. Tell you what. How would you like to play a little trick on daddy?"

At first I was dubious but I heard her out. The trick was this—I was to plead to go to the ladies room after the meal was over. I was to stop at the table before the busboy cleared it up, filch a few bills from beneath stained plates and hide the stolen tip money in my plastic pocketbook. Mother promised to split with me fifty-fifty. She confided in me that she also was skimming money from the household kitty. By taking advantage of my father's absurd penchant for over-tipping, we would be able to build a private bank account of our own. What could be simpler?

"Your father will put us in the poorhouse if we don't do something," she said. Her face was a study in doom. "By the time you'll need it for college, there won't be a penny left." Our little game would remain a secret. After all, thrift was no crime. This way we'd always have a little something put away for a rainy day, just in case the business went broke and my father's gambling debts couldn't be paid.

And so I became a Liberty depositor. Someone had to save my father. Weeks later, my mother explained the intricacies of bank interest and gave me my own bankbook to hide. My father remained too engrossed in his own business to notice our little game.

"Someday you'll thank me," my mother said.

I was proud to meet my mother's high standards of accomplishment. There was no doubt that I was talented at filching tips. If a waiter or busboy noticed me, I'd announce boldly that my father had sent me back for change. I rehearsed various soulful expressions for encounters that never occurred. Nobody dared challenge me. In this manner I acquired nearly fifty dollars a week merely for accompanying

my parents and their cronies to dinner. And so began my life
of crime.

At the convent the nuns began to regard me as a Jewish
Wunderkind who had been fortuitously dropped from the sky
into their midst. Even though they fled past me in their black
robes and starched wimples, like slender herons, I sensed they
were watching me. Even the Mother Superior stopped by the
parlor from time to time to stand in the doorway and listen to
me play. Sister Margaret promoted me to more complicated
pieces with difficult arpeggios, tricky fingering and con-
trolled legatos.

I pretended to enjoy plunking the out-of-tune keys, all the
while dreaming of jet-black Steinway grands on the stage of
Carnegie Hall where I'd sit elevated above crowds of elegant
men in tuxedos and women in ball gowns. My mother
promised to buy me a magnificent ebony baby grand of my
own in a few years, after we had fully established ourselves in
The South. I pictured the piano in the living room of our new
home beside the water in Coral Gables. Someday all of these
finger exercises would earn me great affection and probable
fame and fortune. And so I kept up my lessons for mother's
sake, dreaming of the future.

Sometimes my mother grew suspicious about my long
afternoons at the convent, where the Mother Superior was
offering me lessons and a practice piano for a pittance. Mother
asked me if I was ever required to say prayers. Catholic
prayers. I said no. After that I was careful not to get Sister
Margaret in trouble of any kind for I felt that, in agreeing to
instruct a Jewish child like me, she had already earned the
disapproval of the other nuns. I could tell from their strained
smiles and the embarrassed way they fled by when they
caught sight of me with my metronome and music books.

I assured my mother that I was making fine progress. My
mother had dreamed for years of becoming a concert pianist
but was unable to accept the scholarship offered to her by
Juilliard because she had to go out and earn a living. Every
child has to live out her parents' crushed or discarded
ambitions. I didn't mind piano lessons. I felt proud when my
father pinched my cheek and called me his little Paderewski. I
liked it when he showed off his considerable knowledge. How

many of his Damon Runyonesque cronies like Broadway Bennie or Hialeah Sam knew the names of the composers?

That winter, my mother began to accompany my father to the track every day. Our new maid Elsie hummed melancholy gospel tunes as she ironed. Money was always left on the table beneath the red plastic radio—money for Sister Margaret, money for supper at the old people's cafeteria, money for Elsie which I dispensed according to my mother's instructions. My parents were seldom home. On the few weekday evenings when they returned from the track, I had to join them and their dinner guests at sumptuous restaurants like Ciros and Maxims.

Light-fingered rich girl ready for flight, I had accumulated nearly eight hundred dollars in my Liberty passbook. But my industry was not without penalty. In my dreams, peg-legged pirates slipped me the black spot. Ugly dwarfs fenced my pickpocket tiaras. My Swiss dirndl was now too short for my sprouting limbs and its bodice puckered over my buds of breasts. This made it even easier for me to play our little trick on my father. Nobody seemed to notice. I had them all fooled. I wore my hair over one eye like Veronica Lake. I was a gangster's moll. By now I considered myself the mob's perfect daughter.

When I heard one of The Boys use the term "bookie," I thought at first that it had something to do with library research on those sleek and beautiful horses that my father loved. But from their snickers and whispers I began to realize that "making book" had more to do with gambling than with intellectual endeavors. My father's buddies, fat, broken-nosed men with voices like the gutter, bounced me on their laps while they instructed me in arcane subjects like Daily Doubles and something sinister called *chemin de fer.*

I hated when Broadway Bennie's hands crept up my skirts where they shouldn't be. I had no guilt about jumping off their laps when I felt their fingers wiggle, until I saw my father's dark displeasure. After that, I had to pretend to enjoy their attentions. I wondered if my father knew what they tried to do with their fingers under the elastic of my bloomers. If being nice to Broadway Bennie meant letting him diddle me in secret, then my revenge was even sweeter. My father suffered yet another heart attack. During his recovery he began to put on weight girlishly around the hips. The doctors told him that he had ulcers and diabetes. He laughed and swore he'd bury his doctors.

My mother's eyes were like rooms in which the shades were always drawn. The balance in my Liberty pass book grew steadily, our secret cache against this cruel happiness. My dreams of escape grew unbearable.

As my parents spent more and more time in Havana, leaving Élsie to mind me, I began spending less and less time practicing piano at the convent. Even without weekly practicing, I was able to gain Sister Margaret's faint praise. Unwilling to relinquish her sole pupil, Sister Margaret pretended not to notice that my visits to the convent had diminished. Each week I brought her the envelope that contained the money for my practice time and lessons. She accepted it without complaint.

I began hanging out with my new soda shoppe friends, girls some years older than I. They taught me to store whiskey in perfume bottles and to flirt with servicemen at the bandshell at Flamingo Park. Soon we took up shoplifting in the five-and-dime. The manager at McCrory's once chased me into the street for stealing some lipstick called Crimson Kiss or Bougainvillea d'Amor. Sooner or later, others would find something missing—a comb, a glove, a *Silver Screen*.

I grew bolder in my excursions onto the broad boulevards of Lincoln Road. My friends had devised elaborate schemes for pilfering clothing and costly jewelry from the department stores that lined the shopping street. I stumbled into sex in Flamingo Park while playing child's games like "Spin the Bottle" and "Kiss and Tell" with older servicemen who enjoyed the attentions of schoolgirls. I loved the way kissing and petting made my body feel although I was slow to develop and drew the line at going with men behind the bleachers in the park like some of the older girls. Readily I took to the adolescent mores of the Forties including boys, parties and an obsession with being popular.

The scent of exploratory sex must have lingered on my body because one day after school, as I dressed to meet my friends at the soda shoppe, my mother, home on one of her rare afternoons away from my father, suddenly displayed an unexpected interest in my activities.

"Where are you off to, young lady?" she asked.

"To the park."

In irritation she replied, "Why are we paying these prices to live on Miami Beach if you don't enjoy the ocean?"

"I love to go swimming," I said. It had been months since the two of us had gone down to the beach. Despite my protests, she insisted that I accompany her to Fourteenth Street Beach. The idea of a girl of fourteen going to the beach with her mother mortified me and I prayed none of my buddies would see me trudging down Pennsylvania Avenue with beach chairs and my mother in tow.

Down at the beach, my mother set out the chairs. She removed some papers from her purse and asked me to sign several bank slips for her so that she could transfer some funds. I signed them and she told me that she was putting some of our savings into defense bonds. Then she fell asleep in the sun.

I decided to walk along the shore. Avoiding the indigo stingers of jellyfish and men-of-war, I made my way down the beach all the way to the First Street jetty. The sun was uneven, slipping in and out from behind the clouds. I sat on the rocks at the jetty and watched the fury of the waves. When I returned, my mother was awake and drying herself after a dip in the ocean.

"It's a shame you don't come down here with your friends," she said. "You're a big girl now. You don't need me."

The thought of having to round up my buddies for a day at the beach filled me with dread. I'd be seen as a momma's girl and I'd become a laughingstock, an outcast. Nobody came to the beach during the day; the high school fraternities had beach parties at North Beach at night.

"What about you?" I demanded with uncommon fury. "You never come to the beach either."

"Somebody has to watch your father," she replied.

I felt a chill run through my body and goosebumps rose on my skin.

"I hope you're not coming down with something," she said, and offered me a towel and her chenille robe.

"No," I said, hugging myself, my arms wrapped around me like a straitjacket.

"Well, I hope not," she said. "I have to be with him at all

times. The money's going down the toilet. Or, as your father and The Boys put it, down the crapper."

I shivered again, more at the vulgar term than at the cold breeze that had turned a sunny day into something unseasonable.

"I guess I'm even starting to talk like him," she muttered.

"Why can't we just go back to New York?" I asked.

She stared down at the sand and said nothing. Suddenly I wanted to do something for her. "I do like the ocean. Really I do. I'll go swimming tomorrow." I knew how much it meant to her.

My mother held out her bronzed arm beside mine. "Look how white you are!" she said. "You're as pale as a cracker." I took it as a thinly-veiled criticism of my lack of family feeling. It had been one of the few afternoons I had spent with my mother in months. Hers was a martyr's face as she took me in, a disappointment to her. The lines had started to web beneath her eyes and now, with wet hair, she looked old.

I pretended to lose myself in a sand castle and considered things more seriously. Soon I'd be fifteen. I was learning nothing in school where I sat in rowdy classes with the children of servicemen, divorcees and other Northerners. We were segregated from the children of locals or natives, as they were called. I felt a pang of nostalgia for our old life in the Bronx. At last my mother's absences made sense to me. She was trying to save my father but he was spinning out of control like a car without brakes or steering. I sensed that he was losing heavily at the tables in Havana and at the track. I wondered if the business in New York was in trouble. Now there was only one person left who could save the family and that was me.

On the way home, I promised her that I would come to the beach every afternoon and go swimming. I'd cultivate a rich suntan and bring my friends to share in the bountiful blessings of this tropical paradise in which we now lived.

And, for a time, I did.

Meanwhile, at the convent, I perfected a Kohler sonatina and a piece called "Solfeggietto" which Sister Margaret called my concert piece. I gave up my days at the soda shoppe and my excursions to Lincoln Road and Flamingo Park. Even though I was not playing hookey from my practice time, Sister Margaret seemed distant. I was treated deferentially by the other sisters who, by then, had grown accustomed to my presence at the convent, and looked mercifully with a concern I did not as yet fully understand upon my role in their midst. Sister Margaret said nothing about my recent absences.

Sometimes when I played, I caught her staring out the window and I had the feeling she hadn't heard a note of my lesson. On the few occasions when I tried to draw her into conversation, she changed the subject. With its well-tended gardens and shrubs, the convent seemed indestructible and stalwart to me but I sensed that Sister Margaret was far from sturdy. From her ravaged and ruddy face I assumed she was a secret drinker. Back home in New York I remembered men with the red eye of drink in the junked lots and my mother's admonitions to steer clear of them. I wondered what Sister Margaret dreamed when she closed her pink landlocked eyes at night and inhaled the thick jungle jasmine in the garden.

Between afternoons spent burning myself to a cinder at the beach and my piano practice, I had no time for friends. I prayed my mother wouldn't find out about my playing hookey from the convent and demand restitution for all the money I'd filched from the envelope for Sister Margaret and spent instead on treating my pals to Tropical Pelicans and banana splits.

After a time, Sister Margaret and I fell into a routine. The Mother Superior began to stare at me with a new concern. One day she stopped me as I walked down the hall with my music books and metronome.

"Good morning, Hannah. How are your pieces coming along?" she asked. Still tongue-tied in front of her, I nodded in the affirmative.

"Come now, speak up."

"Fine."

"Fine, Mother," she corrected me.

"Fine, Mother," I replied. When she smiled, I noticed a slight tremor in the corner of her mouth.

That week, Sister Margaret failed to show up at the correct time. I grew worried at this rude departure from our usual regimen. As I sat waiting on a bench in the courtyard, small clusters of nuns in twos and threes sped by like frightened gulls, looking straight ahead. Finally a stout nun strode up, cleared her throat and announced that Sister Margaret had been called away for several days but would return the following Thursday. That week, I found myself missing my afternoons among the shaded banyan trees at the convent.

On Thursday, Sister Margaret appeared as usual, more flustered and nervous than ever. During the lesson, when I glanced over my shoulder, I saw her staring out the window. Her eyes were even redder than usual and I thought she might have been crying. She hadn't bothered even once to correct my incorrect fingering as she usually did. I could sense that she hadn't heard any of my lesson.

"Sister?" I said, to rouse Margaret from her reverie. She seemed startled by my voice. After the lesson, instead of her usual faint praise, she asked me to follow her into the chapel.

Inside the candle-lit chapel, a statue of a baby lay in a mother's arm and a long-haired Jesus Christ dropped on a cross of nails. Tapers flickered in small jars on a low table near the altar. I'd seen pictures of two Madonnas and two Jesuses in my encylcopedia, but not until that moment in the chapel did I realize that there was only one Madonna and Child and that she was also the Virgin Mary and that he was the baby who grew up to be God. I watched as Sister Margaret kneeled at the altar. Then she invited me to kneel beside her. I did so.

While we knelt together, Sister explained that there was a way that let God listen to prayers so that he could answer them. "Come, let me show you," she said. She spoke so sweetly that I would have done anything for her. Gently she unlocked my fingers and placed each fingertip so that it touched the one on the opposite hand. "This way your fingers make a church steeple."

I did as she said but I felt guilty. This was the way Christians prayed. I recalled my mother's admonitions. But, carried away by the soft voices of the sisters, their mumbled prayers and the overpowering aroma of incense, I felt my resistance crumble.

I began to accompany Sister Margaret to chapel after my lessons. As I knelt with her at the altar, she couldn't help but sense my interest. I loved to listen to the Spanish prayers mingle with those in English. When she looked at me, Sister Margaret smiled and a fine dew rose in her eyes. The hard gloss made her look like a doll or plaster saint although her brows remained black and energetic. Her ruddy face perspired in the warmth of the candles.

None of the other sisters seemed to find my presence in the chapel the least bit odd. From time to time I began to think that I really did feel the presence of the Baby Jesus and the Holy Virgin the way Sister Margaret and the others did. I squinted at them in the flickering light and tried to believe that they really heard my prayers. Being Jewish didn't preclude my being lifted on the scales of the angels.

But I saw and felt nothing. No matter how I tried, I knew my heart was empty. I felt only that my prayers might help restore Sister Margaret to the good graces of her superiors at the convent. I was going to return her to her former blessed state, the one she had lost when she began instructing me in piano. I didn't think it was fair for her to suffer because of me. I prayed alongside the others and, while they completed their lengthy devotions, allowed my mind to drift to more earthly matters. I was certain the others believed that I had placed my immortal soul in Sister Margaret's hands.

I used the silence to ask for understanding and forgiveness for my other crimes, especially for stealing my father's tips. I felt sure that Baby Jesus saw how my father devoured my mother and how she had given her life to him. A glimmer of understanding crossed the pallid eyes of Virgin Mary. In them I saw the eyes of my own mother, harried and harassed as she fled off behind my father into the Cadillac, late for the boat to Havana. I knew the Virgin Mary would never wear playsuits with loud cherries and bananas on them or use words like "down the crapper" to refer to money, but I sensed somehow that she and my mother had a special affinity.

After that, I ceased entirely going for piano lessons at the convent. Weeks passed. I showed up once after a long absence, stumbled through a lesson but refused to enter the chapel. Even Sister Margaret had to admit that I had no real vocation for spiritual matters. She treated me impersonally, as one who had betrayed her. I felt myself receding in her eyes, unrepentent and unsaved.

It had been some time since my mother mentioned piano lessons. I knew that my unusual silence was beginning to attract her suspicions. When pressed for information, I was evasive. Finally she announced that she intended to accompany me up to the convent to hear me play. After all, she had been spending good money on my lessons. She wanted to hear what her money had been buying. In anticipation, I practiced my music by drumming on my lap. During the week preceding the visit, I bit my fingernails to the quick.

It was just an ordinary day but I awoke with a feeling of unease. From my mother's conspiratorial look, I knew something was amiss. She led me into her bedroom where I saw an upright piano against the wall. It wasn't the ebony baby grand of my imagination—just a regular mahogany upright, probably second-hand. I ran my fingers up and down the keys.

"Daddy bought it," she said, her face beaming with excitement.

I tried to feign enthusiasm, and asked about the restrictions.

"Don't worry. Your father gave the manager a little something on the side," she replied. "Plus I've found you a marvelous Rumanian woman who has toured all the capitals of Europe." She went on to rave about this teacher of geniuses and prodigies who had recently moved to Coral Gables.

When I asked her about my lessons at the convent, she assured me that, on our visit, she'd wind things up with Sister Margaret.

"What will you tell her?" I demanded.

"We'll just say that we think you're ready to move on to a professional teacher." She went on to describe how the Rumanian had once studied with the great Rubinstein himself.

On the Collins Avenue bus, I felt a vague uneasiness. In her pompadour and upsweep, my mother looked quite regal. Her tan was a deep brown, her nails a glossy scarlet and her dress thankfully had no loud fruits or sombreros on it. For once she dressed like the white-skinned North Beach matrons, in white and seersucker. My dress was starched by Elsie and she had worked hard at the sleeveboard to get the puffed sleeves just right. I drummed my fingers in musical patterns on my lap and prayed that nothing would go wrong during the lesson.

Without realizing it, my fingernails joined in what Sister

Margaret called a church steeple. My mother looked down and noticed my hands as if in prayer.

"Where did you learn that?"

"Nowhere." I looked out of the bus window.

"Don't lie to me."

"I'm not lying."

Then my mother began a tirade more like an inquisition. When she finished imploring the bus ceiling fan, she said, "I should have known not to send you to the Catholics."

I shrugged like an imbecile, as if to indicate that such things meant little to me.

"Don't look at me like that, young lady," snapped my mother, the comb in her upsweep shaking in righteous rage. Hoping she knew nothing of my dark and discreditable fumblings behind the bandshell, I continued to bite my lip and stare out the window.

"Your father won't be satisfied until he puts us in the poorhouse," she muttered. I continued to stare out the window at the Collins Avenue hotels in their creamy Deco splendor. I felt sad to end my convent days, and also to lose the convenient shelter they provided for my other forays.

At the convent, my mother told the Mother Superior the news. She took the news of my new piano teacher rather well, considering, and my mother thanked her for everything. Sister Margaret took out the filigree key and led us to the parlor. Jaw set firmly, she looked down at me with pride. I played well. After my performance, I rose and my mother took the sister aside to discuss my progress. I could overhear them. Sister Margaret said that perfection was too much to ask at this point in my young career, but great things might be expected of me someday if I continued to work hard at becoming a serious musician. Then she locked the room and we were out in the sunny courtyard. She mentioned nothing to my mother about my absences; I said nothing about the chapel prayers. Our compact of silence was complete.

My mother opened her alligator pocketbook. I held my breath, praying that she wasn't going to tip Sister Margaret. She brought out her purse and removed several large bills. "Here's a little something extra for you," she said.

I held my breath in torment.

"I couldn't," said Sister Margaret. She refused to look into either my eyes or my mother's; her own were large with despair.

"Take it. You earned it," said my mother.

Sister Margaret trembled violently and continued to shake her head from side to side.

"It'll only go down the proverbial crapper," said my mother, as she tried to shove the crumpled bills into the nun's hands.

Sister Margaret hid them under her robe and continued to shake her head in the negative.

"My husband wants you to have something for yourself," said my mother. I stared at the terra cotta tiles, appalled at my mother's crude behavior. She was no better than my father after all.

"I couldn't possibly accept any money I wasn't owed," replied Sister Margaret.

"I insist," said my mother.

"Why not give it to the poor?" said Sister Margaret. "Hannah here knows where the poor box is, don't you, Hannah?"

"Good thought," said my mother, heaving a sigh of relief as she handed me the money. I went off in the direction of the poor box which was located just inside the chapel.

Once they were out of sight I examined the bills. I had more than thirty dollars in my hand. I felt a thrill rush through my veins. My hands, deft from finger exercises I had learned for mother's sake, folded the money as I knelt down and slid the wad into the heel of my penny loafer. I rose and glanced outside. I felt the weight of responsibility now on my shoulders. As I saw Sister Margaret's receding figure lumbering down the stone corridor, I blanched and decided to stuff at least one of the bills into the poor box slot. Thrift was no crime. After all, somebody had to save the family. Now it was my turn.

1963

BY JOE DAVID BELLAMY

Jocko had a bad habit of cruising along at about eighty-five in his Gran Prix, and if anyone got in the way, he would close in on their back bumper like some gigantic shark ready to swallow their tailpipe. When the other car finally noticed and swerved out of the way, we would swoosh on by as if we had important business in some other state. Why he never got caught, driving that fast, I'll never know. I was trying not to pay much attention to it. I had my hand under Nadine's blouse in the backseat.

My half-brother Jocko and his newest wife Gloria were up front, and Gloria was humming a little song with the radio and bopping her head to the music. Gloria worked as a bunny at the Playboy Club in Cincinnati. She was a short girl with a blond beehive and big boobs, and she liked to lead Jocko around by the nose. My date Nadine was Gloria's younger sister. Nadine had dark hair and eyes and extremely sexy lips. Overall, she was not as cute as Gloria or one other girl I liked in Yellow Springs, where I went to school, but she wasn't that bad either. She was okay. She was growing on me.

Nadine was in Cincinnati visiting Gloria, and Jocko and Gloria thought they would fix her up with me, since I was home from school and about her age—I was twenty-one then—and not doing anything that night. So we had had this boring dinner at some fake-swank restaurant full of artificial palm trees, cocktails and steaks and after-dinner drinks, with Jocko presiding in his gaudiest blue-glass tie-pin and cufflinks that winked and glittered in the lights every time he raised his fork or sipped his scotch. Then Jocko had driven us back to their little brick house in the suburbs, weaving and speeding like a maniac out Columbia Parkway in his new Pontiac.

As soon as we got in their house, Jocko started pouring drinks for the four of us. We sat around the living room for a while trying to make conversation, then Gloria said she was going to slip into something more comfortable, if we didn't mind; and Jocko went into the kitchen to make some more drinks. After a while Gloria came out in shorty pajamas—and maybe I should have gotten the hint and left at that point—but when she saw that Nadine and I were preoccupied, she joined Jocko in the kitchen. I didn't know what they were doing out there, but they had the radio turned up and they seemed to be talking hotly, and rattling ice cubes, and getting louder and louder, ranting at each other.

They had been married for about six months, and Jocko was in charge of used car sales at Honest Rocky Labaron's Pontiac in Sharonville. For him, it wasn't a bad job, all things considered, including the brand new cars he got to drive; and with Gloria's extra income from the Playboy Club, you'd think they would be doing okay. But it sounded like they were arguing about money, and I know that Jocko wanted her to quit her job, for obvious reasons, and that Gloria didn't want to quit.

Nadine was sitting on my lap, but she was one of those girls who was afraid you wouldn't respect her afterwords if she did anything more than kissing on the first date. I liked her well enough—she seemed kind and sweet—but I thought she was pretty silly. Still, she was trying to tell me things with her tongue that were far more eloquent than anything we had yet managed to say to each other with words. Each time we would come up for air, she would look deeply into my eyes and shake her head and sigh audibly as if she really couldn't believe her conscience had to be such an obstacle—because this was definitely a situation when she would like to make an exception. It was a nice gesture, and I appreciated it.

We were doing a fair job of blocking out the fight that Jocko and Gloria were having in the kitchen, but suddenly we heard a loud bang and the sound of glass scattering and raining on the floor in the other room and then Gloria screaming. As I got up to see what was going on, Gloria nearly ran over me on her way to the bedroom. She bumped into the coffee table, then gave it a good kick, screamed "ouch," and hurried into the bedroom and slammed the door.

Jocko was standing under the fluorescent lights in the kitchen, looking sheepish and dabbing at the blood on his chin with a balled up napkin. He gave me a mischievous little grin. As soon as I saw him, I thought maybe she had ripped him with a steak-knife or I-couldn't-imagine-what. His white shirt had blood all over it, and he had a bloody steak on his cheek and a gouged-looking place on his chin that was dripping blood in a steady stream.

"Are you all right?" I said.

"No problem," he said. "I never liked this shirt anyway."

He was a mess, and the broken glass was lying all around his shoes and sprinkled on the counter and across the table. I grabbed him by the shoulders and started to turn him toward the doorway, where Nadine was standing.

"What happened?" Nadine said, her face registering several stages of alarm as she took in Jocko's cuts and all the blood.

"The goddamned glass just popped," Jocko said. "You never saw anything like it."

"I'll get a broom," Nadine said.

"Let's go into the bathroom, Jock, and get this cleaned up—what do you say?" We started trudging unsteadily together toward the bathroom.

"What's wrong with Gloria?" I said. "What happened, for God's sake?" I got him in the bathroom and turned the cold water on and wet a washrag and dabbed it carefully at his chin.

"Must have been something I said is all. Who knows? The next thing I know her glass is bouncing off the wall. Ban-go!"

"Did she throw it at you?"

"No, she just threw it. You know. Women. She'll get over it."

"You want me to go talk to her?"

"No. She's probably packing her bag or some damned thing."

"This chin looks like it could use some stitches."

"Naw—just a scratch—don't worry about it."

"It's still bleeding like a bitch."

"The Band-Aids are in here somewhere. Just put a good Band-Aid on it. That'll fix it."

I located the tin box of Band-Aids in the medicine cabinet and tore open the biggest one I could find and stretched it out across his jawline and pressed it down. I tore open another one and lined it up next to the first. The blood seemed to be slowing down. I opened a third and crisscrossed the other two parallel to his lip. He checked my handiwork up close in the mirror. The cheek was not as bad, just a slice along the surface. I didn't see how it could have happened from splattering glass; it looked too straight and long. "Are you going to be all right?" I said.

"Hell, yes. Let's drink to it."

"Maybe you'd better change your shirt—get a clean one?"

"Naw—it'll dry."

"Maybe I'd better go home."

"Well, suit yourself, pal."

"I think I will."

Jocko wagged his head and sighed, and his gray eyes unfocused for a second. He put his boozy, mutilated face up close to mine and whispered: "This is what women will do to you, Mike." Jocko held out his hand to show me he also had an ugly gash across his thumb and wrist.

"You'll live," I said, unwrapping more Band-Aids. His big hand palm-up reminded me of when he used to give me bubblegum when I was a kid, just after he joined the Air Force. He certainly didn't have to offer me any, but he always did. None of my friends would have done such a thing. I was convinced it meant he thought I was going to make a good brother in time, someone worthy of the U. S. Air Force and its fighter pilots.

Nadine was standing in the middle of the kitchen with a dustpan in her hand. The clock on the stove said 2:37. She put her arm around Jocko and gave him a soft peck on his good cheek. "Does it hurt?" she asked.

"Not a bit. Can't feel a thing," Jocko said. "Old Mike fixed me up."

I said my goodbyes and started to leave. Nadine followed me to the door and we hugged and kissed goodbye in the dark alcove, but my heart wasn't in it. She told me to be sure to call her tomorrow and I said I would. I walked out to my VW, and she stood at the door and watched me until I had gotten in and slammed the door, started the engine, and pulled away.

The streets were almost deserted, and the full moon was out and everything seemed amazingly bright and clear. I drove hurriedly back across town through the dazzling, empty streets to my parents' quiet house, tiptoed to my room, undressing like a shadow, and fell into bed as soon as I got there.

When Jocko came back from the Air Force in 1953, ten years before, he was twenty-five and I was eleven. My parents and I were living in a maroon-shingled ranch on a lush half-acre in another suburb of Cincinnati and my father was the manager of a radio station, and Dad told Jocko he could live with us until he could put down some roots and get a job and start making it on his own.

At twenty-five, Jocko was a quiet, well-built young man, about five-foot-seven with short, slicked back hair and an aura of sensitivity and refinement and suppressed anguish not unlike the actor James Dean. My father always claimed, often in Jocko's presence like an apology, that Jocko was smaller than he should have been because, as a child, he had had double pneumonia and almost died. Jocko was the smallest offspring in a family whose male members took more than usual macho pride in feats of strength and physical prowess; and in the Air Force, he had been a drill instructor and, later, a military policeman, roles that he must have chosen to prove something, not because he was especially well-suited by temperament to perform them. He was certainly tough enough to have done so, but so laid back that, even now, I have a hard time imagining how he must have managed it. Unless he had been drinking, he was a man who seldom raised his voice. How could he have yelled at fresh recruits and humiliated them and called them names?

Jocko had been away for a long time, and while we were growing up, he was so much older than I was that we had never really gotten to know one another. My only other sibling had died as a baby, so I had grown up as an only child with an only child's self-possession and sense of loneliness. I didn't have a clue about what Jocko might have felt about me.

But I certainly knew what I felt about him. I was just a kid and he was already a man—I thought he was the equivalent of a movie star or a dignified visitor from outer space. I thought it was nifty almost beyond belief to have such a person actually sleep in the other twin-bed in my room and be my brother. I would wake up early in the morning, and there he would be, snoring away in the other bed, and I would get up and creep quietly over there and gaze at his sleeping face, which seemed so peaceful and heroic, and his muscular arm resting across the pillow, and the broad palm of his hand, and the pulse beating in his wrist. Then I would carefully examine the items lying on top of the dresser—his big wristwatch, his wallet, a set of car keys with a plastic Mercury fob, a pack of matches, a pair of aviator sunglasses, an Ace comb—and try to comprehend his unfathomable life in outposts around the world.

As I say, Jocko was my half-brother, and that made him seem even more mysterious. What *was* a half-brother? I couldn't figure it out. I knew a lot of embarrassing things had happened before I was born: the war (World War II), during which my father was badly wounded—he had had terrible nightmares and sometimes drank too much in those days—my parents' itinerant life, moving every year to some new house in some new neighborhood while my father worked for some new company, trying to get rich—we were still doing that even after I was born. I could comprehend those things, if somewhat feebly at first.

But the idea that my father had been married to someone else before he had met my mother, someone named Lucille (whose name was never mentioned in our house, though she was sometimes referred to obliquely as "Jocko's mother")—that idea seemed extremely improbable, seemed almost inconceivable to me.

Judging from his attitude, my father must have felt it was a personal failure he had to atone for, to struggle to live down. He did this by trying to be a model father and husband and breadwinner, by doting on my mother and me, by making up to me in every possible way for what he had failed to provide for little Jocko.

About 4:30 in the morning, the phone rang and it was Jocko on the other end. He sounded a whole lot drunker than when I had left him a couple of hours earlier. He said he was leaving town once and for all, and if I ever wanted to see him again, he was at an all-night diner on Red Bank Road. Did I know the place? I said I thought I could find it. If I was coming, he said, I'd better get there in a hurry because he wasn't staying there long. He had to hit the road. He said even if I made it there before he left, it would probably be the last time I would ever see him because he was never going back to that house with Gloria in it—not if his life depended on it—and he was never going back to that goddamned used car lot, and he was never coming back to this lousy city with its lousy losing baseball team, period.

I said I would get dressed and be there as quickly as I could—I would gladly break the speed limit—but I wanted him to promise to wait for me because I wanted to talk to him before he left. He said he might be able to wait for twenty minutes but he doubted if he could wait any longer than that—he had to be somewhere. I asked him where that might be, where I could reach him, but he mumbled something I couldn't hear and hung up.

I got dressed at lightning speed and tore out to the garage and squealed out the driveway. It was still dark and humid outside. I rolled down the window of my VW and leaned against the door and drove like Mario Andretti, as if my life depended on it, burning up the road as if I had never heard that traffic laws existed. If they tried to pull me over, I would simply tell them the truth: it was a family emergency. As far as I could tell, it was a matter of life and death.

Within a few weeks after Jocko got out of the Air Force in 1953, my father gave him a job at the radio station selling sixty-second spots—his salary based largely on commissions. Even though such work was not at all natural for Jocko, I suppose he had an inclination to do what my father encouraged him to do. But, before too long, it became evident to everyone that Jocko just didn't have it in him to succeed at this kind of sales work. He simply wasn't selling anything, and he hated it.

It was along about this time that Jocko met Rose. Rose was working as a roller-skating car-hop at a Frisches Big Boy, and one day Jocko pulled in for lunch in his big blue Mercury and

Rose skated up to his window and into his life. She was a bleached blonde, a Catholic girl with an angel's sweet face, great legs, and a heart-shaped birthmark on her right shoulder. She knew how to talk to little brothers without a hint of condescension and without hiding a certain natural feminine admiration for the male of the species. Up to that time, aside from my mother, I thought she was by far the most interesting woman I had ever actually talked to.

Jocko married Rose, his first wife, in 1956, and after casting around for a few months to find work, he decided to take out a big loan and buy into a Sunoco franchise and run his own filling station. The work was menial, but the idea of pure independence must have appealed to him. He could open when he wanted, close up when he felt like it. He didn't have to sell anybody anything—they would come to him. He would wash every driver's windshield and make the station a model of friendliness and good service. And he didn't have to follow anybody's orders except his own. He felt he had been taking orders long enough—from both my father and the Air Force.

He figured that after he made a little money and paid off his loan, he could hire some high school kids to man the place and start looking for other investments. He found a station in Middletown, Ohio, about thirty miles north of Cincinnati, and with my father's help, he bought a house within a block of the station and told Rose she could retire from car-hopping.

A parallel scheme he had for making money was to raise purebred chihuahua dogs on the side. He bought four of them, two males and two females, and started breeding them in a little shed in his backyard, and before long, one of the bitches had puppies and he had ten little dogs running around in his backyard, yapping up a storm at anyone who came within earshot.

Jocko would take off for the station early in the morning and knock himself out pumping gas and wiping windshields, and Rose would lie around the house watching soap operas and game shows and doing housework and cooking and tending to the dogs. At noon, she would take Jocko a sack lunch and sit around the station for a while, sharing sandwiches and smoking cigarettes. Then, she would head back to the house and try to find some way to kill the afternoon before it was time to start dinner.

They intended to have babies of their own—Rose, especially, was eager to start a family—but month after month went by and Rose couldn't get pregnant. Within a year, the dogs had another litter, and they sold a few of the pups from the first batch but still had thirteen dogs; and Rose started making sarcastic jokes about how dogs could get pregnant whenever they wanted to but the people who lived there couldn't, for some reason.

Jocko kept three of the dogs in the house by then, and he and Rose both made a fuss over them constantly. Whenever we arrived for a visit, Jocko would make his favorite little dog, Princess, show off all the new tricks he had taught her since the last time we had visited. Without a doubt, that Princess was a smart little chihuahua.

By the end of his third year with Sunoco, it was plain that the station was not going to make Jocko into a millionaire any time soon. The locals had more or less deserted it because it was out of the way and had been through a series of owners. Though Jocko was handy with tools, he was not really a mechanic; so there was very little to be made on anything more complicated than an occasional oil change.

In addition, the dogs were costing more to raise than they were bringing in in income. The truth was that Jocko became so attached to the dogs that he didn't want to part with any of them, and he would ask unreasonable prices for them and deliberately jinx a sale whenever potential buyers would come around to look at the dogs.

He and Rose had several fights over "the dog problem," as Rose started to call it. The dogs were getting on her nerves. She got so mad during one such argument with Jocko that she threatened to go back to car-hopping to bring in more money and get out of the house and away from the dogs once in a while, and Jocko said he didn't give a damn if she did.

So Rose went back to car-hopping, and Jocko started to feel like a failure again, in spite of his best efforts. It nearly drove him crazy to think of Rosie skating around the drive-in in one of those incredible short skirts that was hardly more than a pair of sheer panties with a cloth border around it and flirting with every Tom, Dick or Harry who drove up and gave her the eye, just to make sure an extra quarter tip—even if her disposition did seem to improve at first. He spent a lot of time sitting in his greasy-armed deskchair between gas customers imagining what Rose might be doing and wishing it could be like the old days when she would bring him his lunch and sit across the desk laughing and eating cookies and drawing seductively on her Viceroys.

Then one day, he came home from the station and Rose wasn't there.... She didn't get home until about ten that night, and then when she burst in, she was carrying a pizza and acting far too jovial and sweet and making some flimsy excuse about working a couple hours of overtime because they were so busy at the drive-in.

His mother had deserted him when he was ten—now Rose was doing the same thing. He must have felt that there was something about him personally that was missing, that simply couldn't hold them.

He hired a detective who came back after the first week and said he had followed Rose to a motel three times that week, where she was shacking up with some traveling salesman from Indianapolis.

He had pictures of them going into the motel together, but in order to make it a clean, uncontested divorce, they would have to catch them at the motel together "in the act" and get pictures and serve her with the papers. Jocko could see it for himself and serve as a witness. Looking at those snapshots, Jocko was so overcome with anguish, with a tightness in his throat, that he gave the go-ahead.

Within a few days, the detective called back from the Sunnyside Motel, and Jocko jumped in his Jeep and buzzed on over. The detective was waiting in the office, where he had the warrant and had alerted the proprietor. They walked right down the little sidewalk in front of the units, and the detective quietly unlocked the lock to number 23 and threw open the door and started gunning away with his flash camera.

Sure enough, there was Rose in bed with some creep, Rose, his own true love, screaming and crying and acting injured, and the detective served her with the papers, and Jocko

walked away and got in his Jeep and sped down to a local bar
and drank cheap scotch until he passed out.

After that, Jocko lost the Sunoco station and declared
bankruptcy, sold the house, and got rid of all his dogs. He
came back to live with us for a while and moved back into my
room. Sometimes at night, he would babble and whimper in
his sleep, and I felt so sorry for him, but I didn't now what I
could do. He was a grown man, and I was just a teenager.
Except for the Air Force, it seemed he had failed at
everything he had ever tried, and I, on the other hand, seemed
destined to succeed but be embarrassed by his presence
merely because of my good fortune. It seemed that my very
existence was a constant reminder to him of all that had been
denied him. He had flunked out of school; I was always a good
student, a good boy—I couldn't have been otherwise. Worse
yet, at that time, I was having a growth spurt. I was six feet
tall and still growing. I was good at baseball, basketball, and
track, and brought home trophies and ribbons and district
championships and all-star jacket-patches that Dad was so
proud of he could never stop rhapsodizing. But it wasn't as if I
did those things deliberately in order to make Jocko feel
inadequate. What Jocko had had to suffer was simply not fair.
I didn't blame him for any of it—none of us did.

When I located the diner on Red Bank Road, a thin film of
daylight was just sliding across its aluminum and plate glass
walls and brightening the concrete pavement and the abut-
ment of the distant viaduct. I quickly scanned the cars in the
lot as I pulled in, hoping to see Jocko's Gran Prix. I didn't see
it, but I hurried inside, fearing I had missed him, and found
him sitting at the counter, sipping a cup of coffee. He turned
to look at me, then turned back to his coffee without changing
expression. His hair was uncombed and he was still wearing
the same bloody shirt under his jacket and he still had the
three Band-Aids stuck to his chin. His eyes were like two
bloodshot slits. I sat down on the stool next to him and
ordered coffee.

"You don't look so hot," I said.

"You wouldn't either, brother...."

"You and Gloria have another fight?"

"I don't even want to think about it. I'm never going to see her again, so it doesn't really matter, does it?"

"Why wouldn't you see her? Maybe this is just a bad night. Maybe you'll feel differently about it in the morning."

"No I won't. It *is* morning. See out there—it's almost morning already."

"I mean *tomorrow* morning. You haven't had any sleep. You're not thinking straight. Why don't you come home with me and sleep it off—then maybe you'll feel better about everything."

"Naw—I've got to *be* somewhere. It's time for a change, and this time I'm going to go through with it."

"Where do you have to be?"

"Somewhere.... I can't tell you." Here we go again, I thought.

The waitress poured my coffee and pushed a small ceramic creamer after it. I poured cream in my coffee and brought the hot mug to my lips and blew on it and put it back down.

"Maybe I'd like to be part of it."

"Naw—you wouldn't."

"How do you know without asking me? I might. We could be in on it together."

"I just don't think you would. It's not your kind of situation."

"What the hell does that mean?" I blew on the coffee again and took a sip. I wasn't sure whether this was just drunk-talk or something serious.

"This is something I just have to do alone—that's all."

"Sure."

"I think you should stay out of it," he said.

"If I should stay out of it, maybe you should stay out of it." He shook his head and sighed.

"The way I look at it is this—what have I got to lose? I'm never going to see Gloria again anyway. I'm never going back to that brick house. I mean—why should I? I'm never going to..." He put a hand up over his eyes and bowed his head. We were both embarrassed and silent for a moment. I wanted desperately to say the right thing, something to help.

"Why don't you come back to school with me?" I said. "You could stay there until you decide what to do. I've got plenty of extra room in my apartment."

"In Yellow Springs?"

"Sure. It's a nice town. You'd like it there. You could just take it easy for a while and get your bearings."

"What in the hell would I do there?"

"Hang around with me. You could find a job if you wanted to. We'd have a great time."

"Hang around with a bunch of college kids—sure."

"Hey, it's a big little-town. You could make your own friends. We could hang around. You could stay at my place as long as you wanted to, until you could meet some new people. There are a lot of people there. Then go off with your own friends—call up once in a while to say hello. It's an easy place to live. You'd like it. Eventually, you could get your own place, and I could come over for a beer."

"I don't think so." He tamped his cellophaned pack of Chesterfields on the edge of the counter and held the pack up to his lips and pulled out one weed and lighted up. He showed the pack to me and I shook my head.

"This other thing doesn't sound like such a great deal to me," I said.

"What do you know about it? You don't even know what it is." He blew a thin stream of smoke up over our heads.

"I just don't think you're the kind of guy who would get involved in something like this. I'm surprised to hear about it."

"Maybe I am. Maybe you were wrong about me all along."

"I don't think so," I said. "We wouldn't even have to tell anybody about this, you know. You could just come up there with me, and we could keep it confidential. Gloria wouldn't know where you were, and we wouldn't tell Dad either. Then, later, you could call him if you wanted to. Or maybe you'd decide not to."

He dragged heavily on his cigarette again and exhaled. "Maybe you're right. Maybe that's not such a bad idea."

"It's a damned good idea." I got out a ballpoint and started drawing a map on the napkin. I drew a schematic of the streets of Yellow Springs, Ohio, and labeled them, and then I showed

him where my apartment was, right near the middle with an
X. "It's only a couple of hours on the road. Just head out like
you're going to Middletown."

"What are you doing here, Mike? I mean, why do you really
care what I do or not?"

"Because I'm your brother, that's why." Jocko looked at the
napkin and thought it over. "Right there is where I live," I
said, pointing at the X. "It's easy to find. The key is under the
mat."

"I'll find it," he said, crushing out his Chesterfield butt.
"That is, provided I decide to go up there. It's in the same
direction that I was going anyway." He folded up the napkin
and put it in his pocket.

"So what are you going to do?" I said.

"I'll think about it on the way," he said. "I'll start out and I'll
decide when I get to the turn-off." He stood up from the stool
and laid two dollars on the counter next to his cup and saucer.

We walked out of the diner together and stood for a moment
on the front walk, where traffic hummed from the distant
viaduct. "Give me a call, will you, if you decide not to come,"
I said. "That way I'll know."

"Sure," he said. "I could do that. I'll think it over and then
I'll give you a call." I knew by the way he said it that he
probably wouldn't.

He was only thirty-five, but he seemed so worn out and his
face was so lined and haggard in the eerie morning brightness
that the cuts were more visible—he could have been sixty. His
light eyes seemed bruised but intense as he squinted at me,
friendly but opaque, altogether impenetrable, as always. I
watched him walk around the side of the diner and get in his
car, a small, dignified man, surprisingly handsome. "Don't
forget," I called, "the key is under the mat."

He gave a somewhat nautical little wave, almost a salute,
indicating he remembered, and got in his car and started off.

I got in my VW and drove back to my parents' house across
town. They weren't awake yet; it was only 6 A.M. I lay down
on the bed in my room and fell asleep myself. When I woke
up, it was already noon and the sun was beating down on the
windowsill and bedspread and across my face. I felt disoriented and weak and wasn't sure for a minute where I was.

Then I jumped up with a start, realizing how late it was, and started throwing my things in my suitcase and getting ready to take off for Yellow Springs to meet Jocko.

I drove straight through with only a gas stop. When I got near Fairborn, I passed an accident where someone had run off the road and flipped over and mashed the roof of a red Chevrolet, and a wrecker was up ahead with another car. I had a bad moment when I was certain the car bouncing along on the hoist chain would be Jocko's Pontiac. But it wasn't a Pontiac; it was an old beat-up pickup truck.

I kept thinking about that morning in the diner. I never should have let him go off on his own. I was afraid it was a mistake at the time, but I didn't know what else to do. I should have made him come with me—then and there—but I knew, even as I had the thought, that he never would have come.

I drove on into Yellow Springs and parked in my space beside the apartment building where I lived and went up to my rooms. There was no note on the door, and the key was undisturbed under the mat. Inside, there was no sign that anyone had been there—it was just as I had left it. I made myself a snack and sat there at my kitchen table munching on a sandwich and drinking a glass of milk and staring out the window into the street below.

After a while, it started to get dark, and the streetlights came on. Once I thought I saw Jocko's Pontiac make a slow pass in front of the building, but the car didn't turn around, so I guessed my eyes were playing tricks on me. I was tired, and I figured Jocko wasn't going to show up, and it disappointed me. I wanted a chance to help him out, and now it looked as if I'd missed that chance.

I remembered that I had forgotten to call Nadine. I got her number out of my wallet and dialed it and let it ring twelve times, but no one answered. I dialed it again and let it ring twenty-five times. After that, I must have dozed off.

Along about ten, there was a loud knocking at my door, and I woke up with a start. I couldn't imagine who it might be at this hour. My mind was numb and full of mixed up dreams. I shambled toward the door and opened it, and damned if it wasn't Jocko, grinning from ear to ear, and there was a woman standing there with him out in the hall, her arm draped around his neck like a wounded soldier. She was wearing a sleeveless blouse and she had a little heart-shaped birthmark on her shoulder.

"Hiya, Mike," he said. "Look what this old cat drug in!"

I was so groggy it took me a moment to realize that Jocko's new girlfriend was Rose. Rosie from Sunoco. In the light, she looked amazingly dissipated and angelic. She lurched toward me and reached up and planted a kiss on my startled face. "Hello, little brother," she said. "You remember your Aunt Rosie, don't you?"

Looking for the New Year

BY BECKY BRADWAY

So, she would go East.

Usually she headed West, to open space and dry air, where people wore cowboy hats and string ties, joined the Birchers, skied and sold handmade macramé plant hangers. From Wichita to Cheyenne to San Francisco, the West made her laugh, with its pool and leathery tan in each yard of stone and cactus. And the West made her spin with the joy of viewing the hinge of sky and desert, where nothing man-made limited the scope of the eye. But, as much as she loved it, Angie could never *belong* there—so she decided to try a city where everything moved fast and went straight up, where people traveled underground and lived in sardine-packed apartments for the honor of Making It There. She wanted to sit on curbsides where Woody Allen sulked as a child, bump into Sean and Yoko as they posed for a video in Central Park, stand in the subway of Arbus' dwarves. She wanted to witness art as it was practiced on a scale of success, where writers and painters hung out in famous old bars and parlayed meaningful conversations into the payoff of being noticed—and where some *were* noticed, and where some were great.

Once the idea of a place was in her, she had to go. The need for movement was visceral, like an athlete's need to run, a dancer's need to stretch. For her, it was more than travel—it was desire, adrenaline, dreams.

She danced around the house, singing: *New York, New York, a wonderful town, the Bronx is up and the Battery's down. I wanna be a part of it—New York, New York!* Guidebooks snaked up the

walls of her room. She was even able to convince her friends to
travel with her, by giving them a good reason—a march
against U.S. intervention in Central America.

If she liked the city, she would stay. Angie knew her life
couldn't end in Central Illinois, with its farmers and factory
workers, Lincoln as a souvenir, state employees who spent
their lives in meaningless jobs. In New York, people were
open-minded, creative; they knew what it meant to have
dreams and ideas. It could be her real home, because it wasn't
Springfield, it *couldn't* be. Home had to be somewhere, and
she'd know it when she found it, because ease would come
upon her like a natural fiber cloak, and she would fit in, totally
and completely.

The six of them sat packed in the gray Toyota, Angie in the
back left corner, wedged between the car body and Swenson's
bony shin. Her feet in lace-up leather boots rested on bags
from Hardee's and Taco Bell.

Swenson chewed gum, blowing big purple circles—a bag
filled with Sweettarts, Smarties and Double Bubble rested on
his lap. His round metal-rimmed glasses were smudged with
prints, and wavy red-brown hair trailed to his shoulders and
shone in the early morning light. He wore his special coat,
which was too large and long for him, dotted with buttons
ranging from *Stop Apartheid* to *Fuck Art, Let's Dance* to *Holy
Cow!* His leg jiggled, as if of its own volition. He had been
silent for miles.

Angie, who did not like silence, elbowed him. "Say something," she ordered.

He turned to her, blinking. "Why? What do you want me to
say?"

"Anything. This car is too quiet."

Swenson laughed. Nobody else looked at her; not even Sam
Che, who was squeezed in the space between the front seat
and the back, pushing his toy truck.

"It's six in the morning," said Swenson. "Nobody has
anything to say at six in the morning."

"I do," said Angie, though nothing came to mind.

"The only time you *don't* talk is when you're asleep. And
even then you talk, sometimes."

"You're exagerrating," said Angie.

"Remember the time we went to San Francisco? You talked from the second we left Springfield until we crossed the Golden Gate. I was ready to throw you out of the car."

"You know that was too much coffee. Plus you wanted us to stay with that asshole."

Swenson stiffened. "His name was Greg."

"Greg the asshole. I thought if I talked enough I'd convince you to stay with one of *my* friends."

"Who? Danny the bodybuilder? Give me a break."

"At least he didn't steal my wallet."

Swenson rested his head against the back of the seat. "If you don't mind, I'd like to contemplate the sunrise."

"You can't even see the sun from where you're sitting."

"I'll imagine it." He closed his eyes.

Angie smacked his leg. "You're just deadwood." She looked at the other people in the car. "Isn't he?"

Nobody answered.

Finally, Lucy drawled, "You sound like an old married couple."

Lucy smoked a thin brown cigarette, flicking ashes through a cracked-open back window that let in icy air. Lucy was tiny and wore only black, with an occasional tinge of purple or maroon. Her hair was black and her eyes dark—she claimed Cheyenne blood—and her expression was ferocious. She wrote intense, visual and vicious short-lined poetry, which she performed in a wicked tone that seemed neutral, but carried threats, like the bulge of the handle beneath the waistband of her skirt. For a month, Lucy had been at the house they all shared, having left an apartment where she'd lived for several years with a married couple. Angie didn't know if Lucy had slept with her former roommates. She couldn't imagine anyone screwing her, since she looked as if she might, during foreplay, deliver a chant-poem on the politics of sexual domination.

Angie had been surprised when Lucy agreed to go on the trip. "Sure," she'd said, as easy as that. She'd stuck out her hand, which was warm—not icy, as Angie had somehow expected. "I accept your challenge," Lucy said, shaking. Angie was never certain whether Lucy was kidding.

"The next gas station," Lucy said, "stop."

Up front, Sam, who was driving, coughed. "We just did. You were asleep. We tried to wake you up."

Taking the cigarette between two long nails, Lucy flicked it out the window. Angie watched it fly, spraying sparks.

"I would *like* for you to stop," Lucy said.

Angie knew Sam would.

He mumbled old Stones songs to keep himself awake, since the radio was broken, and constantly pulled on his full brown beard. Though she'd been around Sam for several years, Angie didn't feel that she knew him well. She partially attributed this to his beard; it seemed to her that men who kept half their faces covered with hair had things to hide.

His wife, Faye, leaned against the window, quietly snoring. Faye was obese, with tightly-curled brown hair. She wore custom-made caftans with African designs. Her job at a battered women's shelter made her grim and exacting; when she spoke, it was matter-of-factly, as if checking off lists in her head.

Five-year-old Sam Che, Faye and Sam's boy, pushed a truck along the edge of his mother's seat and sang, under his breath, the theme to "Gilligan's Island." Angie thought he'd been frighteningly well-behaved during the entire trip; when he had requests, he whispered them in his mother's ear, and Faye would order her husband to stop for a Coke, a bathroom, an ice cream. He seemed an angel child, though in the past Angie had seen him drawing on the walls of the farmhouse and smacking other kids with bricks.

Angie had begged them all to come with her. She didn't know why. A year ago, she'd taken a trip alone, and had loved owning the wide road. But that was West; a different direction. For the city, she wanted support. And so here they all were, wedged together, thigh-to-thigh—but the only words Angie seemed to hear were her own.

Yet, they were all friends. They were partners.

Emily Dustin was a friend of Sam's. Calling herself Cocoa, she worked as an actress in cheap horror movies.

"Did you see *March of the Newly Dead?*" she asked, after hellos and introductions. "You *haven't?*" She raised an eyebrow as if to say, 'your loss.' "*I* was in it, and my scream is recorded in the *Big Book of Movie Trivia* as the longest in a feature film."

"Incredible," said Swenson, his tone sarcastic. Angie wanted to kick him—Cocoa was putting them up for two weeks, and it wouldn't do to insult her.

"Yes, it was," Cocoa beamed, seeming to miss the mockery. She waved her arm. "Come, everyone! Let me show you our fine abode." Grabbing their bags, they followed Emily-Cocoa. "Put your things anywhere. Some of you will be sleeping here in the living room. Sam and Faye might be best off on David's bed—he's in the Soviet Union for a month, studying Russian rock groups."

Cocoa lived illegally on the enormous top floor of a former factory, zoned commercial. On the drive, Sam explained that Emily's roommates (he could never remember to call her Cocoa) were two gay actors, a woman who built collages from cans, an historian studying at Columbia and a wealthy woman who did nothing but watch TV. In letters, Emily explained that her roommates were "between gigs," with all but the rich girl waiting tables and answering phones. Hearing this, Angie thought New York must be the place for her, full of people who reconciled their lack of secure jobs with creative goals. She'd been doing it for years.

None of the roommates were in the apartment, except the TV watcher, who ignored them. "Cassie is a recluse," Cocoa explained, when introductions were bypassed. As Angie placed her bags against the wall, she couldn't help but stare at the woman, thin as a thread in leopard-skin pants and fur sweater, with her well-designed face and aloof air. Only total access to or total lack of money, Angie thought, could make a person confident enough to be so casually and completely unfriendly.

"This way!" The factory floor was divided into private rooms composed of cheap plywood, with the exception of the artist's space. Her room was a cave of colored bottles. Throughout the apartment, unframed original art was taped on walls and propped on dressers and tables. The walls were painted with wild swirls of color. (They didn't get to see the socialite's room; it was sealed with a combination lock.) Despite the artistic trappings, Angie couldn't shake the image of sweatship girls who, peering through dim lighting, sewed until their fingers cramped. The fluorescent paint and cheerful, campy objects seemed to say that it *really* couldn't have been that bad here; it couldn't be that bad *anywhere*.

By the time they wound their way to the kitchen, one of the waiter-actors had arrived home. He wore a green silk bandana around his head and greeted them effusively, if skeptically, as if he couldn't be sure Midwesterners could be trusted to act with class. He and Cocoa decided a nice big Tofu salad was just the thing after a long road trip, and set about gathering and chopping vegetables, some of which Angie, a carnivore, had never seen before.

"I'm hungry!" she whispered to Swenson. He nodded. Dinner for them would not be Tofu.

Settling into chairs around the kitchen table, Sam, Faye and Cocoa discussed mutual friends and incidents. Blaine, the actor, mentioned he was in an off-Broadway production of *Krapp's Last Tape*, which he found "delightfully confusing." Sam and Cocoa argued the political significance of Beckett's plays, with Sam asserting that the work had Marxist meanings, while Cocoa insisted Beckett was a fascist. Lucy, lingering silently at the edge of the group, yawned, gathered her Walkman and roller skates from her bag, and escaped. Angie, Swenson and Sam Che decided to make a pagan quest for cheeseburgers and chocolate ice cream.

They piled onto the rickety freight elevator, which quaked as it carried them down five stories. Wooden and enclosed, it was lit by a bare forty watt bulb.

"*Cool*," sighed Sam Che.

Swenson looked as if he might throw up. It was worse going down than up, gathering momentum for the long drop.

When they stepped onto solid ground and into the cool glare of the winter sun, Angie wanted to leap for joy—and Sam Che did. On the street, people surrounded them in infinite variety, and seemed to be going someplace, as if nothing could stop them.

Sam Che squeezed Angie's hand, hard. He was rarely off the farm where they all lived. It was Angie who talked Sam and Faye into letting him go on the trip, for no good reason other than she liked kids, particularly Sam Che. She promised to take responsibility for him, so his parents could pursue their vacation with minimal interference. Sometimes she felt a tugging in her, a need to hug Sam Che, to hold his hand. Something like love.

"You're looking around too much," Swenson whispered to Angie. "Don't act like a hick. You want to get mugged?"

"How else will we see anything?"

"Don't be so obvious. And hold on to your bag."

"Don't you like it here?"

Swenson pushed at his glasses. "This isn't the best neighborhood."

"Snob!"

A woman sat on the sidewalk, her bloated legs hunched to her chin. She asked for money. Angie reached into her bag.

Swenson grabbed her arm and pulled her along. "Don't even start," he said, "or they'll swarm on us like a pack of hungry wolves."

As Angie turned to give him a skeptical look, a tall black man in a Yankees jacket walked up to her, his hand reaching out, brushing her. "Lady..." he groaned, in a tone that was vacant, without hope or even care.

It made her shiver, and she looked to the sidewalk so she would not have to meet his eyes.

"I hate this place," Swenson muttered, as Angie and Sam Che hurried to keep up with him. "It has either rich or poor, with no in between. Someday, they'll burn it down."

"You've only been here twice. That's not much of a chance."

"I like the record stores, the bookstores, and that's it. Crowds make me claustrophobic."

"I think it's tremendously exciting." Angie squeezed Sam Che's hand and looked for something gleaming, choosing the light on a brass gargoyle's face that marked a building of old stone. "Don't you, Sam?"

"Absolutely."

They went into the first restaurant that looked cheap, a neighborhood diner run by Greeks in white T-shirts. The booths were red vinyl and the tabletops gray-flecked Formica. It looked like every diner everywhere, except for the people. They laughed and spoke loudly in different accents and dialects, gestured when they talked and didn't seem to care whether anyone noticed. No one stared the way people did in Midwestern diners, as if as a newcomer you were entering dangerous turf, crossing a line into a Mom and Pop Hell.

"See what I mean?" said Angie, scooting into a booth. "All kinds of people in one place. Not mean and judgmental, like the rednecks in the boonies."

"That's what *you* think," said Swenson, squinting at her. "How do you know they're not sizing you up?"

"They're not even looking at me."

"If that's true, it's only because so many strangers come through that they don't care."

"Okay," Angie began, preparing her argument, "compare it to Chicago. Look how clannish it is. It's a city, but all sliced up—the Irish here, the Germans there, and the blacks someplace else. Check out this ethnic mix!"

Swenson stared morosely toward the front door. "They all have a neighborhood to go home to."

"You can really be a drag, you know it?"

They placed their orders with a dark-skinned man who tapped a pencil on a pad. After he left, Swenson pulled a copy of *Mother Jones* from his backpack and flipped through it. Watching, her annoyance faded into affection: another tip, fighting like old times.

She really loved him—in a sisterly way—knowing they'd be companions until one found a permanent mate.

"What's wrong?" Swenson asked.

"Nothing."

"You were staring."

"You wouldn't want me to stare at the people here, would you? One of them could be a mugger."

"Ha, ha," said Sam Che, putting the ketchup bottle on the napkin rack, and the salt shaker on the ketchup bottle.

Swenson frowned. "You're so disagreeable. Is it too much caffeine? Or are your hormones acting up?"

Jabs. That was the way they talked, as they grew older, knew each other better, took each other for granted. There was a time when she spoke gently to him, when everything he did seemed special. Now there was no need to step around opinions, in fear of offense—she and Swenson couldn't produce insults worse than the ones already given. If they lost each other, it wouldn't be because of argument. It would be circumstance.

"Let's enjoy New York," she said. "This may be the place where I'll spend my life."

"You'd hate it."

Sam Che brushed at his thick Dutch-boy hair with his hand, leaving a hunk sticking out at the top of his head. "Dad says after the march we're going to look at dinosaurs."

Angie smoothed his hair. She wondered what it must be like for Faye, having this being who was a part of her, yet unique and independent. When Angie touched Sam Che, she couldn't help but think of an abortion she'd had at nineteen. Sometimes she dreamt of a hand, waving in a dark sea. Still, there had seemed no choice, with no money, no mate, not even much self, far from home. Had Faye chosen to have Sam Che? Or had she simply gone along with the biological force, the one that begged Angie to follow it, and that she denied? Could Faye have been as intellectual and strong-willed to fight against what was, after all, the natural and right thing to do? And did Faye regret that she hadn't? How could you regret a flesh-and-blood child? Yet women did. Angie's mother had.

"Dinosaurs, huh, Sam?" Angie said. "Big bones, they have. You'll get to see their huge, monstrous bones. They used to live all over the world."

"You mean, they won't have skin on them?" Sam Che's face paled, as he placed his cheeseburger on the greasy plate. "They'll be—empty?"

"The skin is long gone," she said. "It's part of the earth. That's what happens when things die."

"Like all of us will someday," said Swenson. "Remember Raindog? His body is feeding the earth. But his bones remain, right in the yard where you buried them."

Sam Che's forehead crinkled. "Then I can dig him up and put him back together, like the dinosaurs at the museum."

Angie laughed, thinking of what Faye would do when Sam Che brought in the moldly bones of poor old Raindog.

"But what would be the point?" said Swenson. "You can't bring him back. He can't bark or wag his tail. He'll always be dead."

"But when I see the bones, I'll remember him just exactly."

Angie emerged from the room of bottles, wearing a black dress bought at Bloomingdale's with Swenson's father's Master Card. The dress had a low neck and full skirt, and was made from brushed cotton that comforted her knees as it flowed around them. All her life, Angie had avoided dresses, preferring bib overalls, jeans, pants with elastic waistbands. But this was New York, where images were made, and she and Swenson had promised themselves costumes, roles.

He emerged from a bedroom wearing a jacket and baggy wool pants. His hair was clipped, making his face appear angular and somehow more adult. They looked at each other and smiled, a matched set.

"My good Lord," grumbled Lucy, leaning against the refrigerator. Everyone at the table stared.

"Stunning suit!" Blaine breathed. He and the other actor, whose name Angie didn't know, nodded their approval. Swenson, flattered, posed in Oscar Wilde fashion, pretending to display a cigarette holder in his long, thin hand.

"You look like fucking professionals," said Sam.

"It's our new Broadway style," Angie explained, trying to mask her embarrassment, the feeling that she'd revealed something she'd never wanted to show. "We're masquerading as average New Yorkers ready to be pacified by the revival of *Oklahoma!*" Like the gay men, Angie was admiring the new Swenson. He no longer looked like someone prepared to argue about the IWW. He looked like a date. She thought of a game she'd played as a girl, Mystery Date: *will he be a dream (sigh)... or a dud (groan)?*" She'd never been on a real date—casual get-togethers and occasional couplings being more her style—and now felt thrown into the world she'd always been promised: Where men and women were pretty, charming and compatible, meeting on formal ground, rules allowing them to respect one another while maintaining an air of smoldering possibility.

"Who got the stupid idea of going to a revival theater?" said Lucy. "And *Oklahoma!*, for God's sake—we left the armpit of the world for *this?*"

"We thought it'd be a hoot," laughed Angie. "How better to get in touch with the real people of New York, than to see a play where they'll be wrapped up in nostalgia about a Midwest that never existed. It's surreal."

"I'll wear my leather, if you don't mind," Lucy said.

Faye looked at them, tiredly rubbing her nose. "Sorry to bow out, but I hope you'll take Sam Che. He's been looking forward to it all day long."

"Yeah!" he yelled from the floor.

"You don't want to see Times Square on New Year's Eve?" Swenson asked her.

"I was there two years ago. I'm not in the mood for a mob."

Swenson shrugged, then went to the sofa beside the TV. The socialite had vanished, leaving behind the remote control, which he used to flip stations, pausing only a few seconds on each program. He stopped at a loud man in a tiny hat playing a honky tonk piano.

Angie sat beside him.

"You look great." She sniffed. "Smell good, too."

"Thanks." They watched a man dump a bucket of water on the singer's head.

"You never wear cologne."

"It's after-shave. Elegant and alluring, I think the ad went."

"I like it."

He glanced at her. "You look different."

Angie looked at her short legs encased in silk stockings, flaws hidden beneath expense.

"I feel like someone else," she said. "Isn't it funny the way clothes can change how you see yourself? I feel like your average beautiful person going out for a night in the city."

He gave her a thoughtful look. "You are." He walked across the room to the two actors. Putting a hand on Blaine's shoulder, he spoke to him, gesturing. Together, they laughed.

Leaving the revival theater, they found themselves in the midst of a massive crowd in Times Square. They would celebrate the New Year, Angie thought, celebrate survival and the potential for better times. It was culture shock, leaving the saccharine, pastoral world of the play to be enveloped by anxious, drunken, joyous New Yorkers, real New Yorkers whose words grated like nails on a blackboard. She wasn't sure which world was most real. Oklahoma—even the artificial one—wasn't far from home. Every midwestern farmhouse held the possibility of a warm stove, lights in the window. There were no such delusions in the city, to which she thought, let me live in a place where people know what's what. But the child in her kept flaming the dream in which people were loving and smiling and endlessly forgiving.

But this is real: New York, New Year's Eve, the ultimate

experience, Guy Lombardo and Dick Clark displaying the fall
of the big apple, while millions cheered. This was the real
New Year's, the one people traveled to experience. It wasn't
dancing drunkenly with some hated brother-in-law smelling
of whiskey, children tooting plastic horns until you wanted to
strangle them, then rushing to the bathroom to heave your
guts out while people made jokes about visiting the porcelain
God—all the while wishing you were someplace else, wishing
you were in Times Square with Dick Clark, where a momen-
tous thing was occurring, a statement being made. And now
she was there.

Swenson scanned the crowd with a look of intellectual
paranoia. Lucy grinned—or as close as she ever came to it, a
bright-eyed half-smile. Pulling a tiny black notebook and pen
from the pocket of her leather jacket, Lucy wrote. Nobody
jostled her elbow or stepped on her feet; disinterest or
fearlessness made her singular. Angie admired Lucy, as she
admired Sam Che, who laughed and chattered, lost in the sea
of legs. She could neither give herself to the crowd nor stand
against it, and so was afraid in a way she had never expected.
Maybe it was the dress: even hidden beneath her coat, it made
her feel vulnerable, as if bare legs forced a dormant passivity
upon her.

The scent of humanness was apparent despite the cold night
and heavy perfumes. There was the exhilarating possibility of
riot—the need for mass immolation, to wreck and destroy. It
was on the street in the day, tension and threat, adrenaline—
and now in the night, with light cast only by the neon of
Broadway, its musicial extravaganzas and video porn stores,
and the sound of five-hundred-thousand noisemakers and
gunfire and firecrackers from rooftops, alleys and fringes of
the crowd.

They were no longer on the edge, but in the center, pushed
and rocked. Sam Che sat on Swenson's shoulders, high above,
and told of colors, hats. Angie wished she were there, looking
over the people who waved like cornstalks, each stalk different
but the same, she distinct and individual in her own place.

Tiredly, Swenson put Sam Che on the ground. The child
gripped Angie's hand. What a confident kid, she thought—
fearless, not a crier. Not long ago, she was like that, driving
fast and taking dares. What changed her was the awareness of

death—the shock of seeing a friend in a coffin, the realization that it would happen to her, better later than sooner. What Sam Che didn't know was that he could simply not go on.

Swenson must have seen her uneasiness, or perhaps felt it himself, because he put his arm around her shoulders. The surging of the crowd grew more intense as time passed, until finally the lighted apple fell along the building, marking midnight, and the crowd moved together in a high wave, a push of energy. Everyone yelled, kissing and grasping in a spasm of fear and joy at the realization of another year of life. Angie found Swenson's mouth on hers, locked in something that went on and on as the crowd moved and rocked, pressure and release. It was weird, his soft mouth, kiss of friend and something other than friend, as it had always been, promise and denial and hopelessness.

It seemed a long time before the yelling died away, the unified scream of noisemakers fading to scattered shrieks. She and Swenson turned from each other, surprised and sheepish. Then she realized Sam Che had been released and sent whirling.

She heard herself scream his name, saw herself searching for his small, familiar face, pushing through legs and arms for one white bright spot, too small to really be there. She might have looked forever, calling his name, if there hadn't been the pulling on her arm, a sharp pain cutting her shoulder.

It was Lucy, white face inside very black hair. Her smile seemed bored, but her eyes both understood and mocked. She lifted the arm hidden beneath black leather and there was Sam Che, laughing.

"You lost me!" he accused, gleefully. "And Lucy caught me!"

Lucy put a hand on Angie's back and urged her along. "Bet you never thought we'd be the people who salvaged children," she said.

The Crossing

BY SALLY BENNETT

It was less than a year after the end of the war. In early spring, 1946, when I was thirteen and my sister nine, we crossed the Atlantic from New York to Lisbon on the *Algarve*, an old Portuguese freighter that had been in dry dock. Although the worst of the winter was over, the weather was still unpredictable. The owners, eager to get back in business and urged on by a list of passengers waiting to get home, decided to risk the danger of spring storms. Irresponsible perhaps, but not exactly criminal. They surely didn't know about the mines still floating loose in mid-ocean.

We were delivered to the 92nd Street pier in New York City by Mrs. Green, the wife of one of my father's friends, who had met the train from Newton where we had been living with June, our grandmother. Mrs. Green was a nice, motherly woman, who hugged us as we got off the train. She wore a fashionable fur piece around her shoulders; four or five small animal skins complete with heads, each of which had the tail of the next skin in its mouth. I had never been so close to one of these before and stared at it throughout lunch at Schrafft's. The question I was too shy to ask was, had the animals died in that position and if so, what were they doing? They reminded me of the tigers in Little Black Sambo who whirled around and around in a circle until they melted into a pool of butter.

My sister, Jenny, who preferred animals to people, was also interested in the skins. During dessert, she reached over and stroked one. Mrs. Green did not seem the least offended by our interest, and every so often she gave the furs a hitch as if she were urging the animals on to one more lap around her

312

shoulders. After lunch, she bought us a large box of assorted candy for the trip.

The *Algarve*, rocking in its berth, looked small and dirty next to the *Queen Mary*, which was sailing the next day for England. I knew Mrs. Green would have preferred to put us on the *Queen* and kept asking people if the *Algarve* was really the ship sailing for Portugal. Finally, we were taken on board to our cabin, followed by the porter with our luggage. He hoisted the largest case on top of a wardrobe which occupied a third of the small room. My heart sank as I looked around at the few pieces of old fashioned furniture bolted to the floor. Bunk beds, a single chair, chest of drawers and washstand looked dull and colorless in the light struggling to enter the single porthole.

After our luggage was stowed, Jenny and I kissed Mrs. Green goodbye and I reached up to touch the furs. They were soft and warm from her body and I wished we could go back up the stairs with her and her fur piece to wherever she lived and not have to stay in this cold and dim little room. Jenny clung to her a moment longer and I knew that she, too, hated to say goodbye.

After she left, we hung up our coats as we had been taught. Jenny was opening the box of candy, unwrapping and then licking the pieces to see if she liked them. I opened all the drawers in the small bureau, found a chamber pot under the beds and climbed up on the top bunk, which I claimed as mine. Jenny was too engrossed in the candy to argue so I sat up there for a while, swinging my legs over the edge and staring out the porthole. I could only see the sky, which I knew was bluer than it looked.

"Let's go upstairs," I said.

Jenny nodded. Her mouth was full. She tried to put the lid back on the box but her fingers were too sticky so she stood up and the box fell to the floor scattering the candy.

"Now look what you've done." I felt irritated because I knew I should have helped her. "They were supposed to last."

"I couldn't help it," Jenny protested. She started licking her fingers to clean them.

I jumped off the bed and turned on the faucet in the sink. Jenny stuck her hands under the small stream of water and we dried them on my slip.

Outside our cabin were two open doors which turned out to be the bathroom and separate toilet. There were doors to other cabins and a stairway up to the main deck.

A middle-aged woman appeared, dressed in black and wearing flat backless shoes that made a slapping sound on the wooden floor. She was carrying towels and linens and spoke to me in a language I recognized as Portuguese. When I replied in English, she shook her head, smiled and pointed at herself, saying "Fatima." I pointed at myself, said "Sarah," and then at my sister, "Jenny." She repeated both our names, giving them an unfamiliar sound, smiled again and left us. It turned out that she did everything: made the beds, cleaned the rooms, delivered morning tea and meals, and performed any other domestic or personal service required. I never gave her the five dollars my grandmother had told me to give the steward, a man in a white uniform she said would see us to our cabin, but Fatima deserved more than the ship was worth by the end of the trip.

Upstairs, the rooms were clean and bright. The dining room was spacious, its tables covered with heavy white cloths. The lounge and bar was full of comfortable sofas and chairs, and although the deck was too narrow for the shuffleboard games we had been promised, there was room to walk and plenty of rail from which to watch the ocean.

The staff working in the bar and dining room were laughing and talking to each other in Portuguese. I wished I could remember the few sentences I had known when I left five years before but, although the sounds were familiar, I could not understand what they were saying.

The Portuguese captain was a stout, youngish man in a blue uniform with lots of gold braid, who greeted all the passengers in Portuguese or in heavily accented English. He shook my hand and asked after our parents. I explained we were going to join them in Portugal. This seemed to please him and when I told him that we lived in Estoril, he said that he was born not far from there in the Sintra hills.

"You are not going to be seasick?" he teased.

"I don't know," I said, "I've never been on a boat before."

Jenny stared at him the way a puppy stares at its new owner.

"We may have a little roughness," he said, making hand gestures to indicate waves, "Perhaps—some rain," he smiled broadly, showing some large unnatural looking teeth, while waving up and down to simulate falling rain. I nodded to show I understood. He shook my hand once again, patted Jenny on the head and turned to the other passengers.

We were an assorted lot and there were no other children, only two Portuguese seminary students in their late teens. I looked them over carefully. They were thin and scraggly, unlike the sturdy American boys in Newton with names like Boyd, Barry and Mickey who were part of my weekly dance class. After the first six months of lessons, we started going to one of our houses after class for games of post office and spin-the-bottle. We had paired off by then into four couples with two extra boys tagging along. If someone claimed a kiss of another's partner, there was a furor of excitement and protest.

Mickey was older than the rest of us and preyed on all the couples, taking each girl in turn into the closet to plant his wet kiss on her cheek. Emerging, we scrubbed our cheeks with sleeve or handkerchief to remove all illicit traces while Mickey, flushed and hooting with laughter, watched. The other boys sneered self-consciously, knowing Mickey was ahead of them in a place they both longed for and dreaded.

My best friend, Connie, and I made these weekly games the basis of other games in which we practiced growing up, using our dolls as actors in secret lives concocted by our imaginations. Our model was Connie's older sister with her saddle shoes, pleated skirts, sweaters and real boy friends who kissed her when they thought no one was looking.

What impressed us most was their expertise. They seemed unapologetic and confident as they maneuvered her into a corner then tilted her chin up or simply pulled her close. Because of her, we believed that one day we and the boys would grow up and then everyone would know what to do.

Besides the students, there was a young American couple going to Portugal to work for an oil company; an elderly Portuguese woman and her middle-aged daughter going home; and a single man introduced to us later at our table as Mr. Klipp, a Dutch businessman. He attracted my attention immediately because he was the first man I had ever seen who wore a pinky ring: a large square diamond set in gold. My family believed that a man should wear only a sedate tie pin or cuff links. If he wore a ring, it must be a plain gold monogram or some dull stone, never anything that sparkled. I liked his ring because it was pretty but felt embarrassed for him so I looked away when he first sat down at the table that we shared with him and the two students.

Dinner was the social event of the day. The ladies got dressed up and the captain wore his dress uniform with gold braid and medals. The cook was Portuguese and there was always soup to start, fish, meat, cheese and a sweet. There were pickles and olives on the table and fresh rolls and butter. Jenny hated most of it except the rolls, and I didn't like it much more.

At first, Mr. Klipp seemed reserved, bored perhaps with having to sit next to children. The rest of the room became noisier and more festive as the wine bottles emptied, but our table remained a small island of silence. At first, an entire meal passed with hardly a word spoken. Jenny got up and down as she pleased and the students brought their books.

Then, Mr. Klipp began to look out for us with a distant formality. He passed the rolls and butter without being asked and sometimes put a dish aside for Jenny if she happened to be away when something he thought she might like came to the table. Because he and I were the only two with nothing else to do but eat, we began to talk about food. It turned out we shared a love of American ice cream. From that, we moved on to jewelry, which was his profession. I wore the few pieces I had to show to him. He liked my locket with a small topaz and asked if it had belonged to my mother. I said it had come from my grandmother, who was Dutch.

"My poor country," he said. "It has been all but destroyed."

"I'm sorry," I said. Then, "We are going home."

"Your parents live in Lisbon?" he asked.

"Estoril."

He looked thoughtful. "You spent the war in America with relatives."

I nodded and explained that our father was a mining engineer with an American firm. Our parents had sent us to stay with our paternal grandmother, June, because they were afraid Portugal might not be safe for us.

"You love your Grandmother?" asked Mr. Klipp.

I hesitated, not knowing how to answer. I knew you were supposed to love your grandmother. "She didn't expect us to love her," I said, finally, "She was too busy with other things. She just took care of us for a while."

"She does not sound like a very nice grandmother," said Mr. Klipp.

I considered this. June was a vigorous woman of seventy with an active real estate business. She was not used to having children around and cared for us with a casualness bordering on neglect. As we had been brought up with nurses and a governess, we had learned how to keep ourselves occupied and out of the way. June had a weekly cleaning woman but did her own cooking. She introduced us to blueberries and cold milk, which seemed tasteless at first. At home, our milk was always hot because it had to be boiled for drinking. When we were not in school, I was expected to take care of Jenny. She missed our mother and since June was not much of a maternal substitute, made do with the cats and dogs and a cow called Betty and me when I allowed it.

I, too, missed my parents terribly at first but gradually came to feel at home in Newton and over the five years, grew into an American teenager. In Europe, you were either a child or an adult and whatever happened in that twilight period between was never dignified with a name.

When we were told that we were going home, back to Portugal, I felt confused. Home had become a shining fixture on the horizon for almost as long as I could remember, to be called up and dreamed over whenever I was lonely or unhappy. The prospect of finally getting there was like being sent to Heaven, exciting but a little scary. Also, it meant leaving school and my friends. Jenny, being younger, had even dimmer memories of home and did not want to be separated from her animals. We had to hide the cat to prevent his being packed. Twice, she got him in the suitcase and twice he had to be liberated.

However, the day finally came when we were driven well over the speed limit in June's red convertible to the station. Our goodbyes were brisk and businesslike. Remember how many pieces of luggage you have, keep your traveler's checks in your inside pocket, don't take off your gloves or you'll lose them, give five dollars to the steward when you get on board. Then, she pressed us painfully to her bony chest and put us on the train.

Mr. Klipp had listened attentively to all this. Now he sighed. "Portugal is a beautiful country. I will live there for a time; perhaps always."

I asked him where his family lived.

"Rotterdam. But there were killed in the bombing."

I was shocked. I had not known anyone who died in the war. June had a neighbor whose son was killed but I never met him. I wondered where Mr. Klipp would live but didn't like to ask. Suddenly, I realized that if our parents died while we were en route, we would have nowhere to go. Portugal was a foreign country and I had forgotten how to speak the little Portuguese I learned as a child. I looked around for Jenny but she had left the room. The last letter I'd received from my mother before leaving America repeated what she had said when we separated five years ago: to look after my younger sister. I had always taken this lightly as another vague parental dictum like being good and going to sleep. Now, that request seemed ominous, suggesting dangers I had not thought of.

"Where will you go," I asked, "in Lisbon?" My voice sounded frightened.

Mr. Klipp looked at me, puzzled by my tone. "A hotel."

A hotel! Of course. This thought, accompanied by the memory of the checks tucked away in the inside pocket of my coat, produced a wave of relief. "I have some traveler's checks," I said aloud.

A look of surprised pleasure crossed my companion's pink face. "How sweet you are," he murmured. "But I have a lot of money. You must not worry."

He had thought my concern was directed at him. I experienced the very adult emotion of pleasure laced with the guilt of knowing you were taking credit for something you had not meant.

Then two things happened at once: the ship gave a violent lurch and Jenny, who had been approaching slowly, trying to see what food the waiter had brought to the table in her absence, crashed into the back of my chair. Several people screamed, Jenny started to wail and the noise of breaking crockery rose over the sound of many voices speaking at once. Some people had been knocked off their feet and had to be helped to their chairs. The ship had quickly righted itself after the lurch but was still rocking vigorously. I hugged Jenny and tried to see the place on her arm she was holding, saying "Ow, ow, ow," over and over.

"Ladies and Gentlemen," the captain was saying, his voice rising over the din of other voices and objects rolling around on the floor, "Please stay calm; there is no immediate danger—a storm came up suddenly and a strong wind caught us."

Suddenly everyone was quiet except for the urgent voices coming from the crew's quarters below. We all looked out the windows to see rain beating against them and spray rising to wash over the deck. Once again, the boat tipped but not so violently this time. The captain was directing us either to return to our cabins until the storm was over or stay seated in the lounge. The staff would begin cleaning up the room. He finished by inviting everyone to the bar for a drink, reassuring us once again that we were completely safe. Mr. Klipp picked Jenny up, looked at her arm which she was still clutching but which was not broken, and said he would see us to our cabin.

I felt dazed rather than frightened. Up to now, my greatest fear was of being lost. Even during the war when I heard the casualty report on the radio and saw "gold star mother" stickers on windows, it had never occurred to me that I or anyone I loved might be killed. I took the safety of airplanes, boats and cars for granted. Now, death seemed very real and I burst into tears, overcome by a sadness I could not have explained. Jenny looked surprised, then started to whimper again. Mr. Klipp's pink face deepened several shades.

"No, no," he implored, "You must not cry. We are quite safe; you heard the captain. Please." He handed me his handkerchief.

It was no use. My normal reserve was gone. I stumbled after Mr. Klipp, weeping noisily into his handkerchief. Below, we found Fatima running back and forth carrying basins and towels. The Portuguese ladies were issuing directions from their cabin while the American husband tried to get her attention. Mr. Klipp entered our cabin and deposited Jenny on her bunk. It was stuffy below deck and beginning to smell of vomit and urine, a smell which would remain with us for the rest of the ten day trip. We could not open the portholes because of the rough seas, and fresh air did not penetrate below the stairs.

"You must sleep," he told me, "And not worry. Tomorrow

the sky will be blue and we will walk on the deck. I will see you at breakfast, eh?"

I thanked him and said, yes, we would see him tomorrow. I did not believe in the blue sky and the walk around the deck, but I knew he did not want me to cry any more, and I did not want to lose our only friend. My entire world seemed reduced to this smelly place below deck with a small round window to a gray sky. The waves sloshed against the glass, the rain beat down and the boat pitched and rocked.

Jenny was asleep. I covered her and undressed. The bathroom and lavatory were in constant use so I peed in the washbasin (a trick I had learned when staying in hotels) and lay down, wondering if we would still be alive the next morning.

When I woke, light was coming in the porthole so I knew it was day but the boat was rocking and the sky was still gray. I tried to get up but immediately my head began to whirl and I felt sick. I lay back down and asked Jenny to get Fatima. While she was gone, I threw up in the chamberpot. About half an hour later, I had started to doze when Fatima and Jenny returned. Fatima had a basin and towel which she put beside me on the floor. I felt her rough hand on my head and heard her murmur something in Portuguese. A few minutes later she returned with a pot of tea, two cups and some rolls and butter. She poured a cup and helped me raise my head. As soon as I swallowed, I threw it up. She wiped my face and turned to Jenny who was eating the rolls and all the butter with her fingers. She smiled and left.

The rest of the day passed in a blur of sleep and nausea. Occasionally, Fatima would appear to bring me some water and empty the basin. Once when I woke, Mr. Klipp was there with Jenny on his lap. He patted my hand.

"Poor Sarah," he said. Soon you will be better. This *mal de mser* only lasts a short time before you get your sea legs."

I thought this must be what death felt like and made up my mind to live. "Why isn't Jenny sick?" I asked him.

He shrugged. "Too young, perhaps; but some people never are. It all has to do with your inner ear."

I closed my eyes. When I opened them, he was reading a

book to Jenny, who was leaning against him as if she had known him always. His ring shone in the gray light and I found it comforting, like a nightlight in a dark room.

The next morning, the sun was out and the boat had stopped rocking. I carefully got out of bed. My legs felt shaky but I no longer wanted to throw up and my head felt clear. I helped Jenny dress and we went up to the dining room. Mr. Klipp and a student were sitting at the table.

"Good morning," said Mr. Klipp, "How is my friend this morning?"

"Hungry," I said.

"Good." He ordered tea, cereal, bread, butter and milk for us and pushed his own plate of smoked fish away when he saw my expression. Jenny stood next to him and started playing with his ring.

I felt embarrassed. "Jenny," I said, "Sit down."

She pretended she didn't hear. Mr. Klipp smiled and lifted her onto the chair. "After breakfast, we will walk on the deck."

Sooner or later all the passengers appeared. The Portuguese ladies were the last to leave their cabins, but by late morning the fresh air and blue sky were too much for them. They arrived on deck wrapped in scarves and hats and had two deck chairs placed on the only wide space, making anyone who walked by squeeze against the rail. I thought they looked more like sisters than mother and daughter. The younger was the larger of the two and both were dressed in black, like Fatima, but their dresses were made of some heavy cloth with a dull shine on which were pinned gold brooches. Their shoes had laces running up the front. Everything about them looked hard. I imagined that their large bosoms would feel like stones under your head. They carried small black prayerbooks which they studied when they were not talking to each other.

When the captain passed, they bowed and smiled, tilting their heads sideways, glancing up coquettishly out of the corners of their eyes. To the students, they nodded, sometimes putting out an imperious hand to ask a question. Fatima, they merely abused. My mother was always polite and considerate to servants and I was shocked by these ladies' behavior. But Fatima only moved a little faster, muttering, *"Si, Signora, si Signorina,"* as she hurried off for a second pillow or fresh pot of tea.

The American couple were also demanding but at least they asked instead of ordering. The wife was still sick and I heard her husband complain to Mr. Klipp that she could not get used to the food or the bad air in their cabin. There was no ventilation. She seemed to get weaker every day and now could hardly get out of bed.

I wondered if she would die and if she died, what would be done with her. We were midpoint in our trip; at least five days from Lisbon. Once, when we were alone, I asked Mr. Klipp what happened if someone died on shipboard. He said he or she was usually buried at sea. When I asked how this was done, he reluctantly explained.

"The body is wrapped in a blanket or some other covering and lowered overboard. The captain reads the service for the dead or says a prayer the way it is done at a funeral."

Buried at sea! What a lonely phrase. I imagined the boat arriving in Lisbon and the American husband getting off with all his bags and his wife's (or would they throw the bags overboard too?) and going to his job alone when he had expected to buy a house and start a family. I was struck by the extreme oddness of it, how someone could simply disappear forever while traveling from one place to another.

"Mr. Klipp," I said later as we were drinking our tea in the lounge. "What are you going to do until you can go home?" The waiter had put a plate of all yellow cakes next to the teapot and cups. I had been telling Mr. Klipp about life in New England, about June and my friend, Connie. After he had sat by my bed while I was seasick, held the basin and wiped my face, I felt closer to him and talked more openly than I ever had with an adult.

"I have business in Lisbon which may take many months. Holland is no place for me yet; it may never be." He spoke quite matter of factly.

"Why not?" My curiosity made me forget to be polite.

Perhaps he felt safe in the middle of the ocean, and the opportunity to tell his story to someone too young to really judge but old enough to be a listener was too great to resist. Perhaps, like others with an uneasy conscience, he hoped to understand and forgive himself or perhaps it was something else, either better or worse.

"My father was a fisherman in Rotterdam before the war," he said. "A noisy, crowded city. We were poor because there were too many of us. When there was a good catch, my father liked to celebrate. Who can blame him? We all worked by the time we were eight: cleaning, chopping wood, errands, anything. Most of the businessmen were Jewish: jewelers, art dealers, wood merchants." He glanced down at his ring. "The owners had fled or been taken away by the time German soldiers broke into their stores and homes. They hid their valuables but, you see," he leaned closer to me, "I knew the insides of their houses and shops from all those years of cleaning and running errands."

The idea came into my head that his ring was stolen. Unable to meet his eyes, I took a piece of cake. It was plain sponge with raisins. Boring, but it gave me something to do. When I was ten, I had stolen candy and cheap jewelry from a dimestore near our house. Someone had proposed it: a dare, like jumping off the highest branch with the rope swing.

Mr. Klipp must have seen my expression change. He put his ring hand in his pocket. "If I hadn't taken them, the Germans would have and I at least had worked for them. The soldiers were just thieves."

"Did you get caught?" I took a deep breath. It was one thing to steal from a store, another to take things from someone's home. "Suppose they go back," I whispered, "Won't they miss their things?"

"Go back! You must be joking." Then his face softened into its usual kind expression. "I forget how old you are, Sarah. They are all dead. Even the children."

Mr. Klipp was staring at the ocean, which was getting choppy. Whitecaps were beginning to form. The waiter came to see if we needed more tea. Mr. Klipp shook his head. I stared down at the plate of cakes, wishing there was something chocolate.

"Ah, here's Jenny," said Mr. Klipp. He lifted her onto his lap. She had been sleeping and was carrying her stuffed monkey. Then she saw the cakes and reached for one. He caught the monkey as it slipped toward the floor.

"That is not an American toy," said Mr. Klipp.

"No," I said, "She brought it with her." I found it quite repulsive. Most of the once-white fur had worn off the long limbs and tail and now, after a week of being dragged around the ship, it was sticky and dirty.

"It was made in Germany before the war," Mr. Klipp said, examining it, "They were as good at making toys as they were later at making guns. I used to look at them in the windows of the expensive shops in Rotterdam."

I wanted to hear more about Mr. Klipp's life. It was beginning to sound like a book and so far I had found books more interesting than real life. At June's house, they had become the cure for loneliness and boredom. I had developed the ability to lose myself very quickly in a story like the one Mr. Klipp was telling, and I wanted him to go on.

"Where did you go after you..." I couldn't find a way to finish the question.

"After I left Rotterdam?" Mr. Klipp smiled. "To Lisbon as a wool merchant. I had no difficulty getting the papers of one of my former employers, along with bales of woolen cloth stored in his warehouse." Jenny was falling asleep again on his lap. He shifted her position slightly. She sighed but did not wake up.

"It was ridiculously easy," he went on, sounding almost angry. "With my German name and Dutch passport, I could have carried the jewelry in my pocket."

He shrugged as if to rid himself of a troublesome thought. "There was a lot of money in Lisbon in 1941. Old money, new money, honest money, desperate money, stolen money. Everything was for sale: tickets, bodies, lives, food, property and sex. All that is good for the jewelry business. In a very short time I made a lot of money."

For a moment, I was afraid Mr. Klipp was going to cry and my throat started to ache. He sounded so lonely. All this did not sound like the Lisbon I remembered and I said so.

Mr. Klipp smiled. "No," he said. "But it was. Everyone was trying to get to America. You left before things got desperate. I got my ticket because a customer owed me money. The ticket was all he had left."

Jenny woke up and was staring at me. I wondered if she understood what Mr. Klipp was saying. I smiled at her and she smiled back, then buried her face in his chest. He stroked her head and I noticed her braids were coming undone. I touched my own hair self-consciously, wondering what it looked like. We did not pay much attention to our physical appearances.

"Why are you going back?" I asked.

"I never felt at home in America," he replied. "People are too optimistic. They seem so trusting but really do not want to understand. But who knows? Perhaps they will be better than we are one day."

"And you, Sarah," he said after a few minutes. "Were you happy in America with your busy grandmother?"

"Yes," I answered. "Most of the time." For some reason, I felt I had to defend June. "She was not like a real mother," I explained. "But at least she didn't pretend to be one. She wasn't good all the time, either. Sometimes she was mean and bossy. Sometimes she didn't want to be bothered. Mostly, she let us do what we wanted and I liked that."

"There are no flies on you," said Mr. Klipp, smiling.

I was pleased. June had never bothered with compliments and it felt good to know some adult thought I was smart.

That evening the wind was up again and the American husband had a long conversation with the captain. They looked very serious and, at one point, seemed to be arguing.

"I'm afraid the American woman is very ill," said Mr. Klipp after dinner. "Unfortunately, there is no doctor on board. The rules do not require one with only ten passengers."

"What will they do?" I was horrified to think we would have to throw the American wife overboard.

"The captain is trying to locate the nearest ship."

Later that night, the storm got worse. Jenny and I huddled in our cabin and watched the large suitcase slide across the top of the wardrobe, back and forth, back and forth. I did not dare turn the light off in case it fell. Finally, as my eyes began to close, it crashed to the middle of the cabin. Jenny did not wake up and nobody else seemed to hear the noise over the wind and the waves. I went out into the passage several times but no one was about. Fatima was with the American woman in her cabin. I knew where Mr. Klipp's cabin was but was not brave enough to knock. Voices floated up from below, from the engine rooms and the crew's cabins and I tried to imagine they sounded cheerful and reassuring. Then I heard the sound of crying behind the American couple's door. I waited, hoping someone would come out, but the door remained shut. The velocity of the wind picked up and the boat began to pitch even more.

I sat down on the stairs and locked my arms around the railing, feeling like Alice when she fell down the rabbit hole into a strange subterranean world, where she and her odd companions were swimming for their lives in oceans made of her own tears. I desperately wanted my parents and was more and more frightened I would never see them again. However, underneath the fear, there was a thin layer of excitement. I knew something I had not known before and that made me feel less small and dependent. For the first time, I could imagine living without adults, taking care of myself. Finally, I went back into my cabin and crawled into Jenny's bunk. She curled up and I molded myself around her and slept.

The storm was still raging the next morning when I made my way up to the dining room. Crockery, cutlery, and rolls were lying in pools of water from the broken glasses. Butter curls floated on top like the water lillies in the ponds below the Estoril casino. One waiter, already dressed in his white serving uniform, was standing in the middle of the mess. I found it hard to believe what I saw: it was like a dream in which the destruction of order I sometimes longed for had happened, making me feel guilty and ashamed.

I went to the window and stared out over the gray oily ocean, its waves full of violence and saw a dark gray object on the horizon. It had to be another ship. I opened the door to get a closer look and realized then just how strong the wind was. It was tearing and pulling the canvas covers off the four small lifeboats tied to the deck. In a flash of insight, I realized how useless those boats would be. No one could survive in this wind. As I watched the ship approaching on our port side, I felt the relief and excitement I would have felt had I been bobbing around in one of those lifeboats. Just then, I heard someone come up behind me and I turned, closing the door to the deck.

When the American husband saw who I was, his expression became even more morose. His clothes were stained and he had not shaven for days. He smelled of sweat.

"Look," I said, "a ship."

He did not seem to hear. "She doesn't know me."

More excited than worried, I stared at him. Was she dying? At that moment, I almost wished it would happen.

"A ship," I repeated. "To save us." This was the first time I had said those words out loud. He focused one desperate look on me, then rushed past toward the upper deck.

A little later I was in the lounge with Jenny and Mr. Klipp, watching through the window as the ship got closer. The captain appeared. Gone was the full dental smile. He appeared to have shrunk in his clothes. The once immaculate uniform was wrinkled and baggy. He, too, had not shaved that day and a dark cloud was forming around his chin and mouth. He gave us a distracted look and spoke in Portuguese to Mr. Klipp, pointing to the ship through the window. Mr. Klipp nodded and asked a question which the captain answered with a shrug and hand gestures I remember seeing boys use on the streets of Lisbon. I could barely hear him over the noise of the weather.

"It is an American ship," Mr. Klipp said when the captain had turned to the bar, "to accompany us until we reach Lisbon."

"Because of the storm?" I asked.

"The storm and some leftover war debris."

I starred at Mr. Klipp. "Do you mean pieces of metal?"

"Something like that." Mr. Klipp sounded bored and did not want to talk about it any more.

I took a careful breath. Now I could stop worrying about the American wife and whether I would have to see a burial at sea. I decided not even to ask about her. Instead, I hugged Jenny. She looked surprised, then hugged me back.

"You see," Mr. Klipp said to the captain who had poured himself a drink, "Sarah was worried. Just a little."

"How did you know?" I asked.

"Your face. I see there everything you are feeling."

I felt hot and was afraid I was blushing: something I did not usually do. I did not like to think I was such an open book and looked away.

He lifted my chin, forcing me to look at him. "Do not learn too well to hide your feelings or some day you will hide them from yourself. Do you understand?"

"Yes," I said, "I understand."

The storm blew itself out the next day and even though the *Algarve* rose and fell and the cabin deck was once again filled with the sounds and smells of *mal de mer*—Fatima muttering in Portuguese, carrying trays with bread and tea—the sight of the warship behind us flying the American flag kept the mood aboard ship almost lighthearted. I had long since gained my sea-legs and was immuune to the motion of the boat. Mr. Klipp, Jenny and I strode around the deck, making a game out of avoiding the high waves. Once the captain ordered us inside, saying he could not spare the crew to rescue us if we went overboard.

When the sea grew calm again, we found ourselves accompanied by a school of dolphins, leaping out of the water, their dark gray bodies gleaming in the sun. Some approached, sticking their heads out of the water for a better look. Their curved mouths appeared to be smiling and the ocean no longer seemed such an alien and hostile place. The dolphins followed the boat for almost half an hour, sometimes leaping so close I could see the details on their fins. We all waved when they started to move away. Jenny blew kisses.

"Sailors consider them lucky. We are very careful never to harm one." The captain was standing behind us. Shaved and pressed, he had regained his composure and good humor. "They are the true dolphins, relatives of the whale, not the porpoises you see leaping close to shore. You're fortunate to have seen them so close and for so long."

I stared out over the ocean. The sky was blue, becoming grayer where it curved down to meet the water. The waves swelled and flattened but no longer peaked into whitecaps. My own body rose and fell in response to its rhythm, lulled into a new kind of peace, of physical relaxation. I did not know then that this feeling would become a kind of standard by which I would measure contentment, that it would bring me back to the ocean for the rest of my life. The gulls flew around us, screaming and diving, the only visible form of life besides our own, which was dependent for survival on the mood of this great gray giant and on a small ship with its crew of sailors.

When we were within two days of Lisbon, I realized I no longer wanted to see my parents. The thought of them and the home they had built in the hills behind Estoril made me angry. Who did they think they were to send us away? Then, when we were really used to living in America, to bring us back, getting us almost drowned on the way? For a moment, I almost wished we had been. It would have served them right to have been greeted by the news that their children had died and been buried at sea.

That evening, after Jenny was asleep, I told Mr. Klipp I did not want to return to my parents. "Perhaps Jenny and I could live with you," I suggested. "I could help you with your business." We had discussed Mr. Klipp's plans to open a jewelry shop.

I don't know if Mr. Klipp grasped the situation and knew instinctively what I needed or if he allowed himself to believe that such an arrangement might be possible, that our ship-board family might continue once we reached shore, that his loneliness would be lifted from him, that he might even feel forgiven. In any case, he did not argue with me or laugh. He simply accepted my proposal as if it were reasonable and possible.

"I will have to see our parents and tell them of our plan. Then, Jenny and I can meet you somewhere." I had thought all this through. When I was a little girl before the war, my father used to take me to a famous pastry shop in Lisbon for hot chocolate. "We'll meet you there," I said and told him the name of the shop. The mixture of love, hope and disbelief on his face surprised me. I knew that I was responsible for that expression and that knowledge was exhilarating.

As we approached Lisbon harbor, the sun was shining, the sea was calm. The American ship had left us the day before. Everyone was in high spirits. The Portuguese ladies were back in their deck chairs and the two students looked healthier than they had when the voyage began. They had replaced reading with conversation. Sometimes their arguments be-came so intense that the cook (a moody man with high standards, who worked under difficult conditions) would come out of the kitchen to shout at them. The American couple remained secluded. The husband went to the kitchen for food at times when the rest of us were sleeping. I saw him because I got up earlier than most of the passengers.

When the ship entered the harbor, Mr. Klipp, Jenny and I were standing at the rail with our luggage. I could not wait to get through the meeting with our parents so that we could begin our new life. Jenny had been promised a dog, and Mr. Klipp and I were happily discussing the best location for the shop. In my mind, our parents had receded to a vestigial memory, giving off barely enough light to be recognized. I watched the people on shore get larger and larger and finally the ship pulled alongside the pier, the engines stopped and the gangplank descended.

Uneasily, I scanned the faces. As the crowd began to move, I saw the American couple ahead of us. She was wrapped up in a coat, hat and scarf, leaning heavily on her husband. Behind them came Fatima, looking like a stranger, in her dark coat and hat, carrying a suitcase. They seemed to be leaving the boat together. I felt a vague sense of relief. The American wife was still alive and Fatima was being liberated from her abusive job. I imagined them living together in Lisbon. Fatima would bring the wife cups of tea and raise their children.

I looked up at Mr. Klipp as we started down the gangplank. He gave my hand a squeeze. It did not occur to me to say goodbye. As we stepped onto the pier, onto land for the first time in ten days, I felt dizzy. Then I saw my mother and father. They waved and started moving toward us. Jenny dropped my hand and ran. I did not move until they were so close I could smell the familiar scent of my mother's perfume. Suddenly, as if someone had thrown a switch, everything changed. These strangers became my mother and father again. I was hugging them and crying, no longer grown up and self-sufficient.

Within the next half an hour, we got the bags into our car and drove away from the harbor and Lisbon, toward home. Our old car had the same smell and scratchy seats I remembered. The sights and smells of the country swept over me with a remembered familiarity and the child I had forgotten seemed to reenter my thirteen-year-old body.

For the first few days, I did not think about the trip. Then it all came back, but as though from a great distance. It was months before I really thought about Mr. Klipp: although, I often thought I saw him out of the corner of my eye on the street but it was always someone else, someone with his coloring or build or gait. When I turned, startled, he had disappeared.

Gradually, I started telling my mother and father about our ten days at sea. They knew about the storms and told me they had heard rumors about the mines suspected of drifting loose on our path. They had not really begun to worry until they heard the American ship had been sent to accompany us, and by that time we were safe. I was shocked to hear about the mines as I had assumed the "war debris" were pieces of wrecked ships or planes. Mr. Klipp had known, of course, and must have been pleased that I had not guessed the truth. I felt a surge of love for him but could not find the right words to explain and so I said nothing to anyone, but I thought about him often and for a long time.

During this period, I felt neither happy nor unhappy but somehow elevated in a different space from those around me from where I could see and hear what was going on but could feel nothing. I often stared at myself in the bathroom mirror, looking away then quickly back, trying to surprise my reflection into revealing something. Sometimes Jenny interrupted what she was doing to lean against me the way she'd leaned against Mr. Klipp. Sometimes I liked it, sometimes I pushed her away.

Our parents no longer treated me like a child but instead with a slight formality which never entirely left our relationship, even though I became an English schoolgirl in a green uniform, wearing a tie and hat and carrying a satchel. There were boys but no dancing class and no kissing games. Instead, there was field hockey and elocution lessons. We had to recite John Masefield's "Cargoes," which I found stirring, and Shelley's "Ode to the West Wind," which made me want to cry. I don't think I was happy again for a long time.

Twenty years later, married and living in America, I returned to Lisbon where my mother was then living. We spent the afternoon at the Guilbenkian Museum and afterwards, wanting some coffee, found ourselves in front of the famous old chocolate shop.

"Do you remember this place?" my mother asked. "You used to love the hot chocolate they served before the war."

"It was like drinking melted chocolate candy," I said. "No wonder I couldn't get out of my chair." We had a snapshot that had become a family joke of a plump two-year old trying to get out of her potty chair. "Let's go in."

We pushed open the old fashioned door, starting the bell ringing that announced our arrival. A case filled with chocolates and pastries ran along the left side of the small room. To the right were perhaps a dozen round tables with chairs. As we were removing our coats, I glanced over the room and was stopped by the figure of a man in a dark overcoat sitting at the furthest corner table, bent over his newspaper.

"My God," I said. "Mr. Klipp!"

"Who?" asked my mother.

"Mr. Klipp," I repeated. "The man on the *Algarve* after the war."

My mother looked puzzled but turned to look at the table in the corner. The figure meant nothing to her so she started talking about the museum, how much she admired Rodin's Burghers of Calais. Then, the waiter appeared, took our order and left.

I listened but my attention was riveted on the man in the corner. He did not move much and it was impossible to see his face from where I sat. He had removed his hat and his head had a thin covering of reddish brown hair. His coat looked heavy and rather old fashioned. He was reading a Portuguese newspaper. The more I stared at him, the more I became convinced it was Mr. Klipp. As the time we had spent on the *Algarve* had once seemed to stretch out like a rubber band, the twenty years between, now seemed to retract.

I had not thought of that experience or Mr. Klipp for a long time but now I could again smell the cabin deck of the boat, hear the waves as they crashed against our sides and see the dining room floor littered with broken crockery and glass, the white-coated waiter standing helplessly in the middle. Mr. Klipp was as clear as if he sat next to me. I saw his ring, smelled his shaving cream and felt the warmth of his presence. I thought of my plan to live together, the elaborate cover I created to avoid the anger I felt toward my parents and how he accepted this without question. I remembered his loneliness and felt a deep sorrow that I had been too young to understand and had lost a friend. It was suddenly imperative that this be

Mr. Klipp, that I see him once again. For what? To thank him? To reassure myself he had really existed?

After we put on our coats, I walked over to the corner table. "Excuse me," I said nervously, leaning toward the figure in the dark coat. The newspaper lowered and a middle-aged man's face looked at me in surprise. He had the same coloring as Mr. Klipp, the same blue eyes, now paled with age. We stared at each other for a moment.

"Mr. Klipp?" I asked.

He made no sign of recognition and I saw nothing I remembered in his face. I looked down at his hands but the left one, on which he had worn his ring, was hidden by the paper. The thought came to me that that had not really been his name, after all; that he had taken it as he had taken the jewelry and other things. I drew back. "Excuse me," I said again. "I thought you were someone else."

For an instant, I thought he was going to speak but he only nodded before turning back to his paper.

"Well?" said my mother when we got outside.

"It was someone else," I said.

"How could you tell, after all that time?"

"I don't know," I said. "But he was not there."

Leaving the World

BY ANN COPELAND

And at once they left their nets and followed Him.

For years, those words had rung for Claire Delaney with the seductive power of the absolute. In early childhood they had been simply words, part of a story as familiar as the furniture in her home, the contents of her closet. As she grew older in the Church, however, she began to hear echoes. *And the Lord said to Abram: "Go forth out of thy country, and from thy kindred, and out of thy father's house, and come into the land which I shall shew thee." And the Lord said to Moses: "I will send thee to Pharaoh, that thou mayst bring forth my people, the children of Israel out of Egypt."* So often the command was to go into another country. *"Take the child and go into Egypt."* To leave. *"Arise and go into the city, and it will be told thee what thou must do."* Depart. Venture forth into the dark, the unknown. *"Go ye forth . . ."*

And so, as years passed and she became what they called educated, worked her summer jobs, matured as a Catholic young woman did in those days, she knew all along that there was more to life than this. The gospels said so. Saints proved it. The very nuns before her dramatized it, albeit imperfectly. Leaving the familiar everyday world was the greatest adventure. Every explorer knew that. And what greater path to embark upon than the path to holiness? What greater world to discover than the world of God Himself?

He who loses his life will find it.

I.

When the novice mistress, a holy woman, spoke to her fifteen novices gathered for two and a half years away from the world to learn a new way of life, she put before them the response of those hardy fishermen, James and John, to the Lord's invitation "Come follow me." *And immediately they left their nets and followed Him.* Magnetic words to Sister Claire Delaney, encased now in her trappings of adventure, starch and black serge.

Occasionally, as she dusted them in the morning, Sister Claire would look through the mullioned windows of the novitiate library—misnomer for a room that housed books to dust, not read. She might glimpse a cardinal or bluejay swooping toward the apple tree, a squirrel nibbling away at acorns, or simply the shaded patch of clover and wild daisies at the far end of the sloping mowed lawn. Sometimes, on summer mornings when the novices sat outside making their meditation from five-thirty to six-thirty, a deer would emerge from the forest surrounding the novitiate house. Alert and wary, it would stand poised, staring at the odd spectacle of fifteen white-veiled figures dotting the lawn on camp stools, eyes shut, hands folded, a book balanced on their black laps. Then, with a turn and a flick of the tail as if to say "Phooey," it would bound back into the woods.

The novitiate was well situated for those who would put hand to plow. Its only approach—an unmarked dirt road plunging through dense woods—wound past scrub brush, alders, wild berry bushes, an immense corn field, cow pastures, an apple orchard and a small mountain before it finally reached the large half-timbered house with its attached chapel. By some stroke of cosmic humor, the original owner had been Margaret Sanger.

Yet even here, so far removed from the world, Claire Delaney soon learned that will has limits. Desire does not so easily die. Kneeling to dust chair rungs, window sills, she yearned to see the tail flick of a fleeing deer—something unbidden, unexpected, a vision to cherish, gift unsought.

Such longings would grow suspect.

Novitiate days are outwardly simple: hours of prayer, manual labor, strain to learn this other way, care about the letter of the law in hopes of one day moving into that freer realm where one lives by the spirit. How many worlds are there to leave? Too many to number. The journey to leave, to begin, grows endless, like rings on a tree, waves in the sea. One longs to be done with the purgative way. But to hope for higher—the illuminative, the unitive—might be pride. For when does aspiration become ambition? The last shall be first. Jesus wasted no sympathy on one mother ambitious for her sons.

Nonetheless, these were the enlightened late Fifties and everyone, even nuns, knew that educators must keep up.

So it was that, two and a half years later, on a January morning aglitter with diamond-crusted snow, the novice mistress gather her black-veiled, newly professed sisters on the freshly dusted library chairs for their last conference before leaving the novitiate womb.

"The Order has built a new House of Studies in Washington, D.C.," she told them. "To this house all of you who have already completed college will be sent in order to go on with graduate training in whatever field the Order deems suitable."

Another departure.

Would Sister Hillary be sent with her? They'd been together from the beginning. And what academic field would the Order "deem suitable" for Sister Claire? Departures were part of God's plan. What country would open out before her, now that she had crossed the threshold of her first vows?

"We must live each day as if it were our last, Sisters," said their new superior two days later, by way of welcome to the Washington House of Studies.

A woman esteemed for remaining humble even with a Ph.D., Reverend Mother Dominic projected pain through a resolutely joyful face. "I know you have been well trained in the novitiate. This is a time of further testing. We must live, Sisters, in the world but not of it. You will be pursuing studies on a university campus. You must carry with you everywhere the presence of God. And to help you in this, you will have all that the Order can give you, including the monthly retreat Sunday required by rule."

This was the day they lived eschatology, as if each breath would be their last, a day of intense preparation for the final departure.

Claire anticipated higher studies with apprehension. Novitiate efforts to erase secular knowledge, to wipe out what sixteen years of Catholic education plus tuition and fees had so deeply imprinted, had left her newly minted religious mind a *tabula raza* suspended above a pit of exhaustion. Names and dates were Back There, back in the world of Martha, ah Martha, so busy about many things that she missed the One Thing That Mattered. For where your treasure is, there will your heart be.

Now, with her newly professed sisters, Claire Delaney had reentered the world of moths and corruption. New person, new garb, new place. Returned. She must cross the bridge of sighs, ascend Mount Snowden, suffer Bosworth field, head for Canterbury, sail once more into the heart of darkness. (For they had decided, thank God, that she'd study English literature.) Surveying anew those literary texts she'd struggled to forget, she must test how completely the scales had fallen from her consecrated eyes.

But first (God's ways are not ours) they were set to painting. It was early February. University classes would not start for the latest group of arrivals until the following September.

"I will mix the paint for you, Sisters," said Reverend Mother Dominic.

They saw it as an exercise in humility.

The house, newly completed, smelled still of plaster and paint and gyp rock and sweet wood shavings. Their task was to transform the small square room on the first floor into a sickly rosy-pink chapel.

"Even though we will use this room for only one more year, Sisters, if our building progresses according to plan, it is still the house of God."

Each morning, Mother Dominic gathered her five new arrivals in the basement laundry room for paint-mixing. Nothing is insignificant in the eyes of God. The shade must be just right. She pinned back her veil, her large outer sleeves, donned a bibbed gingham apron, and hungrily eyed the cans through her bifocals. Then, with muscle one would not have expected, she took a long flat stick and stirred. "Just a little more white, Sister." Stir. Stir. "And now some yellow, please." Stir. Stir. "Now, just a bit of red." All these directions given in the silent tone. Thick ribbons of color swirled and blended into a uniform rosy-pink.

Claire watched the grim intensity of her superior's stirring and felt depressed. Despite the smiling face, the unflagging energy, the brisk walk and expert enthusiasm, she made you feel like such a slob. You knew you were sandpaper to her soul. She suffered you nobly.

Her inner life, Claire would think years later and a life away, must have been riddled with pain, one raw wound, for about the house she cast a pervasive gloom, a soul-eroding anxiety that even after twenty years could make those who'd survived her formation flinch to recall. Too long a sacrifice can make a stone of the heart.

During the weeks of chapel painting, she left them alone, morning after morning, once the paint had been perfectly mixed. In the presence of the God to Whom they were vowed, they worked silently, transforming His dwelling-place to a sickly rosy-pink.

What, they wondered, had this to do with becoming educated?

They rolled on the paint, prayed for perfection, and perspired in silence. God's ways are not our ways. Beneath black serge, their T-shirts were soaking.

After two months, when painting was done and chairs in the chapel had all been refinished, Reverend Mother set them to learn how to bind and patch the library books they were not yet permitted to look at. That would come in the fall when they were formally admitted to the university.

These things bear telling because leaving the world, one discovers, is immensely complicated. An act never completed.

Gone the woods and orchards and pastoral simplicities of novitiate days. Gone the simple earnest hopefulness of beginning. The tree of knowledge had begun to cast its shade.

Daily, as sizzling summer melted into burning September, they went out now to the university, a stream of black-veiled young nuns walking silently each morning toward the groves of academe, readying themselves for the challenge by meditating, or saying their rosary as they walked.

The world seeps in.

"You are to keep the rule of silence at all times, Sisters. Especially when you are on campus. You are not to speak to men. Any lapses you are to report to me."

"What's your name, Sister?" he asked, as he bent to pick up the pencil she'd clumsily dropped that first day in Romantic Poetry.

"Sister Claire." The hair on the back of his hand was red. He bit his nails.

How could she refuse to give her name? Besides, he reminded her of her brother, now off somewhere in uniform. Such occasional contact surely did not merit reporting to Reverend Mother.

Except for time in the university library, they were to study in common, in the convent, never alone in their cells. Eventually, when the new chapel was completed, they would have a large study hall beneath it.

For now, they had to study each evening after supper in the small library, crammed around one long table. Claire writhed at pages turning noisily on either side of her. She couldn't concentrate. The breathing of others sounded so steady, so untroubled, compared to the addled workings of her own print-fogged brain. Sister Jude, a student of American history, was permitted to look at the daily *New York Times*. Who would have thought the rustle of news could so shatter Wordsworthian solemnities, so dilute the epistolary anguish of Keats? Staring at her poetry anthology, Claire fought the urge to make marginal notes. She did not, could not, own the book. It would be returned to their library shelves at the end of the course. In the name of poverty, she was permitted only its *use*. She longed to write a note, cast her bottled message onto the unknown sea of the future. "I sat here in December 1960. I survived. I was discouraged, too. Hang in there." Or maybe, beside the "Preface to the Lyrical Ballads," one simple word: *Nuts*.

"You must pursue your studies with purity of heart, Sisters," admonished Reverend Mother. "There is a variety of gifts."

But everyone knew she expected A's. As if veil and beads

conferred on newly sanctified gray matter the capacity for excellence. As if brain power thrived on privation. *Amor vincit omnia.*

The world seeps in.

It lies within you, along with the kingdom of God. Discovering the two so deeply intermixed brought Sister Claire Delaney up short with a start, almost pain. It was her second summer in the House of Studies. The chapel had just been completed.

Throughout that spring they'd suffered the pounding, drilling, sawing and sanding with resignation. Each evening in June, at the end of recreation, Mother Dominic had brought her junior nuns to the threshold of chapel to see what progress had been made.

And one had to admit that the sunken flagstone nave, the oak choir stalls, the stone sanctuary with its austere lines, its plain marble table, had about it a simplicity, a form that appealed. It avoided clutter, bespoke a sensibility aimed out and up. Transcendence. Aspiration. Leaving. Climbing. Departing. Sister Claire liked it. She could hardly wait to leave the rosy-pink room where they'd knelt for a year and a half, shoulder to damp shoulder, breathing air that grew fetid in Washington heat as twenty-two nuns meditated for an hour each morning or chanted their blurred way through Divine Office. Gone the long sloping lawn of the novitiate. No fleeting glance here from a wayward deer. One longed instead, futilely, for Reverend Mother to turn on the fan.

At Saturday chapel the day before July Visiting Sunday, Reverend Mother spoke to them about the meaning of the new chapel. She took as her text "I will go unto the altar of God, to God Who gives joy to my youth." She spoke, rather grimly, of joy. The crucifix, she told them with something that bordered on exultation, would represent the risen Christ. And then she announced that tomorrow some would be having parents for a visit.

Sister Claire's heart leapt. She had not seen her parents for a year and a half, not since Profession Day in the novitiate when she'd emerged from the vow ceremony radiant beneath her new black veil, proudly conscious of heavy beads rattling against her knee, the large crucifix tucked into her leather cincture. She kissed her father and the lingering smell of his shaving lotion smote her heart. If she were to die that very day she'd go straight to heaven. They wanted her to go on living.

And so, in truth, did she.

Now they would see her halfway through her juniorate, halfway toward her final vows, the day she would say "forever" and receive the ring.

"I have prepared descriptions, Sisters," Reverend Mother was going on, "of the two statues and the crucifix that are available for donation, should any of your parents wish to be remembered in our chapel. It is a rare opportunity."

Claire stifled a tremor.

Next morning, after breakfast, she surreptitiously picked up from the table outside Reverend Mother's office the small folders describing the new chapel and available memorials: a statue of Mary, of Joseph, a crucifix of the risen Christ, a small pipe organ, choir stalls. In the interests of economy, Reverend Mother had decided against stained glass.

When her bell rang, Claire slipped the folder into her pocket, left chapel, and went to meet them.

He looked sallow somehow, and smaller. Not the man she remembered from a year and a half ago. He'd been ill. Gallbladder operation, persistent trouble with blood pressure. The shoulders inside his blue and white striped cotton jacket stooped ever so slightly. The small hands that once had commanded attention by their quietly graceful gestures, their magic on the keyboard, looked unsteady as he took out a pack of cigarettes and then, at her look, put them away.

Hugs accomplished, they took their places in the three-seat parlor not far from Reverend Mother's office. Clackety clack, clackety clack. A speed typist, Mother Dominic was at it all day, her door wide open in case a sister needed to see her. Clackety clack. No escaping this insistent background to their visit. In the novitiate, even on coldest Visiting Sundays, Claire had always taken her parents outside. They'd walk up toward the barn or apple orchard. Her father would smoke, observing her, while her mother rattled on.

"So, how's the scholar doing?" he asked now, somewhat formally.

"Surviving." Was he hinting about her grades? "This summer we're all taking two courses at the university—one in kerygmatic theology from a wonderful German theologian and the other in the sacraments from a Benedictine monk."

Her father's eyes glazed over.

What then to tell them?

"Now, Claire, I've brought you something," chortled her mother, rummaging through a bulging straw purse. "I've been saving them for months."

"You know your mother," said Burt Delaney. He shifted weight on the straight chair, stretched out one leg.

Claire remembered the wrinkled ankles of her mother's stockings, the overstuffed quality of her enthusiasms. He hid his worries, let them slide over into angers often hard to decode. She, on the other hand, defeated introspection. A chirpy lady with something of a nesting robin always about her even now that the nest was empty, she loved to bake, play cards (not too seriously), crochet layettes, and visit. Dauntless, she carried her thawing power into settings more subtle souls would tremble to invade.

Happy now, Monica Delaney pulled from her purse a bundle of folded newspaper clippings. "I saved what I thought you'd be interested in."

With pudgy ringed fingers, she began to straighten out the clippings, laying them on the small glass-topped table between her and Claire, her daughter, so recently of this world.

"But, Mom—"

"Now, there's one about Lucie Barnes.... She got married—when was it, Burt? October, I think. To Billy Meehan. Remember him? His youngest brother went to school with you at St. Jerome's. And yes, that's right... I brought the whole account of the fiftieth anniversary at St. Jerome's. Father Hurley put on a buffet with the help of the ladies of the parish, and..."

Claire saw them, the nuns of her youth—pleated bibs, starched headdresses, marshalling segregated recess lines, drilling on *The Baltimore Catechism*. Why did God make you? God made me to know, love, and serve Him in this world, and to be happy with Him forever in the next.

"But, Mom—"

"Remember Sister Geraldine?"

"Monica, maybe Claire has some things she'd like to tell us—"

"Mom, we're not allowed to read the papers."

"Good God, Claire!" His anger blasted her like hot air, scorching her soul. "You're in graduate school!"

She eyed him staunchly. He always made sense. A kind of sense. At least with him she could argue. "But we still require permission, Dad. We're still in formation. And my field isn't history, anyway. I'm busy reading poetry."

"Now, here's one for you," trilled Monica. "Remember Jackie, dear? Well, he finally got married. And who would you guess was the lucky girl?"

Lucky girl!... Jackie of the heavy breath, sweaty hands, big feet on the dance floor... Jackie Halloran whose mother thought it would be so lovely if only...

"Sheila. Oh, here it is—"

She handed Claire the picture. June bride. Frozen smile. Satin princess. Bouquet held loosely, just so. *Come to me all you who labor and are heavily burdened and I will refresh you.* They'd been close friends.

Suddenly, at the door, Mother Dominic.

Anxiety gripped Claire as she stood, but Reverend Mother seemed not to notice the worldly clippings. She greeted them, invited them to see the new chapel, offered to show them the inside way toward it.

"After next Sunday's dedication, I wouldn't be able to take you this way," she said as they hurried down the corridor beside her. "Papal enclosure, you know. The entrance for seculars will then be from the outside only."

At the back door of chapel she stopped. "I'll leave you here. I'm going into chapel, Sister. You can take your parents to the gallery." She shook hands and disappeared.

Claire led her parents up a few steps and into the small gallery. She pulled down the kneeler in the second row. They knelt together, looking down at the heads of five or six meditating nuns in the chapel below. Although it had not been dedicated yet, the nuns were permitted to pray here. Most elected the other room, where the Blessed Sacrament remained. This was cooler, however, and today the mercury had hit ninety-five degrees Fahrenheit.

For a few moments they were quiet.

Monica stirred, leaning her rose linen back against the seat. "It's so... bare," she whispered.

"It's new, Mother. Monastic. This is not a parish church." No garish Stations of the Cross, no rouged plaster statues. Claire felt inside her deep pocket for the folder. Quietly she handed this to Burt.

"Claire," whispered her mother again, louder. "I've never seen a crucifix like that. Why is it like that?"

Reverend Mother was kneeling in her stall at the rear of chapel, her head just a few feet away from them.

"Look at this," said Burt to his wife. "We could make a contribution, Monica. Though one might argue we already have."

Claire's heart beat faster. Had Reverend Mother heard? They sat back in the pew and together looked at the brochure. *Why should this matter to her?* He was not rich.

"Oh, Burt, wouldn't that be nice." Monica took the brochure to study it.

"Let's get out of here," said Burt, standing up suddenly, jarring the kneeler.

Claire quickly pushed it back.

They left the gallery and this time, instead of heading back through the convent, she opened the door to the outside. Ten cement steps would lead them out of the cloister, down to the street.

Burt pulled out his cigarettes. Lighting up, he seemed to relax.

"Well, Claire, what do you think?"

They began to walk in front of the long cinderblock building. Sister Anthony had cut the grass just yesterday. The small lawn looked trim, cared for. A few weeks of this heat would leave it parched and yellow.

"About what?"

"Shall we donate something... more? What do you think?"

Opaque. That's what he could be when he chose. This was one of those maddening moments.

"Oh, Burt, wouldn't it be nice to know something was here that we'd put here?"

"It already is."

"Oh, not that. You know what I mean. A part of our daughter's life has been here, after all."

"Exactly my point."

"And then, even after she's gone...wherever they send her..." her mother had in mind perhaps Rome, the first female pope, "There'd always be something here. I like that idea, don't you, Claire?"

"Your mother excels in looking forward to looking back," he said, sprinkling ashes in the freshly swept gutter. "What about you, Claire?" His eyes bored into her. "Does it matter to you?"

How to answer? *She wanted their donation. She wanted to knock at Mother Dominic's door later today, enter her office, kneel by the tidy desk and announce quietly, modestly: "Reverend Mother, my parents wish to donate..." She wanted to see the light of surprise erase pain in those blue eyes. She wanted the secret pleasure (surely it would remain secret) of knowing when she knelt in the new chapel that her parents had contributed...that she, Sister Claire Delaney was needed...that but for her...*

Her father was watching.

She reddened.

"Well, maybe, Dad. If you and Mom really want to...you might—" it came out in one tremulous daring breath, "consider the crucifix."

Except for the organ, the most expensive item on the list.

The afterbirth brought pain.

Because it entailed looking up at the resplendent carved crucifix with its priestly robed Christus, that patient face, that strong noble figure suspended before her above the main altar, and knowing, with a tinge of sadness, that the world was still definitely within. She'd known that before, of course. But this knowing was new and sharp. Outsides and insides, the simple squares of her eschatological bookkeeping, had deceived, would deceive. Leaving the world—strange phrase—meant confronting it. In oneself. And the possibilities of discovery, confrontation, were endless.

She prayed for detachment, for a spirit of poverty, for purity of heart. She prayed to recognize the truth when she saw it, whatever its guise.

And several months later, courses over, dissertation completed, she rejoiced to learn that she would rejoin Sister Hillary, already in the community of Holy Name, a flourishing girls' high school in southern Massachusetts.

Sister Claire Delaney prepared her soul to reenter the world.

II.

"It's a fantastic story how we got this place," says Sister Dorothy, settling down to darn the heel of a stocking.

Three summers later now, seventeen nuns of various ages and dispositions are easing into a rhythm Sister Claire thought she'd forsaken forever. Vacation.

After prodding freshmen through Latin I, walking sophomores and juniors through *The Thomas More Anthology of Prose and Poetry*, and threading the labyrinthine intricacies of community life, she isn't protesting.

Late June sun, locust buzz, shimmering humidity, the heavy dampness of black serge against human skin reminds one, even a resolutely mortified one, that some skins can be shed, that people do, in some worlds, shed layers in summer, shed in fact as much as possible. They might leave their skins, if they could. Though that, of course, is in the world. That other world, the one left behind.

So here, at Lake St. Mary, high up in New York State, a narrow lake two miles long, a quarter mile wide, surrounded by dense pine woods and bordered by clots of lazy wildflowers, here the nuns from Holy Name vacation.

There is a spacious central house with cathedral ceilings, a large kitchen, a dining area and a large living room, and five small bedrooms off the upstairs walkway. This main house also boasts a broad veranda with wicker chairs. But the best part, so Sister Claire thinks, is the smaller cottages with one or two bedrooms, some four or five of them stretched in among the trees along this side of the lake.

To one of them she has been assigned with Sister Hillary. A kind fate put both their names on the same vacation list. And Sister Edwin, a sympathetic woman assigned as this week's vacation superior, has arranged for the two of them to share the same cabin, St. Catherine's.

Sister Hillary will be working this summer on an M.A. in Greek. Sister Claire, fresh from *amo amas amat*, *David Copperfield*, and *Mill on the Floss*, is ready for anything. Anything, in this case, will be reading through the *Oresteia* in translation with Sister Hillary.

For a couple of hours each day, reveling in the coolness of the students' blue gym suits which they wear at all times except for meals and hours of prayer, they will set chairs by the side of the lake and muse on the rashness of Orestes. They will explore the mystery of *hubris*. And they will have a chance to talk.

With minimal exceptions, the rule of vacation is To Each His Own. Prayers remain, of course. Otherwise, days are pretty open. Every morning, Sister Luke goes off in gum boots with her fishing rod and pail. Sister Josephine disappears with her flute. Sister Stella sits beneath the huge ash tree near the main house composing a learned article on "Lycidas." Some knit. Some crochet. Some stare at the lake. Some cook.

Hours of prayer in the specially built chapel, a square building with a screened side facing the lake, constitute a special pleasure. Morning birdsong and a cool lake breeze against one's back confer a gentle edge on the gospel. Divine Office is said in private, perhaps as one walks around the lake.

If this is spiritual childhood, it's okay.

The story of how they got the place comes out now, all in one piece, at evening recreation on the second night. Reclothed in habits, they sit in a large circle on lawn chairs between the main house and the lake. Some laps hold piles of stockings to be darned. Faces inside the starched vises are already red or brown, freckled, peeling. Bodies seem to have loosened. There is a quiet tolerance here that Claire never feels in the convent at home.

"So how did we get the place?" asks Sister Hillary, who is resisting any thought of darning.

Sister Dorothy smiles, eager to tell. "She got the whole place—lake, cottages, main house, everything except the chapel which we built—lock, stock, and barrel...free."

"Providential," murmurs Sister Beatrice. She is hooked on Divine Providence.

Sister Eleanor, a square-jawed nun with a rugged athletic look, stretches a measuring tape across the width of a small crocheted baby blanket lying on her lap. "Tax break," she murmurs.

"One day, inspired by the Holy Spirit perhaps, who knows..." Sister Dorothy sets down her darning egg, "Reverend Mother just went upstairs without saying a word and got the big statue of the Infant of Prague. You know the one just outside the upstairs chapel?"

Claire knows it to the motes of dust on His crown, for which she is responsible.

"Reverend Mother had great devotion to the Infant," says Sister Beatrice. "A blessing."

Once again, Claire feels her lack of a sense of history. She never knew the legendary Reverend Mother William. It puts one at a disadvantage.

"So she carried Him down to the portress booth," continues Sister Dorothy, "set Him on the table in front of her, and asked the portress to dial a number for her."

"None of us knew until later," chimes in Sister Eleanor, folding her pink blanket. "Not even Mother Gerard who was sub-mistress then. Only Mrs. Borgia, the portress. She's the one that told the story."

"Anyhow," Sister Dorothy sends abroad a shushing look, "when Mrs. Borgia had made the connection, she handed the phone to Reverend Mother who identified herself as from this convent. She explained her mission. She had a houseful of nuns, eighty of them. They were tired. They worked hard all year in a large girls' high school and two parochial schools. They taught, they studied, they prayed. They needed a vacation, some arrangement that would make getting away for a few days each year possible. Until the past year, they'd shared a summer house on Long Island with another convent in the province, but that could no longer be. It was a case of overcrowding. And somehow—who knows, maybe she'd seen it advertised in the real estate section of the *Times*—she'd heard this lake in upper New York State was for sale. She understood he'd built the houses for his family, a regular compound, and it was no longer used."

"Here she touched the Infant," breaks in Sister Beatrice. "And she asked how would Mr. So and So like to donate the whole thing to a worthy cause."

Lake water laps nearby. Behind chapel, a falling orb fires leafy green tips. Somewhere out in the lake a loon laughs.

This is a moment I shall never forget, thinks Claire.

For although she'd never known Reverend Mother William, she can see it all—the polished oak top of the portress booth table, the kind discreet portress, Mrs. Borgia, being helpful, moving aside, tactful. And Mother William, daring. Taking them all on. Was she wise as a serpent, simple as a dove? Perhaps that's what the passage meant. As she and Hillary had once agreed—back in the days when Hillary had been Patsy Molloy—Christ's words, "The children of this world are wiser in their generation than the children of light," were a colossal putdown if ever there was one.

Tax break or not, charity or greed, whatever his motive, bless him, thinks Claire, in these days of water and sun and talk and something indefinable she would call "community." Bless the rich donor. Thank God for Reverend Mother William's nerve... There's a word for that, isn't there? Vaguely, she dredges it up from somewhere. *Chutzpah.* That's it. *Bless Mother William for her chutzpah.*

She says it to herself dreamily, floating on her back in the middle of the lake, or rolling over into a dead man's float. *Chutzpah... chutzpah... chutzpah.....* Water fills her ears. Hanging onto the far side of the raft, she looks over at the opposite, deserted shoreline with its waving fireweed, its clumps of strange yellow and purple flowers, its darkly clustered cat tails. *So many things in nature I cannot name*, she thinks with something like regret. Then dives deep, parting the black waters, seeking the depths until her ears hurt and her head feels funny. With a panicky frog kick, she pushes herself back to the top and breaks the surface, gasping for air. *Chutzpah... chutzpah... chutzpah.* Any deep dive takes nerve. *Chutzpah.*

For languid hours she lies in the rowboat, letting it drift among lily pads as she stares straight up at the sky of soft white and blue. The book she's brought along out of a vague sense of duty lies unread. *Giles Goat Boy.* The mother of a student lent it to her. But time for drifting is too precious to waste. The book is tedious. Far more tedious than Aeschylus.

Whether or not others join her, she forces herself into the water every day, letting numbness steal her toes, her feet, her shins, her thighs, nerving herself up for the cold finger against her stomach, her breasts. It has been so many years.

One day, when she is swimming alone, a sudden idea grips her. She is careful to stay on the far side of the float, out of sight of the house. Sister Anthony is tatting down near the water's edge. Several figures sit on the veranda, reading.

Claire loosens the buttons of her water-logged gym suit, no easy task, and eases it down from her shoulders. Back and forth she swims, half naked fish streaking through the lake underworld. The cold water icing her breasts, her nipples, her back, feels strange and wonderful. Her skin becomes satin, or is it the water against her skin? The heavy gym suit drags about her waist like a deflated tube. If she could, she'd shuck off the whole thing, swim about immersed in this alien thrilling embrace. Too complicated. It would be just her luck to lose it. She sees it happening...the blue cloth slowly sinking out of sight, away, her desperate plunge to retrieve it as it moves toward the other side of the raft, her waiting, hopeless, growing cold, skin going pruney, shivery, until at last she can wait no longer, twilight is coming, the peepers have started, the sun has sunk behind the trees...and she swims to shore, bursting forth in pink embarrassed splendor, an accidental Venus, shaking all over, oh so naked. The sisters run for towels, averting eyes...

Giggling, she blots out the picture with a quick underwater duck and swims forward. Through the clear water she sees her pale breasts following, swinging mysteriously in bubbles created by her own breath. She remembers now nights at the Connecticut shore when she and her friends would sneak out from their cottages after dark. Modest, as young Catholic girls would be, they'd slip into the black water quickly, ducking out of the cold night air, dive into a mouthful of salt, then strip off their suits and stash them atop a barnacled rock. Swimming about in total liquid joy—screaming, teasing, giggling— they'd float down watery moonlit paths, dive to the slimy touch of seaweed ribbons, shrewdly gauge their strength against the undertow and seek out elusive warm spots.

So many years later, so far way, in this cloistered lake, out of her sisters' sight, half naked, she swims about in an unknown donor's gift, swims to joyous release, surprised to feel so little guilt.

It feels almost natural.

Directly opposite the raft, on the uncloistered side, a huge willow tree hugs the edge of the lake. Its elegant filmy branches hang out over the water, weeping downward, creating another tree below, a water tree, on the dimpled surface. From her spot beside the raft, Claire can see the water tree. It moves slowly, almost dances, as a soft breeze stirs the yellowish green above. Yet it holds its shape, a large uneven darkness on the lake's surface.

Praying no one will come and discover her, she swims toward the shade. Bit by bit, as she approaches, she loses the outline, but the cool darkness tells her she has arrived. She turns over and floats, looking up into the pale green canopy blocking the sun. Then she turns again and dives, down, down, leaving far behind on the surface the dancing shadow tree. Near the bottom, white pebbles glisten in murk, and tiny quicksilver fish dart about like slim silver coins, avoiding her pale feet, racing away from this intruder.

Then she is above again, inside the water tree, swimming along its branches, scissor-kicking its trunk, diving through its leaves, playing discreetly amid the rippling foliage. Limp lance-shaped leaves above become flat dancing shadows all around her. Exhilarated, she swims about in them, joyous, almost content. Reveling to frolic half naked in the watery shade, gift unsought, hers alone to explore, to dive beneath, to embrace, hers alone to swim through, to leave behind, to remember.

She cannot see the future, cannot dream the world of time ahead, prepare for new wildernesses, new shades. Nor is it required.

Enough to be here... floating... diving... swimming... in the secret water tree she has found, a tree she can never possess, never encompass, that from time to time she can only see and swim to meet, divining its shadow against a distant shore, aware that in the moment of her arriving it will already have disappeared.

Plans

BY SUSAN S. HUCKLE

September 19

Sinclair bent over the stainless steel counter and teased back layers of fibrous capsule with scissors and forceps. This fist-sized ram's testicle was normal, though the other of the pair had been as large as a football. For the sake of completeness, he needed to dissect them both through the stroma to the mediastinum and epididymis. The task required rhythm and delicacy. Sinclair hummed along with Doc Watson singing from the radio, and reminded himself to check the time in a while. He needed to get home early, having volunteered his five-acre yard again for the fall student party.

"You coming to the barbeque tonight?" he asked, to which the young man at his shoulder answered, "Yes sir!"

Sounds as if he's been in the military, thought Sinclair, but he didn't remember seeing it in the boy's record, not even ROTC. Yet here's a kid who probably should have joined up before he got this far this fast. Kirt was serious to a fault.

Sinclair liked to keep it light with his apprentice-students. In fact, he preferred conducting his research alone; in this arena, he tended to get so involved he sometimes forgot to teach. And his new apprentice didn't make it easy; Kirt's precision seemed robot-like, his intensity calculated. Ones like this sometimes never get it through their heads in the course of four years that they're on no royal mission, that it's just a job waiting for them at the end, a lot of hard work rewarded with more of the same.

Sinclair handed Kirt a slice of tissue on a scalpel and said, "Tomorrow I'll show you how to make sections for slides."

The position Kirt filled was one of a number of jobs available throughout the college to third and fourth year veterinary students. Every fall, Sinclair was assigned a third year student who had aspired to the few surgery apprenticeships, but had lost out to some fourth year favorite. Pathology, Sinclair's area, was thought to be a distant second best. He was sure Kirt's opinion reflected the consensus. At least the young man was willing and brawny; he could easily lift an animal his own weight from the necropsy table.

"That's it for now. If you would, hang the carcass in the freezer and hose down in here. See you at the barbeque!"

In the locker room Sinclair stepped out of his rubber boots and his overalls, and took a shower. He reflected for a moment on his own time in the military—how he had joined the Army, intent on fighting in Korea, but found himself stationed in Germany where he did nothing more than chauffeur a colonel around and coordinate his company's intramural sports. It was not what he'd expected, but then, he'd had the advantage of a sense of humor. Maybe playing soldier wouldn't have helped Kirt at all.

Sinclair wondered what else might loosen up this kid, this new apprentice, and was reminded again of the barbeque. He must get home and start the coals.

Cold storage was full of hanging cow quarters, half-horses, and odd legs and heads propped along the walls or sitting on shelves, along with trash bags containing opossums, birds and rabbits that the public felt compelled to bring in from road kills. Kirt had difficulty finding a place for the ram. He had to rearrange the hanging specimens on the overhead track to make room for the gaping, shaggy body. It was late when he finished cleaning up, leaving him time for only a short workout in the weight room.

The lanolin odor of the ram's wool was still with him as he pressed. He concentrated on upper body, thighs and stomach, those muscle groups he felt were most vulnerable to thinning. He wore long navy sweats and closed his eyes while he worked. Then he showered and dressed quickly, guarding against being randomly viewed. People often stared at him, even other well-muscled men. But he had worked too hard for the pectoral definition, the biceps, the washboard stomach to waste them on locker room bravado. Kirt preferred keeping his body hidden beneath long-sleeved shirts and loose trousers. Thus when his physique was discovered at some moment of his choice, the astonishment it created in the viewer was all the greater.

He drove to his apartment for fresh clothes. His roommate had already left for the barbeque. Kirt entered his room and checked it in case he should bring a girl home. His bed was tightly made. There were the requisite piles of textbooks and stereo equipment on his desk, dirty laundry on a chair. He tossed the laundry in his closet.

He left the two reloaders bolted to their positions on the edge of his desk, but cleared away the cans of powder, boxes of brass shells and copper bullets, the scales, the tubes of resizing lubricant and several wire brushes; placed them all in a drawer. He propped the twenty-five pound bag of chilled lead shot in a corner. The Browning 30.06 and the Anschutz .22 lay unostentatiously enough in the gun rack on the wall, but Kirt removed his burly 12-gauge shotgun, put it in its case and placed it under the bed. The room had better balance now. He dressed and left, carefully closing his bedroom door.

Alice watched them. They formed two groups, one around the beer kegs, and the other around the clutch of faculty. This is why they're here, she thought, to brown-nose teachers and get drunk for free. In her library job at the university, she spent every day dealing with students and felt little tolerance for the assembly before her. Alice had been helping her parents protect their house from the unruly ones by escorting them inside to the bathroom and out again, during which she overheard jigsaw bits of their conversations, mostly harsh complaints about veterinary school. If it's that bad, she wanted to say, why did you people sweat blood to get here? Why must you moan so, when you swear there's nothing else you'd rather do?

She used to enjoy the fall barbeque. When she was a teen, she spent the whole evening deciding which of the handsome male students to have a crush on. When she was in college, she would come home for the event and tap a keg with the best of them. Then one year, her parents hadn't been so careful of the house as before. As a result the hall carpet had been ruined with dropped cigarette ashes and mud. One student had fallen through the porch screen door and demolished it, and, unbelievably, their aging terrier had somehow been shut away in a closet where he died from the stress of trying to escape. Since then, Alice had not attended the annual fall party; she had been living in Canada. And even though now she was home again, she agreed to help tonight only at her mother's pointed request.

The crowd seemed to swell as twilight deepened. Suddenly the invasion was too much for her to watch. She had to leave. Her mother would have to understand. Alice slipped through the seldom used, formal front door and jogged across the yard, avoiding the house flood lights. She had planned a means of escape, should the need arise, by parking her car half a mile away so she would not be blocked in by student cars. As she neared the end of the long driveway, a man's voice sailed out from the dark.

"Excuse me, are you first year?"

"Far from it," said Alice. Spare me, please, she thought. The question had come from someone leaning on a car. She couldn't make out the man's face. She kept walking.

"I didn't think I'd seen you around before."

Alice walked on.

"This is quite a place," the man said to her back. "Listen to the crickets. They're getting slow in the cooler air. You know, the frequency of their chirps is a pretty good thermometer. You can equate chirps per minute to degrees Fahrenheit, up to a point. I think it must be about fifty-five degrees now. I've been counting."

Alice turned and stopped, trying again to see the speaker's face.

"My name is Kirt." His handshake was brief.

"Alice."

"Can I drop you off somewhere?"

"You're leaving the party already?"

"I've got no use for big parties. Besides, I should study some tonight. Do you need a ride?"

"No, my car's down the way, thanks."

"Well, if you're leaving too, care to join me for some coffee?"

"I thought you had to study."

"I do. That's why I need the coffee."

Alice found herself perversely curious, though her last, most serious lover had left her hard-shelled and unhappy with men. But the cricket line was unique in her experience. She agreed to meet Kirt at a coffee shop in town.

After an hour with Alice, Kirt returned to his apartment alone. He studied his Clinical Practice notes until midnight. Then he pulled out a strong box from under his bed which contained his revolver and a thick, well-thumbed notebook. The notebook had ceased to be his diary years ago; now it was where he mapped his plans. Recording progress on his agenda helped him stay on track. He wrote.

1. Have feeling Sinclair doesn't like me.
   Have to win him over. (Try pulling extra necropsy duty.)

2. Notes on Alice Sinclair:
   —almost thirty (too old?)   (−)
   —seems smart, but confrontational (be careful)   (+/U−)
   —recently moved from Canada, don't know why(find out)   ?
   —M.A. in library science, works at university   (+)
   —lives at home with mother and father *Dr. Sinclair*   (+)
   —a small woman   (−)

October 17

It was still early evening when Alice met Kirt in town, as she had tentatively agreed to do on four other occasions since the barbeque. He would call her on his study breaks, and they would have coffee and talk. Alice was careful. Kirt was an intimidatingly large man, as well as her least favorite kind of student. Yet he tempered his physical presence and his status with a gentle voice and gentlemanly gestures that involved no contact between them. She was also leery of the absolute attention with which he listened. He was only twenty-three years old. At that age, could he possibly know how to contrive such patience, such fine-tuning for seduction, she wondered? Alice felt her wariness thin somewhat.

They sat at a back counter in the shop. Alice had finished her French roast and was stuffing her napkin in her cup when Kirt asked if she would like to come with him to the college. In laboratory class that day, he explained, student teams had performed intestinal surgery on dogs. Team members were then supposed to take turns checking their animals every four hours to record vital signs, and administer fluids and medication.

"So it's your turn now?" she asked.

"I took all of tonight's checks. First night's the worst, you know."

"Sounds like you're either very dedicated or you don't trust your teammates."

"I am, and I don't," said Kirt.

Alice laughed but Kirt didn't look like he was kidding, so she stopped.

"Besides," he said, "I was surgeon this time. I want to be the one to watch him for the first twenty-four hours."

"I'll go with you," said Alice.

The pens inside the narrow animal shelter were lined with wood shavings and placarded with clipboards; in each lay a different variety of dog. Most of them were very still. Alice had to breathe through her mouth for a few moments to prevent the sour, gastric smell of the place from gagging her.

Kirt walked evenly down the aisle until he stood before the last pen. The dog within did not respond to his voice. Alice watched him write on the clipboard sheet and enter the pen. He produced a stethoscope, listened, wrote on the sheet, produced a thermometer. The dog moved slightly when the thermometer was inserted. Kirt ruffled the dog's fur, lifted a pinch of skin, looked in its mouth, gently prodded its abdomen. With his brow locked down in a line over his eyes, Kirt looked so deliberately grave that Alice had to smile.

"We discontinued the fluid drip late this afternoon, and I think it was premature," he said. "He's still dehydrated. Can you hold him while I set up another I.V.?"

"Of course."

The dog was a mongrel, chestnut-backed, with a creamy belly and whorl on his chest. His head lay flat and his mouth was opened slightly, exposing a pale, dry tongue.

"Kirt, is he dying?"

"No. The fluids will help, I promise. Just hold him still while I get the needle in."

She leaned down and held the dog against her. Kirt whispered to the animal as he worked. It didn't flinch. Alice stroked the chestnut head, rubbed behind ears and under chin; the dog's eyes half-closed.

"What's next?" she asked.

"We recover them for a week, then go back in and see how our sutures are holding up." Kirt hung the bag, adjusted the drip, taped the tube in place.

"And then?"

"They get put down on the table. It's the most merciful thing."

"I've heard that sometimes people sneak their animals out of lab and take them home, to keep from putting them down."

Kirt didn't reply.

Alice shook her head.

"It's training, Alice. There's no other way. But I can tell you I don't plan on doing this for a living with a small animal practice. Large animal surgery is where I'm headed."

Kirt snapped the dog's pen shut and followed Alice down the aisle, silently passing several other students where they knelt, ministering to their own patients.

Outside, the night air felt quite clean. Alice hadn't noticed before how it smelled deliciously of the fresh wood shavings used for bedding, stockpiled high in a nearby shed. They walked beside other animal shelters and down past the open kennels, sending up a wave of howls and barks from dogs as they passed. Then without warning, a Doberman rushed at Alice, snapping and barking as it threw its body against the fencing at the end of the run. She gasped and uttered a little scream, inaudible in the din; Kirt sprang between Alice and the kennel, pressing her behind him.

"He's inside the fence—" he shouted after a moment, and then said more quietly, "You're safe."

"Good God, I thought he had me!"

"I did too, for a second." Kirt stepped away from her.

Alice stood still, heart tumbling in her chest. She tried to read Kirt's face by the dusk-to-dawn lights overhead. Those few seconds of unyielding, protective pressure of his body on hers had thrown her. His action had been wholly spontaneous, if melodramatic. He couldn't have planned this to impress me, she thought, and allowed herself to be impressed.

Kirt concealed his surprise when Alice said she would go back to his apartment with him for awhile. He thought it would have taken longer. It was awkward when they first arrived; Kirt introduced Alice to his roommate, Roger. But Roger was on his way out. He was seeing a first year student, one that he had met at the fall barbeque, and he was now embroiled in helping her through her first round of tests. Kirt had warned him of such complications, dating a first year. It had done no good.

"Guns," said Alice when she glanced into Kirt's bedroom. She stopped in the doorway. "Guns?"

"It's a hobby. I like to load my own ammunition, like to target shoot."

"And hunt?"

"A few weekends in the fall. Not much time for any of it these days."

"I've never shot a gun before."

"You would like target shooting."

"I don't know about that." She had turned cool, looking up at the gun rack.

"I'm not a fanatic, Alice. I was raised with guns."

"Oh?" She crossed her arms and leaned against his desk. "I was just thinking of the contradiction: how you wear one hat to help animals, then another to stalk and kill them..."

"It's something my brother and I used to do with my grandfather. That's all."

"You're sensitive about this."

"I just don't want to put you off. You know, my grandfather's the one who taught me about crickets."

She smiled at that. It was time. Never having touched Alice romantically, letting the anticipation build to this moment, the tactile flood should be powerful. He leaned down to find her lips. And he was right. After several kisses she warmed predictably in his arms. Kirt locked the door, lit a candle. He wanted just enough light to see by. Removing his shirt, having a woman first look at his naked torso was always exquisitely arousing. The expression on Alice's face did not disappoint him. She began to disrobe.

"Let me do it," he said.

She had smaller breasts than he had hoped. She was tiny waisted, tiny wristed. But her hips had some girth; enough, he guessed, for childbearing.

"Do your parents know we're seeing each other?" Kirt asked when their lovemaking was over.

"No. I want to see how it goes, Kirt. My parents worry about me." Alice sighed. "Several years ago, I started seeing an older man in graduate school, one of my professors. Now here I am, seeing a younger man. One of Dad's students."

"You think that's cause for concern?"

"It was in the other case. I ended up going with him when he took a position at the University of Toronto. It turned out to be a big mistake. I mean a terrible mistake. Dad tried to—"

"You don't have to go into it. It doesn't matter now."

Alice turned over and looked at him quizzically in the candlelight.

"I know your father at school, but I want to meet both your parents, as your parents. Soon. Put everybody's worries to rest. Because," Kirt said soberly, "I can see how it's going between us, Alice, can't you?"

October 21

Sinclair had left word on the message board for Kirt to find him in the lab prep room, where he had spent the morning rummaging through jars of preserved specimens, picking out the ones he needed to use for this week's embryology practical. Overhead was suspended the serpentine length of a heifer's digestive track for next semester's anatomy class. It had been cured to the color of amber and was now being inflated and dried with pumped air. The pump motor sat on the counter beside Sinclair, vibrating the formaldehyde in his jars and rattling so that he could hardly hear himself humming.

"This thing's awful damn noisy, John. Doesn't it get on your nerves?" he asked, thinking the person behind him was one of the lab prep techs.

"You wanted to speak with me, sir?" It was Kirt. John was

bleaching bones at the far bench and didn't hear Sinclair over the noise of the pump.

"Yes, I wanted to tell you how much I appreciate the extra time you've put in lately on necropsy. But, uh, how's your schedule? Could you fit in a few more hours for me?"

The young man said something and glanced up at the ballooning stomachs that swayed over his head.

"Speak up!"

"I could try," Kirt said more loudly a second time. He appeared to be ill at ease. He must think I'm about to play the protective father now that Alice has let us know about the two of them, Sinclair thought. Maybe I should give him a break and tell him I've learned my lesson: we've only just gotten Alice back with us thanks to my meddling. I'll be staying out of this romance.

"Let me tell you what I'm proposing," Sinclair shouted. "Seems they've got more rams than ever going down with epididymitis in Gilbert country. I thought we could take one of the ambulatory units up there the next few times they call, perform the necropsies on the spot, and then look over the herds."

"I do have midterms coming up."

"I wouldn't take you away from classes, don't worry. Just a few more afterschool or weekend hours, if you're game. Here." He reached into his overalls' pocket and handed Kirt a small black box. "I can have you paged with this. You give the switchboard a call back and let them know if you can make it. Simple as that."

Kirt's mouth broke into a grin that was so broad, his lips paled as they pulled across his teeth. "You've got a deal."

Sinclair observed him curiously.

"Is that all, sir?"

"That's it. See you later."

Kirt clipped the pager to his belt as he left. John winked at Sinclair and switched off the air pump.

"I believe you just made that boy's day. Now he gets to brandish his new beeper in front of his classmates."

Sinclair laughed. "What do you think of that one, John?"

"Don't know. The other kids say he's a real loner. Doesn't seem to be tight with anybody, not even his roommate. But you should see him in surgery lab."

"Good?"

"You bet he's good, better than good. I expect you'll lose him on necropsy; he's a cinch for one of the surgery jobs next year."

October 27

In surgery lab, Kirt had taken his turn performing ana-esthetist, assistant-anaesthetist, and assistant-surgeon duties on his team. This week he had been slotted for surgeon again. But when the moment came to direct the team, to execute the orderly manipulations of the procedure, it did not empower him as it had before. He'd had little time for follow-up on the animal; Dr. Sinclair had scheduled field trips on three con-secutive afternoons. And there was still one midterm exam left to be taken, Pharmacology, the most difficult yet. Kirt had propped notes on the dashboard of the truck and tried to study as Sinclair drove them to designated farms, his favorite country-western music blaring on the radio. The sheep farmers hit it of well with Sinclair. They always offered supper. Then after the meal, they liked to push back from the table and chew the fat. Kirt had been consistently late getting home.

His weight room work had suffered. Kirt felt his muscles were already showing neglect. He used the early morning to prepare the necessary work for his daily seven hours of lecture and lab classes, and then ate chili beans from a can and white loaf bread while studying late at night, when Alice usually called.

"I'd like to see you," she said this evening. "I think I'll ask Dad to give you a break. Sounds like he's taking too much of your time."

"No. Don't say anything. This has just been a bad week. Lots of sick sheep."

"I'd like to come over."

"My Pharm study group will be here in an hour."

"Spare me thirty minutes."

She brought him cookies and a tape of classical guitar music to study by. She was moist-lipped and insistent, but obli-gingly dressed quickly again, ready to leave before the study group arrived.

"Call me; let me know how the exam went. Oh, I haven't told you. I've got a new telephone number." Alice slipped a piece of blue stationery on his desk with seven digits penned on it.

"What's this?"

"I'm moving into an apartment tomorrow. It's overdue. I've needed to leave the nest again for some time. And now we can have some privacy—how about seeing a play with me Saturday night? I've got tickets. I could fix dinner for us at my new place."

"This Saturday?"

"Why not?"

"The Halloween party's that night, the big blow after midterms. People go all out on costumes. It's really something to see; I thought we could dress up and go. Can't you give the tickets to your parents?"

Alice rolled her tongue over her lips. "I thought you didn't like big parties."

"I've been strung pretty tight. I need a night out. Something like dinner and a play isn't going to do it for me."

"Maybe not." Alice's voice tightened. "But that doesn't give you the right to make all of our plans. I work hard, too, you know. What if something like the Halloween party isn't going to do it for *me*?"

"This is really not a good time to get into it, Alice."

The telephone rang in the kitchen. Kirt's roommate answered.

"For you," Roger yelled.

"Take a message," Kirt yelled back.

Alice cooled off fast. She said she'd go to the party if she could find someone to take the tickets for the play. She wished him luck on the exam and left. Roger waited until she was gone to place a cashier's tape from the grocery store on Kirt's desk. He had scribbled a long-distance telephone number on it, and beneath the number, the name "Kathy."

November 13

She had been his first pick. He had seen her only a few times the previous summer before deciding Kathy was the perfect choice. She worked in the local bank, sat like a centerpiece in the lobby. Her abundant lengths of leg were always crossed just so, calves parallel and full, beneath a mahogany library table, and her hair was as richly glossed as the table's deep red wood. Kathy used a devastatingly uniform smile when directing customers to the appropriate service areas. Her nameplate said "Lobby Officer for Public Relations," and was pinned to a bustline that formed a large, even shelf across her chest.

Just after daybreak at the shooting range, Kirt watched Kathy take aim with his .357 magnum Dan Wesson revolver. Her stance was flawless. When she fired, she did not stiffen against the blow, but moved with it, her upper body taking the linear shock better than many men he'd seen fire the gun. He had taken her to his back country range often in the summer; Kathy's aim was consistently poor, but she loved to shoot. This was when they would come—quite early on Sundays, when no one else was there. He had scarcely been back himself since Kathy broke with his plans, deciding in September to return to college, and to her boyfriend there.

She had said little when he picked her up. She seemed different, almost shy. They walked without talking to retrieve the paper target. Three of her five shots had missed entirely.

"It's been a while," she said.

"Is this your first weekened home, Kathy?"

"Yes. No. Well, I'm not going back. I've finally decided to quit. They're going to give me back my old job at the bank. It's just crazy for my folks to be paying out-of-state tuition when I don't even know why I'm going to college. I'm flunking three classes."

"What about Charles?"

"We broke up. Things weren't the same this year between us. I think he could tell there had been someone else, you know, over the summer." She handed the revolver to Kirt. "I guess you're seeing someone."

"Yes."

"I thought so. From the way you've been acting."

"It's nothing serious."

She nodded at the ground.

"What I mean is, you've been awfully hard to forget."

Kathy looked up with her perfect smile.

Kirt smiled back. His strategy had finally worked, though it had taken considerably longer than he had thought. As the months of fall had passed, he had given up expecting Kathy to come back. But here she was. And so luxuriously tall, he had forgotten. Almost his own height.

"It's cold," he said. "Let's go to the car."

He found a sequestered place to park beyond the end of the dirt road. The property was heavily posted, so that he doubted if any hunters would stumble upon them. His back seat was narrow and small for two their size; Kirt and Kathy had to work at coupling there, under blankets. Yes, yes, he thought with their rhythm. This one, yes.

That afternoon, Kirt studied lecture notes. He washed his laundry and had a long workout in the weight room. Two hours before dusk, he put his deer rifle in his car and drove to a tract of land where he had permission to hunt. It had been a wet fall, and the ground was soft. The undergrowth lay flat and did not betray his progress. He produced only the minor sounds of rubber soles grabbing tree bark, rifle stock rubbing against camouflage jacket, and once he was set in his tree, the slow unzipping of a pocket to yield his gloves. He waited. He saw no bird or rabbit, doe or buck. No other living animal. The light finally thinned so that he could not see the ground below him.

Last season, he had shot a buck from this blind. It hadn't been a clean shot, but the deer was dead when he discovered it, its eyes already filmed over like blue pearls. Since then, he had found himself watching the eyes of animals on the surgery table as they were put down. It was such a frictionless act for the animals, to die. Wholly without message in the eyes, this private, unintelligent mystery.

He must make a note to stick to business from now on. Surgery was no place for such distractions. Back at his apartment, Kirt retrieved his agenda book from its strong box for the first time in weeks and wrote down the reminder. Then he paged through his plans for third and fourth years, which were the most difficult he had yet set forth. First of all, during the third year he must lay groundwork for obtaining a residency in large animal surgery at the college, which meant earning consistently high grades, demonstrating skill, making connections, landing the right fourth-year apprentice job.

Secondly, he planned to be married in the third year, or by the beginning of fourth year at the latest. It was obvious he was not alone in this strategy; there had already been a rash of weddings in the third year class, and many more were scheduled. There was simply no time to keep dating. Third year was notoriously difficult. Third year students needed domestic support. Additionally, one's perceived maturity was enhanced by marital status; in this way, the second goal worked for the first. It was a sound agenda.

Kirt wrote a comparison list in his book:

Alice	Kathy
well educated	----
influential father	----
only conditionally supportive	devoted
a small woman	a large woman

The morning's encounter with Kathy made it all but impossible for Kirt to remember making love with Alice. This lapse seemed prophetic. And Kathy would give him the large, strapping children that he wanted, not gazelle-like creatures such as Alice was likely to produce. His children were included in his five-year plan. For reasons he did not question, they were essential to it. He circled Kathy's name.

They could be quietly married over Christmas break. He would need to stay in the background at school while the gossip ran its course. And he would have to give up his job with Dr. Sinclair, although he could truthfully say the hours were taking too much of his study time.

As far as next year was concerned, Kirt doubted if Sinclair would try to make trouble by keeping him from one of the apprentice jobs in surgery. But after that, out of spite, the man could easily vote him down for a residency at the college. Sinclair chaired the committee that awarded them. There were other residencies at other schools, however. They would be more difficult to obtain, but Kirt was certain to receive excellent recommendations from the rest of his teachers.

Nevertheless he felt apprehensive. He should break it off with Alice tomorrow. After all, they had already begun to quarrel. He could point that out; she deserved better, certainly. Kirt rationalized for an hour and composed a speech which he felt addressed the essentials, but would protect the truth and thus Alice's feelings for the critical interval, through Christmas break. By then she would be over it.

With that decided, he made a note to cash some savings bonds in the morning. He would buy a diamond for Kathy right away. She wasn't going to slip through his fingers again.

December 5

His wife had gone to bed early. Sinclair took his time reading the newspaper in the evening's quiet. When he finished, he poured himself a glass of juice in the kitchen and started to whistle a soft, twangy tune. Then he heard someone shuffling in the front hall.

Alice's voice called out, "It's just me, Dad." He found her climbing the stairs with a bulging overnight bag.

"What's this, Alice? Come for the holidays already?"

"Where's Mom?" she asked, her voice wavering.

"Mom had a long day; she's already gone up. Why don't you keep me company down here for a while?"

He waited for her at the bottom of the stairs. Alice walked slowly down each step, then sat in the darkened living room.

"Don't turn on a light, please Dad."

"All right." He sat down.

"You did it this time," Alice eventually said. "You stayed out of it. And now I wish you hadn't."

"You and Kirt?"

"He dropped me."

"I guessed as much. Couldn't think of why else he would resign from his job with me in the middle of the year. What did he say?"

"All about how different we are, and how he's too busy; the whole load." She sniffed. "I was dealing with that. It's what I found out tonight that sent me home."

He watched his daughter's form in the semi-darkness. She had always confided in her mother and he had always been glad of it. Sinclair could probe the most putrid of diseased animal flesh more easily than he could bear his daughter's anguish. But this time he felt responsible. Perhaps in Alice's eyes, he had conferred approval by working with the young man, and that might have influenced her involvement.

"I think you should know this," said Alice. "Kirt talked

about marriage quite early in our relationship. And apparently, he was seriously considering marriage, but not with me. He ended it and got engaged to some other girl all in one day. He'll be married to her by next semester."

"How did you find out?"

"I called his apartment tonight. I, uh, just wanted to talk, but his roommate kept giving me the runaround about where he was, when he'd be back. Finally, Roger said he was tired of covering for Kirt, and told me the truth. I suppose Roger's guilty conscience was the only thing Kirt didn't plan on. It would be comic if it weren't so sinister."

"I'm not sure I follow you."

"The guy's got big plans, Dad. He's decided he doesn't need me to make inroads, that's all."

"But maybe Roger misinformed you. Maybe it's not what it seems."

"No. Everything fits. I think it's exactly what it seems. And I'd like to see Kirt pay for it."

Sinclair said nothing more, but moved onto the sofa and pulled his daughter under his arm. They sat together in the dark. He petted her arm and hummed to her, and she soon fell asleep. Her nose was congested from crying and she snored intermittently, finally waking herself with the noise.

"Dad, I would like to stay here for a day or so, until I get my bearings."

"As long as you want."

"Just a couple of days. I wouldn't ask except that this has come along so soon after Toronto. Can you believe it—two disasters in a row? Shall I try for three?"

Sinclair couldn't tell in the dark if she was smiling.

"I don't think it'll happen again," he said.

"I don't either."

"Hey, why don't you stay through the holidays? I'm getting your mother a puppy for Christmas."

"Another terrier?"

"Wait and see. Now, to bed with you."

After Alice went upstairs, Sinclair continued to sit in the unlit living room. He wept soundlessly for his daughter as he had for every occasion of trauma in her life, including birth. His weeping always ended abruptly. When he finished, he mopped his face with his hands and returned to the kitchen for his briefcase. In it was the latest draft of his research article, which detailed the fall outbreak of ram epididymitis in Gilbert country. He had credited his apprentice student as a co-author, knowing that his enlistment of a scientific publication among his credentials would enhance Kirt's resume nicely. And regardless of his motivation, the young man had done excellent work on the project.

God damn this, Sinclair thought. Every student has youthful ambitions. He had himself, that was natural. Most of the kids he taught were decent people, however. Some were even exemplary, but he and Alice had to pick this one for their favorite.

Sinclair gripped a pen in his hand. Perhaps listing Kirt's name beside his own on the article overstated the student's contribution. Yes. Kirt doesn't deserve this, he thought, rationalizing his fury. He held the pen tip poised over Kirt's name to strike it from the paper, clasped it tightly there for many minutes until he got a cramp in his thumb. At length he lay down the pen. This would take some careful thought. Sinclair rinsed the juice pulp from his glass, and a great deal more slowly than usual, went up to bed.

Lourdes

BY DIANE STELZER MORROW

When the time came for Preston to go into the nursing home, Caroline drove him there herself. Preston wore a dark gray suit and a gray hat with a small blue feather in the hatband. On the floor between his feet was a duffel bag. A map was spread out across his lap. Caroline kept turning from the road to look at him. From the very beginning, from the first time one of the children had mentioned it, she'd been against the idea of a nursing home. She believed, still, in the vows she and Preston had taken at their wedding; she believed they were binding: until death do us part. Now, each time she glanced over at Preston—at his duffel bag, the map—she had the same thought: What do you believe, Preston? And how in the world could you ever have agreed to this?

Yet it was, in spite of everything, a beautiful drive. They rode for a half hour through the low hills of southern Ohio—the farmhouses looking weathered, the thick green tobacco leaves yellowing the the September heat—to Pennsylvania and the mountains. At sharp curves in the road, Preston's body leaned towards hers and then, on the straightaways, righted itself.

Preston spoke. "I think we should talk."

"Talk?"

"About what happened."

"Oh, Preston." Caroline kept her eyes fixed on the road. "We know what's happened. You got sick. Don't you remember?"

"I mean before that," he said. He shifted his duffel bag between his feet.

"No, Preston." Her voice was sharp. This was, it seemed, the hundredth time he'd brought this up. Ever since last month, the operation on his hip, all he wanted to do was talk, and always about the same thing—the past. The past, which for both of them had come over the years to mean a specific time—the time just after the birth of their second child when Preston had left the house one morning and been gone for six months.

When she thought of that time now, it seemed as much a part of their lives as their house—the house they had lived in for sixty years. Or the children even. It seemed as important as that. Yet except for the first few days after Preston got back, they had never spoken of it. She believed they shouldn't. That speaking of that time could hurt them, could damage the agreement they'd come to about their life together—that theirs was, after all, not such a bad life.

"Not now," she said. "Please."

Before he could argue, she reached over and turned on the radio. She had to fiddle with the dial, moving it back and forth between the static, before she found the station she wanted—WAKJ in Dayton, a station they got at home which claimed to play fifteen straight country hits every hour without stopping. When he could still keep track of them in his head, Preston had liked to count the songs. Several times he counted sixteen, and once only fourteen. She'd told him an average was good enough, that surely that's what they must have meant, but each time he had gone on about it. Preston hated country music. He said it reminded him of the sound a man might make when he was dying, and that, besides, it wasn't serious music. By serious music he meant classical music. She disagreed. The singers, or at least the people who wrote those songs, had real troubles; at the same time, there was a sense of keeping going, moving forward against all odds, that she admired. Wasn't that serious? Wasn't that just exactly what they were trying to do now?

"Did you pack your razor?" she asked him.

He turned around toward the back seat where both his suitcases were stacked. "I'm sure I did."

She shook her head. She would have to check when they got

there. She'd wanted to pack for him; she'd been able to go so far as to lay some of his clothes out on the bed, but when it came time to packing his toiletry kit, to actually putting everything into the suitcase, he'd been insistent—he would do it. It had taken him forever. He used a walker now; because of it, all his movements were awkward and inefficient. It pained her to watch the deliberate way he moved across the room. Sometimes he was carrying only one thing at a time—a bar of soap or a tube of toothpaste—and it had taken every bit of restraint she could muster not to get up off of the bed and take it from him. "I'm sure they'll have soap at the place," she told him. That's what she called it—the place. All the time she watched him, she knew there were really important things he was forgetting.

He'd been forgetting things more and more over the last few years. This last year it had been worse, as if he could no longer hold anything new inside his head, and then in the winter it had come to a kind of a crisis: he'd forgotten to come home.

On the afternoon of his eightieth birthday, he'd gone out for a walk while she was taking a bath. It was snowing. By the time the police found him, it was already early the next morning—he was walking down a back road on his way to the next town. They brought him to the house. "I'm sorry," Preston said. He looked at her and then down at his feet which were bare and had a white unnatural sheen. "I lost my boots. I'm sure I had them on when I left." He seemed to consider this. Then he turned to the police officer. "Could I get you some coffee?" he asked him.

Before the man could answer, Preston had disappeared into the back of the house. When he came back, he wore socks and shoes both; he'd come through the kitchen and put the coffee on. "You'll stay?" he asked the officers. It was the kind of lucid moment Preston sometimes had with strangers—when a part of his mind realized what he'd come to and needed, often in a desperate sort of way, to make up for it.

Caroline glanced away from the road over at Preston's feet, at his duffel bag settled between them. She shook her head. The duffel bag was something he'd decided on at the last minute. The car was packed and they were ready to pull out of the driveway when he'd decided he hadn't put in any hand-kerchiefs. "You can use Kleenex," she told him. "People do that now. All the time. It's more sanitary." She'd hardly finished suggesting it when she saw that he was already opening the car door. "I couldn't," he said. So she'd waited while he went back into the house and came out finally, his duffel bag set on top of his walker and balanced uneasily against his chest. The bag was one he had used to take with him on business trips.

"Did you put anything else in your bag?" she asked him. They had come up to a town and were stopped at a red light. "Besides the handkerchiefs?"

Preston leaned over and unzipped the bag. "Two oranges," he said, lifting the handkerchiefs and rummaging beneath them. "A jar of coffee."

She started to ask him why—he never even ate oranges at home, he hardly drank coffee—but then she thought better of it. Certainly, those were harmless enough things. "Are you comfortable?" she asked.

He nodded.

The light turned green. They started moving again. "Your foot too?"

"My foot's fine," he said.

This was the same thing he always said, the same thing he'd said to her in fact after the policemen left. She'd taken him to the emergency room anyway. The doctor said he had severe frostbite—the four small toes on his right foot—that he'd have to have an operation or the frostbite would turn into gangrene. The operation, as it turned out, was an amputation. Still, the doctor said, Preston was lucky—at least he'd have the big toe on that foot for balance.

He told her the operation would take an hour. While she waited, she paced back and forth in a room that looked out over the hospital parking lot. Every few minutes, she'd hear an ambulance, and each time she'd go over to the window, fearing, for reasons she knew were illogical, that one of these times it would be Preston—he would be the emergency. After two hours, when the doctor still hadn't come out, she found a pay phone, and, though she hated to worry them, called the children. There were three girls, all of them long distance; as it turned out, only Mary was home. She was the youngest child, the only one of the three who hadn't married. She lived in Texas.

"That's it," Mary said. This after Caroline had explained everything. "You can't go on like this."

"Like what?" she asked her.

"He needs to go into a nursing home."

It was the first time anyone had said this, and Caroline was silent for several seconds, trying to remember why it had at first seemed like a good idea to call the children.

"Are you there?" Mary asked.

"I can't. It would kill him. All cooped up like that."

"Mother. He is going to kill you otherwise. What about your own health? Think of that."

"I think of my husband," she told her. "We have a good life."

"Mother. He'll leave you again. Something will happen."

"He won't," Caroline said.

But then he had.

It was the beginning of the summer. The operation was long over. His foot was almost healed. He could get around without crutches if he were careful. She went into his bedroom one morning with his breakfast on a tray, and he was gone.

This time it was raining. When the officer called, he said they had found Preston but that he was breathing hard; he said they couldn't bring him home but that they were going to take him straight to the hospital.

That second time, he had double pneumonia and an infection in his blood besides. He was in the hospital for months. It seemed that every morning when she went to see him, something new had happened—first a rash from the antibiotics, then a blood clot in his calf from lying in bed for so long, and finally, after several weeks, what was certainly the last straw, Preston got up in the middle of the night one night without calling the nurse and broke his hip.

The hip required surgery—a pin inside the joint to hold the bones together. It was after this second surgery that Preston really began to change. While he was recovering, it seemed that nothing of the present—nothing of his days, nothing of their time together—stayed in his head longer than five minutes, but the past became clear, urgent even. Twice she asked the doctor about it; the second time, she asked him if he thought it could be the pin. "I don't think so," he said. "I've never seen it." He told her it was probably an effect of the anesthesia, that it would pass. She wanted to believe him.

But each morning when she visited Preston, it was the same. She'd stand out in the hall, the door closed, imagining him lying on the other side of the door like bad news. Then she'd open the door, walk into his room. He'd ask her to press the button next to his bed and she would, raising the head of it so he sat at an angle looking out across the room. "I want to tell you a story," he'd say.

"Tell me about your night," she'd urge him.

Sometimes she turned on the television or the radio, even classical music if that would divert him. She knew, from the few times he'd begun, what story he would tell. It was a story she couldn't hear.

Now she looked over at him. He was looking out the window at the billboards. The sun was shining and his face was outlined against the light.

She cleared her throat. "Have you seen any signs for the place yet?"

"Not yet," Preston said. "I'm looking."

She glanced over at the map. If the doctor was right, they should be coming up on one of the signs any minute. She held out her hand. "Why don't you let me look at the map for a minute, Preston?"

Instead of giving her the map, Preston began smoothing it with his hands. They rode without speaking for a few minutes. Every now and then Preston would look at the radio; then he'd look out the window and back at his map; each time he seemed more confused. Finally he spoke. "If I could hear myself think."

"What's that, Preston?"

"That music." He raised his voice, something he rarely did. "If I could hear myself think."

She hesitated.

"Caroline. Please."

She reached over and turned the radio off.

But Preston, it seemed, had forgotten about the map. He took off his hat and began to examine the inside of it. "I remember when you were pregnant with Lily—"

"No, Preston." Lily was their second child. She felt the

sharpness come into her voice, and made an effort to soften it. "We've had a good marriage, Preston."

He was still for several seconds as if considering this. Then he turned his hat over, sharpened the crease, and put the hat back on his head.

"Don't you think so, Preston? Sixty years and we're still together. And the girls too—it's not as if they've turned out so badly."

He turned toward the window. She waited. "That's it," he said finally.

"What's it, Preston? Say it."

But Preston was rolling down his window. "The sign," he said. "That's it."

She slowed down. He was right. Set between two billboards was a small white sign with narrow black letters: OUR LADY OF LOURDES, 1 mile. The first three words were faded—you could hardly read them. So maybe this was what Rose had meant. Rose, their oldest daughter, had told her most people just called the place Lourdes.

Rose had also told her how it had once been a convent, a place where people came to take water, that in fact many people believed miracles had once happened there. Saying this, Rose, who was a sensible woman, like her mother in that way, had added that she herself did not believe in miracles. Caroline told her Preston did. He did. As they came up on the second sign for the place, it occurred to her this had always been part of the problem—how he couldn't just settle for life the way it was already.

She turned down the gravel road where the arrow pointed; it felt as if they were driving into a forest. Dense woods lined both sides; every now and then a tree branch would scrape the window with a high unsettling sound. "Maybe we're lost," Caroline said at one point. Preston didn't answer. It was another quarter of a mile, several curves, before they came to a clearing and one final sign: LOURDES. There was a lot out front with a couple cars and a white truck of the kind that laundries use. Caroline parked.

She hated marigolds. Seeing them now in the window boxes across the front of the nursing home, she thought of dandelions. For an instant she considered telling Preston she had changed her mind—that she'd thought she might like the place but she didn't now, that what they really needed to do was drive out of there fast. But before she could say anything, Preston had opened his door. She turned off the ignition. That morning after Preston had broken his hip, the doctor had stopped her after rounds. He'd told her he thought a nursing home would be the best thing. She told him no—they weren't ready. He touched her arm. He told her he had talked to Preston already—that Preston agreed. At that instant she'd known: something had started which was out of her control. Now it was only continuing.

She got out of the car. Taking both suitcases out of the back, she slammed the doors, and followed behind Preston, who was already starting up the walk.

"I could take your duffel bag," she said.

Preston shook his head. "I've got it."

She slowed her pace so she wouldn't pass him.

Red and white geraniums lined the walk up to the front door, and next to the porch, glinting in the sun, was a pool with goldfish. Preston set his walker on the porch, and steadying his duffel bag with his chin, rang the doorbell.

A nurse opened the door. "You must be the Grangers," she said. She was a young woman, tall and thin and somehow prettier than Caroline had expected. Behind her, through the doorway, Caroline could see into a large room.

The room resembled the waiting room of a doctor's office: it was dim but clean with straight-back leather chairs, coffee tables, and against the far wall, a television set where two old women sat in wheelchairs close to the set, blocking the picture. Preston spoke and then the nurse did again. Caroline didn't hear them. She imagined Preston sitting with those women.

The nurse ushered Preston inside. There was a step, and she took the duffel bag from him, holding him under one arm while Preston maneuvered his walker. Caroline started to follow with the suitcases.

"I'll take them," the nurse said. As she said this, she reached forward with both hands to take the luggage from Caroline. But Caroline, ignoring her, walked inside.

The nurse shook her head. "Didn't they tell you?"

"Tell me what?" Caroline asked. She was looking around her, trying to imagine how the place would look to her if she were Preston. This was a way she had used to look at places just after they were first married.

"Our policy," the nurse said. "The first month. We ask the family to let the patient settle in first." She made a motion with her hand. "After the first month you can visit as much as you like."

Caroline set Preston's suitcases down on the floor; then, crouching down next to one of them, she began to unzip it. A twitching sensation had begun in her eyelid. The twitching was something that had started on and off in the last year. At first she'd been certain it was some kind of palsy, and she'd gone to the doctor about it. He'd told her not to worry—that it was only nerves and the best thing for it was to relax. Now, whenever she felt the twitching, she closed her eyes for a few seconds and tried to imagine herself relaxing.

She opened her eyes and finished unzipping the suitcase. "I need to check this," she said. "God only knows what he brought."

The nurse touched her arm. "It's better for them if you leave," she said. "Really. It's easier." She squinted then, wrinkling her nose. She was actually a very young woman, still unsure of herself; maybe she would change her mind.

But then Preston spoke. "It's okay," he said.

Caroline turned. "Preston."

"I have your phone number," the nurse said. "It's Mrs. Granger, right? I'll call you. Twice a week. Let you know how he's doing. And you can call any time you like." She pointed to her name tag. "Ask for Beth."

Caroline looked at Preston. He nodded. It seemed there was nothing to do but let him decide.

There was nothing to do. That was the hardest part.

The next morning when Caroline woke, it was raining. She could hear the rain, the sound it made against the windows and rushing out of the spouting. It was dark yet. For some time now actually she had been waking like this before dawn, startled awake as if by an alarm, as if there were some work for her, some place she had to be. Before Preston had gone into the hospital, she had used this time to get up and clean the house, make his breakfast, so that by the time he woke, the house was tidy and there was always coffee ready and pancakes or bacon and eggs; after he got sick, there was herself to get ready, her own breakfast, before she went to visit him at the hospital. This morning she awoke and heard the rain and was at first worried by it; then she remembered all at once—it didn't matter—there was no place she needed to be. As she got up and went into the kitchen, she tried to imagine how she was going to use all this time.

Time invited brooding, regrets. It invited dwelling on the past—something she would not do. After that first morning, which she spent mostly wandering around the house, looking out the windows, she developed a routine.

The first thing each morning, she took a bath. Then she fixed breakfast—coffee, half of a grapefruit, one soft-boiled egg. From the kitchen window she could see the neighbors' house. It was the same house as theirs actually, except that it was the mirror image—the kitchens faced each other. A new couple had recently moved in. They were young, handsome people. Often in the mornings their curtains would be open, and while she waited for her egg to cook, she would watch them. They'd be sitting at the table, drinking coffee, reading the newspaper; she imagined them talking. When she and Preston were first married, they had spent a thousand good mornings just like that before he left for work.

While she ate her own breakfast, she watched the "Today Show." She had never watched much television in the morning, but now it seemed necessary. She liked in particular the part after the news when Jane Pauley would move from behind her desk to one of the more comfortable chairs for an interview. Jane was so handsome and calm, so happy, that somehow, just watching her, Caroline could almost believe her own life was going to get better.

After the "Today Show" she would call the nursing home and ask for Beth.

"He's fine," Beth would say. "Healthy."

Often Beth used the word adjusting. This disturbed her. In the hospital, when she and Preston had discussed the nursing home, they'd agreed it was temporary, until Preston got better and could come back. After she'd hung up and was cleaning the house, she'd count in her head the number of weeks she believed it would take for a hip to heal.

Though before she'd always kept a nice enough house,

cleaning was now something she needed to do. Most mornings she did the bathroom first. When she was finished, she'd linger in the doorway. The sight of the clean bathroom pleased her, as if there were some place in her life now that was orderly.

Afterwards, she'd do her few dishes in the kitchen, make her bed. Often she'd remake Preston's bed. She'd arrange pictures on the top of dressers, put out clean towels. When the house was just exactly the way she wanted it—perfect—she would stand in the middle of the living room and look around her. Sometimes she would speak to him. "Preston Granger, you should see the house now. If you could, you would not even think of adjusting anywhere else. You would get better. You would come home."

Then it was October. Caroline awoke one morning and it had been one month exactly since she'd driven Preston out to Lourdes. She got up and took a warm bath and dressed quickly in the dark bedroom, expectant.

She left the house early before the morning traffic. On the road it was quiet. The farmhouses were dark. As she drove past them, she was able to imagine him still asleep; she imagined walking into his room, standing next to his bed, waking him; she pictured the look on his face—some form of gratitude, or relief even, that she'd finally come for him. Picturing him like this reassured her. As she crossed the line into Pennsylvania, she decided that when she got to the place, she would not tell any of the nurses she'd come, but would try to find Preston herself and surprise him.

In Pennsylvania, the mountains, the leaves had mostly changed. This was especially true near Lourdes. At the point where she turned onto the gravel road, the yellows were brilliant in the early sun. She wound through the trees and came to the clearing. The marigolds were gone and the geraniums—they must have had a frost here already. Smoke rose out of the chimney. She parked around back and walked across the gravel to the back door.

The door led onto a screened-in porch that was cold, like the morning outside. At one end was a Coke machine, and next to that a diagram of names and numbers. Caroline walked over to the diagram. Preston's name was written in blue ink on the second floor. The ink surprised her. Though it was a small thing, it made his move seem somehow permanent. She left the porch, and, trying to avoid being seen, found some stairs. They were slats really, uncarpeted; she guessed they were stairs the maids used, and perhaps the nurses; as she started up them, she felt like an intruder.

Upstairs the hall was carpeted—a rose-colored carpet that was worn clean. At the end of the hall, a nurse stood next to a medicine cart. Caroline walked toward her, looking in each of the rooms, trying to pretend she was a patient, perhaps from another floor, lost. The nurse seemed not to notice her. At the end of the hall, disoriented now and trying to imagine the diagram, Caroline turned and started down a second hall. Midway, a man's voice called out from one of the rooms— "Swee-ty." It was a cry really—each of the syllables drawn out—and it occurred to her, he might be crying out for her; perhaps he had mistaken her for someone. She kept walking. The next room was Preston's—a small white card next to the doorjamb: Granger. She walked inside. It was empty. There was one small window, a dresser, and a narrow bed, already neatly made. She looked into the bathroom. It was clean and empty too.

"Preston," she called. As if just by calling him he might appear. Then she came back out into the hall.

Further down she recognized Beth standing next to a medicine cart. Caroline walked over to her. "I'm looking for Preston."

Beth looked up. "Mrs. Granger." She seemed anxious, and Caroline decided she must feel bad now for how abrupt she had been on the first day.

"Could you tell me where he is?" she asked.

"He's in Jessie's room," Beth said. She pointed behind her down the hall.

"Jessie's room? So he's been moved? He has a roommate then?"

Beth shook two capsules out of the bottle into a small plastic cup. She seemed distracted. "It's at the end," she said. "You can't miss it."

Caroline looked into each room as she walked past. At the very end, facing her as she walked toward it, was a room with the door half open, a wooden sign on the door—Jessie's Room.

Caroline stood in the doorway looking in. A woman was sitting in a wheelchair by the window. She was an old woman: white hair, red nail polish, and on her wrist, two wide gold bracelets, one of them with two rows of small glittering red stones. Next to her on the windowsill was a jar of coffee and a basket of fruit. "Oh, Preston," Caroline said, but under her breath. Then she saw him. He was sitting on the bed, propped against the headboard, his legs stretched out, drinking coffee and reading the newspaper. He looked at home.

Caroline pushed the door the rest of the way open. Before either Preston or the woman could say anything, she was standing next to his bed. She had stayed away too long. She never should have listened to Beth. If he only saw her, he would stop this nonsense and come back with her—to his room, or home even.

"Preston," she said, leaning over and kissing him on the side of the forehead.

He looked up at her, puzzled. "Yes?" For an instant she could have sworn he didn't recognize her. But then he shook his head as if to clear it. He pointed to a straight-back chair next to the window. "Why don't you sit down?" he said. "Could we get you some coffee?"

He looked over at the old woman. "Jessie," he said. "Maybe you could do that."

Jessie turned away from the window. Then, as if noticing Caroline there for the first time, she held her hand out across the bed. "I'm Jessie," she said. "So pleased to meet you." Caroline shook her hand without speaking and watched then as Jessie maneuvered her wheelchair around the bed and out the doorway.

When Jessie was halfway down the hall, Caroline went over to the window and sat in the chair, shaken. "I stayed away too long," she said. Now, with that woman gone, he would say something. He would tell her he missed her. Things would go back to the way they had been before.

"It's not so bad here," Preston said. He folded the newspaper and laid it across his lap. "The nurses take pretty good care of us."

"Us?" Caroline asked. She shifted in her chair.

Preston looked down the hall, and then back at her. She could see his mind working—trying to piece together the parts of things he could remember into one thing that could make sense of it. It was painful to watch. More painful when his eyes cleared—as if a circuit had connected.

"Caroline," he said. He did know her. "I want to talk."

She stood up. The twitching in her eyelid had started. She closed her eyes. What could they possibly talk about now that would not hurt them?

"It's okay, Preston," she said. "Really." She kissed him again, this time on the cheek. "I've got to go now. There's a new woman who moved in next door. I told her I'd go shopping with her this afternoon." This was a lie, and as it came out it surprised her; at the same time, she knew it would satisfy him. Before Jessie could come back with the coffee, she was walking down the back stairs. She was driving home, taking the curves faster than she ever would have on a good day.

When she got home she called Lily.

Lily was the second child. She lived in Chicago. Both she and her husband had been married before, and between them they had four children, all boys.

"Maybe Dad's just sick," Lily said.

"Sick. Why do you say that?"

"There's a lot of flu here. The boys have all had it. They were sick as dogs."

Caroline nodded. Lily was always blaming something on a virus. Last winter, after Preston's amputation, Lily had said more than once how she thought Preston had left the house because he had caught something. And though Caroline didn't believe this, there was always a certain comfort in talking to Lily—knowing that Lily did.

"But if you could have only seen them," Caroline said. "The room is nothing—a bed, a chair, one small window. To see her there, you would think she is the Queen of Sheba."

Lily made a small murmuring sound. "The pneumonia," she said. "He's barely had time to recover. Who's to say the infection's not still in his blood?"

"I don't think so," Caroline said. She wrapped the telephone cord around her wrist. "It couldn't explain it."

After she hung up, she put a pot of coffee on. While it was brewing, she called Mary, and then Rose. Mary said the same thing she always said—that Caroline should think of herself, her own health. Rose remembered a story—it was a story of the grandfather of one of her students—how he had come home one day from a ride in the car and forgotten his wife's name.

"And then what?" Caroline asked her.

But Rose couldn't remember. "I should fly home," Rose said. "Stay with you for a while."

"No," Caroline told her. "I'd rather you didn't. Please."

It shamed her that the children knew. At the same time, she could not keep herself from calling them. Once a day she would phone one or the other of the girls just to talk, to ask them what they thought. "Why has he done this?" she asked them.

If they answered her, she didn't hear them.

There was a mirror in the hall just down from the phone. After she hung up, she found herself stopping in front of it, touching her hair, trying to figure out what had gone wrong.

And two, sometimes three mornings a week, she went out to Lourdes. The two of them sat in the same places as if these had been ordained—Preston on the bed, the Queen of Sheba in her wheelchair. As soon as she walked in the door, Preston would point to the chair next to the window and ask her if she wanted to sit down. The Queen would head down the hall to get her a cup of coffee.

After that first time, Caroline was able to make herself wait for Jessie to come back, able to sit next to Preston without asking him to say anything. After awhile, she expected nothing more when she visited but that she would sit there. A few times Preston didn't recognize her. Jessie would roll back into the room with a cup of coffee, and Preston would look back and forth between Jessie and herself, confused, until finally, several times Caroline had to stand up close to his face and tell him her name. "Your wife, Preston," she would say. "Caroline. Me." Other times, it was as if he knew her too well. He would complain bitterly, saying it had been a big mistake to marry a woman who was so cold she couldn't forgive—not even after all these years.

Forgive? Does a man who wants forgiveness move into the room of another woman? Does he? She asked herself this in the car on the way home. But in Jessie's room, she was quiet, watching them.

Sometimes, Preston read aloud from the newspaper. Those were his clear days. He would read distant news mostly— stories about horrors in other countries. After each story he would look up at Jessie. She would run her finger around the rim of her coffee cup and shake her head; it was as if she shared with Preston some special sense of what had gone awry in the world. Driving home at dusk, the windows up against the cold, Caroline felt as if her whole life with Preston had been cancelled somehow—erased.

One afternoon, she dug up all her old jewelry as soon as she got home. She put it on until she was weighted with it— necklaces and bracelets and rings and two brooches, one on either side of her dress. She painted her nails. She walked out of her bedroom and stood in front of the hall mirror and looked at herself—this new image. Then she took it all off, the nail polish too, and she bathed and put on her pajamas and got into bed. The wind was blowing at the windows, and it had begun to snow. Before she fell asleep, she tried to remember what it had been like to have Preston there in the bed next to her on nights like this.

The next morning when she woke up, the snow had stuck— three inches or more. She called the Highway Patrol. There had been even more snow in the mountains, and ice; the man on the phone told her that the road that went up to Lourdes was slick. He asked her if she had a four-wheel drive. When she told him she didn't, he told her the best thing for her would just be to stay at home. For days that stretched into weeks, and then a month, she couldn't visit.

It was a bad time. The house was cold. In the mornings she found herself staying in bed sometimes for hours after she awoke. When she did get up, she had no energy. She stopped cooking breakfast. For a while she made a pot of coffee, but after a time even that seemed like too much, and she began to make only instant coffee. It was decaffeinated—Sanka actu- ally—and had a flat muddy taste. She drank it standing at the kitchen window. Often, during the week, the neighbors would have already left for work by the time she got up, but on the weekends she watched them.

The man liked to read the paper. He could sit there for an hour, or two hours sometimes. While he read, he held his mug of coffee up to his face for warmth. The woman was more restless. She got up and left the kitchen and came back, often several times in the same morning. On Saturdays, she did laundry. After she had finished her breakfast and while the man was still reading the paper, she would bring a basket of clean laundry into the kitchen and begin to fold it, right there at the table. The man, used to this, hardly looked up. If he did look up, it was to tell her something—usually it was something funny, because the woman would laugh then or shake her head or sometimes hit him even, usually on the back or shoulder with a clean shirt. Though Caroline knew it was unreasonable, she began to feel angry with them for the way they excluded her from this.

She stopped calling the children. Though they called occasionally and she would talk with them briefly, the only calls she made herself anymore were to the nursing home. Like the rest of her morning, these left her feeling vaguely unsettled.

Beth seemed more terse when she answered, more clinical than before. She told Caroline that Preston was eating well and had no fever, no signs of infection, but if Caroline asked her any other questions, she brushed them aside. "Don't worry," she said. "We're taking good care of him."

This went on for a month, and then in the very dead of winter, when Caroline could not even get out of the driveway, Beth began to tell her that Preston seemed more confused than he had before.

"What do you mean?" she asked her. She felt the twitching start in her eyelid.

"I don't know how else to say it," Beth said. She seemed embarrassed to be saying this. "He's just more confused."

Caroline called the doctor. He told her the nurses often exaggerated. He told her he had seen Preston. He said he thought Preston seemed only a little more confused, that it was from the cold, and that it would pass.

"Are you certain?" she asked him.

He said he was.

The next time Lily called, Caroline asked her if she had ever read anything like that in one of her health books. Lily said she couldn't remember exactly, but that it made sense. "Temperature," Lily said. "Can affect all kinds of things."

Caroline began to watch the weather. The year before, at the children's urging, she and Preston had gotten cable. Before this she had never paid it much attention—the sheer number of stations overwhelmed her—but now, having found the weather station, she kept it on in the living room almost continuously. Sometimes she sat in front of it for an hour, two hours at a time, just waiting for a break in the cold.

The house seemed larger than it had when Preston was there. It expanded around her, so that sometimes when she sat there in the living room in the late afternoons, the weather flickering on the screen in front of her, she felt as if she had shrunk.

Often she fell asleep in her chair. One afternoon she found herself in bed, a young mother. The bedroom was dark, except for a shaft of light from the hall. She heard a noise. The baby crying, or Rose—sick or frightened and wanting to come into bed with them—and she jumped out of bed and was to the doorway when she saw him. He was standing in the hall, fully dressed. He even had his hat on. And this confused her, because usually she was the first one up in the morning; usually Preston came down and had breakfast in his pajamas before he got dressed. "Where are you going?" she asked him. He started away from her. A noise again, this time clearly downstairs, and she leaned over the railing to look. Sitting on the landing was a woman. She was a young woman—not beautiful, but pretty, with nice skin. Her hair was a light brown, almost blonde, and it shone in the hall light. Though she looked innocent enough—harmless really—Caroline was suddenly frightened.

She woke up shaken. The memory was intact: as powerful—as powerful to hurt—as ever. Only the woman was new. When Preston had come home after being away all those months, he'd told her it was important that she understand. He'd gone to Kentucky, he told her. Kentucky. A harsh name. She'd told him that was enough to know. When he protested, she set two fingers up against her own mouth. "No, Preston." What was it about men that they believed talking could change things?

He gave up trying to talk about it after the first week. By

then she'd already begun to picture Kentucky as a woman. A nice woman in a small neat house, no children. A woman who had something to offer Preston that she couldn't offer.

She fixed an early supper and ate it sitting in front of the television. In the bathroom, getting ready for bed, she stopped in the middle of washing her face. What would have happened if she had let Preston go on about this Kentucky of his? Would the memory have blurred a little? Would the edge have rubbed down? Would he have needed to do this all over again?

A few days later, she woke in her chair, the house dark except for the television set and one light she'd left on over the stove in the kitchen; in that minute before she was fully awake, she believed Preston had come home. He was standing in the kitchen doorway, straight and beautiful.

"What do you want?" she asked him.

He didn't answer. He never did.

"What is it you want me to do?"

The phone rang. She shook herself awake and went into the kitchen. He wasn't there. She picked up the phone. It was Rose. "When are you going out again?" She called every week to ask this, but this time the words took on a new meaning, as if they were some sort of a message.

"When it melts," she told her.

"I'll fly home," Rose said. "I'll drive out there with you."

"No. You stay there. I need to do this myself."

In February, the ground thawed. The road into the mountains opened. Caroline packed a picnic basket with cookies, new underwear for Preston, and warm socks. Then she drove out to Lourdes.

The place had endured the winter. Behind the bare trees it stood white and exposed. She parked and went in at the back door. Inside, beyond the porch, it smelled close and stale, of sickness. She took a deep breath and held it and walked up the stairs and down the hall toward Jessie's room.

Jessie was not in her room. Instead, a man in striped pajamas was lying on her narrow bed, asleep. His skin was white and shiny and it covered his bones closely; there were hollows in his cheeks and behind his collarbones. At first she feared it was Preston. Her heart skipped as if to stop. Was it already too late? She set her picnic basket down on the floor next to the bed and touched his shoulder. He opened his eyes. They were vacant like glass—and not Preston's. "Good morning, sir." The words came out in a kind of rush of gratitude. Then she picked up her basket and left him.

In the hall, a nurse Caroline had never met before was standing outside one of the rooms writing in a chart. Caroline asked her where Jessie had been moved to.

"Jessie?" The nurse's stare was nearly as blank as the old man's.

"Jessie," Caroline said, pointing. "An old woman with painted nails. She used to stay there in that room, but now there is a man there."

"Jessie," the nurse repeated, tapping her pen on the chart, and then remembering. "Oh, Jessie. She died."

"When?" Caroline asked. The news chilled her—more than she would have expected.

"I'm not sure," the nurse said. Then, as if fearing she had already said too much, she turned back to her chart. "It's been a hard winter here." She said it not without feeling. "A lot of the folks got pneumonia."

"Preston?" Caroline said, feeling her voice rise.

The nurse touched Caroline's arm. "Don't get excited." She probably said that a hundred times a day. "Preston Granger is sitting downstairs in the day room watching television. Where he always sits now." She began writing again. "I believe I've noticed you here before. You're his wife?"

Caroline nodded.

"I should warn you. He's not been well lately." She hesitated, her pen hovering over the chart. "I mean, physically, well—he's fine."

Caroline started to ask her what she meant. But she couldn't quite form the necessary words. Instead she turned and, without speaking, started down the back stairs, shifting the picnic basket to her left hand so she could hold the rail.

Halfway down the stairs she turned. "Thank you," she said.

The nurse looked up. "You're welcome."

At the soda machine, Caroline stopped and bought a Coke. "Just give me a minute," she said—aloud, as if someone were standing there on the porch expecting something of her. The

Coke burned the back of her throat and down into her chest. She stepped out onto the parking lot. It was chilly, but the sun was out and there was a sound of water in the distance—the kind of day that when the children were small they'd be begging to go outside and she'd go with them.

She looked around for a sidewalk that might lead to the front of the building. When she couldn't find one, she cut through the grass. It was still wet from the morning and cold against her ankles. She passed the pond. The goldfish were darting back and forth—gold and flashes of orange. At one edge of the pond, a fish floated with its belly swollen and turned up.

She stepped up onto the porch and stopped in front of a heavy wooden door with a pane alongside it made of a thick corrugated glass. She didn't remember the glass from her first visit. She cupped her hands on either side of her face, trying to peer through it. When she couldn't, she jiggled the doorknob. It was unlocked. She leaned against the door with her shoulder and pushed. The door opened.

Inside it was dark—only one light at the far end of the room—a bluish light which was the television. A man was sitting in front of it. She walked over to him. The floor down here was linoleum, and her footsteps made a clicking sound, but if he heard he gave no notice of it. When she reached him, she stood behind him for a moment without speaking. On television, a man and woman were sitting next to each other on a couch. That Preston had begun to watch soap operas since her last visit seemed not at all surprising.

"Preston," she said. She set a hand on each of his shoulders.

He tipped his head back to look at her—a thinner man than she remembered.

"I brought you something," she said. She set the picnic basket on the chair next to him and opened it. First, she unpacked a tin of cookies. She took the lid off the cookies and held them towards him. "You could use one of these."

He took one. "Thank you." He bit into the cookie. "They're very good."

She was taking out the underwear and his socks when he stopped her, touching her on the wrist. "Who are you?" he asked.

"Preston." She set the socks down and stood close, directly in front of him. This had always worked before. "Preston. It's me."

He looked at her face and hands and then his eyes traveled down the length of her body to her shoes, but still he looked confused.

"Oh, Preston. Your wife. Me."

Preston cleared his throat. "That's impossible," he said. He looked back at the television. "My wife is dead."

He meant Jessie. But still she felt the words as if he'd hit her. She stepped back, the impact—the possibility—moving from her stomach into her chest and outward into the rest of her body. Dead? She looked at her arms and legs. She touched her face. What did he see when he looked at her? What had she become?

"No, Preston." She moved so that she stood between him and the television set. "Look, I'm here." She held her hands out in front of her, palms up. The palms were reddened, cracked, definitely hers.

Preston nodded. "I see. But I told you. My wife is dead. She died with pneumonia."

She stepped towards him and, without thinking now about what she was doing, knelt down in front of him so that their faces were only a few inches apart. "How am I going to do this, Preston?"

He shook his head. He looked past her at the television set, and then down at his lap, not understanding.

"Look, Preston." She put her hand beneath his chin. Then, gently, she lifted his chin so that he had no choice but to look at her. His pupils were dilated—like deep black pools. She imagined that somewhere, perhaps at the very depths of them, he could understand—even forgive. "Look, Preston. It's me. Caroline. The one you left. Remember?"

Contributors

JOE DAVID BELLAMY grew up in Cincinnati and now teaches at St. Lawrence University. He has published a novel, *Suzi Sinzinnati* (Pushcart/Norton), as well as numerous stories in literary magazines. His other books include *The New Fiction*, *American Poetry Observed*, and *Superfiction*.

SALLY BENNETT has been the Coordinator of the Creative Writing Program at Syracuse University. Her work has appeared in *Poetry*, *The Seneca Review*, *The Montana Review*, and *Viva*. She has also completed a novel.

BECKY BRADWAY makes her second appearance in *American Fiction*. In addition, she has published stories in *Greensboro Review*, *Crescent Review*, *Cottonwood*, and *Four Quarters*. She works as a training coordinator at the Illinois Coalition Against Sexual Assault.

CATHERINE BROWDER began writing fiction while teaching in Japan. Her stories have appeared or will soon appear in *New Letters*, *Kansas Quarterly*, *Shenandoah*, and *Prairie Schooner*. In 1988, she received a Writer's Biennial Award from the Missouri Arts Council.

ANN COPELAND'S short fiction has appeared in *The Best American Short Stories*, *Best Canadian Stories*, and *Ontario Review*. Three collections of her short fiction have been published by Oberon Press—*At Peace*, *The Back Room*, and *Earthen Vessels*. A fourth, *The Golden Thread*, was published by Viking/Penguin in 1989. She lives in New Brunswick, Canada.

ELIZABETH EVANS is the author of a collection of stories, *Locomotion*, Currently at work on a novel entitled *Ancient History*, she teaches fiction writing at the University of Arizona.

JELENA BULAT GILL was born and raised in Yugoslavia where she received her Ph.D. in Mathematics. She has lived in many

MARIA NOELL GOLDBERG has an MFA from Sarah Lawrence College. The recipient of a *Transatlantic Review* Award for fiction, she is at work on a novel.

PAT HARRISON also makes her second appearance in these pages. A native of Oklahoma, he is a graduate student in the MFA program at Sarah Lawrence College. A chapbook of her fiction was published by Brick Lung Press.

URSULA HEGI'S earlier story, "Saving a Life," was first published in *American Fiction*. She has published a novel, *Intrusions*, and a collection of short stories, *Unearned Pleasures and Other Stories*. Her work has appeared in *North American Review, Prairie Schooner, The Boston Globe*, and many other magazines. She directs the MFA program at Eastern Washington University.

MARCIE HERSHMAN'S work has appeared in *Ms., Massachusetts Review*, and *The Beloit Poetry Journal*. She has recently completed a novel, *The Salt Marsh*. She teaches writing at Tufts University and at Emerson College.

JOANNA HIGGINS has published work in *MSS, Passages North, Prairie Schooner*, and *The Best American Short Stories 1982*. She recently finished work on a collection of short stories and novel, and received an NEA fellowship for 1989. She lives in Pennsylvania.

SUSAN S. HUCKLE, a native of the Blue Ridge Mountains of Virginia, has pursued a career in clinical and research science and has recently graduated frm the Iowa Writer's Workshop. She written a collection of short stories called *Air and Space*.

THOMAS E. KENNEDY'S work has appeared in a number of literary journals, including *The Literary Review, Kenyon Review, North American Review*, and *Sewanee Review*. His novel—as yet untitled—will soon be published by Washington Square Press. He makes his home in Denmark.

JOANN KOBIN has had stories in *Massachusetts Review, Virginia Quarterly Review, North American Review, Ploughshares*, and many other magazines. She lives in Massachusetts.

ROBIN LEWIS lives in Fairbanks, Alaska, where he recently graduated from the MFA program at the University of Alaska. "Jet Pilot for the Sandinistas" is his first national publication.

DAVID MASON has published work in *The Threepenny Review, Sewanee Review,* and *The Literary Review.* A chapbook of his poetry was brought out by Aralia Press. He lives in Minnesota.

CRIS MAZZA'S story collection, *Animal Acts,* was released in 1989 by Fiction Collective. Her fiction has also appeared in *Fiction, High Plains Literary Review, Kansas Quarterly,* and many other magazines. A second collection of stories, *Is it Sexual Harassment Yet?* is forthcoming from Fiction Collective Two. One of her stories was cited in *The Best American Short Stories 1988.*

FLORRI MCMILLAN, recipient of this year's *American Fiction* $1000 First Prize Award, has published a novel and a short story collection, as well as numerous stories in places such as *Redbook, Greensboro Review* and *Quarterly West.* She teaches Creative Writing at Northwestern University.

DIANE STELZER MORROW practiced medicine in a clinic in Washington, D.C., before leaving to attend the writing program at George Mason University. She lives in Gaithersburg, Maryland, and is working on a novel.

DAVID MORSE has just returned from Shropshire, England, where he was gathering material for a novel. He lives in Storrs, Connecticut, and has work that will appear soon in *Northeast Magazine.*

MARK NIEKER lives in Seattle Washington. "Elvis" marks his first published work.

JANE RUITER has been a social worker, lyricist, journalist, and bartender. Her work has appeared in *Special Report: Fiction, Other Voices,* and *Florida Review.* A sequel to "Trees" is being syndicated by Fiction Network. She lives in Michigan.

BARBARA UNGER'S short fiction will appear in *Midstream* and *Esprit,* and a collection of hers is forthcoming from Kendall/Hunt Publishers. She is also the author of four books of poetry, and lives in Suffern, New York.

The Editors

Guest Judge ANNE TYLER is the author of a number of books, including *The Accidental Tourist*, which received the National Book Critics Circle Award in 1986, and *Breathing Lessons*, which won a Pulitzer Prize in 1988.

MICHAEL C. WHITE, Editor, has had work appear in *The Laurel Review, Cream City Review, Folio*, and *Northeast Magazine*. He also has stories forthcoming from *Redbook, Green Mountain Review*, and *Spectrum*. He teaches writing at Springfield College in Massachusetts.

ALAN DAVIS, Assistant Editor, has had stories appear in numerous magazines and journals, including *The Quarterly, Kansas Quarterly, Denver Quarterly*, and many other magazines. His fiction collections have been finalists in both the Iowa Short Fiction and Drue Heinz contests. A frequent book reviewer, he lives and teaches in Moorhead, Minnesota.